Lyn Andrews is one of the UK's most popular authors, whose books have appeared many times on the *Sunday Times* bestseller list. She has now written thirty-two enormously successful novels, which are all available from Headline.

Lyn Andrews now lives on the Isle of Man but frequently visits Merseyside to see her three children and four grandchildren.

By Lyn Andrews and available from Headline

Maggie May
The Leaving Of Liverpool
Liverpool Lou
The Sisters O'Donnell
The White Empress
Ellan Vannin
Mist Over The Mersey
Mersey Blues
Liverpool Songbird
Liverpool Lamplight
Where The Mersey Flows
From This Day Forth
When Tomorrow Dawns
Angels Of Mercy
The Ties That Bind
Take These Broken Wings
My Sister's Child
The House On Lonely Street
Love And A Promise
A Wing And A Prayer
When Daylight Comes
Across A Summer Sea
A Mother's Love
Friends Forever
Every Mother's Son
Far From Home
Days Of Hope
A Daughter's Journey
A Secret In The Family
To Love And To Cherish
Beyond A Misty Shore
The Queen's Promise

LYN ANDREWS

The Queen's Promise

headline

First published in 2012
by HEADLINE PUBLISHING GROUP

First published in paperback in 2013
by HEADLINE PUBLISHING GROUP

1

Cataloguing in Publication Data is available from the British Library

ISBN 978 0 7553 8671 0

Typeset in Janson Text by Avon DataSet Ltd,
Bidford-on-Avon, Warwickshire

Printed and bound by
CPI Group (UK) Ltd, Croydon, CR0 4YY

Headline's policy is to use papers that are natural, renewable and
recyclable products and made from wood grown in sustainable forests.
The logging and manufacturing processes are expected to conform to
the environmental regulations of the country of origin.

HEADLINE PUBLISHING GROUP
An Hachette UK Company
338 Euston Road
London NW1 3BH

www.headline.co.uk
www.hachette.co.uk

Acknowledgements

I would like to thank the Duke of Northumberland for allowing me access to the Duke of Northumberland's Collection of Manuscripts at the British Library and to Christopher Hunwick, the Duke's archivist, for his invaluable help and advice. To Anne Williams, Associate Agent at the Kate Horden Literary Agency, I owe a huge debt of gratitude; I couldn't have done this book without you! But for your encouragement and guidance I would never have completed it. I would also like to thank my editor of ten years, Marion Donaldson, not just for her support and advice on *The Queen's Promise* but for her help on all the novels I've written in that time. My thanks also to Jane Morpeth, Managing Director of Headline Publishing, for having enough faith in me to agree to publish this novel, which is a departure from my usual genre. To Caitlin Raynor and the staff of Headline Publicity; Aslan Byrne, UK and International Sales Director; Lucy Mustoe, Consumer Director; and the staff of sales and marketing and production: you really are a great team. And last but not least, my husband Robert, who has made me endless cups of coffee, chauffeured me to the various castles and other destinations and who has given me unfailing support in my thirty-year writing career.

Prologue

<hr>

1507
Wressle Castle, Yorkshire

I‌T WAS UNSEASONABLY HOT for May. The late-morning sun blazed down from a perfect sky, casting parts of the crenellated battlements into deep shade whilst illuminating others with its brilliant rays. The air was still and heavy and sound carried clearly: the drone of bees in the blossoms on the fruit trees in the orchards beyond the courtyard wall; the scrape of a shovel against stone as a boy mucked out in the stable block; and the faint, mournful lowing of cattle in the distant water meadows beside the River Derwent. Muted by the thickness of the castle walls, the voices of servants could be heard as the hour for dinner approached.

Sir William Percy swatted away the flies that, attracted by the steaming pile of dung from his horse and the beads of sweat that stood out on his brow, were annoying him. He leaned forward in the saddle, his gaze fixed on the figure of his young nephew some yards away in the centre of the tilt yard. The boy was clad in a short dark blue tunic bordered with gold thread. Around his waist he wore a belt of Spanish leather and his hands were tightly clasped around the hilt of a sword, the blade of which was equal to his height. A slight, pale child with short brown hair covered by a hood of mail, he fixed his eyes on his opponent, a lad not much older than himself.

'Again, Henry! Again! Feign to the left this time and put more of your weight behind the thrust.' Sir William shouted the instructions with a note of impatience in his voice.

The child struggled to raise the weapon but with an effort managed to do so; he doggedly swung it in an arc towards his opponent, who parried the blow easily, causing the child to lose his balance. He staggered and then fell heavily, dropping the sword. A cloud of dust rose to sting his eyes and cling to his lips. Spitting the dirt from his mouth he drew the sleeve of his tunic across his face, trying to ignore the pain that was searing his cheek and blinking rapidly to stem the tears of humiliation and frustration that filled his brown eyes. The sword was too heavy, too large and unwieldy. His arms were aching and he could feel the sweat trickling down his neck beneath the tight hood of metal links. He lacked neither the courage nor the will for combat, just the strength and the skill.

Sir William leaned back, shook his head and sighed heavily before turning to his older brother, Henry Algernon Percy, Fifth Earl of Northumberland, who was seated beside him on a fine chestnut gelding, its saddlecloth and trappings also of blue and gold damask. 'There are times when I think his heart is just not in it, Henry. He makes little improvement despite my tutoring and the hours spent in practice.'

His brother frowned, shifting his position slightly and adjusting his dark blue velvet bonnet which was growing increasingly uncomfortable in the heat. 'He will learn, William. In time he will improve. He is five years old.'

'And Harry "Hotspur" was eight when he accompanied his father to France as a page in the campaign against du Guesclin,' his brother reminded him succinctly.

Irritated by the comparison of his eldest son and heir to their illustrious ancestor, Henry Algernon flicked the rein and turned the gelding's head towards the stable block. 'There are other ways of gaining esteem and favour, William. Am I not assembling the greatest collection of literature and learning in the North? Have I not advanced our position at court; does the King not look with affection upon our loyalty? Did our sovereign lord not choose me to escort the Princess Margaret to her wedding with King James of Scotland?'

Sir William urged his horse forward, his lips set in a line of disapproval. He did not agree with his brother. The Earl's ways were not the ways of the Border. In his view his brother had spent too much time and money in London, courting the favour of a suspicious and watchful King. He well remembered how much money it had cost to escort King Henry's daughter, Princess Margaret Tudor, to her wedding, for his brother had spared no expense. Accompanied by a dozen knights, the Northumberland Herald, the Percy Herald and four hundred mounted gentlemen all clad in velvet and damask bearing the Percy arms of the crescent and manacles, the Earl had led the procession wearing a surcoat of crimson velvet, the collar and sleeves of which had been thickly encrusted with precious stones and pearls set in goldsmith's work. His black velvet boots bore his stirrups of gold, his horse's crimson velvet saddlecloth had been bordered with gilt and reached to the ground. He'd heard it said the Earl had looked more like a prince than a subject and that was a comment that had reached the ears of the rapacious Henry VII, who abhorred such displays of wealth and power by a subject. In consequence – under the guise of a wardship dispute – that display had cost the Earl a fine of ten thousand pounds. No, he did not approve of Henry Algernon's ways or his wasteful extravagance. And what use were fine clothes, books, manuscripts and illuminated texts in fighting the Scots or marauding moss troopers?

'He will have to learn, for what use is a Percy – a Warden of the Scottish Marches – if he cannot fight? Would you have the Scots mock us? Would you have them reiving the Marches at will?'

The Earl dismounted and passed the reins to a groom. 'I say he *will* learn and when the time comes he will not dishonour the name of Percy,' he snapped. 'Now, let us eat.'

Sir William remained silent as he followed his brother into the castle. He was a veteran of numerous violent and bloody border campaigns and he grudgingly admitted that his brother's courage and fighting skills could not be lightly dismissed either. Ten years ago the Earl had led the Northern Horse in the royalist army's victorious assault on the pretender Perkin Warbeck's army of rebellious Cornishmen at Blackheath, capturing the causeway at Deptford Strand. Sir William hoped that when the time did indeed come, his young nephew would not be found wanting in courage, skill or leadership.

Blickling Hall, Norfolk

The chamber was uncomfortably hot and stuffy. Outside the sun bathed the courtyard and gardens in a golden light and sparkled on the small diamond-shaped panes of the windows of the old manor house. The new green leaves on the trees that surrounded the rear of the building rustled in the soft warm breeze. The scent of flowers – violets, gilly flowers and early roses – filled the air but their perfume did not drift in through the window for no window in the chamber had been opened for days. No sunlight penetrated the room; heavy curtains covered the windows. The tapestries and painted cloths that hung from the walls increased the oppressive, stifling atmosphere and not even the sweet herbs that had been strewn on the rushes on the floor could dispel the cloying odours of sweat and blood.

Her nightgown and the sheet on which she lay were soaked with perspiration; her light brown hair was plastered to her skull. Her skin was clammy with sweat and her throat felt raw and dry. Her lips were sore and bloody for she'd bitten them as she'd fought to stifle her cries of agony. The palms of her hands bore the deep indentations of her fingernails. As the pain diminished she fell back on the pillows, gasping for breath.

'Sweet Virgin! How much longer must I bear this?' she begged.

'Be of good cheer, my lady. It will soon be over and you can rest. Take a few sips of wine, it will help.' Mistress Tyndall, the midwife, held the goblet to her mouth but she shook her head, turning away.

'I cannot. Take it away, it sickens me. It was the same when I laboured with George.'

'I remember now, my lady. Maybe it is an omen – a good omen. Maybe the child will be another boy.'

She tried to smile but the pain tore through her again and she writhed, sinking her teeth again into her ragged bottom lip. She was a Howard, a daughter of the Earl of Surrey, and she would *not* scream out in her agony . . . but it had gone on for so long now and she was close to exhaustion. Surely, surely the child must come soon.

The pain became unbearable, as was the urge to bear down. She was being consumed by this agony, it was tearing her apart and yet she knew she would not die from it. With a rush of blood and mucus that stained the damp sheet the child was thrust out and she felt waves of dizziness, relief and exhaustion wash over her.

'My lady, it is a fine healthy girl,' Mistress Tyndall cried, lifting the baby and giving it a slap on the tiny buttocks. The child immediately wailed loudly and fretfully. The woman laughed. 'See how strong and lusty she is.' The midwife tied and cut the cord and wrapped the baby in a clean linen sheet.

The maids had gently lifted her up and slipped more pillows behind her. They stripped off her stained nightgown, bathing her face, neck and shoulders with rose water. Then they changed the soiled bedding and dressed her in a clean, sweet-smelling robe and Mistress Tyndall handed the baby to her. She smiled down at the little scrap of humanity in her arms. The child waved tiny fists and briefly opened her eyes. They were dark brown and her head was covered with soft, downy hair that looked almost black in the flickering candlelight.

'You will send word to my lord husband?'

Mistress Tyndall nodded. 'I have already sent a girl to find Sir Thomas and inform him of the news.'

Lady Elizabeth Boleyn nodded slowly. 'He will perhaps be disappointed it is not another son.'

Mistress Tyndall frowned. 'We should all praise God that the child is healthy.'

Elizabeth sighed, feeling wearied almost to death now the ordeal was over. 'But girls are of little use to an ambitious father and a dowry will cost him dear.'

Mistress Tyndall nodded as she went about overseeing the tidying and sweetening of the chamber. 'There will be a goodly time before Sir Thomas needs contemplate that, my lady. Have you a name for her?'

Lady Boleyn nodded. 'She will be christened Anne.'

Chapter One

———◦◦◦———

1513
Alnwick Castle, Northumberland

WINTER SEEMED TO COME very early to the northern counties of England and particularly to Northumberland, Henry thought as he sat shivering on his horse in the inner courtyard of the castle. At eleven he was still a slender boy with a pale, often wan, complexion, and he would have preferred to have stayed at Wressle, his father's castle further south beyond the city of York. It was far more comfortable than Alnwick, whose sandstone walls towered above and around him, glittering in the frosty November morning.

Alnwick was an impregnable fortress built on a natural bluff above the River Aln and the small town that bore the same name. The curtain wall was ten feet thick in parts and rose to forty feet in height. The turrets of its many towers were adorned with heraldic shields and medieval figures of knights and men-at-arms carved from stone which, from a distance, looked lifelike and were intended to deter potential raiders, be they marauding Scots or the thieves and brigands that infested the valleys of Redesdale and Tynedale to the north-west. Alnwick was impressive, Henry thought, but it was far from comfortable.

He pulled the collar of his heavy, fur-lined cloak up around his ears and then reached out to pat the neck of Curtall, who was becoming restless, pawing the ground with an iron-shod forefoot. He glanced around at the two dozen men who waited with him. Their horses also becoming restive; metal bits and curb chains clinked as heads were tossed and their breath rose like steam from a cauldron into the cold air. The riders were all his father's men, their weather-beaten faces grim beneath thick cloth hats and hoods of chain mail. Born and bred in Northumberland, they were marcher men all. Beneath their heavy felt cloaks they wore padded tunics and steel breastplates. They were armed with swords and short battle-axes; heavy leather gauntlets protected their hands and high leather boots their feet. They waited impassively and in silence and he felt safe within their company.

Frowning, he tried to sit taller in the saddle and control the shivering, which was compounded of both cold and apprehension. He hadn't wanted to be part of this expedition – he was content to sit with his books in the comparative warmth and comfort of his chamber above the gatehouse – but his father had insisted.

'By God's blood! Is it a weakling I've bred?' the Earl had demanded angrily when he'd tried to excuse himself. 'When I am dead the Wardenship of the Marches will be yours. As Earl of Northumberland it will be your duty to administer justice on behalf of King Henry. Since William of Normandy came to this land we have protected the King's realm against the Scots. It's time you looked to your duty and responsibilities! You are eleven years of age, Harry Hotspur was of that age when he was knighted by King Richard and at twelve his father granted him the honour of leading the victorious assault on the castle at Berwick.'

Henry had ceased to protest but he still felt ill at ease and apprehensive. He was fully aware that he did not have the warlike temperament of his illustrious ancestor, who had fought the Scots at Otterburn two hundred years ago and become the most acclaimed knight in the realm. His younger brothers Thomas and Ingram did. Arrogant and strutting, they both would have relished this opportunity; instead they were inside the castle sulking and posturing because they were not accompanying their father this time. Now a hard day's ride lay ahead, followed by what would be a very cold and cheerless night spent in Ros Castle, which was little more than a fortified tower house near Chillingham, before their return to Alnwick.

The looting, burning and murdering by the brigands of Redesdale, behaviour known throughout the Borders as 'reiving', had increased of late and the Earl was determined to show by force of arms that the House of Percy would no longer stand for such flagrant disregard of the law. In the minds of the inhabitants of this wild and inhospitable part of the country London was far away and King Henry VIII but a vague, distant figurehead. It was the Earl they feared rather than the King.

The comparative quiet of the crisp November morning was disrupted by the sudden clattering of hooves on the cobbles as a groom led out the Earl's destrier. Seventeen hands in height at the shoulder and as black as the night, it looked gigantic beside Curtall and the mounts of the marcher men. It was truly a magnificent beast, young Henry thought. His father strode out behind, preparing to mount, and the familiar mixture of respect and fear filled him at the sight: 'Henry the Magnificent' inspired awe; a tall, strong man on whose features were etched grim determination and pride. His clothes were the most fashionable and expensive to be seen outside of London. He was dressed for hard riding in a dark green doublet, slashed to show the white shirt he wore beneath, and padded breeches. Italian leather boots encased his muscular legs and over his fine clothes he wore a cape of soft russet leather lined with sable fur. His hat was of black velvet – a flat bonnet adorned with a black feather – which would be covered by the furred hood of his cape when the journey commenced. At his side hung his two-handed sword of tempered steel and upon the horse's saddle was strapped a battle-axe.

The Earl acknowledged Branxton, his sergeant, with a brief nod and then stared down at his eldest son. Henry tried hard not to quail beneath that hard, speculative gaze.

'Ride close to Branxton,' his father instructed him sharply before urging his horse forward. 'Come, we have delayed too long,' he commanded.

They moved off under the iron-studded portcullis, the horses' hooves clattering upon the wooden drawbridge, and rode quickly through the parkland that surrounded the castle. Riding next to Branxton Henry realised they were heading in a north-westerly direction towards the Cheviot Hills and the border with Scotland. A border where an almost constant state of war had existed for hundreds of years.

He felt the warmth begin to creep slowly back into his limbs as eventually the moorland stretched out before them, deep purple in places where the heather grew thickest but grey and stark in the distance where the hills rose, etched against a pale duck-egg-blue sky.

Although he rode well it was far from easy going for frost had turned the ground iron hard. By mid-morning a wind had sprung up and the watery sun was hidden behind sullen, lowering clouds the colour of gunmetal. The first icy drops of rain stung his cheeks and the biting wind made his eyes water. Thomas would be welcome to this, he thought miserably as the rain became heavier and began to soak into his cape. He would be chilled to the bone and aching all over before this day was out and then no doubt he would be laid low with an ague to which he was prone. Ahead of him rode his father, his back erect, his head unbent in the face of the elements, as though disdainful of them. The soldiers, familiar with both the terrain and the harsh climate, kept up with the Earl's relentless pace, hunched and silent in their saddles.

At noon, to Henry's relief, they reached the village of Hepburn and the Earl halted. It wasn't a very prepossessing place, he thought, peering through the curtain of rain; it was poor and miserable, a huddle of daub and wattle cottages, their thatched roofs held down securely against the winter gales by boulders and ropes. A road that was little more than a muddy track led to a barn of sorts and the ubiquitous midden heap, but a few yards beyond that there did appear to be an inn.

'Branxton, ale and such food as they can furnish and water and fodder for the horses,' the Earl instructed curtly as he dismounted a little stiffly.

'And a good fire, my lord. Lord Henry's face is the colour of parchment,' the sergeant informed his master in a low voice.

When they reached the inn, Henry slid slowly down from Curtall's saddle, his knees buckling with the numbness of fatigue. The man nearest him held out his arm and the boy clutched it tightly to steady himself.

'A pot of spiced ale will soon warm you, Lord Henry,' he said, not unkindly, for he thought the boy looked ill and wondered if the rigours of this expedition would be too much for him. The young lord was reputed to be of a sickly disposition, unlike both his brothers Thomas and Ingram.

The inn comprised one long, dark, low-ceilinged room, the roughly hewn beams black with smoke from the fire that burned at the far end, the floor hard packed earth. The furnishings consisted of a few crude benches and stools; empty upturned barrels served as tables. Upon being informed of the identity of his illustrious guests the landlord hastily beat his wife and daughter into a flurry of activity to prepare the small room beside their kitchen for the Earl and the young lord.

As the landlord ushered them in, grovelling before them, the Earl looked askance at the old and rancid rushes on the floor, which were probably alive with vermin and lice, the hastily cleared table devoid of any covering and the two battered stools. Henry, despite his wretchedness, wrinkled his nose in distaste at the smell of sour ale, stale food and sweat, animal fat and dung that seemed to permeate the room, the latter wafting in from the midden heap behind the building.

With the dubious benefits of a pot of hot spiced ale and the warmth from the fire, however, he began to feel a little better. The landlord's daughter, an unkempt slattern overcome with awe to the point of dumbness, served them with flat, coarse trencher loaves and thick wedges of strong-smelling cheese. This, her father explained with abject humility, was all a poor but God-fearing man such as himself could provide. Had his lordship sent word ahead he would have killed some chickens and his wife would have cooked them.

'Plain fare will suffice. You will be paid for your hospitality,' the Earl informed him, before slicing up the bread with the jewelled knife he had drawn from his belt.

It was a brief respite but when they departed an hour later Henry felt stronger. The rain had ceased and the entire population of the village had turned out. Many had never seen the Earl before and were staring in open astonishment at the richness of his clothes and the magnificence of the horse's saddle and trappings. Men doffed shapeless hats; women bobbed curtsies while small, grubby children clung wide-eyed to their stained skirts. A ragged cheer, instigated by the landlord of the inn went up as the Earl and his men prepared to depart. Henry was still cold and stiff but his teeth had ceased to chatter, he wasn't shivering so hard and his belly was full.

They resumed their journey, which took them with each passing mile ever closer to the notorious valley of Redesdale. The landscape grew more desolate. The few trees that had survived were stunted and twisted by the prevailing winds. Steep hills strewn with huge boulders slowed them down and a chill numbness again penetrated Henry's bones. His head had begun to ache.

'My lord! Look! Smoke! Over to the left!' Branxton cried.

The Earl reined in his horse and peered in the direction of the sergeant-at-arms's outstretched finger. Many miles away on the distant horizon, thick black smoke rose in a column and then appeared to be absorbed by the heavy cinereous clouds.

'The work of those murdering bastards of Redesdale, I'll warrant!' Branxton muttered grimly. He had only contempt for the thieves and cowards who skulked in these remote valleys and terrorised the poor peasants.

The Earl did not reply but his mouth was set in a hard line and his eyes were the colour of flint as he turned his horse's head in the direction of the steep, gravel-strewn path that led towards the column of smoke.

Henry's throat felt dry and his heart lurched. He just wanted to go home; to crawl into a soft bed, pull the thick warm blankets around him, lay his aching head on a soft pillow of goose down and have his mother soothe and fuss over him. With an effort he straightened his back and swallowed hard. He was not a mewling child. He must put aside all the discomforts. He must not shame his father or his ancestors. He was a Percy of Northumberland, the great border lords who upheld the law and kept the King's peace. He must remember that above all else – whatever lay ahead.

Chapter Two

—◆—

Redesdale, Northumberland

'WILL, LAD, TAKE IN that bundle of kindling to your mother. I'll chop up this blackthorn trunk; it will burn well when seasoned. It's not often such a stroke of luck falls to us.'

Will Chatton grinned at his father, squinting up through the unkempt fringe of brown hair that was always falling into his hazel eyes. His rough homespun tunic, tied around the waist with twine, and the dun-coloured leggings, also bound with twine around his calves and ankles, did little to keep out the cold blasts of wind that blew down the valley. His feet were encased in badly fitting, patched old boots and his hands were rough, chapped and ingrained with dirt. He was a hardy if rather skinny lad of eleven and had never in his life known the comfort of warm, serviceable clothes, good boots or a full belly. He worked hard helping his father to wrest a meagre living from the poor patch of land that surrounded the cottage and barn, which nestled in a hollow at the base of a rocky outcrop. 'I'll help you drag it into the barn out of the weather,' he offered.

'After you've done as you are bid. Your mother will need that kindling for the fire if we're to have any hot food inside us today,' Jed Chatton reminded him. 'Get off with you, lad.' Then he picked up the axe and turned his attention to the fallen blackthorn. The stunted old tree had come down in the wind two nights ago and he'd thanked the Blessed Virgin for such good fortune. It was hard, back-breaking work scratching a living in this barren country. Times had been better some years ago when they'd had a cow, a sow and her litter and some sheep and goats but they'd all been taken from them. All that was left now were a few scrawny chickens, he thought bitterly.

'Here's the kindling, Ma. What be there for the dinner?' Will asked as he hauled the bundle of twigs into the single room where his mother sat at a bench scraping and chopping the few vegetables she'd pulled from the stony garden patch beside the barn earlier. The smoke from the fire had blackened the squat stone walls; the floor was strewn with reeds gathered from the edge of one of the many burns that coursed down the valley. The one small, unglazed window let in little light and the air was dank and chilly. A pile of dried bracken in one corner served as a bed for them all, with a few sacks as bedding. Rushes dipped in animal fat gave them scant light at night for even cheap tallow candles were beyond their means.

Will grinned at the antics of the two young bairns squabbling beside the open hearth, over which was suspended a small black pot of steaming water. John, his brother, was seven and Margaret, or 'Meggie' as he called her, was five.

'Vegetable broth and I've a few handfuls of barley to thicken it, but it's the last of it,' his mother informed him. She sighed heavily. It wasn't much for the only hot meal of the day, barely enough to keep body and soul together, and no coarse bread to go with it. 'Would you go out and try to snare a coney, Will?'

He nodded. 'I will, Ma, after I've helped Da to drag the trunk into the barn.' He grinned at her, pushing his hair out of his eyes. 'You hear that, Meggie? We'll have a great fire this Christmas.'

Mary Chatton smiled tiredly at him. He was a good lad, he worked hard and seldom complained. But her smile faded and a worried frown creased her brow as she heard shouts coming from outside. 'Go and see who that be, Will!' she urged, getting to her feet and pulling her coarse wool shawl tightly around her thin shoulders.

Will felt a shiver of fear run through him as he ran to the door for travellers were few and not always welcome. Then he cried out as he saw the band of mounted men emerging from the track and heading rapidly toward the cottage. 'Da! Da! What be they coming here for now?' He ran to where his father stood beside the tree trunk, gripping the axe tightly. Jed Chatton's thin, sallow face was flushed with anger but there was fear, too, in his eyes.

'We'll find out soon enough, lad,' he said grimly as the group grew closer. There were six men mounted on small, sturdy, shaggy ponies. He knew them well enough. They were all villainous-looking individuals, their hair and beards long and matted. They wore jerkins of leather over rough woollen shirts. Three of them wore cloaks of a green and brown woven tartan over their jerkins and all were armed with knives and swords. They drew to a halt a few paces away and two of them dismounted. The bigger and more thickset of the pair grinned at Jed, revealing blackened teeth. A jagged scar ran from the corner of his mouth to his ear.

'Good day to you, Farmer Chatton! It's time for the dues to be paid to us,' he announced.

'What dues be they?' Jed asked sullenly.

'For our protection should the Scots come raiding across the border.'

'We've seen no Scots in these parts for two years and more,' Will retorted, stepping closer to his father and wishing he had some sort of weapon, if only a stout stave. He hated these men, as did every poor farmer and labourer for miles around. Because of them there was never enough food or money. Because of them they all went cold and hungry and had to break their backs working just to exist. They were thieves and brigands and did nothing to protect anyone from the Scots when they came killing and burning and driving all the livestock before them back across the border.

The man uttered a harsh laugh. 'The whelp has guts! There're no Scots reivers, lad, for they know the men of Redesdale protect you.'

Jed Chatton gripped the axe harder. 'We cannot pay. We have nothing.'

The man took a step forward, his pretence of good humour vanishing. 'Do not play me for a fool, man! The harvest is gathered.'

'And what little we had that wasn't spoiled by the rains went to pay the tithes on the land. You took all the sheep and goats the last time you came this way. We have nothing to tide us through the winter. The bairns will go hungry.'

'It's the truth he be telling you. We have nothing left!' Will added, glaring at the man, who, he'd noted, wore two rings, one of gold and one of silver, on his fat, dirty fingers.

The other men had now dismounted and with a jerk of his head their leader dispatched them in the direction of the house and the barn.

'Take whatever is in the barn and the chickens and then search the house! Dig up the floor, pull down the thatch! That's where coins will be hidden.'

'No! I tell you we have *nothing*!' Despite his fear Jed started to raise the axe. He couldn't let them take what little they had, but the thickset man was quicker. He grabbed Will and held a dagger to his throat.

'I'll slit his throat and he'll die like a pig if you don't drop that axe!'

Jed let the axe fall to the ground and Will struggled free and ran to him. They would take their precious few sacks of corn and oats that were stored in the barn. Crops they'd laboured hard to grow and harvest and save. They would be left to starve through the winter. Blind fury swept over him and he lunged for the axe and lashed out at their tormentors. 'You are worse thieves and brigands than the Scots! You're cowards! Filthy low cowards!' he yelled. He caught the man on the shin, an ineffectual blow delivered with little strength and deflected by the thick leather boots, and then he cried out as his head seemed to explode in pain and he was sent sprawling to the ground. He tried to sit up but a heavy boot slammed into his side and he pitched forward groaning.

As he lay trying to gather his wits he could hear the shouts of the brigands as they ransacked the cottage and then, finding nothing of value, began to tear down the roof thatch. He could hear his mother screaming and the bairns howling in terror. Despite the dizziness he dragged himself to his knees. He had to do something to help them. He heard their leader bellow at his father, 'You're a liar, Chatton! The dues will be paid!'

'There's nothing left to give you. Have pity – don't destroy the house. We'll die without shelter!' Jed begged.

The thickset man struck him hard across the head with the flat of the sword blade and Jed staggered and fell to his knees. 'Liar! You think to defraud me of my dues?'

Through a haze of pain and fear Will saw his father try to rise and grapple with the two men. His efforts were hopeless for both were much stronger and heavier than Jed but his attempt at resistance goaded them to fury. Will hauled himself to his feet, swaying as waves of nausea washed over him. He tried to run towards his father, who was being savagely beaten to the ground; if he could just get to the axe which lay forgotten a few feet away … Then he was knocked flat on his back again by a fist smashing into his belly as a third thief came running to join his compatriots, having deduced the lad's intentions. He rolled over, fighting for breath. The blow had winded him but he could make out the figure of his mother beside the door of the cottage, bending over the two sobbing children, but then she uttered a shriek of terror as the three men seized his father and began to drag him towards the barn.

'Hang the lying bastard! It will be a lesson to others who might think to cheat us!'

Still screaming, his mother ran towards his father. 'No! No! Don't harm him. For the love of Almighty God, have pity. Have pity!' she begged, trying to cling to Jed's arm. One of them lashed out and caught her a vicious blow across the side of her face, sending her sprawling in the dirt, the blood spurting from her nose and lip.

With a supreme effort Will was on his feet. His brother and sister were on their knees beside his mother, wailing hysterically. He stumbled across the rough ground to the doorway of the barn. He heard his father's desperate pleading and saw his face, bloody and bruised, one eye already swollen and half closed.

With every ounce of strength he could muster he hurled himself at the men, kicking, clawing and scratching, but he was already weakened. Two massive blows felled him. Lights danced before his eyes and he could taste the blood in his mouth. There was nothing more he could do except lie in agony and watch.

They bound Jed Chatton's arms behind him. His feet were tied and one of them put a rope around his neck and threw the end over a roof beam. They were all shouting and swearing and laughing and slowly Will dragged himself away. When he reached the doorway again he pulled himself up and sat clutching the doorpost, his bleeding, broken fingernails digging into the wood. His chest heaved painfully as sobs convulsed him and he was blinded by tears. He was powerless to do anything at all to save his father and mingled with the horror and grief was impotent fury at his own helplessness.

He didn't know how long he crouched there, dazed and crying, but eventually his mother's voice, shrill with hysteria, penetrated his numbed mind. He looked up. Her eyes were wild, her face contorted, tears were coursing down her cheeks mingling with the blood from her nose and mouth.

'Will? Will! Help me. Help me to . . . cut him . . . down, lad. Please, you've got to help me. Oh, God help us! They've set the house and barn alight.' She pulled frantically at his arm.

He struggled to his feet, drawing the sleeve of his tunic across his streaming nose and eyes. Between them they managed to get Jed's lifeless body down and Will knew he would never forget the sight of his father's bloated and battered face. They dragged him outside for flames were licking at the dry timber of the roof beams and dense smoke was filling the barn.

In what had been the vegetable patch, now trampled and rutted by hooves, Mary Chatton sank to her knees, clasping the body of her husband to her, rocking to and fro, keening in her terrible anguish. Will staggered towards the cottage but it was engulfed in flames, and he sank on to his haunches in the dirt. They would all perish now for there was no shelter and no food and no Father to work their land.

He didn't hear the riders approach. It was the shrill cries of his brother and sister that finally made him aware that they were no longer alone. Had they come back to finish their work? Had they come back to murder them all? A wave of fury surged through him. He'd kill them with his bare hands or die trying! They were going to die anyway, so what had he to lose now?

'There be nothing left, damn you to hell! I'll kill you! I'll kill you!' he screamed as he staggered towards them. Tears made clean furrows down his blood and snot-stained cheeks.

Branxton dismounted and ran forward to catch him. 'We're not Redesdale men, lad! Is this their doing?' he asked, taking in the scene before them. The cottage, now a smouldering ruin; the small barn still burning fiercely, although the roof had collapsed; the woman half sitting, half lying on the ground, cradling the lifeless form of a man, her face covered in dried blood; two young dirty, terrified bairns clinging to each other; and the young lad, also bruised and bloody and half demented with grief and terror.

The Earl beckoned and Branxton led Will towards him. 'Have courage, lad. It is the Lord Percy himself,' the sergeant urged.

The Earl's furious expression softened a little as he took in the boy's appearance. 'Is this the doing of the thieves and murderers of Redesdale?'

Will nodded, gazing up through his tears at the big man on the enormous black horse. 'They . . . they came this morning and said we had not paid the dues for protection against the Scots, but they had already taken the sheep and the goats. Da . . .' He drew his sleeve across his eyes, fighting down the sobs. 'Da told them there was nothing left. They . . . they said he lied, but it were true. We had nothing. They . . . beat him. I . . . I tried to help him but I could do nothing to stop them! They . . . they . . . hanged him and they . . . they laughed!' He choked, tears now streaming down his cheeks. 'If I could have got to the axe . . . If I had had a sword, I would have killed them!'

The Earl nodded and Branxton patted Will on the shoulder. 'They would have killed you too, lad. Leave justice and retribution to his lordship.'

The Earl dismounted and walked over to the boy's mother. Cold fury at the arrogant flouting of the law and the wanton destruction and murder filled him. 'Mistress, have you kinfolk hereabouts?'

At his voice she raised her battered and swollen face and nodded. 'At Holystone. A hamlet some miles distant.'

'Then pack what little there is left. We will bury your man and two of the soldiers will escort you safely to them.' He dropped a small bag into her lap. 'This will tide you through the winter.' He turned to Will. 'What is your name, boy?'

'Will. Will Chatton, your lordship.'

'How old are you, Will Chatton?'

'I seen eleven summers, sir.'

'And you would have your father avenged?'

Will nodded, finding a spark of courage. 'Give me a sword, sir?' he begged. 'And let me ride with you?'

'You haven't the strength to lift a sword, boy, but you may ride with us. Branxton, take him up behind you. If we hasten we shall catch up with them.' He was impressed with the boy's courage and spirit, qualities not often found in the poor peasant classes, who for the most part were bovine and subservient. The boy had already proved himself fearless and determined; a place would be found for him at Alnwick.

Mary Chatton struggled to her feet. 'Sir! Your lordship, he be only a child! He is all that's left to me, for the bairns can do nothing for themselves!'

Branxton turned towards her. 'Fear not, mistress, no harm

will come to him while he is in the service of his lordship – for that is what I suspect Lord Percy has in his mind – nor to yourself or the bairns.'

'You have my oath on it, mistress. A place will be found for him at Alnwick and you will not be left destitute by his absence. The brigands of Redesdale will pay for their crimes. You will have justice, mistress. You have the word of a Percy.' The Earl turned to his men. 'Mount up, there's little time to spare!'

Almost before he realised what was happening to him Will Chatton was hoisted into the saddle and for the first time in his life he was astride a horse. It was an experience that in other circumstances would have amazed and delighted him, as would the unheard-of good fortune of having a place at Alnwick, but all he felt was a sense of utter relief as he clung tightly to Branxton and rested his bruised and aching head against the man's heavy riding cloak. Relief and infinite trust in his benefactor: Henry Algernon Percy, Earl of Northumberland.

Chapter Three

———◆·◆·◆———

Redesdale

WHEN THEY HAD RIDDEN into the small, smoky clearing young Henry had stared around him, shocked at the destruction the brigands of Redesdale had left behind. He was sickened by the needless violence. The family was desperately poor, that much was obvious. His father's horses were better housed than this woman and her children. As he learned of the evil perpetrated that day, he felt pity for the young boy who had been so badly beaten trying to defend his family. Sitting a few paces behind his father listening to Will's words, he'd tried to imagine how he would feel if his father had been dragged away and hanged and his lady mother beaten until her face was bloody but he'd failed, for such a thing could never happen. There was no one, except the King, who had the power to harm his family. However, he had begun to understand why his father had insisted he accompany him on this expedition. The lives of these poor, ignorant, helpless people would one day be his responsibility. It would be his duty to protect them from the murderers of Redesdale and Tynedale and from the Scots.

As they rode off, leaving two men to bury the murdered farmer and escort his widow and children to their kinfolk, Henry glanced across to where the boy, Will Chatton, rode behind Branxton: an uneducated peasant, his clothes dirty and torn. He was the same age as himself, he thought, and yet he'd had the courage to pit himself against evil, violent men without thought for his own safety. He was glad that his father intended to find a place for him at Alnwick for as well as pity he felt admiration for the lad. He realised that the boy was staring back at him.

'I am sorry for what has happened. At least you did try to stop them. You must take comfort . . . from that,' he said haltingly. He was unused to uttering condolences.

Will nodded. 'If I had had a sword . . .'

'But you have no training in the use of arms.' Henry replied, thinking of the hours he and his brothers spent with their Uncle William, who instructed them daily in the art of warfare.

'It wouldn't have mattered,' Will said vehemently. 'I would have killed one or two of them. That would have been enough.'

Henry's estimation of the boy rose further. He would almost certainly have been killed himself yet he would have taken that risk.

Henry began to shiver: the raw dampness was making his bones ache again. Then he frowned. He should not complain of such things; he had warm clothes and a fur-lined cape, leather boots and gauntlets. Will Chatton had only a thin homespun tunic and breeches, which offered no protection at all against the cold.

They rode on in silence and as the light of the November afternoon began to fade Henry realised that they couldn't be far behind the brigands. His apprehension began to increase as the craggy outline of the hills surrounding the valley came into view and his father signalled that they should stop.

'From here we will go stealthily. They will not be expecting us but there is no sense in making our presence known,' the Earl said quietly.

'My lord, there is a pass which leads down the western side and into the valley. Only a few know of it,' Branxton informed him.

'Then lead us on,' his lordship instructed.

Henry rode beside his father as they followed Branxton, with Will Chatton still riding pillion behind him, to the narrow pass. They progressed slowly and cautiously down and when they reached its foot and entered the valley the Earl ordered half of his men to work their way silently on foot to the further end of the gulley that lay ahead. He watched as the soldiers disappeared into the gathering dusk and then the Earl urged his horse on. Henry glanced across at Will Chatton. The cold and the rigours of their journey seemed not to have affected him and he was disconcerted to see that the boy's face was now a cold mask of fury. He felt the sweat break out on his forehead and the trembling in his limbs increased, knowing more violence lay ahead and praying he could find the courage to face it without flinching. Will Chatton would; the boy's face told him that.

They had ventured a few hundred yards into the gulley when the Earl again halted them. Ahead Henry could see the orange glow of flames that came from a camp fire. Shadowy figures were grouped about it.

'Stay a dozen paces behind me. Keep the boy with you and keep him silent,' the Earl instructed Branxton before riding on.

Sound carried clearly on the cold air and the clatter of the war horse's hooves on the stony valley floor caused the outlaws to get to their feet, snatching up their weapons and peering into the gloom.

'We have a visitor and a fine bird with fine feathers,' the thickset man with the scarred face muttered to his companions, grinning wolfishly.

'Alone too. Easy pickings,' his closest companion replied as he prepared to move forward.

The Earl was much closer now and the leader of the group hesitated. 'Hold back. What fool would come here alone after dark? For what reason be he here?'

'Perhaps he's lost his way,' someone muttered.

'Halt, stranger! What brings you to these parts? Have you strayed from the path?' the man shouted.

The Earl did not draw rein but carried on towards them steadily and in silence.

The thickset brigand felt even more apprehensive as he began to realise that this was no ordinary wealthy traveller as he'd first assumed. The saddle and trappings of the horse – a horse such as he'd only ever seen in woodcuts and carvings of knights – and the man's clothes were of a magnificence he'd never seen before and denoted someone of more importance than a wealthy merchant.

At last the Earl drew to a halt before them. 'I seek the men who flout the laws of our sovereign lord, King Henry. Think you it's your right to burn and pillage and murder at will?'

'We be peaceful, honest men!' the leader of the group protested warily.

The Earl leaned forward in the saddle and the horse moved a pace closer, tossing its head and pawing the ground with its feathered forefoot. 'And I say you are a liar! Is that not what you called the man Chatton, before you murdered him?'

'No. No! We know no one who goes by that name. We be honest men!' Again the thickset outlaw protested but his men were all afraid now, unconsciously drawing closer to each other.

The Earl was becoming angry at their craven denials. 'And I, the Lord Percy, say you are liars, thieves and murderers!'

They could now see the soldiers advancing and at the stark horror at finding that they were confronted by the Earl of Northumberland himself they huddled together, their faces ashen, all pretence of bravado and innocence gone.

'My lord, have pity. Have pity!' one cried, falling to his knees.

'You beg for pity? By God's blood, you are little better than cringing dogs!' the Earl shouted. 'What pity did you show to the man Chatton and his family?'

Two of them turned and tried to run, only to be caught and dragged back by the soldiers who had advanced unseen behind them.

'A trial? A trial! It's the law, my lord,' their leader begged.

'The law for which you have scant respect. But there is a witness to the murder and pillage you committed this day. You should have killed him too but in your arrogance and ignorance you did not think that I would hunt you down. Branxton, bring forward the boy.'

The sergeant rode to his lordship's side and the Earl turned to Will.

'Are these the culprits, Will Chatton?'

Will was shaking with anger and hatred burned in his eyes. 'These be the ones, my lord. Those three hanged my father and it was him who beat me. See, he wears two rings on his right hand, I remember them well.'

The Earl nodded. 'That is proof enough. Hang them!'

Henry braced himself as the three were seized, tied and dragged screaming and struggling towards a gnarled and misshapen hawthorn tree. His stomach heaved but he fought down the nausea. They did not die well, coughing and choking, their eyes bulging, their faces turning black.

The Earl was not yet finished. 'Bring forward the others.'

The remaining three were dragged forward, crying with fear and terror.

With an effort Henry held himself upright and forced himself to look straight ahead, keeping his eyes averted from the three lifeless bodies hanging from the boughs of the hawthorn. It wasn't over yet.

'You are but a few of the craven blackguards who infest this valley and that of Tynedale, but you will live to tell the rest that the Lord Percy metes out the King's justice. Yet you shall not go unpunished for your crimes. Hold forth your right hands!'

One man protested but the others were silent and trembling. None of them moved to obey the Earl's command. The soldiers seized them roughly and forced them to the ground and at a nod from the Earl, Branxton severed the hand of each man in turn.

Henry felt the sickly blackness creeping over him as their screams filled his ears and the blood poured from their wrists while the severed hands twitched on the ground beside them. It was what they deserved, he told himself. It was justice. Justice. Justice. Justice. Over and over he repeated the word until at last he felt the dizziness receding. He turned his head and looked for Will Chatton. The boy was sitting on the ground a few feet away, his arms wrapped around his head, his shoulders shaking. Slowly and stiffly Henry dismounted and went to him. The boy's obvious misery had come as a surprise and he forgot his own feelings as he bent down and touched the boy's shoulder.

'It's over. Does it not comfort you that justice has been done?' he asked.

Will looked up, his bruised face wet with tears, and shook his head. 'I did think I would be glad to see them suffer but it doesn't help and I don't know why. It doesn't take away the . . . feelings.' He struggled to put his conflicting emotions into words. The death and mutilation of his family's tormentors could not bring back his father, nor undo the vicious harm that had been done to his mother, himself and the bairns.

Branxton stood beside the two boys. 'It's the grief, Lord Henry,' he explained. 'He will need time to accustom himself. Give me your hand, lad. We ride now to Chillingham. There is nothing left for us to do here.' He helped Will to his feet and Henry walked beside them back to where the horses stood waiting. He kept his eyes averted from the still moaning figures on the ground. 'Will they . . . ?'

'Aye, they'll live,' Branxton said grimly. If he'd had his way he'd have hanged them all, they deserved nothing less, but only in his heart would he disagree with his lordship's decision. 'You will both be better for a hot meal, a good fire and a night's rest,' he added, knowing that the wagons had set out yesterday for Ros Castle, carrying food, wine and ale, furniture and bedding and firewood.

Henry nodded; he was in dire need of such comforts. And he had made a decision. 'I shall ask my father if you can serve me as my squire, Will Chatton.'

'What be a squire, my lord?' Will asked, surprised.

'A servant,' Henry answered, looking to Branxton for confirmation.

Will was confused and perturbed. 'I be country born and bred. I be unused to the ways of gentlefolk.'

'You can learn. It's an honour for a lad such as you,' Branxton said, although he wondered how the young lord's suggestion would be received by his father.

'Then I thank you, Lord Henry,' Will replied. This day had brought about so much change in his life, he thought dazedly as Branxton hauled him up on to the horse and one of the soldiers helped Henry to mount.

There was more than enough room for another servant in his father's household, Henry thought. The boy had had so little and this day had seen him robbed of both his father and his home. He was a brave lad, he deserved a small chance in life.

Chapter Four

◆━◆━◆

Hotel de Bourgoyne, Malines, Netherlands

S HE WASN'T IN THE least bit overawed now. Not by the rich, beautiful, brightly woven tapestries depicting biblical and classical scenes that hung on the walls, or the intricately carved cupboards with their displays of finely chased gold and silver-gilt plate studded with precious gems that lined the chamber, or the leather-bound books and illuminated manuscripts that were on display or the floor tiles of Italian marble. When she had first set eyes on such splendour she had been wide-eyed and incredulous. Her home had been large and comfortably furnished, she had always had good food and fine clothes, but it had been but a manor house and she was the daughter of a knight. She had never imagined that there could be such wealth, but she had grown accustomed to it.

She did not hang back shyly now in the presence of the Regent of the Netherlands, Margaret, Dowager Duchess of

36

Savoy and Archduchess of Austria, seated at the end of the chamber beneath the cloth of estate, as she had done six months ago when Claude Bouton, Captain of the Guard to the Prince of Castile who was betrothed to the Princess Mary of England, had brought her to Malines. She was familiar now with this lovely town with its wide, clean streets and many picturesque canals. She felt at ease in this pretty yet sumptuous palace on the Keyserhof, and she enjoyed her lessons in the schoolroom with Eleanor, Ysabeau and Mary, who were the granddaughters of the Holy Roman Emperor, Maximilian. Why should she not? It was a very great honour to be educated with the Archduchesses who would all one day be queens; her father had impressed this fact upon her.

He had worked very hard to obtain such a position for her, he had said, even though she was only six years old, and she had replied that she was very grateful and would be an obedient daughter. He was a very clever man, her father, Sir Thomas Boleyn, she knew that, and the Regent held him in high esteem, as did King Henry. Young as she was she knew that both her father and mother were descendants of King Edward I and her mother, Elizabeth Howard, was daughter to the Earl of Surrey, raised after his victory at Flodden to Duke of Norfolk, and that it was her duty to learn as much as possible while she was here so that they would all be proud of her.

Of course it had saddened her to leave her lady mother and Hever Castle in the Kent countryside where she had grown up with her younger sister Mary and George, her older brother, but both her parents had told her how fortunate she was and how she must work very hard so she would not be a disappointment to them. Mary had been jealous and had sulked but that had not upset her for Mary was often silly. George had teased her, saying she would become such a great lady that they would have to bow down before her when she returned home.

She had reached the foot of the dais and she curtsied to the Regent, holding the folds of her green damask skirts out daintily and bowing her head. She was a fashionably dressed lady in miniature with her green hood, edged with gold lace, covering her long, dark hair and the fine gold chain around her neck. The ladies of the Regent's court smiled and looked at her kindly for she was a popular little figure.

The older woman smiled at the child, her kind blue eyes full of approval and affection. 'You may rise, *la petite Boulain*. I have some good news for you.'

Anne smiled up at her, her own eyes bright with curiosity. 'Some news of my father, your grace?' Her father travelled a good deal as an envoy for King Henry and she wondered was he now coming to visit the Regent?

Margaret shook her head, thinking what an attractive child she was. She had a natural grace, a pleasing demeanour and pretty manners. She worked diligently at her lessons and her French was improving rapidly, as was her self-confidence. In fact she was so delighted with the child that she had written to Sir Thomas Boleyn, for whom she had much respect, thanking him for sending his elder daughter to her. She glanced at the parchment which lay in her lap. 'You are to have a companion, *ma petite*; she is of an age with yourself and from your country. Does that please you?'

'Very well, your grace,' Anne replied, bowing her head deferentially, a gesture that served to hide the quick flash of speculation which filled those expressive dark eyes. Who was this 'companion' to be and would she be happy to share her privileged position with her? She raised her head, her eyes wide and filled now only with interest. 'May I ask her name, your grace?'

'Anne Brandon, the daughter of Viscount Lisle. She is seven years old and, poor child, motherless.'

Anne tried to look suitably sympathetic as she nodded. She had heard of Charles Brandon, Viscount Lisle, her father had spoken of him, but she did not know this other Anne, his daughter. So, she was seven, a year older than herself. She hoped she would not prove to be quarrelsome, but she must try to feel sorry for her for it must be a terrible thing for your mother to die.

'She will join you next month, in time for the Christmas festivities. William Sidney, his lordship's servant, is to accompany her here. She will be in the care of the Mistress of the Archduchesses' Chamber, as you are. You must make her welcome.'

Anne smiled. 'I shall try very hard, your grace,' she promised. 'May I now return to Semmonet? I am copying a letter to my father which she has written out for me.'

Margaret smiled, dismissing the child with a nod. 'Soon, perhaps, you may be able to compose a letter to him yourself. That would give him great pleasure and pride in your accomplishment.'

Anne curtsied. 'I shall work diligently, I promise.'

When she returned to the schoolroom, which overlooked the formal gardens at the back of the palace, it was to find Eleanor, Ysabeau and Mary all dutifully at their books. Semmonet, her French teacher, was in quiet conversation beside the fireplace with Marguerite de Poitiers and the Spanish gentleman, Louis de Vaca, both of whom were charged with the education of the Habsburg girls and herself.

'I am to have a companion. Anne Brandon, she is seven years old. She is the daughter of Viscount Lisle and her mother is dead,' she informed them.

Fifteen-year-old Eleanor nodded sympathetically. 'It is a great sorrow to lose a parent, as we know well.'

'We must pray she will not be too distressed at leaving her home,' Ysabeau added kindly.

The Frenchwoman raised a dark eyebrow and looked speculatively at her companions before setting down the quill, inkpot and two pieces of parchment before Anne.

'Then let us hope she will soon become accustomed to us and apply herself diligently to her lessons. And we do not wish to hear you chattering to her in your English tongue, Mistress Anne. You are here to learn to converse and to read and to write in French,' she commented a little sharply.

The child was not perturbed by this remark. 'And to learn to play well upon the lute and the clavichord and to sing. Master Bredemeres has told me I am making excellent progress.'

Semmonet's features relaxed into a smile; she had grown fond of her youngest pupil. 'You have the gift of music, little Anna Boulain. The Regent herself thinks so too and she is the greatest patron of the arts in all Christendom. Master des Prez has told her you have a clear voice with a sweet pure tone and that if you continue to practise and to improve, you may be permitted to sing at the festivities at Christmas.'

Anne's face lit up with a smile of delight and her dark eyes sparkled with excitement and pride. This was praise indeed for

Josquin des Prez was the greatest composer at this court. Would that not be wonderful? Perhaps she might have a new gown and hood too for such an event? She would certainly spend more time at her lessons with Master Bredemeres. Anne Brandon's father might be a viscount but she was certain that she would not have a voice as sweet and clear as hers. As she settled down to complete the letter to her father she had been copying she determined that from then on all the time she could spare would be spent sitting in the chamber that served as a music room with the beribboned lute on which she accompanied herself. Master Bredemeres had selected a trio of songs for her to practise, her favourite being a poem composed by the Regent herself and set to music by des Prez. This she was certain would delight her benefactress.

Christmas was drawing ever closer and on a dark afternoon in mid-December, with the candles burning in their sconces on the wall and the fire in the hearth making her small chamber glow, Anne was trying on her new scarlet and gold gown. She was delighted with it for it had a tight, laced brocade bodice with a square neckline and a full skirt over a plain gold underskirt. The long wide sleeves were also of brocade and cut in the French fashion. Her kirtle was of scarlet and gold cord. Carefully she placed the matching hood, edged with tiny pearls, over her hair which fell like a shiny dark curtain down her back, almost to her waist. She gazed at her reflection in the polished metal hand mirror and nodded with satisfaction. It was beautiful and made her feel very grown up. Her mother had sent her a pair of soft scarlet velvet slippers adorned with gold tissue rosettes on the front. They were her special gift for Christmas.

'Do I look like a fine, grown-up lady, Semmonet?' she asked, gazing up intently and seeking the assurance of her mentor.

'You do, little Mistress Anne, and you look very pretty,' came the reassuring reply, delivered with a fond smile.

She touched the square neckline of the bodice and her dark eyes clouded a little. 'I shall have to wear my gold chain. I had hoped that my father might send me something else, something . . . finer, as a Christmas gift.'

The older woman shook her head and tutted impatiently. 'You are too young for jewelled collars or necklaces. Your chain will be sufficient. Do not frown and pout, Mistress Anne. It does not become you.'

The child did not have time to reply before Lady Anna de Beaumont entered the chamber holding by the hand a child still dressed in travel-stained clothes, her face pale, dark rings of fatigue beneath her eyes.

Both Anne and Semmonet curtsied to her for Lady de Beaumont was of the royal house of Navarre and Mistress of the Archduchesses' Chamber, a position of great responsibility.

'Little Mistress Brandon has just arrived. Come, Anne, greet her,' Lady de Beaumont instructed.

'You are most welcome,' Anne answered pleasantly, scrutinising the girl who was to be her companion. She had heard that she was to come today but in the excitement of her new gown and hood she had forgotten. The girl was pale and tired, that was obvious. She had blue eyes and fair hair showed beneath her hood. In her plain dark blue travelling cloak and the heavy, awkward-looking gable hood she did not look very pretty, Anne thought. But I must be kind, she told herself. She herself had arrived here very tired, still feeling queasy from the sea journey and the jolting litter, confused and unhappy at being so far away from home. She reached out and took Anne Brandon's hands and drew her towards the fire.

'You will be cold and tired. Come, sit here close to the warmth. Was the journey over the sea rough? I was very sick, I thought I should die,' she confided.

Anne Brandon nodded. She had been terrified.

'Your trunks and boxes will be brought up and I shall order water for you to wash and food and spiced wine to warm you. You will share this chamber with Mistress Anne Boleyn,' Lady de Beaumont said kindly, smiling at both girls. 'I am sure you will find Anne to be a kind and merry companion,' she added before leaving, accompanied by Semmonet, to instruct the servants to bring the necessary comforts for her newly arrived charge.

'You will feel much better soon and you will like being here, I do. It is a wonderful palace and the Regent is a kind and gracious lady,' Anne informed her companion affably. 'But we must speak French and not English and we must work hard at all our lessons.'

Anne Brandon had unfastened her cloak, revealing a dark crimson gown embroidered around the neck and sleeves with white knots but which was as stained and dusty as the blue cloak. She was feeling warmer and Anne's words had calmed her a little. She knew that Anne Boleyn was younger than herself and yet if she was happy here then why should she not be too? And her young companion was dressed in a very fine gown and hood. 'After I have washed and changed my clothes, will you tell me about the Archduchesses and the ladies of the

43

court and what is expected of us and what is planned for Christmas?' she asked hesitantly.

Anne nodded enthusiastically. 'I shall tell you all that and while you are eating I shall sing for you. I have been practising very hard for I am to sing at the festivities,' she announced, her dark eyes shining with pride.

'You are? Even though you are only six? You must be very gifted.' There was astonishment and a little envy in the older child's voice.

Anne looked serious. It would not be kind or courteous to repeat Master des Prez's words. 'My father will be pleased that I am being honoured so.'

Anne Brandon looked perturbed. 'Do you miss him and your lady mother?'

Anne shrugged. 'I do, although I did not see my father very often.' She looked wistful. 'I miss my sister Mary and George, my brother.'

Anne Brandon's lower lip trembled and her blue eyes misted with tears. 'I miss my mother. She died.'

Anne felt sorry for her and she reached out and took her hand. 'I know, but I am sure you will be happy here and we will be friends, will we not?'

For the first time her companion smiled. 'I am sure we will.'

Anne smiled brightly, all thoughts of sadness forgotten. 'And when we grow up we will both be beautiful, accomplished ladies and so our fathers will be pleased and proud of us and will seek to find us good husbands, which is important. That is what my grandfather of Surrey says. It is important for our families.' She laughed excitedly. 'Maybe we will even go to court and see the King and Queen.'

Her companion looked a little apprehensive. 'Does that not make you a little afraid?'

Anne shook her head. 'No, why should it? Already we are here at the court of the Regent. We will be taught all the ways of great ladies. We will copy the Archduchesses. What is there to fear?'

Chapter Five

1516
Alnwick Castle, Northumberland

WILL WAS LEADING HIS horse towards the blacksmith's shop situated outside the barbican. The animal had cast a shoe and he would need to have it replaced before he could attend the morning's practice at the quintain. With wholesome food plentiful he had grown taller and sturdier and he enjoyed the pursuits of armed combat, supervised by Sir William Percy. He could now wield a sword and battle-axe, shoot an arrow and tilt with a lance equally as well as Lord Henry's younger brothers Thomas and Ingram. Lord Henry, however, preferred his books and his music, although he rode skilfully and enjoyed hunting, and hawking too, having patiently trained his own peregrine falcons.

Will had come to know his young master in the time he'd been in his service and the respect and loyalty he felt for him had deepened into affection. Henry Percy was quiet, sensitive, honorable and considerate, whereas his brothers were arrogant and dismissive. He had soon become aware that Thomas in particular was jealous of his elder brother, who would one day succeed to his father's title. He was also aware that both Lord Henry's brothers resented the fact that he, a commoner, was allowed to join their instruction in the use of arms and that he was on such affable terms with their brother.

He shivered a little in the chilly wind that was now blowing in from the coast. Spring was late in coming this year, he thought. It was now mid-April but when he had arisen at five that morning there had been a light frost covering the ground.

'Master Newson, I have need of your services,' he called as he tethered the horse outside the blacksmith's. Upon entering the forge a fierce blast of heat hit him, momentarily taking his breath away.

Alfred Newson turned towards him, the muscles of his arms and shoulders glistening with sweat, his heavy leather apron bearing the singe marks of the fire and the white-hot metal he worked with every day.

'What be wrong now, young Chatton?'

'My horse has cast a shoe, master, and I have only half an hour before practice,' he replied respectfully, for he was aware that the man had more pressing work.

Newsom nodded and grinned. He liked the boy; he'd adapted to life in the Earl's household well and there was no malice or insolence in him.

'Bring the animal in, lad, and I'll see what I can do.'

Will did as he was bid and as he stood watching the smith at work replacing the shoe, he deliberated on the good fortune that had come out of the loss of his father and his home. He was more than adequately clothed. He took his meals in the great hall, at one of the lower trestle tables, with servants of a similar standing to his own. The Earl's household was large; he employed a Chamberlain of the Household, a Comptroller, a Treasurer, a Secretary, a Master of Horse and Clerks of the Kitchen and Signet who all ate at the Knights' Table in the great hall. There was a Dean of the Chapel and ten priests, a Master of Grammar and a Riding Chaplain, who accompanied the Earl on journeys, plus seventeen choristers and – so it seemed to him – hundreds of domestic servants.

He slept on a truckle bed in the same chamber as Lord Henry. Daily he rose at five, as did everyone, and attended six o'clock Mass with his master, but he had been truly astounded when he'd learned that he would be paid three pounds eleven shillings and sixpence a year to purchase his food and drink. He doubted his poor father had ever seen so much money in his life.

Master Newson gave the last nail in the shoe a tap. 'There now, good as new.'

Will thanked him, taking the reins and leading the animal out. At last the watery sun had broken through the ragged grey clouds, he noticed as he approached the tilt yard.

All three boys were already mounted and were talking to their uncle as Will hastened towards them.

'Is there a reason for your tardiness this morning, Squire Chatton?' Sir William asked, frowning, while Ingram Percy smirked behind his hand.

'Sire, my horse cast a shoe and I am sorry for it,' Will excused his lateness.

Sir William nodded curtly and then instructed Thomas to take up his position.

Will watched as the boy tested the weight of the long wooden lance and deftly found its balance, eyeing the quintain carefully. If the lance did not strike the dummy in the centre it would swing round and the rider would be struck by the heavy sandbag.

Thomas spurred his horse forward and galloped down the lists, striking the dummy mid-centre. Sir William nodded his approval whilst eleven-year-old Ingram cheered his brother's efforts. His horsemanship and balance were impressive.

Will knew from experience he would be the last to attempt the feat. Ingram Percy rode next and he also struck mid-centre; then it was Lord Henry's turn. Beside his brothers he appeared slight, for both Thomas and Ingram were strong, sturdy youths. Will thought that for Lord Henry the lance seemed heavier and far more awkward to handle.

Sir William shouted for him to commence his ride and he dug his heels into the animal's flanks. The lance seemed to waver and when he reached the dummy his thrust missed, the sandbag swung round and he was knocked sprawling from his horse.

Will instantly ran to him to help him up. 'Are you hurt, my lord?' he asked anxiously.

Henry shook his head ruefully, trying to get his breath. 'There is naught broken, I think, just bruised.'

'Lean on me, my lord,' Will said for Henry had winced as he'd taken a step forward.

Will glanced at Sir William and sighed inwardly, seeing the look of annoyance on the older man's face. Both Thomas and Ingram were doubled up with laughter and he glared at them.

'I see my efforts have afforded you great amusement, brothers,' Henry said, wincing again.

'Would the Scots could see you, Harry. I wager they would split their sides with mirth,' Thomas gasped.

Will's face flushed with anger but he held his tongue.

'Have no fear, Tom, when the time comes the Scots will have no cause to mock,' Henry replied quietly.

'If you continue to fall from your horse they will have good cause!' Ingram jeered.

Henry's refusal to reply only added fuel to Ingram's spite.

'Have you no answer? Has the fall bereft you of speech? Or is it you lack the stomach?' he taunted cruelly.

The colour flooded Henry's cheeks and anger filled his dark eyes but before he had chance to reply Will shot forward and grabbed the bridle of Ingram's horse, pulling it sharply around so that the boy was facing him. Almost every day he'd stood silently seething as Lord Henry had been mocked by his brothers. Now a fierce rage surged through him. Lord Henry did not lack courage. It was true he had no stomach for jousting but he tried hard not to let that deter him and to Will's mind that was a much harder thing to do.

'Because you can wield a sword and strike true with a lance you think you are a better man than Lord Henry, but his lordship will be a better man and a better earl than you could ever be!'

Ingram's face contorted with fury and yanking his sword from its scabbard he raised it menacingly above Will's head.

Sir William's arm shot out and he grabbed Ingram's wrist

tightly until the boy cried out in pain and dropped the sword. 'There will be no murder done here, no matter the provocation!' he roared.

Ingram's face was puce with anger. 'You think it right for the like of *him* to insult me!' he yelled back at his uncle.

Will knew he had gone too far. There would be a terrible punishment exacted for his outburst. He could expect dismissal at the very least.

'You insolent young fool! Get to your chambers, both of you!' Sir William snapped at his two young nephews.

Will looked pleadingly at Henry but before either Henry or his uncle had time to speak a servant came running towards them, consternation etched on his face. As the man reached them he dropped to one knee.

'My lords! My lady the Countess wishes to speak with you immediately. She has received ill news from London,' he gasped.

'News of my lord father?' Henry asked, feeling a frisson of fear pass over him. The Earl had been at court for a month now and there had been no news of him. The man's obvious distress was unsettling.

Sir William took his nephew by the arm. 'Come, Henry. We must hasten to your mother. Chatton, you will await your master in his chamber,' he instructed grimly.

Will followed them slowly towards the castle. Obviously the news from London was far from good, but what had happened? He also wondered what would happen to him now. Would he be beaten or flogged – or worse? Should he start to collect his few belongings? Should he run – and run now? He was the son of a poor peasant farmer whilst Ingram Percy was the son of an earl and one of the greatest in the country. He frowned and squared his shoulders. True, he was a fool, but he was not a coward. He would not run from whatever punishment lay ahead.

It had seemed like hours before Lord Henry came to his chamber and Will had cursed himself over and over for allowing his anger to get the better of him. He would bear a flogging if only he could remain here. Pain he could stand but to be cast out into the world with only his meagre savings filled him with fear. He stood with his back to the wall, his hands clasped tightly behind him so Lord Henry would not see that they were shaking.

Henry looked at him, puzzled. After the terrible news his mother had just imparted to both himself and his uncle, Will's outburst had been driven from his mind. 'Will, have you not gone to the great hall for dinner?'

'I . . . Sir William told me to wait here,' Will answered, equally puzzled. Why was Lord Henry asking him such a mundane question?

Henry nodded slowly. 'I remember now.' He sat down on the edge of the bed.

Will began to realise that there was something very wrong and that it had nothing to do with that incident in the tilt yard. 'My lord, what has happened?'

Henry was still dazed. 'My lord father has been sent to the Fleet. He . . . he is in prison, Will. My lady mother is distraught.'

Will's jaw dropped. 'In *prison*! What has he done, Lord Henry? Has the King commanded it?'

'No, not the King. Not directly. The Cardinal . . .'

Will was confused. What right had Thomas Wolsey, Cardinal Archbishop of York, to send the Earl of Northumberland to the Fleet prison? 'Why? How can this be?'

Henry's eyes darkened with anger at the injustice. 'My lord Cardinal bears great malice towards the noble houses of the realm because he is but the son of a merchant of Ipswich. He has risen high in the King's favour, so my uncle says, but he cannot forget that my lords of Buckingham, Surrey, Oxford, Norfolk and my father have mocked him for his base birth. When my father's true friend Cardinal Bainbridge of York died, did not Wolsey foist himself into that high position and ever since has caused nothing but annoyance to us?' Henry was repeating almost word for word his uncle's remarks: remarks the blunt and outspoken Sir William had uttered with the contempt Henry, too, felt for Thomas Wolsey.

Will still did not really understand. 'And so because of this . . . great malice he has imprisoned the Earl?'

Henry stood up, clenching his fists in anger yet at the same time filled with fear for his father, whom he had always considered to be above such treatment. 'No, that would not suffice. He has claimed that my father has seized the wardship of four northern knights. I know not who these persons are but he claims the right of wardship for them belongs to the King and that my father should give them up. It is but an excuse to humble him, or so my lady mother believes.'

Will had heard of this practice of noble families entrusting the upbringing of certain of their sons and daughters to the aristocracy in the hope that they would learn better manners and advance themselves through good marriages.

Henry turned away and stared bleakly out of the window. 'My father has refused and for that he has been imprisoned.'

'For how long, my lord?' Will asked, thinking that the Cardinal must have had the King's permission to do this for surely he had not risen *that* high?

'We do not know. The King was present in the Star Chamber while my lord father was examined, so he must believe the Cardinal. We must pray God that King Henry will relent and soon.'

'And if he does not?' Will asked.

Henry shivered and the colour drained from his face. 'I fear for him, Will. It could be the Tower next.'

It was Will's turn to shudder at the mention of that fortress for he knew dark deeds had been committed there. 'I will pray for him, Lord Henry.'

'We must all pray for him, Will.'

Chapter Six

HENRY WALKED SLOWLY ALONG the leads of the curtain wall towards the Postern Tower, which looked out over the countryside to the north-east. Apart from the Barbican Gatehouse it provided the only entrance and exit from Alnwick Castle and he sometimes walked here on fine days and when he was troubled for it was generally quiet.

He stopped and leaned against the stones of the crenellated wall, his expression grave, the pallor of his complexion heightened by the dark brown velvet tunic he wore, slashed to show the white shirt beneath. Before him stretched the parkland, tranquil in the sunlight of the May morning. Clumps of daffodils and primroses formed splashes of bright yellow beneath the hedgerows where the birds were nesting. Patches of gorse and broom glowed like gold and the paler rays of the sun dappled the trees on which leaves and buds were beginning to unfurl, but he hardly noticed the beauty of nature's blossoming. It was as if a threatening cloud of uncertainty and gloom hung over the castle, he thought.

There had been no further word from London regarding his father's plight and he knew that both his uncles, Sir William and Sir Jocelyn, were seriously worried. His mother had written to her husband, begging him not to persist in antagon- ising the all-powerful Cardinal. But what if his father ignored her pleas and the similar advice of my lord of Shrewsbury who, he had heard from his Uncle William, had also written to the Earl? Men had been committed to the Tower for less. What if the Cardinal suggested to the King that the Earl's obstinate refusal amounted to treason? What if Wolsey whispered in the King's ear that his father was in fact defrauding and openly defying him? He knew King Henry would not – could not – tolerate that and the penalty for treason was death.

He began to shiver but this time it was not a sign that the ague, by which he was so often afflicted, was about to beset him again. He was afraid for his father's safety and it was a fear that was with him constantly, causing him to wake sweating during the hours of the night. He gripped the cold stones of the wall to try to control his emotions. If anything happened to his father the enormous responsibility of his father's title and estates, the care of his mother, his brothers and sisters would instantly become his and that was so daunting a prospect that he could hardly bear to contemplate it. He was too young, too inexperienced.

He had always known that one day he would become the Sixth Earl but he'd thought he'd be much older and have gained more experience of life and duty and even border warfare. He'd envisaged being married by then, with a wife who would have supported him and overseen his households. But now . . . now he was but fourteen years of age, he thought, a feeling akin to panic rising in him.

His knuckles became white as his fingers gripped the stone harder, remembering that his father had been even younger when his grandfather had been killed. His father had been just twelve years old at the time the Fourth Earl had died, fighting the rebels in the hall at Cockledge.

He leaned his head on his hands, trying hard to dispel the fear. He would have the support of his uncles, he told himself. They would help and advise him, especially in quelling the frequent raids of the Scots and in the management of their vast estates, not only here in Northumberland but in Yorkshire, Cumberland and in the southern counties too. But what if those estates were confiscated? How would he care for his mother and his siblings then? Doubt threatened to swamp him but he struggled against it. Maybe the King would not listen to the Cardinal after all. King Henry reigned supreme in this realm, not the son of a merchant from Ipswich, and the Percys had always been loyal to the Crown. He must draw some hope from that fact, no matter how slight.

He straightened up, taking deep gulps of the clear, fresh air. It was just the uncertainty and the strain of waiting that was unnerving him, he told himself. His father had been in prison now for nearly a month and it had seemed as long as a year. He prayed it would all end soon.

By the time he had walked back to the octagonal towers of the keep he felt more resolute and the shivering had stopped. He must show no weakness, no sign of giving in to anxiety and despondency, he told himself firmly. He must continue to hope and to pray and go now to his studies of Greek and Latin, for his tutor would be waiting and would be displeased that he was late. He was ready and prepared for his lessons, if nothing else.

The following day was Saturday and there were no studies to occupy him. He had no wish to join his brothers in the armoury and yet he could not settle to read or to play upon his lute. His mother and his eldest sister Margaret were still in the chapel, praying for his father. Little Maud was in the nursery. He wandered slowly across the inner bailey until he at last made up his mind to do something that he hoped would take his mind off his predicament. Spotting Will Chatton in conversation with a young groom, he called to him.

Will quickly hurried across to his master; he would seek out the groom later to finish their conversation for the boy regularly brought him news of his family. They now lived nearer to the castle and he gave the boy a few groats to call on them when he could not make the journey himself.

'We shall go down to the mews, Will. I shall take my falcon out and you will bring your goshawk,' he instructed.

Will nodded his agreement. As a squire a goshawk was the bird allotted to him; only the Earl and his sons were allowed to hunt with the long-winged peregrine falcons.

They rode out through the postern gate and across the parkland towards a line of trees. The peregrine, its head covered by a hood of black velvet to keep it calm, was perched on Henry's wrist, which was protected from its talons by a gauntlet of padded leather.

'There should be good sport this morning, Lord Henry,'

Will said, trying to sound cheerful. Everyone in the castle had been affected by the Earl's imprisonment and he knew, perhaps better than anyone, how heavily his father's predicament weighed on Lord Henry's mind, for when his young master awoke in the night it was he who fetched him wine, infused with valerian, to help him sleep.

'I hope so, Will. God knows I have need of something good to occupy my thoughts,' Henry replied as they halted. He had changed the jesses attached to the bird's legs before they'd left the mews, for the mews jesses were made of heavier strips of leather and would affect its flight. He removed the hood and released the bird, which instantly spread its wings and took flight, rapidly climbing higher into the sky, the thin hunting jesses trailing behind and the sound of the bells attached to its leg becoming fainter. Henry watched it as it sighted its prey, a wood pigeon breaking slowly from an elm, and felt his admiration increase as the falcon, glorious in its control, swooped and swerved in pursuit of its now desperate and terrified prey. His spirits rose as they always did as it dropped like a stone at a speed that was almost beyond belief.

After two hours in which Henry succeeded in thinking of little else but the skill and ferocity of the bird and the beauty of the day they turned for home, the falcon once more hooded, his despondency lifted. He knew that the Earl of Cumberland was due to visit his mother that day, which would be a diversion. There had been talk of negotiations between his father and my lord of Cumberland regarding the betrothal of his sister Margaret to the widowed Earl, but he now wondered if Cumberland was still in favour of the match. Perhaps the purpose of this visit was to inform her that he was not, or maybe it was to try to bring some solace and support to the distraught Countess. He hoped it was the latter.

After leaving the horses in the care of a groom in the stables, Will followed Henry across the inner bailey to the castle. It was almost time for dinner and whilst he would eat in the great hall he knew Henry would join his mother and uncles in the small dining room set off it.

'Lord Henry, there must be news.' Will ran to catch up with his master. 'Sir William is with her ladyship and he looks pleased. And see: her ladyship is smiling.' He had caught sight of the two adults who were about to enter the small dining room before Henry had.

Hope surged through Henry as he hastened to join his mother. If she had indeed been smiling it could only mean one thing for she hadn't smiled in weeks: his father must be safe.

'My lady mother, is there news?' he begged as he joined them.

'Oh, Henry. It is the most joyful news of all. Your father has been released from prison and will be coming home within days.'

'Thank God!' Henry was so elated that he took his mother's hand and kissed it.

'After we have eaten I have asked that a special Mass be said to give thanks for my lord's safe delivery,' the Countess informed him, unable to hide her own relief.

'Have I leave to tell Will Chatton the news? He has been as sorely worried as I have?' Henry asked.

The Countess nodded as Sir William escorted her to her seat at the table, amused that her son's first thought was for his servant.

'But do not linger too long, Henry,' Sir William instructed.

Will had been standing just behind the door to the chamber and he grinned happily at his young master. 'I could not help overhearing, Lord Henry. The Lord be praised! It is great news; it will lift the cloud of doom we have all lived under these past weeks.'

Henry clapped him on the shoulder, smiling broadly. 'You must tell everyone that my lord father is free and is coming home.'

'I will and no doubt there will be great rejoicing when he arrives safely,' Will replied. He was relieved and thankful, but could not help wondering what effect his imprisonment had had on the Earl.

The news ran like wildfire and within hours everyone's spirits had risen. Laughter and jesting were once again heard in the chambers and passageways of the castle and in the yard of the inner bailey. That evening Henry informed Will that there was to be a banquet when the Earl returned and that my lord of Cumberland would prolong his stay to welcome his fellow peer home.

'I think that perhaps we shall soon see Lady Margaret betrothed,' Henry had mused happily.

'More good news, my lord. It is amazing how quickly luck changes,' Will replied, knowing that although Lady Margaret was only twelve years old and would not become a wife until she was at least fourteen, the alliance would be sure to please the Earl and Countess. It seemed their fortune's tide was on the turn.

When Henry Algernon returned home almost a week later the entire household greeted him. As he rode into the inner courtyard with his small entourage all the officers of the household and the servants of the Earl of Cumberland cheered him. His cloak and bonnet were stained and dusty from the long ride and he looked drawn and had lost weight but it was obvious that he was happy to be home.

At supper that evening Henry studied his father closely. His experiences had changed the Earl. He seemed more withdrawn in his manner, less full of confidence and bluster. Henry felt sure that the threat of the Tower and even death could not have crushed his father's pride but obviously the prospect of years confined in the Fleet prison had taken its toll. And he felt that the malign interference of the Cardinal was still weighing heavily on his father's mind.

He hoped that in time, away from the court, his father would regain his spirits and become once more the man he respected, admired and even feared a little. His father still had friends such as my lords of Shrewsbury and Cumberland, who would remain faithful and whose patronage might help to raise his father's standing in the eyes of King Henry. And at least for now life had returned to some semblance of normality; for that Henry gave thanks.

Chapter Seven

—◆—

Wressle Castle, Yorkshire

THE EARL DID REGAIN some of his old fire and spirit, or so it seemed to Will, although Henry was not too certain about it. The household had removed to Wressle at the beginning of June and his father had gone on a pilgrimage to Canterbury to give thanks for his delivery from the Fleet, accompanied by my lord of Shrewsbury.

'But of what consequence is it? Surely there is nothing wrong with making a pilgrimage?' Will had asked when Henry had confided his doubts to him.

'He has never done it before,' Henry had replied, his tone anxious.

Will had shrugged. 'He had never been in prison before and let's hope he never is again.'

The day after the Earl returned from his journey he sent for

Henry. Dinner was over and Thomas and Ingram were out riding in the park with their uncles.

'You wish to see me, my lord?' Henry asked as he entered his father's chamber. He was surprised to see his mother seated beside the open window, her needlework resting on her lap, her tray of brightly coloured silks set to one side.

It was a large room with a high vaulted ceiling. A screen of tapestry stretched on a wooden frame stood in the hearth of the empty fireplace and woven rush matting covered the floor. A set of Flemish tapestries depicting the birth of Venus covered the walls, the colours of the wools vivid and bright in the sunlight that streamed in through the window. A rich Turkish carpet covered the top of the large oak table at which his father sat, dressed in a doublet of black and gold brocade, the white shirt beneath embroidered around the collar with gold thread. His expression was sombre and thoughtful.

'My lord of Shrewsbury and I spent many hours in discussion, Henry, whilst on our journey to the shrine of St Thomas Becket.'

Henry nodded respectfully and patiently. Obviously there was something of importance his father wished to announce about his discussions with George Talbot, Earl of Shrewsbury.

The Earl glanced across at his wife, who nodded and smiled.

'You are now in your fifteenth year, Henry, and we have agreed that it is time you were betrothed. My lord of Shrewsbury has suggested that his youngest daughter, the Lady Mary Talbot, would be a suitable wife for you and so that match has been agreed.'

Henry was a little taken aback at the news. Of course he

had always realised that he would one day have to take a wife but he had never really given it a great deal of thought. 'I . . . I understand, my lord,' he replied cautiously.

The Countess rose, laid her needlework down beside the silks and came to stand beside her husband, placing a hand on his shoulder. Her expression was kindly, but as she stood there, the wide sleeves of her silk gown turned back to reveal the lining of white and silver tissue, the white silk lappets of her gable hood framing her face, enhancing her fair complexion and light brown eyes, she was every inch the great lady, not to be gainsaid. 'So that you will have the opportunity to become better acquainted with the Lady Mary, Henry – and she with you – she is to come and reside here.' She smiled at her eldest son, noting the look of caution in his brown eyes. 'I am sure you will welcome her and she will have Margaret as a companion too, until she is married to my lord of Cumberland of course.'

Henry nodded. Margaret's betrothal had been announced when his father had first returned home from London so he really should not be surprised that a match had been arranged for him too. 'How old is the Lady Mary, Mother?'

'She is, I believe, twelve, the same age as your sister.'

Henry wanted to ask what she looked like. Was she pretty? Was she of a pleasant and lively disposition? Did she like books and poetry, music and dancing? Was she intelligent and witty? But he remained silent, knowing these were not things his father would consider important. The alliance between the Houses of Percy and Talbot would be paramount in his father's thoughts.

'There will be no marriage until she is fourteen or fifteen

but she will be aware of the position she will hold and of her duties as both a wife and one day a countess,' his father announced. He did not inform his son that Mary Talbot would bring no dowry to the marriage. She was the youngest of George Talbot's five daughters and there had been lengthy discussions on the subject but Talbot was one of the most parsimonious men in the country and had managed to marry off his other four daughters with the minimum of expense to himself. He had driven the hardest of bargains.

'When is she due to arrive?' Henry asked. He was beginning to realise that his life was about to change.

'Within the fortnight. Her father will accompany her.' The Earl drew some rolls of parchment towards him and the Countess turned away to resume her needlework. 'You may go now, Henry, I have other business to attend to. You may speak with your mother later on the matter if you wish,' the Earl instructed him, abruptly ending the interview.

Henry went in search of Will Chatton and at last found him in the armoury, restringing his bow of yew, which was as tall as he was.

'What news did my lord your father have for you, Lord Henry?' Will asked.

It was much cooler in the armoury for the thick stone walls and narrow window slits kept out the heat of the sun. Henry leaned against one of the pillars that supported the roof, folding his arms across his chest. 'I am to be betrothed. I am considered to be of a suitable age.'

Will sucked in his breath. This was indeed news. 'Who is she?'

'Lady Mary Talbot, Lord Shrewsbury's youngest daughter.

She's coming here to reside with us so we can get to know each other. She's twelve.'

Will had laid aside the bow. 'What's she like? Is she pretty?'

'I didn't ask. I suppose I shall find out soon enough. She'll be here within the fortnight.'

It surprised Will that Henry hadn't asked the question that was most obvious to him. 'If I may make so bold, you don't seem very interested or pleased, my lord.'

Henry shrugged. 'I knew I would have to take a wife one day but . . . but I'd not given a great deal of thought as to who it would be.'

Will wondered what the Lady Mary's feelings were on the matter. 'Can you not choose a lady for yourself? When perhaps you are older, my lord?'

Henry shook his head and smiled wryly. 'That is not the custom, Will. Not for someone of my station in life. These matters are always arranged by parents. It's all bound up with land and titles and power and politics, things I neither know nor care a great deal about.'

'Always?' Will probed.

Henry frowned in concentration. 'Not *always*. I expect sometimes it's possible to choose for yourself.'

Will picked up the bow and his quiver of arrows and looked thoughtful. 'Perhaps there are *some* advantages of being low born,' he mused. Then he grinned. 'But not many.'

The Earl of Shrewsbury and his young daughter arrived early the following week with a small entourage. A chamber had already been prepared for Lady Mary and Lady Margaret Percy at least was looking forward to having a new companion.

'We will have much in common, for we are both betrothed ladies now,' she'd informed her brother.

Henry had laughed but not unkindly. 'Oh, indeed! Very grown-up ladies of twelve, Margaret.'

He had dressed with more than usual care on the morning of Mary's arrival. His white shirt of finest lawn was richly decorated with silver thread around the neck and cuffs and over it he wore a doublet of emerald green silk slashed and bordered with silver lace. His breeches were of matching silk and his hose were white. He'd selected a flat bonnet of deeper green velvet adorned with a white feather held in place by a brooch of intricate goldsmith's work. Flat black velvet shoes with a squared toe completed his ensemble. He looked with some satisfaction at his reflection in the polished steel mirror and adjusted the bonnet. He liked fine clothes and thought he looked well. He hoped his future bride would agree.

'The Lady Mary will have naught to complain of in your appearance, Lord Henry,' Will complimented him, handing him the slim silver dagger which Henry slipped into the matching scabbard at his waist.

'I hope so, Will. A first impression is always important.' It was a warm day and Henry felt beads of perspiration form on his forehead, which were not due entirely to the heat. He was beginning to feel nervous about meeting this girl who one day would be his wife. But he supposed it was only natural.

Will nodded his agreement as he followed his master out of the chamber and down the narrow stone stairs for Lord Shrewsbury's party had arrived and had been conducted to the Earl's chambers to take refreshment after their journey from

Sheffield. He was as eager as Lord Henry to see Lady Mary Talbot.

Will announced his young master quietly and then respectfully drew back and stood with the Countess's ladies and Lady Margaret's maid at the back of the chamber, ready to wait upon their masters and mistresses.

Henry swept off his bonnet and bowed formally to the Earl of Shrewsbury and then his daughter, a small figure on whom he found himself looking down. 'You are most welcome my lord, and my lady Mary. I hope you will find your time with us pleasant and our company congenial, my lady.' He had spent some time choosing and rehearsing these words of greeting. A dart of disappointment struck him as he looked into the girl's pale grey, expressionless eyes. She was slightly plump and her gown of pewter-coloured damask did little to enhance her appearance. Her complexion was pale, her eyebrows and lashes so fair they seemed almost invisible. She regarded him steadily but he was unable to deduce anything from her flat mask-like expression and she did not speak. At length he moved his gaze to his sister's face and returned Margaret's smile, relieved to have some response to his performance even if it wasn't from its object. Mary Talbot seemed without any humour or spark of vitality. As they proceeded towards the great hall he tried to be charitable. Of course she could just be shy: overcome by being brought to live amongst strangers and by the rigours of the journey. It must be very daunting to be faced by the prospect of a future husband, his family and a new home. Maybe she'd been instructed by her father to give no indication of her feelings? Talbot had a reputation as a wily, calculating individual.

As Henry sat beside her at the table he toyed with the wine and food that was served whilst his father and Lord Shrewsbury engaged in conversation. His mother and sister were both valiantly attempting to put his betrothed at ease. She answered their questions in a voice that had a distinctly sharp edge. When she laughed, albeit briefly, at some jest of Margaret's, the sound grated on him.

He sipped the sweet hippocras slowly, his feelings of disappointment and dislike of this girl growing stronger. He watched as she cut her meat with her knife. Her small hands were the colour of putty and her fingers were short and pudgy. They were not the fingers of a girl who would play well upon the lute or virginals, he thought miserably. He caught Will Chatton's eye and turned away, his mind in turmoil.

Will felt his master's disappointment as if it were his own. She was far from what could be termed comely, let alone pretty. His own little sister Meggie was more attractive and lively. She appeared to be making no effort at all to get to know Lord Henry, seeming to prefer conversation with his sister. He thought her clothes too dark and unbecoming for a young girl and her manner appeared cold and aloof.

He'd watched as Lord Henry had turned to her and smiled, offering her more wine from the silver jug and trying to put her at her ease, only to receive a cold glance and a curt shake of her head before she turned once more to Lady Margaret. He couldn't help a surge of anger at the rebuff. Nor did it bode well for the future, he thought. Unless of course, once her father had returned to Sheffield, her attitude changed. For his young master's sake he sincerely hoped it would.

* * *

Christmas had arrived at last and the frenzied preparations in the kitchens, the bakery, the buttery, the pantry and the brew house were finally complete. On Christmas Eve the whole family went to Midnight Mass. The chapel was ablaze with hundreds of candles of the purest white wax, the altar and the beams of the roof adorned with garlands of holly and boughs of evergreen and the perfume of incense filled the air. The priests in their vestments of white brocade and velvet embroidered all over with gold and silver thread had solemnly commenced the service and the choirboys in starched white surplices sang the old Christmas hymns.

The Earl was resplendent in a surcoat of cloth of gold over a doublet and breeches of crimson and black velvet. The Countess too was wearing a gown of velvet, the sleeves and the underskirt of gold damascene, her matching hood bordered with pearls and precious stones. Lord Henry wore royal blue velvet edged with silver lace and his brothers looked like young noblemen in black and gold velvet. After Midnight Mass there was the customary lavish banquet in the great hall with the Earl and his family seated on the raised dais. Their table was covered with a fine embroidered white linen cloth; their chargers and goblets were of gold and silver. Set in front of the Earl was the beautifully engraved golden salt, set with rubies and emeralds. The great Yule log burned in the massive stone hearth and scores of candles, set in sconces on the walls and in the wheel-shaped candelabras suspended from the ceiling, illuminated the room with their flickering warm golden light. The level of noise rose as the household celebrated the joyful occasion.

Will had become accustomed to this Christmas banquet although he still marvelled at the sheer amount of food, wine and spiced ale that was provided. There were always at least three courses and each course was ushered in by the Master Cook, beaming with pride and satisfaction upon his masterpiece of a sugared marzipan device. These devices never ceased to astound Will with their ingenuity. The first was a large tableau depicting the Virgin Mary and the Angel Gabriel, tinted and fashioned so they looked lifelike. The second was a tableau of the angel appearing to the shepherds, the third the Three Wise Men. They would all be eaten at the end of the meal and Will always half regretted their destruction even whilst enjoying pieces of the sticky confection.

Each of the devices was followed by dishes of brawn and mustard, broth, boiled and baked joints of beef, roast mutton, stewed pheasants and capons, pork, and baked venison pasties. There were dishes of rabbit, kid, stork, peacock, heron, woodcock and plover. Almond cream, snipe, quail, perch in jelly and crayfish. Then came bream and carp and baked lampreys and finally sweetmeats, amber jelly, baked quinces, poached fritters, nuts and wafers and then a swan or peacock, the feathers gilded and replaced so that it appeared alive. The Earl and his family were presented with the dishes first, helping themselves to whatever took their fancy, and then the plates were passed down to the lower tables. Whatever was left at the end of the meal was given to the poor and to the beggars at the castle gate and Will had heard that at times the Earl had had two oxen roasted whole on a spit for the benefit of these lowly souls.

Henry helped himself to some roast beef and mutton and a venison pasty. His brothers were eagerly devouring their food but today he just picked at his, despite the oblivious festive spirit that imbued everyone else in the hall. He felt far from cheerful. He had had yet another quarrel with Mary Talbot that afternoon. It was all they ever seemed to do, he thought miserably. She had a waspish tongue and considered little else but her own welfare and happiness and her existence at Wressle offered a meagre supply of the latter, she frequently told him. She did not like to read, she played the lute badly and the virginals not at all. She danced without grace and was indifferent to the poetry he enjoyed so much. She had mocked him openly on numerous occasions for his love of books and music and his lack of skill in jousting, so much so that he had finally lost his temper with her and called her uncouth, ungainly and semi-literate. He disliked her intensely and she assured him the feeling was mutual.

The beef tasted like sawdust in his mouth and he drank deeply of the wine in his goblet to mask it. That afternoon she had come upon him as he'd been trying to make the stanzas he was composing rhyme.

'Composing a ditty for the Christmas feast, I see. And I suppose we will all have to listen to it and then no doubt applaud your feeble efforts,' she'd said cuttingly, her grey eyes full of scorn.

He'd remained silent, determined not to be goaded by her remarks and wishing she would go away and gossip with his sister instead. But his silence had served only to infuriate her.

'And what, my lord, have you as a gift for me this Christmas? A jewel? A kirtle of silver? A cup of gold? A fine saddle for my palfrey?' She'd laughed derisively. 'I pray it is not a book or a score of music. I shall be bitterly disappointed if it is such a gift.'

'I would not offer you such a thing for its worth and beauty would be wasted upon you. Perhaps a jewelled knife would be more appropriate.'

'I should know not to expect anything more than such a paltry gift,' she'd snapped at him.

'It is an apt one for you have a tongue as sharp as any blade,' he'd replied.

She'd snatched the parchment from his hands and thrown it to the ground. 'And how, pray, would you know? You who are such a dolt with a sword and a lance that your brothers turn away for very shame and your lack of manly skills shames me, too! Tis a fine husband you will make! A fine Earl and Warden of the Marches, who cannot even stay upright upon his horse in a joust!'

He'd jumped to his feet, his cheeks flushed and his eyes filled with anger as he'd picked up his half-finished poem. 'And a fine wife you will make! You are far from a beauty, you have a tongue and a nature that would better befit a hornet and you lack any grace. And it is I who am shamed for you bring nothing with you. You have no dowry and it is known the length and breadth of the land that your father is too miserly to provide you with one. It is I who am getting no bargain, madam!'

She had burst into tears of rage and humiliation for she knew he spoke the truth. 'I hate you! I will not stay here to be insulted and humbled!' she had raged and had turned and fled.

There had followed an uncomfortable interview with his parents and his mother had instructed him firmly that this latest quarrel was in no way to mar the festivities.

He signalled that his now-empty cup be refilled with more wine and glanced surreptitiously at his betrothed, who sat beside him. There was no sign on her plain, pale face of any pleasure. Her lips were set in a tight line and she, too, was toying with her food. The damson velvet of her gown had drained what little colour there had been in her cheeks, her matching hood looked ugly and cumbersome and her eyes were puffy from weeping. Around her short neck she wore a gold chain set at intervals with river pearls. He knew she felt just as miserable and unhappy as he did and he tried to feel some pity for her but it was useless.

He clapped dutifully as the second course was ushered in and then caught the look of concern on his mother's face as he realised she'd been watching him. He smiled at her and she smiled back but he could see she was perturbed. He sighed and helped himself to a dish of woodcock; surely his parents could see that he and the Lady Mary were unsuited and far from happy?

Countess Catherine was not the only one who had been watching him. From his seat at the lower table Will caught sight of his master signing for his wine cup to be refilled. Lord Henry was drinking far too much, he thought, but he could not blame him. He had overheard the quarrel that afternoon and had wondered, not for the first time, why the Lady Mary insisted on taunting and provoking Lord Henry. True, his lordship did not like her but he never deliberately set out to pick an argument with her. Most of the time Lord Henry tried to avoid and ignore her but maybe that did not please her either. He shrugged. There was little he could do to help his master and meanwhile there was the feasting to enjoy. When the meal was finished there would be jugglers and acrobats to entertain them and on St Stephen's Day he hoped to pay his mother a long overdue visit. Perhaps he could salvage some marchpane from one of the devices for his sister? If little Meggie had had all the privileges Lady Mary had he was certain she wouldn't be sitting at this Christmas feast looking so sour and disgruntled.

Chapter Eight

1519
Wressle Castle, Yorkshire

I F THERE WAS A single room in the castle that Henry loved
most it was 'Paradise', so dubbed by his father, a refuge from
the constant commotion engendered by his teeming household
of 160 servants. It was the Earl's library, a circular room in one
of the five towers. The walls, lined with oak bookcases filled
with expensive leather-bound books and illuminated manuscripts, seemed to insulate the room from the incessant noise
and chatter of the servants going about their daily tasks in the
many chambers below.

Henry was aware that all these volumes had cost his father a
great deal of money and that some were virtually priceless.
There were manuscripts hand-embellished by the monks with
brightly coloured inks and gold leaf, others that had been
printed by the new process invented by Master Caxton. A good

fire of seasoned logs burned in the ornate stone fireplace above which hung a tapestry worked in coloured wools and gold thread. His father's desk of carved oak with its folding ledges used to support the heavy volumes stood beside the narrow glazed window and fresh rushes covered the floor.

It was a room where peace and solitude reigned, where it was a delight to the soul and the spirit to sit and to read from the classical works of Cicero and Livy, and the modern works of Erasmus and Thomas More. It was a room that one day would belong to him – but not yet, he thought as he stood waiting for his father's arrival.

Will Chatton had come to him and informed him that the Earl wished to see him and now he stood wondering why. What was so important that it would not wait until they were at supper, when just the family would be present?

It was some minutes before he heard the door open and he turned to greet the Earl. 'You sent for me, Father?'

The older man nodded and set down on the desk the sheaf of parchments he carried. He was dressed in a black velvet doublet and breeches, his hair and beard neatly trimmed, a large ruby ring adorning his right hand.

Henry, trying to judge his mood, thought he seemed preoccupied. Since his imprisonment his father had changed. He had become much quieter and often morose, content to spend more time in this room with his books than at court. There had been no raids to pursue the border brigands of late.

The Earl looked across at his eldest son and sighed heavily. His heir was still a pale, gangly, shy boy whose apparent sensitivity, which he often thought bordered on squeamishness, hardly suited a future Warden of the Marches. Henry was still a callow youth, despite his education, but the Earl had decided the moment had come to remedy that.

'It is time you went to London,' he announced flatly. 'You are seventeen, Henry. I would have sent you a year or two since had I thought you capable of conducting yourself in a manner befitting your station in life.'

Henry flushed and fidgeted with the edge of his doublet. He knew full well he did not come up to his father's high expectations, particularly in the fields of politics and warfare, and even more now that his betrothal to Mary Talbot had been set aside. Things had reached such a pass between them that they practically ceased speaking to each other and whenever they did it ended in a quarrel. At last it had reluctantly been agreed that she return home to her father. Henry had not been sorry to see her go but the episode had not endeared him to his father who had greatly desired the alliance with George Talbot.

'So, you are to go to the Cardinal's court as a page to his lordship. A little older than is usual, but . . .' He shrugged.

Henry was completely taken aback at this news. Cardinal Wolsey had certainly been no friend to his father in the past. 'But, Father, I thought that after—'

'That is past,' the Earl interrupted sharply. He wished for no reminder of his time in prison or of the fact that Wolsey had the ear of the King and it was only a fool who believed he could mock or defy him. Wolsey was all powerful; it was whispered that he ruled both the country and the King himself, but it was only whispered. The Earl had learned a hard lesson through bitter experience and he still suffered the Cardinal's interference in his affairs. 'You will learn the manners and customs of the court and I trust you to take especial note of how the Lord Cardinal conducts affairs of state. And I expect you to cultivate those at court who will be of value to you both in friendship and allegiance in the future.'

He beckoned the boy to come closer.

'You have important lessons to learn, Henry. You must be alert at all times and study the ways and the words of the men about the King for he does not fully trust the Houses of Percy or Neville. Between us we can raise the whole fighting force of the North and I think it is in his mind that one day such an event may occur and threaten his position.'

'But we are loyal to the King,' Henry stated firmly, unable to grasp where this was leading.

The Earl nodded. 'We are, but do not forget that the Tudors have come to the throne comparatively recently and that so far there is only the Princess Mary in line of succession. You must not waste your time at court; you must do all you can to secure the stability and advancement of the House of Percy. Your time must not be spent in idleness. I want to hear no tales of foolishness or foppery or wastefulness. You will be there to watch and learn and to make useful alliances, Henry, do you understand?'

Henry nodded. His father's remit sounded rather daunting but he could feel a sense of excitement rising in him. He was going to London! 'I understand, Father. When am I to go?'

'At the beginning of next month. You will accompany me for I have business to attend to there.' The Earl frowned as he picked up a sheet of parchment. 'A meeting between the King and King Francis early next summer in France is being mooted – a meeting of grandiose proportions. I am commanded to accompany King Henry, as will many noblemen, and to furnish an entourage of five hundred, which is deemed suitable to my estate and to the King's Majesty.' He frowned again, glancing down at a letter. 'But by God's wounds! How I am to pay for it all, I do not know,' he confided. He was beset by debts. The extravagances of the past were catching up with him and these latter years he had had to borrow heavily from the wealthy merchants of York and Beverley; he had even pledged some of his plate to the monks of St Mary's in York. 'But that is no concern of yours. You may go now.'

There were many questions Henry wanted to ask but he bowed politely and left; he could see his impending departure had already been replaced in his father's attentions by other matters.

He went down the narrow stone staircase, pausing to look through a window down into the tilt yard below. Henry had lost count of the number of falls he'd taken and the cuts and bruises he'd sustained. He'd been fortunate not to have broken a limb. Thomas was riding at full gallop towards the quintain. His Uncle William stood watching critically with Ingram at his side. Thomas hit the dummy squarely in the middle and Ingram cheered loudly to Thomas's obvious pride and delight.

Henry continued his descent. A thought struck him. As a page to the Cardinal he wouldn't be expected to take part in jousts or any other such sports. No doubt he would watch them, he wouldn't mind that, and he might even see King Henry himself joust, but he would have time to indulge in the things he enjoyed most: his literary and musical pursuits. A shiver of anticipation ran through him at the thought.

When he reached his chamber he sat down on the edge of

the bed with its coverlet of green velvet and satin and carved and gilded tester. The heavy damask curtains had been pulled back. He was to go to London! Excitement welled up inside him. He would see for the first time in his life all the fine buildings, the churches, the palaces, the Tower, the bridge and the traffic on the river. He would see the King and the Queen and observe at first hand the fashions in dress, music and literature in one of the greatest and most lavish courts in Europe. He would mingle with ambassadors and bishops and other noblemen and -women.

He got up and walked over to the window and gazed out. Beyond the castle walls were the gardens and orchards, clad now in the colours of autumn, and beyond them the deer park which ran down to the River Derwent. Beyond that the land-scape was becoming shrouded in mist as the sun set. Soon he would be leaving all this, the cold, grey, bleak country of the North, and he wouldn't be at all sorry. He would be far away too from the constant jealousies and jibes of his brothers. London would suit his tastes very well indeed.

He looked up as the door opened and Will Chatton entered. He smiled at him. The bond that had been forged that day in Redesdale had strengthened over the years for Will had proved intelligent, loyal and quick to learn the ways of life at Alnwick, Wressle and Leckenfield.

'Lord Henry, your uncle is asking, should your audience with his lordship be over, that you attend him below in the tilt yard.'

Henry grimaced. 'I have no mind to go, Will. You know only too well I have no stomach for jousting. I end up bruised and aching.'

'But what am I to tell him, my lord?' Will asked, with his

usual mix of deference and familiarity, acutely aware of his young master's dislike of such sport. He had never addressed Henry as anything other than 'Lord Henry' or 'my lord'. Will's manners, his speech and his dress had all greatly improved but he never forgot he was a servant or that he had been plucked from poverty, ignorance and obscurity to enjoy a far better life than he could ever have envisaged.

'Can't you think of some excuse, Will?' Henry pleaded. 'I have other more important matters to think about now.'

Will shrugged. 'Should I tell him that I could not find you and think you are still with his lordship?'

Henry nodded. His father would be preoccupied with his correspondence and probably would not come down from his library until it was time to eat. 'I am to go to London at the beginning of next month, Will. As a page at the court of Cardinal Wolsey.'

Will's eyes widened in surprise. Did not Lord Henry fear and mistrust the man who had caused the Earl to be imprisoned? 'Is that a great honour, my lord? Do you trust the Cardinal?'

'I suppose I must for it is my father's wish that I go and I am looking forward to it. And I shall no longer have to make excuses to escape practice in the tilt yard. Quite a blessing.'

Will's forehead creased in a frown. 'Am I to be dismissed, Lord Henry? You will have no further need of me then.'

Henry looked surprised and shook his head. 'No. You will come with me. I will have need of one servant at least and you are my squire.'

Will could hardly believe his ears. He too was to go to London! He was to accompany Lord Henry to the court of the great and powerful Cardinal Wolsey!

Seeing the look of pure amazement on his squire's face Henry grinned. 'Does that suit you, Will Chatton?'

'It does indeed, my lord. I never thought I would have such a chance to see with my own eyes such a great city!'

Henry laughed and clapped him on the shoulder. 'It will be a new life for us both. A better life, a more exciting life, far away from this dour and miserable place.'

Will nodded, still unable to believe his luck. 'And we are to leave in three weeks? May I have some time to see my mother before we leave, my lord? I don't know how long it will be before I see her and the bairns again.'

Henry was reminded that he should see his own mother too. 'You may go tomorrow, Will. Now, I must pay a visit to my lady mother. No doubt she knows of this but I shall need to discuss it with her in greater detail.'

Countess Catherine was sitting in her solar with her eldest daughter Margaret and two of her ladies. Her gown of dark blue velvet, the cuffs turned back to reveal the brocade lining, suited her fair complexion. Fifteen-year-old Margaret was reading aloud from a Book of Hours while the ladies worked on a cloth for the altar in the chapel. The room was lit by many candles and the smell of wax mingled with that of the sweet herbs that had been strewn on the fire and the fresh rushes on the floor.

At Henry's appearance Margaret stopped reading and the Countess laid aside her needle and smiled at her son.

'Henry. I see your father has informed you that you are to attend my lord Cardinal's court.'

Henry bowed and then went to sit beside her on a faldstool. 'He has, Mother.'

'And are you pleased?'

'Indeed, I believe it is a great opportunity.'

'And you must make the most of it, Henry. You must learn well.'

He nodded. 'I promise I shall Mother.'

Catherine sighed. 'It is a long journey and at this time of year the roads will be hazardous. You will be travelling for almost a week, but you will rest at monasteries on the way.'

'Will we reside at the house in Newington Green for a while?' Henry asked.

'I think perhaps just to recover from the journey for your father has important business to attend to and he wishes to be back before Christmas.'

'Am I to have new clothes, Mother? I should not wish to appear in any way rustic.'

Catherine smiled. 'I shall order them at once. We must ensure your appearance befits the heir to one of the greatest earldoms in the country.' She studied her eldest son thoughtfully. 'I think a blue satin doublet and breeches, a black velvet doublet trimmed with gold lace and a matching cap, a green velvet riding cloak with silver fringe: that should be a start.'

Henry looked delighted. He didn't want to appear at the Cardinal's court looking like a country bumpkin.

'Will you miss being here at Wressle, Henry?' Margaret asked.

He smiled at her affectionately. 'I shall miss you and Maud and you, too, Mother.'

Catherine nodded, although she doubted very much if he would miss them, there would be too many new distractions in London. And she noted that he had not mentioned either of his brothers. She sighed. Her three sons were so different in nature and temperament but Henry, so quiet and self-effacing, was the most vulnerable, suffering as he did from agues and fevers. He did not have Thomas's brashness and obstinacy or Ingram's swaggering self-confidence, nor did he enjoy their good health and robust constitutions. She loved him perhaps above all her children, but she feared for him the most.

Chapter Nine

※

Lund, near York

WILL SET OUT AT noon the following day wrapped in his heavy felt riding cloak, in his saddlebags the food he had begged from the kitchens. He had portions of the broken meats from the previous day's dinner – pork, mutton, beef, capon and pheasant – wrapped in a cloth as well as round flat trencher loaves and some marchpane as a special treat for Meggie. The horse was his own, given to him last Christmas by Lord Henry, and he was proud of the animal and tended it assiduously.

His mother had moved from Hepburn some years ago. He had persuaded her to move nearer to Wressle where she would be safer and would be able to find work, as would his brother John who was now thirteen. They lived in a small cottage in the nearby village of Lund and his mother had found work in the kitchens of a manor house a few miles from Selby. It wouldn't take him long to get there, passing through the villages of Hemingbrough and Cliffe, and he had promised Lord Henry he would be back at Wressle before the castle gates were closed when darkness fell.

Despite his thick cloak and the padded dark green tunic he wore beneath it, emblazoned with the Percy badge of the silver crescent moon, he was cold when he at last alighted outside the small wattle and daub cottage. It wasn't as substantial as their stone cottage in Northumberland had been but it was warmer and more comfortable, he thought as he dismounted and tied the animal's reins to a small bush. It immediately began to graze on the short coarse grass of the roadside verge and Will knocked loudly on the door before pushing it open.

'Mam! Meggie! It's me, Will. I've come to visit,' he called.

Meggie uttered a cry of delight and rushed and threw her arms around him, her big hazel eyes shining. 'Will! Will! It's so long since I've seen you!'

He caught her up and swung her around, laughing. Her long brown hair was neatly plaited and her blue wool homespun gown was clean and tied around the waist with a length of twisted cord. 'You've grown, Meggie, since I last saw you.'

'I am almost eleven now, Will,' she reminded him.

'Where's Mam? Is she at her work?'

She nodded. 'And John is with her. He works in the stables now, helping to muck out.' She grinned impishly. 'Master Tamford, the head groom, has taken a liking to Mam so she asked him to give John work.'

'Is that so?' Will mused. It was the first time he'd heard this piece of news.

Meggie giggled. 'But John isn't so fond of Master Tamford, for he makes him work hard.' Leaving her brother to digest all this, the child went and put more kindling on the fire, poking at it vigorously with a stout stick so it blazed up.

Will frowned. So John was proving to be lazy. He would have to speak sharply to him. His mother needed every groat she could get and he wished she didn't have to work at all. He looked around the room. At least they did have more in the way of comforts than they used to have when his da had been alive, he mused. On the clean flagged floor stood a table, a bench and a three-legged stool. A small cupboard set against one wall boasted two candlesticks of base metal each holding a candle. There were three bowls and three earthenware mugs on the table. The hearth was also tidy and the place was warm. A wooden ladder led to a loft where he knew there were mattresses stuffed with straw and covered with coarse wool blankets. His mother was thrifty and at each quarter day he made sure that a portion of the amount of money he had managed to save was paid to her for his needs were few. With what she could earn and what he sent she managed well but he still would have preferred her to have spent her time at home. It was obviously Meggie who kept the house neat and tidy and he felt the child shouldn't be alone so much although he knew that the neighbours would watch that no harm came to her.

'I'll take a pail of water to the horse and then I'll show you what I've brought,' he promised as he went out to tend to the animal.

When he returned his sister was carrying one of the earthenware mugs to the table. 'Hot ale, Will. It will warm you.'

He sat down on the bench beside the table, thankful for the warm drink. 'We'll ride over to the manor to see Mam, Meggie. I can't stay until she finishes her work and gets home. I'll take you up behind me.'

His sister looked apprehensive. 'You won't let me fall?'

Will laughed. 'Of course not. You'll be safe enough if you hold on tightly to me. Now, see what I have for you in here.' He opened his bag and brought out the sugared confection.

Meggie cried out in delight. This was a rare treat. 'Marchpane! You remembered how much I like it.'

He grinned as she broke off a piece and popped it into her mouth. In a few years' time she would be a bonny enough lass and then he'd have to think about finding a good husband for her. He put the loaves and the meats back in the bag and placed it in the small cupboard, and then, bidding her get her shawl and follow him, he went outside and untied his horse.

It didn't take them long to cover the distance to Redeshall Manor and in the courtyard Will dismounted and lifted his sister down. As he did so his cloak fell back; seeing the silver crescent moon on his jerkin a man came quickly towards him.

'What business have you here, master?'

'I've come to see my mother, Mary Chatton. I'm her son, Will. Squire to Lord Henry Percy.'

The man nodded. 'I know Mistress Chatton well. I am Thomas Tamford.'

Will held out his hand and the older man shook it warmly. 'I have heard of you, Master Tamford. And I thank you for giving work to John.'

The man's expression changed. 'The lad be in need of taking in hand.' He fell silent but he looked as if he could say more.

Will nodded and glanced at Meggie. 'So I've heard. I intend to speak to him.'

'Walk with me to the kitchens, that's where Mistress Chatton be.'

As they crossed the courtyard Thomas Tamford called to a boy to take Will's horse. Will had taken an instant liking to the man and decided to confide in him. 'Master Tamford, I am to go to London very soon with Lord Henry. He is to reside at Cardinal Wolsey's court at York Place and I do not know how long it will be before I see my mother again. It would be a great relief to me to know that someone is looking to her welfare.'

His companion nodded. Mary had told him that Will had been with Lord Henry for six years and although she did not see him very often he made sure she was safe and provided for her to the best of his ability. Now, having met him, he judged him to be a good lad who had done well for himself, for he spoke well and his manners and dress were those of someone of a higher station than the son of a poor border farmer. Tamford reflected that young John would do well to emulate his brother. 'You can put your trust in me, Master Chatton. I have come to admire your mother. She is a good, hard-working woman. And I will make sure she has no need to fret over your brother.'

They had reached the door to the big kitchen and Will and Meggie followed Tamford inside where he quickly caught the eye of Mary and beckoned to her.

'Will! Will, lad!' she cried, wiping her hands on her coarse apron.

Will hugged her, thinking she looked well – a little older than last time he'd seen her perhaps, her hair beneath her plain linen cap was greying and there were a few more lines on her face, but despite that she seemed content. 'Can you spare some time away from your chores, Mam?'

Mary looked up at Thomas Tamford and he nodded, smiling. 'I will tell your master that Lord Percy's squire has come to see you, Mary. Take the lad and Meggie to my quarters above the stables. You will have some privacy there.'

Will took his mother's arm and led her back towards the door while the older man went in search of the master cook.

'Will brought me marchpane, Mam, and I rode behind him on his horse,' Meggie informed her mother.

'I brought food from Wressle too. I put it in the cupboard for safe keeping. You will have a feast for supper tonight, Mam.'

'You're a good lad, Will. Did the young lord give you leave to come?'

He nodded and they climbed the narrow stairs that led to the loft above the stables. Mary sat down on the bench beside the window and indicated that Meggie should sit beside her. 'Let me have a good look at you, lad.' She sighed and smiled sadly. 'You remind me of your da, especially about the eyes. May he rest in peace.'

The image of his father's face, black and bloated as he had been hanged, flashed through Will's mind. Six years it was now since Jed Chatton had been murdered and he still occasionally had nightmares about it. 'You are safer here, all of you, and Master Tamford has promised to look out for you while I am away.'

'He is a good man, Will. He's a widower and he has shown me much kindness.'

Will smiled. 'I'm glad, Mam. And I'm glad he is getting some work out of John.'

Mary's expression changed. 'John worries me, Will. He be not like you. He resents your good fortune and he will not work for he says why should he break his back shovelling dung when you have an easy life at Wressle? I don't know what's to become of him.'

'Don't worry, Mam. I have the feeling that Master Tamford will be watching him closely.' Will felt he could have confidence that Tamford would be as good as his word and he was eager to make his mother less anxious now that he would be leaving. 'I have great news. Lord Henry is going to London to the court of Cardinal Wolsey and I am to go with him.'

Mary's eyes widened. 'You be going to *London*!'

Will grinned. 'To York Place. I've heard it is as magnificent as any of the King's palaces. It's a great opportunity for me, Mam. To see all the fine houses that line the river and the bridge over the Thames and the Pool of London where the merchant ships lie, bringing riches from all over the world. And Westminster Hall and the Tower of London – Master Henry says it's a palace and prison too. Think, Mam, I might even see King Henry himself and Queen Katherine, the little Princess Mary and all the noble lords and ladies.'

Mary shook her head in amazement. She knew no one who had even been to London, never mind seen their great and magnificent King, who it was rumoured, was taller than all other men and very learned and whose clothes were of very rich materials. And the Princess Mary was said to be a fine, delicate child, as pretty as a daisy.

For the next hour they discussed with excitement Will's forthcoming adventure until reluctantly Mary got to her feet.

'I have to go back now, Will. Take care of yourself and God bless you,' she said. She smiled, the pride she felt for him shining in her eyes.

Will hugged her and kissed her on the cheek. 'God bless and keep you too, Mam. I know Master Tamford will keep his promise, so do not fret about John. I will take Meggie back to Lund and then take the road to Wressle.'

When he set his sister down outside the cottage she hugged him tightly. 'Will you bring me something back from London, Will?' she begged.

'I'll bring you something fine, Meggie, I promise. Go on in now and stir up the fire and choose which meats you will have for the supper when Mam and John get home.'

She stood at the door and waved until he disappeared around the bend in the road. Will felt a shadow of sadness pass over him as he wondered how long it would be before he saw her again.

Dusk was falling rapidly as he drew closer to Wressle but he drew rein as he caught sight of a figure ahead of him. The man appeared to be examining the hoof of the horse he was holding. Will's hand went automatically to the short sword he carried and he slowed his mount to a walk. It wasn't unheard of for brigands to be found in these parts. As he drew closer he could see it was a young man, decently but soberly dressed and he relaxed his guard a little.

'I see you have trouble,' he called politely.

'A stone lodged in his hoof, I think. I can't ride him any further and I'd hoped to be home before nightfall,' came the reply.

Will dismounted and examined the animal's hoof, and then shook his head. 'You're right. He's lame. Where are you bound?'

'To my father's house in York.'

Will whistled through his teeth. 'Even on a sound horse you would have to ride through the night to reach York. Who are you?'

'Robert Aske. My father is Sir Robert Aske of Aughton, a wool merchant. I have journeyed from London where I am studying at the Inns of Court.'

'You are a lawyer?'

'Not yet but I hope to be one day. And you?'

'Will Chatton. Squire to Lord Henry Percy. I'm bound for Wressle; you'd best come with me for you'll get no further tonight. You will find a night's board and lodging and be welcomed there but we must reach the castle before the gates are closed for the night.' He held out his hand and Robert Aske shook it. He was a stocky young man, Will saw, about nineteen or twenty. 'You'd better ride pillion and we'll lead your horse.'

'I thank you, Will Chatton. I lost the sight in one eye in childhood and would have spent a cold and miserable night wandering alone in the darkness.'

Will smiled at him. 'Lord Henry and I are bound for London in a few weeks' time, Master Aske, and should I ever need a lawyer I will seek you out.'

'Do so, Master Chatton. I should be pleased to be of service,' Robert Aske replied affably as they rode off into the deepening dusk.

Chapter Ten

Palace of Vincennes, near Paris

'YOU MUST MAKE HASTE, Mistress Anne, for there is terrible sickness throughout the country.' Semmonet looked flustered as she entered the girl's chamber early that October morning.

'I had heard that it was growing worse. Is it the plague?' Anne demanded, frowning. Were they to move their abode yet again?

'It is, *ma petite*, and the King has ordered that the Queen and the royal family are to go to the château at Amboise and that all who have no business to attend to are to be denied entrance until the sickness has abated.' Semmonet had hastily begun to gather the girl's belongings together.

'And what of me?' Anne asked, her dark eyes wide and full of concern.

Semmonet looked at her in surprise. 'You are to go with

them – what else? You do not wish to remain here, surely?'

Anne shook her head. Everyone feared the plague. 'But what of my father, Sir Thomas? He is King Henry's envoy and I know his business here is not yet completed.'

'I do not know, Mistress Anne. I was instructed only to oversee your packing. Everything must be ready by this noontide. We set out this afternoon.'

Anne turned away, twisting her blue and gold plaited silk kirtle between her fingers. She had no wish for her father to be exposed to this danger and he would be if he were left behind. She had become accustomed to him visiting her as often as he could for he had arrived in France last November to conduct affairs of state. He had told her that he was to negotiate the betrothal of the Princess Mary and the Dauphin and he had stood as proxy for King Henry at the christening of little Prince Henri in March. Now he was in the midst of the plans for a grand meeting between King Francis and King Henry here in France next year.

'Come, do not stand in a trance like a dullard. Make sure all your chains and necklaces are secured,' Semmonet instructed as the trunks were brought in and the girl's clothes were taken from the presses and laid across the bed, ready to be packed.

Anne lifted the small box from its resting place on the chest beside the bed and opened the lid. She didn't have a great deal of jewellery to secure, she thought ruefully. Two gold chains, one of silver and a link of pearls. No; she lived in the most opulent court in Europe, she shared the schoolroom and was the close companion and attendant of nine-year-old Madam Renée, Queen Claude's sister, and yet she had few costly adornments. She sighed as she closed the lid and locked the box, slipping the key on to her kirtle. She had become accustomed to moving from palace to palace on her father's instructions.

She had been sorry to leave Malines and the Regent but her father had impressed upon her how great an honour it was to be the youngest of the new French Queen's ladies. She had been nearly eight years old then and had tried to be obedient and dutiful but inside she had felt confused and upset to be leaving. The Regent too had been upset when Sir Thomas had requested that his daughter leave her court. She had expressed a hope to Semmonet that Mary Tudor, the eighteen-year-old bride of the ageing King Louis, would not ignore or neglect the child's welfare and education. Young queens had more on their minds than the wellbeing of even younger girls.

Anne handed the box to Semmonet. 'It is secured and I have the key safe about my person.'

The woman nodded and then turned her attention to supervising the maids.

Anne wandered to the window and leaned on the sill, gazing out and ignoring the flurry of activity that surrounded her. Queen Mary's arrival in France had been delayed by terrible storms. She had not gone in the party to meet her; she had been taken directly to the French royal nursery in Paris and here she had first met Madam Renée. They had become friends quickly, she recalled happily, for she had felt a little sorry for the four-year-old child who was small and walked with a slight limp, as did her older sister Claude. They had watched Mary Tudor's triumphal entry into Paris together from a private window, and they had marvelled at all the decorations which adorned the streets of her route from Porte Saint-Denis to

Notre-Dame. Neither of them had ever seen anything so magnificent.

It had been Renée who had informed her that they were to move again. Claude had told Renée that the Dauphin Francis was giving a tournament in the Parc des Tournelles in his new stepmother's honour, but that, alas, they would not be attending for they were to take up residence in the Palace of Vincennes outside the city. And so they had moved, but to their delight Queen Mary had sent some of the desserts from the banquet at the Hôtel de Ville for them. A smile hovered around her lips as she remembered how sticky their faces and fingers had become after eating the sugared plums and comfits and the little birds and butterflies made of marchpane, and how they had been scolded for it.

She slowly traced the letters of her name in the mist of condensation on the window pane, trying to ignore Semmonet's voice, shrill with annoyance at some misdeed committed by one of the servants.

After that the celebrations had ended, Anne thought. After just eighty-two days of marriage King Louis had died and Francis had become King in his place. She had ridden in a litter in the procession behind the young widow, the King's mother and Madam Renée and not long after that Mary Tudor had married the widower Charles Brandon whom she had always loved but who, for the sake of duty to her country, she had abandoned in favour of the now dead Louis.

It had caused a terrible scandal; both she and Renée had heard the whispered conversations of how furious King Henry had been at his sister's outrageous conduct and it was feared that Charles Brandon would be executed, but King Henry had finally forgiven his sister. Charles Brandon was now the Duke of Suffolk and because of that Anne Brandon had a new stepmother. She began to trace her surname on the glass, thinking that she had not had Anne Brandon as a companion for long. Her friend hadn't been happy at the Regent's court; she had never settled and barely a year later her father had asked that she be sent home and so she had gone out of her life. She wondered idly if the now thirteen-year-old Anne liked her stepmother. Probably not, for she had mourned her own mother deeply.

Semmonet's voice broke into her reverie. 'Mistress Anne, wipe your fingers and straighten your hood. You have a visitor.'

Obediently she pulled her blue and gold hood further forward over her dark hair and wiped her damp finger surreptitiously on the skirt of her gown, and then her face lit up as she saw her father standing in the doorway of the chamber, surveying the untidy room with an expression of annoyance.

'My lord, we are instructed to be ready to depart for Amboise with haste because of the plague,' she informed him, crossing to his side.

'I already know that, daughter. Which is the reason I have come.'

She looked up anxiously at him. 'And you, Father?'

'I am to accompany you. My discussions with His Majesty are not yet complete.'

She sighed with relief. 'I would not have wished you to run the risk of catching the plague, my lord.'

He smiled, his thin lips beneath the brown moustache lifting at the corners. He was a man whose countenance was always serious, his dark eyes calculating and often cold. His thick short neck was half hidden by the collar of his richly embroidered doublet and his hair was trimmed neatly in the French fashion.

'I would speak with you, daughter, but this chamber is too full of noise and idle gossip for my liking.' His sharp, wary gaze flickered over Semmonet and the maids.

Anne took his arm and led him through the chaos of trunks, shoes, gowns and cloaks into a tiny room in which she said her prayers or read from her Book of Hours.

Sir Thomas gazed around it in disapproval. 'Such a poor, close place, but it will suffice. I have two pieces of news to impart to you, Anne.'

She waited in expectant silence. 'The first concerns you, daughter. You are almost a young woman: it is time to put your childhood days behind you and leave the schoolroom. I have spoken to the Queen on many occasions and she has agreed with me that you should take your place at court but in the household of the Duchess of Alençon as Her Majesty is often indisposed due to illness and childbearing and is unable to supervise your welfare as closely as she would wish.'

'The Duchess of Alençon is a gracious lady, Father,' Anne answered politely. The Duchess was only fifteen years older than herself and she felt a stir of excitement at last being able to leave the schoolroom. But close on the heels of this thought came regret that then she would not see nearly so much of little Renée.

'You must watch and learn how to conduct yourself at court, Anne. To behave as the ladies of the nobility do, so that when it is time an advantageous marriage may be made for you.' He fervently hoped that she might be looked upon favourably by a French nobleman. She was attractive and he had heard she had many accomplishments already. She sang, danced and played well. Her French was excellent; she was already showing signs of becoming a graceful young woman and was fond of fashionable clothes, as his accounts bore witness. It all augured well for his plans for her.

'I shall do my best, Father, I promise,' she replied solemnly, wondering when, if ever, she would be allowed to remain in a place long enough to think of it as her 'home'? But if she did perhaps she would become tired of it. New ventures were to be welcomed, were they not?

'And whilst we are speaking of marriage, I have news of your sister,' Sir Thomas continued.

'Mary?' she queried, surprised.

'She is to be betrothed to William Carey.'

'But she is younger than me,' she answered more abruptly than she had intended. Her pretty, blue-eyed, blond-haired sister, as she remembered her, was rather immature and ill educated.

'I am aware of that but the marriage will not take place until at least next year and she will be wife only in name until she is older.'

Anne digested this but then frowned. It was not such a grand alliance for Mary as far as she could see. Carey held no exalted position that she had heard of.

Sir Thomas could read her mind. 'Indeed he is but a younger son of Sir Thomas Carey of Wiltshire but he is a gentleman of the privy chamber. He has daily contact with King Henry and can provide lodgings at court for your sister and opportunities for her to take part in the revels and entertainments and perhaps to be considered as a maid to Queen Katherine.'

Carey would also be his means of gaining information regarding the King's plans before they became more common knowledge and both Mary and his son-in-law would be in a good position to perhaps persuade the King to look more favourably upon him and grant him even higher offices.

So, it seemed as if little Mary would go to court and maybe even become one of the Queen's ladies, Anne thought, feeling a pang of jealousy. But would Mary be able to behave appropriately at court? Of course their mother would have instructed her, when she herself was not attending court, but she doubted her sister had the same accomplishments as herself, not having had the advantages of her upbringing.

'I shall take my leave of you now, daughter, for I have much to occupy me,' Sir Thomas announced, turning to the door and running his finger around the embroidered neck of his shirt. The room was unbearably stuffy and quite dark.

Anne laid a hand timidly on his arm 'Father, this great meeting of King Francis and King Henry . . . ?'

'The Field of the Cloth of Gold, as it is to be known, is to take place next June when the weather is deemed to be most clement.'

'Will my lady mother be attending?' Anne asked.

Sir Thomas nodded. 'Every nobleman and -woman in the kingdom will attend, including your grandfather of Norfolk and of course your brother George.'

'Would it be possible for me to go too? It is so long since I have seen my family,' she pleaded.

Sir Thomas frowned and shook his head. 'I fear not. There

will be great demands upon my time and I shall have scant opportunity to make such arrangements for you. I bid you farewell and God speed to Amboise, daughter. I will endeavour to speak with you again when the royal household is established there.'

The heavy oak door closed behind him, leaving her alone. The atmosphere felt even more oppressive and she was bitterly disappointed and hurt by her father's perfunctory dismissal of her request. Everyone, it seemed, would be going to this Field of the Cloth of Gold – everyone but herself. And she had longed to see her mother and George. She wondered would Mary be allowed to go? William Carey would be certain to be going as a gentleman of the King's privy chamber and so would he take his new wife? She felt a wave of jealousy sweep over her. Mary would be able to view the splendour, to take part in the festivities, to be received as Lady Carey by their friends and relations, while she would have to remain behind in Paris. She clenched her fists so tightly her fingernails dug painfully into the palms of her hands. It was not fair! She was the more accomplished daughter, she had more style and grace and wit, she knew how to behave in the presence of the nobility of the two great nations, unlike her silly, simpering, vacuous little sister who would still be a child of twelve and the wife of a younger son who held no lands or fortune. She swore to herself she would marry a man far above her sister's husband in station and wealth and then she would be the one who would be fêted and admired.

Semmonet's voice carried clearly through the open doorway: 'Mistress Anne, all is nearly ready. Come change your gown for travelling.'

Her jealousy died as suddenly as it had come. Oh, let Mary enjoy her brief moments of pleasure next June, she thought, for she had been kept confined at home for so long and it could not be enjoyable to be betrothed so young and have to face living with a husband and doing his bidding daily. Her composure recovered, she readied herself to do Semmonet's bidding.

Chapter Eleven

1522
York Place, London

'WHY SO GLUM, HARRY? Has my lord Cardinal been upbraiding you for your tardiness yet again?'

Henry, dragged from his reverie by the question, looked up and caught the sardonic gaze of Francis Bryant. Bryant was an accomplished poet, something he himself aspired to be. He was fully aware he had little of the talent possessed by either Thomas Wyatt or Bryant and while he admired and enjoyed the sonnets and poems they wrote (as he appreciated the writings of Erasmus, More, Homer and the classical authors) he never felt totally at ease in this young man's company. His rakish behaviour was common knowledge; the 'Vicar of Hell' was the sobriquet Bryant had earned for himself. Henry disliked his sardonic attitude and the often cruel way Bryant mocked the people he called his friends.

Bryant's utter disregard for the position and sensitivities of others was something Henry failed to understand. He himself was always considerate to his companions; at least he hoped he was.

'You are aware there are to be revels in honour of the Imperial Ambassadors when they attend the banquet here on Shrove Tuesday?' he replied tentatively, not really wishing to divulge what was troubling him to his companion.

Francis raised an eyebrow. 'I hear my lord Cardinal is planning a very elaborate masque, but then isn't everything his lordship plans elaborate beyond all measure?'

Henry ignored his companion's barbed innuendo. 'The King is also to attend and must be very royally entertained.'

Bryant threw back his head and laughed. 'By God! Your puns don't improve, Harry.'

The colour rushed to Henry's cheeks. Bryant had the knack of making him feel a fool. 'The pun was not intended,' he replied sullenly.

Bryant sat down beside him, throwing his arm carelessly across the back of the bench. He cut an elegant figure, the scarlet velvet of the collar of his doublet contrasting handsomely with his dark hair. 'So, what is it about this elaborate masque that has you looking so dour?'

Henry began to explain. 'Eight very fair ladies are to take part and eight boys from my lord Cardinal's choir are to be disguised as Indian women and all are to be besieged in the Château Vert.'

'Oh, a truly original idea! I assume this castle will indeed be green?' Bryant interrupted.

Before Henry could comment further they were joined by

Thomas Arundel, the younger brother of William FitzAlan. Henry relaxed a little for he knew Thomas was a friend he could trust.

'Go away, my dear "vicar", and annoy someone else,' Thomas instructed pleasantly. He knew Henry's opinion of Bryant and could see his friend was uncomfortable.

Bryant looked indignant. 'I was not annoying Harry. He was imparting to me the fascinating details of my lord Cardinal's forthcoming masque, entitled I presume *The Siege of Château Vert.*'

Thomas shrugged. 'Oh, that,' he replied, trying to sound uninterested. 'No doubt we will hear so much about it in the coming days that we shall be sick of it by Shrove Tuesday.' He directed his attention to Bryant. 'I came to tell you that Tom Wyatt is seeking your advice on some lines he has just penned to the fair Mistress Shelton.'

'Are you sure of that? I did not know he thought Madge "fair" at all.'

'Certain,' Thomas replied firmly.

Bryant screwed up his face in disbelief but got up and left them.

'He has a knack of twisting my words and making me appear foolish,' Henry confided. He was irritated with Bryant but more so with himself for allowing his cocksure companion to penetrate his defences.

'Take no heed of him. Were you discussing this proposed masque?' Thomas enquired.

Henry nodded. 'When he came upon me I was looking downcast and it intrigued him.'

Thomas sat down beside his friend. They were the same age

and had been drawn together as soon as Henry arrived at the Cardinal's court. 'Why downcast?'

'This masque: I am to be one of the gallant knights.'

'As am I. It might prove entertaining.'

'I would enjoy it more were it not for the fact that we must wear coats of cloth of gold, buskins of blue velvet and a cloak of blue satin and I do not have the means to purchase them.'

'Ah . . .' Thomas began to understand his friend's predicament. While the Cardinal was closeted with the King there was very little for them to do except while away the time with poetry, music and games of chance. Henry must have gambled and lost all his allowance but there was no question of him being able to refuse to take part in this masque. 'You have no funds?'

Henry shook his head. 'I lost heavily to Jamie Butler at cards. What is there to be done, Tom? I dare not refuse my lord Cardinal and I dare not ask my father for more money.'

'Then you will have to sell something,' Thomas stated flatly. 'Send a servant you can trust into the city to sell some items for you.'

Henry looked relieved. 'Of course. There are some clothes I have no use for and I shall have to part with two rings. I will instruct my squire, Will Chatton.'

Thomas stood up and smiled. 'I am to have the part of "Sir Youth" in this masque. What name have they given you?'

Henry grinned. ' "Sir Pleasure". There would not have been much "pleasure" about the role if I could not have purchased the costume. Now, I think it will be a fine entertainment.'

As he went in search of Will Chatton Henry wondered why he hadn't thought of this solution himself. He was uncomfortably aware that Will himself wouldn't have needed to find money to pay his gambling debts for Will saved his money. His squire didn't indulge in such pursuits the way he and his companions George Boleyn, Thomas Wyatt, James Butler and Henry Norris did. But what else was there to do? The hours of waiting were tedious. He had no desire to take part in any of the jousts or archery tournaments or games of tennis for they taxed his strength and his health sorely; he was still struggling to overcome the illnesses of his childhood. So he gambled. He had never done so until he'd come to court. His thoughts turned to his father. The Earl would be furious if he found out how much of his allowance he wasted for he had become aware that his father was deeply in debt. Money: neither he nor his father had enough yet here it was all around him.

When he'd first come to York Place he had been astounded at the riches with which the Cardinal surrounded himself. His court numbered eight hundred people; York Place was only one of his palaces and was comparable to any of those of the King himself. The first time he had accompanied the Cardinal to Greenwich he had been overawed by the pomp and magnificence of the Cardinal's procession. Wolsey's scarlet robes had been of the finest damask and satin, the collar of his surcoat trimmed with sable. A procession of knights had preceded him, one bearing the Great Seal of England, another his cardinal's hat, both on cushions of gold taffeta. Two carried the great silver crosses, two more the silver pillars and a third the silver-gilt mace emblazoned with the Cardinal's arms. When the procession had reached the water stairs the Cardinal's painted and gilded barge had been waiting, a dozen yeomen in scarlet and black livery ready to take up the oars. Since then he had witnessed many more such displays: whenever the Cardinal rode from York House through the city to Greenwich or Whitehall the trappings of his mule would be of scarlet velvet and the stirrups of gold, the knights would bear all the emblems before him while the gentlemen of his household rode behind.

He had never dreamed a man of the Church could acquire such wealth and status but in the time he'd been here he'd begun to realise that what many dared to whisper was indeed true. It was the Cardinal who ruled the country and it seemed as if it was the Cardinal who ruled the King. Thomas Arundel had warned him that Wolsey's spies were to be found everywhere and it would be wise to keep a guard on his tongue for my lord had his finger in every pie and little escaped those hooded eyes. Henry shuddered as he thought of that cold gaze, which seemed to see into his very soul. He had no desire to cross Wolsey, remembering his father's treatment at the Cardinal's hands.

He well recalled his first meeting with Wolsey in the gallery that led to the King's chief minister's Privy chamber. He had felt ill at ease, wondering if the Cardinal would show any animosity towards him but the older man's attitude had been almost dismissive. Wolsey had made it quite clear that he thought him just another gauche page. He'd inwardly quailed as the Cardinal's hard, calculating eyes had swept over him.

'Your father has sent you here to learn, Lord Henry. See to it that you do not disappoint either of us.'

He'd nodded and had replied tentatively, 'I shall be most

studious, my lord, I promise.' He had then been dismissed with a gesture of the Cardinal's beringed hand, as Wolsey had turned away.

He left the wide gallery and went down the stairs. Crossing the courtyard and climbing the stone steps he entered the wing of the building where the young men had their chambers. He made his way along the passageway to the room he shared with Thomas Arundel and George Boleyn and rummaged through one of the presses that contained his clothes, picking out those he intended to sell. He laid the garments he would dispose of on the bed and took two rings from a box and put them in his pocket. Then he went in search of Will Chatton once more.

He found him with Brother Thaddeus, one of the many priests and monks who resided in the Cardinal's household.

'Good morning to you, Lord Henry,' the elderly friar greeted him pleasantly.

'Good morning. Brother, I have need of Will's services,' he explained.

'Then I must not detain you any longer, Will. Remember, my son, with practice will come perfection,' he advised, smiling.

'What progress are you making, Will?' Henry asked as they made their way back to Henry's chamber. He had been surprised when he'd first found out that while he spent his time attempting to write poetry or playing at cards or dice, Will was spending many of his free hours with Brother Thaddeus, learning to read and write. It had never occurred to him that Will Chatton might want to better himself in this way. Will was the son of a peasant farmer and his pursuit of literacy had taken Henry aback, but it had also increased his admiration for his squire.

'I find it slow and laborious, my lord. I struggle with the words in English let alone in the Latin Brother Thaddeus insists I learn too.'

Henry nodded. 'Latin is the language of the Church and the law. French, the language of the courts of Europe, and English the language of the people. I'd ask the good friar to let you master your native tongue first. It seems to me that he is confusing you.'

'He is so, Lord Henry,' Will agreed, looking at his ink-stained fingers. Sometimes his head reeled and he wondered if he was mad but he wanted to be able to read things for himself and to master writing. The first time he'd written his own name he'd felt such a surge of pride that he would no longer be forced just to place a cross on a document, he'd become imbued with a fierce determination to be literate. Even though neither his mother, nor Meggie nor John would be able to read the letters he would send them in due course, the village priest would read the letters to them. It would give them all a sense of pride in his accomplishments.

'I require you to go into the city, Will,' Henry informed him as they reached the chamber and he caught the lad looking at the clothes with a puzzled expression. 'I need you to sell these things for me – and these too.' He held out the two rings in the palm of his hand. 'I have need of the funds.'

Will nodded slowly, concerned. So he's been gambling again, he thought, wondering why his master seemed to care so little where his money went.

'I lost at cards to James Butler and I had to honour the debt although it was the last of my allowance.' Henry paused. 'You disapprove. I can see it in your eyes,' he said, feeling both irritated and guilty.

'It is not my place to approve or disapprove, my lord,' Will replied mildly, folding the clothes into a bundle after pocketing the rings.

'But you think it, I can tell,' Henry persisted.

'My thoughts should not trouble you, Lord Henry. I will take the rings to Goldsmith's Row; I will get a better price for them there.' He did not blame his master for engaging in such pursuits, Lord Henry was young and still seemed amused by the diversions the court afforded. The environment his master now found himself in was very different to that he'd experienced in the North.

'Don't let them cheat you, Will,' Henry warned.

Will looked him squarely in the eyes. 'No one cheats a marcher man, my lord.' There was a note of pride in his voice that Henry did not miss.

When he'd gone Henry sat before the fire that burned in the hearth and stared into the flames. He was twenty and had been here now for three years but he could not help thinking he had not accomplished very much. He'd made some friends: the young men of his own age and background who might or might not prove to be allies in the years ahead. He'd tried to carry out his father's commands to secure and advance the interests of the House of Percy but in reality there seemed little he could achieve in that respect. He was not privy to the Cardinal's more important affairs; he did not have the ear of the King, nor was he likely to have it in the future. His life was aimless. At first he'd relished the constant round of banquets and revels, everything had been such a novelty after the quiet and often dull days at Alnwick and Wressle, but after a time they had paled, and he had wearied of the many hours in between, trying to find things to occupy his mind.

Most of the young women and girls he came into contact with were empty-headed and semi-literate, could sing and dance only passably well and thought of little else but clothes, entertainments, idle gossiping and giggling frivolity. They reminded him forcibly of Lady Mary and he was still thankful that his father and Lord Shrewsbury had agreed to set aside their betrothal. Unfortunately there were all too many like her at court, interested only in themselves and their transient pleasures.

He got to his feet slowly. It would be time for dinner soon and after that hopefully Will Chatton would have returned and he would be able to go about ordering the clothes he would need for the masque. Perhaps that diversion would lift his spirits.

Chapter Twelve

———◆———

City of London

WILL MADE HIS WAY through the labyrinth of corridors and galleries and across the courtyard and then the gardens and lawns, down to the water stairs where he hailed a passing lighter. The river was always crowded for it was easier to go by water than traverse the rutted, potholed roads and the filthy lanes. The cheapest fare was one penny but it would cost him three to be taken from York Place to the city. The bridge was always the most dangerous part of the journey for the tide race between the narrow stone arches was very strong. But 'shooting the bridge' was something the Thames lightermen faced many times a day. As he watched the barges and wherries and the scores of other lighters crisscrossing the river he wondered if he would ever get used to life here. True, there was always something to enjoy – bull-and bear-baiting, cock-fighting, freak shows and fairs – but at times, especially during the warmer months, the noise, the flies, the stench from the sewage and garbage rotting in the open gutters in the narrow streets and lanes nauseated him and made him long for the cool, fresh air of the border country and the salty tang of the Northumberland coast.

When he had first arrived, after he had become accustomed to the grandeur of the palace and the hustle and bustle of the city, he had been shocked at the behaviour and lack of manners of many courtiers who considered themselves well bred. They seemed to have little or no respect for the sumptuous public apartments. Window panes were frequently smashed, furniture broken, the paintwork that decorated windowsills and panelling defaced and the Office of Works was kept busy with repairs. Tankards and dirty dishes – often still containing the remains of a meal – were left lying around, which encouraged the numerous dogs, cats and rats. He'd seen instructions from the Comptroller of the Household forbidding visitors to wipe their hands or their noses on the expensive tapestries that lined the walls of many rooms or to leave dirty dishes or food on any of the beds, which would stain and ruin the rich coverlets. Theft was rife and not only amongst the hundreds of servants. He'd been brought up never to touch anything that did not belong to him on pain of severe punishment, yet these gentlemen and ladies seemed to think nothing of helping themselves to any trinket that caught their fancy and a blind eye was turned to their larceny.

But what had appalled him most was the unashamed and, in his opinion, disgusting practice of men and boys pissing in the fireplaces or against the walls. His mother, poor and uneducated though she was, had always maintained that the hearth was the heart of the home. It gave warmth and comfort and a place to cook their food and as such should be tended with care. There were garderobes adjacent to most large rooms and in the courtyards there were stone and lead urinals so there was no excuse for such behaviour. He'd noticed the red crosses painted on the walls of the buildings that surrounded the courtyards and when, out of curiosity, he'd asked a fellow squire why they were there, he'd been told offhandedly that they were to stop people from pissing against the walls. 'My lord Cardinal says it is a sin to so desecrate the cross,' the lad had informed him, shrugging carelessly.

He no longer shared a chamber with Lord Henry. He and all the other squires slept in the great watching chamber on pallets that were rolled up and stored away when not in use, for the chamber was occupied during the day by the yeomen who formed the Cardinal's personal guard. He ate with the other squires at a trestle table in the great hall while Lord Henry ate with his peers at a table higher in the room, but below that of the Cardinal who dined in state on plate as rich and fine as anything the Earl possessed. Wolsey also provided food that was the equal of any at the King's court, so he'd been told.

He alighted at the water stairs at Thames Street, taking care not to slip on the slimy stone steps around which lapped the dirty waters of the Thames. He then made his way through the narrow lanes where the half-timbered upper storeys of the houses and shops jutted so far out that they almost met and blocked out most of the sunlight of the spring morning. Avoiding the open sewer that ran down the centre of the streets and the mangy dogs and cats that foraged and fought amongst the piles of rubbish, he sought out a row of shops. He stopped outside one bearing the arms of the Guild of Drapers above the low doorway and went inside. It was very dimly lit but even in such a poor light he had no difficulty in convincing the master draper of the quality of his master's clothes and so negotiated a good price. He secured the coins he received in the small leather bag hung around his neck beneath his tunic, for the city abounded with thieves and cutpurses. After some haggling he got a good price for the rings in the second goldsmith's shop he called at and then made his way back towards the river, stopping to look at the tall masted ships in the Pool of London. Leaning against the stone parapet he watched the stevedores as they loaded and unloaded the many merchant ships.

'A hive of activity is it not, Master Chatton? Like bees around a honey pot.'

Will turned and smiled as he caught sight of the familiar stocky figure of Robert Aske approaching, clad as usual in the sombre black of a student of the Inns of Court. He had met the young lawyer on half a dozen previous occasions while he'd been in London and he liked and respected him. In fact it had been Robert Aske who had first encouraged him to seek the help of Brother Thaddeus.

'I was thinking that there must be fortunes to be made from the goods that are shipped in and out of here,' Will mused.

'Indeed there are. Are you on business for Lord Henry or is it an errand of your own that brings you away from York Place?'

'Lord Henry's business, if you can call it that. He has need of funds. He has lost his allowance gambling and dare not ask the Earl for more. So I was sent to Goldsmith's Row.'

Aske nodded. Life at court encouraged both idleness and wastefulness and he'd heard his father say that the Earl himself had squandered a fortune at court in his younger days. His own feelings on the cost of the much famed library, the magnificence of the Earl and his entourage on occasions such as the journey of Margaret Tudor to Scotland, and the sumptuous banquets provided for the merchants of Beverley and York were unforgiving. The Earl was known throughout the North as 'Henry the Magnificent', and with some justification, but he considered such extravagance very imprudent.

Will was still staring at the stevedores. 'If I had but a fraction of Lord Henry's allowance I would try to invest it in something that would bring me some reward.'

'Have you any money of your own, Will?'

Will tore his gaze away from the ships. 'A little. Not very much, though I try to save. Why do you ask, Robert?'

The young man leaned forward, resting his arms on the top of the worn stones. 'My father's agent has dealings with the captains of ships that trade with Spain and the Netherlands. If you could purchase some commodity I could perhaps persuade him to place it with a cargo and sell it for you. It would be a start.'

Will stared at him. Did he mean it? To become involved in trade, to perhaps add to his savings, was a rare opportunity. Of course there were the risks to consider. If the ship sank, if there was a sudden decline in trade or sickness decimated either animals or people, he would lose everything. He remained silent for a few minutes debating it and then he nodded. 'What should I buy?'

'The finest woollen cloth you can afford. That is always guaranteed to bring a good price, especially in the Netherlands,' Aske advised.

Will became apprehensive. 'But that is so very expensive I doubt I should be able to afford to purchase even a yard.'

Robert Aske thought for a moment. 'My father's agent may let you have it a little cheaper or maybe extend you some credit.' He smiled encouragingly. 'Great things can grow from small beginnings, Will. I shall see what can be arranged. Can you meet me here at this time tomorrow?'

'Indeed.' Will seized his hand and shook it. 'I thank you most heartily, Robert. I too will see if there is anything I can sell to increase my funds.'

Aske tucked his books under his arm. 'Until tomorrow then.'

All the way back Will thought about Aske's proposition. The prospect of being able to accumulate more money was exciting, but credit could also mean debt and that was something he was uneasy about. Yet if things went well, could he then look forward to a better life for both himself and his family? He could go back to the North Country and maybe buy a small house of his own, continuing his trade from there through a London agent and in time become respected as a merchant. His heart began to pound as the ideas filled his mind. An even greater determination to learn to read and write hardened within him. He was already good at calculating; he had a firm grasp of figures and money. Was it really possible that the son of a poor border farmer could one day become a rich and respected man? But wasn't the great Cardinal himself the son of a merchant from the Suffolk town of Ipswich and look at the wealth he had amassed and his eminent position! He heartily disliked and mistrusted Wolsey but he grudgingly admired his achievements – and those achievements had been founded on education and trade.

These thoughts absorbed him as the lighter ploughed its way through the now choppy waters of the river. When he alighted he stood for a moment looking at the lawns and gardens that stretched before him and then up at the sprawling buildings of the palace. All this belonged to the Cardinal. He certainly couldn't aspire to such grandeur. To have a modest house of his own, an income and savings: that was his dream, and now he hoped he had been given an opportunity to realise it.

He crossed the inner courtyard and went up the wide stairway to the long gallery with its tall bay windows that overlooked the gardens and the river. He found Henry standing in one of the bays, deep in conversation with George Boleyn and Thomas Wyatt. Upon catching sight of his squire Henry left them both and came towards him.

'Did you get a good price, Will?'

'I did, my lord.' Will passed over the gold coins.

Henry noticed that Will's face was flushed and his eyes bright. 'You have some news?'

'I met with Robert Aske, you remember the young lawyer from York?'

Henry nodded. Aske had come to the Earl's house in York on occasion, some years ago, seeking his father's advice on border law.

'He is going to help me to purchase some cloth to send to the Netherlands to sell. I hope to make a profit to start me in trade.'

Henry stared at him in astonishment. 'Why do you wish to become engaged in trade?'

'So that I can make money, my lord,' Will answered, thinking that surely it was obvious.

'Are you not satisfied with your position here?' Henry asked.

'I am, Lord Henry, I am most grateful for it, but I would like to have money to give both myself and my family a better life.' He hoped Lord Henry would not think him ungrateful or over-ambitious. When they had first arrived here they had grown closer for they had both been strangers in a new and vastly unfamiliar environment, and he felt that perhaps his master now looked on him as more than just his squire. But he reminded himself quickly that he must never forget his place or overstep the boundaries of degree. He feared that in divulging his plans to Henry he had done just that.

Suddenly Henry grinned and clapped him on the shoulder. 'Then I wish you luck. When your ship comes home, Will, you can perhaps lend me some of your fortune.'

Will grinned back in relief but he hoped Henry wasn't being serious. If he had been in his master's position he would have spent the gold coins he'd just passed over on a part cargo which might have brought a handsome return, not on an elaborate costume for a masque. But he supposed it would not have been considered appropriate for a nobleman of Lord Henry's standing to engage in trade. The costume was a necessity for his master. And as for the masque, he certainly did not envy Lord Henry such pleasures.

The following morning Will took the same route into the city, taking with him his small hoard of savings and some things he hoped to sell, although he knew he would get nothing like the same amount as he'd obtained for Lord Henry's belongings.

He was waiting impatiently at the wharf when finally Robert Aske, grey-cloaked and wearing a flat black felt bonnet, appeared.

'Good news, Will! I have managed to get you half of a small bale at a good price and it's to go on the next ship out on this evening's tide.'

Will thrust the small bag containing the coins into his hand. 'Here is all the money I possess. Is it enough, Robert?'

The young man opened the neck of the bag and quickly gauged the contents. 'It is but I am to give you the option of a few shillings' credit should you need it. Captain Fanshaw is an honest man, he'll not cheat you, and when he returns you can purchase more cloth and so on until your money increases. Come, we'll share a tankard of ale to celebrate your first venture into trade.'

Will took his arm and they made for the nearest tavern, Will feeling almost giddy, as if he was walking on air.

'I hear the Imperial Ambassadors are expected in the city soon?' Aske remarked when they had been served with the ale in the dark, noisy Waterman's Arms.

'There are to be banquets and festivities when they come to York Place,' Will informed him.

'It is to be wondered how long this allegiance will last. At times it is the French who are our allies, at others the Holy Roman Emperor, but treaties are always broken and new ones made.'

Will shrugged. 'I have little knowledge or interest in such affairs.'

'You might if you had to go to war with Lord Henry. If I were called upon to fight I would prefer to know what I was fighting for.'

Will looked alarmed. 'Is such a thing likely to happen?'

'Not at the present, but who knows? You know as well as I

do that there is always war on the Border and Lord Henry will one day be Warden of the Marches. He will have his obligations, like his father before him. But fear not, let us hope that the Earl has many long years ahead of him and that by then you will no longer be in his lordship's service.'

Will smiled and nodded. 'I'll drink to that.' The thought of a life spent in the pursuit of his own destiny rather than in service sent a small thrill of excitement racing through his body.

Chapter Thirteen

———•✦•———

Greenwich Palace, London

A S THE ROAD BECAME steeper and finally topped the rise in the ground Anne slowed her horse's pace to a trot. The Palace of Greenwich sprawled in a vast T shape before her. The red brick of the twin towers of the new armoury beside the tiltyard and the battlements that faced the river seemed to glow in the watery March sunshine; the myriad of diamond-shaped panes of glass in the numerous huge, tall windows sparkled in the pale light.

A smile lifted the corners of her mouth and her dark eyes were bright with excitement. After nine long years she was finally home. She had travelled from France with her father for there was now the very real prospect of war between France and England and Sir Thomas, returning from his first meeting with the Emperor Charles V, had instructed her to meet him in Calais. It had been a long, arduous and cold journey but now she could forget all the discomforts for she was to be lodged for a while at Greenwich.

'Don't dawdle, Anne. This wind is chilling me to the bone,' Sir Thomas complained, pressing onward.

She kicked her heels into the mare's flanks and caught up with him. When they at last reached the courtyard nearest their lodgings two grooms appeared and helped them dismount, while two more took the bags containing the possessions they'd brought with them. Anne looked around at the red-brick crenellated walls, thinking of the beautiful pale grey turrets and walled gardens of Amboise in the Loire valley. Life here would be very different but she was determined that she was going to be noticed and admired just as much as she had been at the French court. What use would all the years of schooling and all her accomplishments be if she dressed, spoke and behaved just like every other girl who lodged within this palace? She intended to marry well to please her father and elevate her family. She did not wish to be plain 'Mistress' Boleyn for ever. As she followed her father along the wide passageway towards his chambers she was looking forward to seeing her mother and Mary and George again. Her grandfather, elevated to the title of Duke of Norfolk after the great battle of Flodden, was not in residence but her uncle, Sir Thomas Howard, was.

As Comptroller of the King's Household her father's chambers were spacious and well furnished and a good fire had heated the room. Fine tapestries covered the walls and silver plate and candlesticks adorned the tops of the heavy carved chests and cupboards. Food and wine had been set out on the table and a servant brought water and napkins for them to wash.

Anne removed her heavy wool travelling cloak and sat down. 'When will I be able to see my lady mother?' she asked, deftly cutting off a slice of meat from the breast of the roasted capon.

'When Queen Katherine gives her leave,' Sir Thomas replied, filling a goblet with fine wine.

'The Queen knows I am here?'

'Your mother will have informed her of the fact and the King expects me to wait upon him before dinner with news of my mission.'

Anne took a sip of the sweet Rhenish wine. She had no duties here. At fifteen she was considered too young to wait upon Queen Katherine but she would surely see her and the King too. 'Father, will there be a place for me here?' she asked tentatively. She had wanted to ask him this on the journey but had refrained, aware that travelling and all its inconveniences had soured his mood. She had decided it would be better to broach the subject after they had arrived when he would, she hoped, be in a better frame of mind. After all, Mary was at court and she was a year younger, even though she was now married to William Carey.

Sir Thomas frowned, concentrating his thoughts on the news he was about to impart to her. 'In time I might be able to arrange something but I wish to speak to you on another matter.'

Anne tilted her head, her eyes alert and fixed enquiringly on his face.

'The King and my lord Cardinal have agreed to a marriage between you and James Butler.' He delivered his announcement in a tone that brooked no argument. It had taken a great deal of time and effort to arrange this. James Butler was the son of Sir Piers Butler, the Earl of Ormonde, a title disputed by Thomas Boleyn for he himself had claim to the Irish earldom through his mother and aunt. When the Earl of Surrey had returned from Ireland, Ormonde had been made Deputy Lieutenant of the country in the hope that he would curb his homeland's tribe of their frequent rebellious behaviour. James Butler was one of a group of young men residing at the Cardinal's court, ostensibly to advance his education but in reality little more than a hostage to ensure his father's loyalty to the Crown.

Anne's eyebrows rose for this was the first time this had been mentioned. 'James Butler,' she repeated.

'Son of Sir Piers, Earl of Ormonde.'

She nodded slowly. '*Bien!* Then I am to be a countess?' The thought pleased her greatly. It was a better match than Mary's.

Sir Thomas nodded, his speech restricted by a mouthful of mutton. 'In time,' he at last managed to reply.

A frown creased her forehead. 'How old is this James Butler and is he well mannered and can he be called handsome?'

Sir Thomas stared at her. Anne had a keen grasp of politics for her age and sex, she was intelligent and curious, and he had expected her to be above such girlish concerns. 'What matter such things? He will inherit a title and lands and it will provide the solution to both the question of Irish loyalty and your grandmother and great-aunt's claim on the Butler earldom.'

She should have anticipated such an answer, she told herself. Her father was not a man to have his decisions questioned and she was not someone whose opinions would sway his plans. 'I see, Father. Is he here in London? Is he at court?'

'He is at my lord Cardinal's court.'

She said nothing. Maybe Mary would be able to enlighten her as to the age and nature of her future husband. She would have to hold her impatience in check until she could cross-question her sister. Anne resumed her meal, struggling to master her agitation.

It was early afternoon before she saw her mother and Mary. Both had been with Queen Katherine, although as they were both married neither were ladies-in-waiting.

'Let me look closely at you, child,' Elizabeth Boleyn instructed after Anne had dutifully curtsied and then kissed her.

Anne pirouetted slowly, holding wide the skirts of her claret velvet dress bordered with gold thread. She had had plenty of time to change from the clothes she had travelled in. She had washed and brushed her dark hair for the pearl-trimmed French hood revealed more than the heavy gable worn by both her mother and sister would have.

Her mother's face softened with approval. 'You have grown tall but you present well and you have the demeanour of a French lady.'

'Thank you, Mother. I am happy to be back in England,' Anne replied demurely.

Mary was staring at her with something akin to astonishment. She was so *different*. So very stylish. The cut of her gown, the long, wide elegant sleeves that gracefully half covered her hands. The pretty horseshoe-shaped hood that flattered her oval face and showed off her dark, glossy hair. Her expressive, elongated dark eyes with their thick black lashes. The ropes of pearls around her long, slender neck, the graceful line of which was enhanced by the gold 'B' she wore on a chain. Mary knew she herself was considered to be one of the prettiest girls at court but her sister's style made her feel dowdy. Anne was going to cause a sensation.

'Mary will take you to your chamber,' Lady Boleyn instructed, ending the brief interview. She intended to find her husband to learn how her elder daughter had taken the news of her proposed betrothal.

'You look so . . . different. And you sound different. You have an accent. Are you really glad to be back or did you want to stay in France?' Mary asked as she sat down on the bed which took up most of the room in the small chamber that had been allotted to Anne.

Anne shrugged her shoulders elegantly and sat beside her. 'You know as well as I do that we have no say in where we go. But I think I am pleased to be back. If I can stay at court I shall be happy.' She smiled fondly at her sister. 'And tell me, did you enjoy your visit to France? I heard that the field of the Cloth of Gold was a magnificent occasion. I was disappointed not to be there, the reports of the banqueting, masques, tournaments and the splendour of the garments of both courts was marvelled at by everyone. It was *tout à fait magnifique*!'

Mary was enthusiastic. 'It was wondrous, Anne. Everyone was so ... so elegantly and richly attired. The King and King Francis vied with each other in everything: clothes, jewels, sporting and dancing and in the masques. I was sad when it came to an end.'

Anne nodded; she had heard as much. She had also heard that her sister had turned a few heads and had unwisely gained something of a reputation as a flirt. Perhaps it was as well that she had not remained in France. 'And what of you? How does marriage suit you, Mary? What's he like, this William Carey?'

Mary blushed prettily. She was the exact opposite of Anne, blonde with wide blue eyes and a pink and white complexion. She was also smaller and decidedly plumper. 'He suits me well enough. He is kind and considerate and he is young too, twenty-six. I think him handsome.'

'And do you share a bed with him yet . . . in that way?' Anne probed. She could not think of Mary as anything other than her little sister.

Mary giggled. 'I do.'

Anne lowered her voice. 'And what is it like? Does it hurt? Is it uncomfortable? Is it embarrassing?'

Mary rolled her eyes expressively. 'It was all those things the first few times but . . . but . . .' She giggled again.

'But *what*?' Anne demanded curiously.

'But now I enjoy it. I can't describe the feeling . . . but wait until it is your turn. Then you will understand.'

Anne drummed her heels irritably against the coverlet and then, hitching up her skirts, pulled her feet up on to the bed and tucked them beneath her. She came to the subject that had been filling her mind since the morning. 'It seems I am to have a husband too, so I shall soon find out.'

Mary too pulled her feet up and, stuffing a pillow behind her back, sat facing her sister. 'Who is he? Who told you?' she asked, her eyes wide with curiosity.

'Father did, after we arrived this morning. I am to be betrothed to the son of the Earl of Ormonde. I will be a countess.' She pronounced the word carefully and with deliberation.

'Jamie Butler? You are to marry him?'

Anne nodded, dropping her air of superiority. 'Do you know him? I asked Father how old he is and what he is like but I was told such things are not important.'

Smiling knowingly, Mary helped herself to a sugared comfit from the dish beside the bed.

'You will get fat if you eat too many sweets and your teeth will rot, then your William's eyes will wander to other maids,' Anne chided. 'But tell me of this Jamie Butler.'

'He is young, I think maybe twenty or twenty-one. He is pleasant enough in nature from what I have seen of him and he has grey eyes and his hair is gold like the King's, but of a darker shade. And he is of course Irish but his manners are goodly enough.'

Anne smiled. He didn't sound too bad at all. At least he wasn't an old man with a bad temper and worse breath.

Mary looked a little downcast as a thought struck her. 'But you will have to go away again. When you marry him you will go to live in Ireland and I will have no one to gossip with.'

Anne's eyes widened in horror. That was something that hadn't occurred to her. 'You mean I shall have to go and live in that *terrible* country? But . . . but it is barely civilised! I have heard that the people have wild, matted hair and they paint their faces and their bodies like the people of Queen Boudicca did in ancient times. They are always rising in arms against their lords and each other. Why, they are little more than savages. Mary, I couldn't stand to live in a place like that! Not after living in France. *Non! Non!* I won't! I won't go and I won't marry him! *Je refuse! Absolument!*'

Mary caught her hand and squeezed it. 'What else can you do? We can never challenge Father; we must do as we are bid.'

Anne's brows rushed together in a frown as she contemplated Mary's words. She thought bitterly of all the years she had spent away from her home and her family. Nine years spent in the palaces of foreign kings and archduchesses, learning the accomplishments of a noble lady. For as long as she could remember it had been impressed upon her that she must marry well for the advancement of her family, yet now it seemed as though all that time away, all the hours of practice and learning were to be thrown away. Yes, she would have the title of 'Countess' but it would mean very little in such a wild country.

'I won't! I won't be forced to leave court to live in that Godforsaken land,' she answered determinedly.

'But, Anne, you have no choice,' Mary insisted.

Anne stared back at her mutinously, furious that her father should choose to discard her so.

The door opened and George Boleyn put his head around it. 'Is it safe for me to come and greet my sophisticated sister newly arrived from France?'

'Oh, George! Come in and help me to try to talk reason into her,' Mary cried, relieved. George had always been able to make Anne see sense.

A look of concern crossed nineteen-year-old George's handsome face as he closed the door behind him. 'Surely my sister is not being unreasonable?'

'Father has told me I am to marry James Butler and then I shall have to go to Ireland. But I refuse to live in *that* place!' Anne informed him resolutely.

George held up his hands in mock horror at her outburst.

'Such rebelliousness! Is that how you have been taught to behave in France?'

Anne stared at him steadily. 'Indeed, why then did they *send* me to France to learn how to be a noble lady if now they intend me to live amongst savages?'

George sat at the foot of the bed and shook his head. 'Don't be a fool, Anne. You were sent not just to learn how to speak and how to behave or how to sing and dance. Father sent you there hoping you would catch a French lord or even a duke, but now that Francis and our sovereign lord Henry are no longer bosom friends his plan must change. Father can only react to circumstances and circumstances have a habit of altering. We must marry to advance the fortunes of the family. Little Mary has William Carey, who has the ear of the King and therefore may wheedle favours from him for Father. You must settle for Jamie Butler to ensure his father's loyalty and to keep Grandmother Boleyn and her dear sister content—'

'But you seem to be able to please yourself,' Anne interrupted sharply.

George shook his head. 'Alas, there you are wrong, sweet sister. I am to be married too.'

This news surprised them both. 'Who?' Mary demanded.

'Jane Parker, God help me,' George said, grimacing. 'The daughter of Lord Morley.'

'Oh, poor George,' Mary commiserated. 'She is such a plain girl and she has sly ways and a sharp tongue too.'

'It chills me to the bone to think I must share a bed with her,' George confided miserably. 'She watches me like a hawk hovering in the sky.' He shuddered. 'So you see, Anne, having to marry Jamie Butler might not be too bad. Or it might come to nothing. Until Father has haggled over the dowry he will pay and the terms and conditions of the contract he will agree to, nothing is certain.'

Mary, never downhearted for long, echoed George's sentiment. 'You might remain here after all! Now, let me tell you my news. I am to have the part of "Kindness" in a masque my lord Cardinal is giving and you, Anne, are to be "Perseverance". There will be other ladies and we shall all have gowns of white satin embroidered with gold thread and our headdresses will be adorned with jewels.' She clapped her plump hands together. 'It will be a wonderful revel.'

Anne's ill humour began to evaporate as Mary elaborated on the plot and the costumes. Next to them, George sat listening but unusually he didn't join in. He already knew all the details, including the fact that his future bride Jane Parker was to have the part of 'Constancy'. He heartily wished to avoid her but knew it was a futile hope. Disconsolately, he helped himself to a goblet of wine. It tasted sour in his mouth.

Chapter Fourteen

———◆———

Greenwich Palace, London

THE FITTING OF THE costumes they were to wear for the masque caused the first disagreement between Anne and her sister.

'We must take a bath for we do not wish them to be soiled before they are even finished,' Anne urged as Mary brushed out her long, dark hair.

'A bath!' Mary cried, her blue eyes wide with surprise. 'A wash will surely suffice?'

Anne turned and took the brush from her. 'No it will not! In the time I have been here I have observed . . . and *smelled* . . . how little time is spent on cleanliness. *Enfin!* Compared to the French court everyone here is so malodorous, including you, dear sister.'

Mary pouted and two spots of colour appeared on her cheeks. 'I am not!'

Anne stood up and resumed brushing her hair. 'When was the last time you took a bath, Mary?'

Mary shrugged, not wishing to reply that she couldn't remember.

'When was the last time you washed yourself all over, including your breasts and belly and secret parts?'

'Last week,' Mary replied defiantly.

Anne rolled her eyes expressively. '*Mon Dieu!* You should wash all over each day.'

'It is not the custom here and there would be high words indeed if hot water and bath tubs were to be demanded with such regularity,' Mary snapped irritably. 'I change my body linen frequently, as does William.'

'I should hope so. And do you instruct your maids to hang up your gowns so that the air may sweeten them? It is bad enough trying to combat the fleas and other vermin that are such an annoyance without encouraging them with the stale odours of the body.'

'William has confided to me that the King wears a small piece of fur next to his skin to trap such pests,' Mary said sullenly.

Anne nodded. With the close proximity to the King his position afforded, William Carey would know of such things. 'That is a good idea. Take off your hood, Mary,' she instructed firmly.

'What for?' her sister asked suspiciously.

'I don't suppose you have used a lice and nit comb on your hair this week either?' Anne dropped her officious attitude and smiled. 'You have such beautiful hair, Mary. It is the colour of ripe corn and you should take more care with it.'

Mary sighed, thinking her sister's attitude to cleanliness was bordering on the irrational for she knew of no one who washed so often, but she removed the hood and submitted to having her long blond hair meticulously combed with the fine-pronged steel comb, which thankfully harvested nothing.

Anne then commanded the maids to bring up the wooden bath tub, lined with canvas sheets. They both watched as linen sheets were draped over the canvas ones and the maids sweated and strained with the heavy buckets of hot water.

Anne took a small glass bottle from a chest and dropped oil of lavender into the water. Then they both undressed and climbed in and Mary was quite surprised to find that she enjoyed the sensation of the warm, sweet-smelling water on her body.

'You see, Mary. It is very pleasant, is it not?' Anne smiled as she splashed the water on to her neck and shoulders. 'And the smell of lavender will linger on our skin.'

Mary watched Anne submerge her head, her hair floating around her on the surface like a cloak of black silk. When she emerged with rivulets running down her face she was laughing. 'I suppose you thought I might drown?' She pushed her hair away from her face and with a small tablet of perfumed soap that she had brought from France, began to wash her hair.

The water was rapidly cooling when they both stepped out and wrapped themselves in clean linen sheets and went to sit before the fire while the maids emptied the bath tub and then hauled it away.

'Do you feel better now? Your hair and your skin will smell so sweetly that I wager your William will not be able to curb his desire for you.'

Mary giggled and she grudgingly admitted that she had enjoyed the experience, although she secretly vowed it would not become a frequent occurrence for even the King did not bathe every week and many ladies said it was unwise to bathe more than two or three times a year for it weakened the constitution.

The costumes, when they arrived, were very becoming, both girls agreed. The full skirt of white satin, the tight, square-necked bodice and flowing sleeves were embroidered all over with flowers and leaves in gold thread. But Anne complained vociferously about the style of the matching hood.

'I will not wear something as old-fashioned as *that*!' she stated flatly, refusing to allow the seamstress to place the white satin gable hood on her head. Despite the opulence of its pearl decoration, it was ugly and Anne would not tolerate ugliness.

'But we have to wear them. They are part of the costume, modelled on Queen Katherine's,' Mary urged.

'But Queen Mary doesn't wear such a monstrosity!' Anne retorted. 'And I will not appear in front of so many important people looking as if I have a small house on my head! *Non!* Take it away! I will wear only a French hood.'

In the end it was resolved that they would all wear French hoods and Anne felt a quiet satisfaction at her victory. She had no wish to resemble Queen Katherine, whom she thought was starting to look old and tired and faded, despite her lavish gowns and matchless jewels.

They had practised their parts in the masque a great many times under the direction of the Master of the Revels. There had been some squabbling, of course, and Mary Carey blamed Jane Parker, insisting her future sister-in-law instigated the rancorous outbursts each time. Anne had watched Jane closely and she had come to the conclusion, as had both Mary and George, that the girl was poisonous. She seemed clinging, envious and petty-minded in the extreme. Poor George indeed, she mused after one of Jane's jealous outbursts.

The only 'Fair Lady' who didn't take part in these rehearsals and was therefore spared the attendant arguments and often cruel jibes, was Mary Tudor, Dowager Queen of France, now Duchess of Suffolk, with the plumb part of 'Beauty'. Royalty brought many privileges, great and small, Anne mused. She wondered why her former companion from Malines, Anne Brandon, had not been chosen to take part in the masque. Perhaps her stepmother had not wished it, she thought, as she was helped out of her costume after the final rehearsal. She had hoped to renew her friendship with Anne Brandon but to her disappointment she had so far not seen her and inferred that she was not at court, even though she had seen Anne's sister Mary on numerous occasions. Perhaps her old friend had elected to remain at home. Anne knew she was fortunate to have her family to support her in this new and challenging world, but a trusted companion like Anne Brandon would have been a welcome blessing.

York Place, London

'Have I secured the mask firmly enough? It won't slip?' Henry asked Thomas Arundel when they were both dressed in their knight's costumes. He had no wish to embarrass himself by revealing his face before the allotted time.

Thomas checked the fastenings. 'It's secure.' He ran his

finger around the satin collar of his cloak. 'I'm over-warm already and it will be hot in the great hall. They've lit hundreds of candles and there is also a good fire.'

'No doubt after all our exertions we will be even warmer. Still, there will be plenty of wine to refresh us,' Henry replied happily as they went in search of the other knights.

'Remember we must let the King lead the attack. Don't get carried away with the spirit of the thing and rush ahead of him,' Thomas warned. 'He does not like to be upstaged.' The King loved taking part in these revels but he also loved to be the centre of attention and as he towered above everyone else in both height and magnificence he always was. But one had to be ever vigilant where King Henry's sensitivities were concerned.

'Let us hope that the aim of the Fair Ladies of the castle isn't very accurate, otherwise these clothes will be ruined. Comfits, rose water and sugared plums don't mix well with satin and velvet,' Henry reflected, thinking of the efforts he'd had to go to to secure his costume.

Thomas shrugged carelessly. 'No doubt they will be too caught up in their excitement to aim true. I have heard that Her Grace Queen Mary is one of the fair Ladies; Mary Carey is another, as is Jane Parker—'

'And I heard George Boleyn swear he would be avoiding her like the plague,' Henry interrupted.

Thomas grinned impishly. 'I think he wishes the plague would take her. Then he won't have to marry her.'

'Who else is taking part?' Henry asked, still fiddling with his mask for it was not easy to see through the eye slits.

'George's other sister, Anne. Just returned from France, I hear, and not at all impressed that negotiations are in hand for her to become betrothed to Jamie Butler. She's refusing to go and live amongst "savages", so George says; she is quite adamant about it.'

It was Henry's turn to shrug. 'I think I'd sooner do that than have to lead Mary Talbot down the aisle. She's not one of the ladies, too, is she?' he asked in alarm.

Thomas grinned and shook his head. 'Not that I've heard. I have a feeling that Mistress Anne will not remain long at court voicing her opposition to the match for all and sundry to hear, not if Sir Thomas has his way.'

'Come, let's not spoil the evening with all these sour thoughts,' Henry urged as they joined the group of young men in an ante-chamber to await the arrival of the King.

A castle of shiny green sateen had been erected in the great hall at York Place, complete with towers in which each of the ladies in white and gold had been installed. The young choristers, their faces darkened with walnut juice and dressed in brightly hued garments and turbans to represent Indian women, were torn between embarrassment at their appearance and excitement at taking part in the masque. Nonetheless they dutifully took their places at the foot of the castle.

'I hope they can all remember what they are supposed to do and don't start fighting with each other,' Mary called from her tower to her sister.

'Let us hope that all of *us* can remember what we are supposed to do,' Anne replied, looking pointedly across at Jane Parker before turning to watch the audience arrive. Jane studiously ignored her.

There was a volley of small cannon fire from the river

beyond the palace gardens, signalling the entrance of the knights in their blue velvet and satin and the masque's commencement.

To Anne's satisfaction it was obvious that their performances delighted the Queen, the Imperial Ambassadors and the other assembled dignitaries. There were gales of laughter and cheers when the knights, all wearing masks and led by the King (although no one was supposed to know it was Henry himself), bombarded the Indian women with dates, oranges, apples and pears after William Cornish, who had devised the revel and who as 'Ardent Desire' was the knights' spokesman, pleaded for the ladies in the castle to surrender. They had of course refused, and the Indian women and the Fair Ladies had gone on the offensive, throwing sugared plums, comfits and sachets of rose water until the battle was deemed over and all masks were removed.

'Is not the King a very handsome man and so tall and . . . awe-inspiring? His garments are magnificent. *Mon Dieu!* But my hands are so sticky!' Anne laughed, collapsing breathlessly against George.

'Then be careful you don't attach yourself to the Ambassador who I see coming to lead you into the dance,' he replied, his gaze going to the gentleman dressed in black velvet and silver lace approaching them.

Anne smiled encouragingly at the courtier, her dark eyes shining, thinking it would be the perfect opportunity to show how fluent was her French. She could hold the Ambassador's interest by regaling him with her knowledge of the court of the Regent of the Netherlands and anecdotes of all the people whose acquaintance she had made whilst there and in France, instead of just simpering and flirting and giggling as most of the other girls were now doing with their partners. She particularly wanted her father, the Cardinal and perhaps even the King himself to notice her confidence and superior behaviour. Then maybe they would all think again about trying to marry her off to that nobody James Butler and banishing her to live in Ireland. Lifting the skirts of her white satin gown daintily between her fingers and casting her eyes down before raising them alluringly to his gaze, she swept him a low and elegant curtsy.

With the masque over and the dancing commencing Henry led Margaret Fairfax out. She was a plump girl with green eyes and hair the colour of ripe barley. She had not been one of the ladies of the castle but he liked her, finding her easy company, although she did have something of a reputation amongst the young men at court.

'You look well in that disguise, Harry,' she said, laughing up at him. They were surrounded now by dancing couples as the musicians, seated in the gallery above, played on lutes and pipes. The men were all resplendent in velvets, silks and damasks, their bonnets sporting plumes and fine brooches; the ladies wore a myriad of brightly coloured gowns like gorgeous butterflies, jewels twinkling at their throats, ears, fingers and from the borders of their hoods. Hundreds of pure white candles illuminated the hall, the light enhancing the ceiling, beams and carved heraldic devices painted in scarlet, blue and gold. On the raised dais sat the Cardinal in his robes of crimson velvet and satin and beside him the Queen, her gown of purple and scarlet velvet and cloth of gold far more elaborate and expensive than anyone else's. Her purple velvet hood was encrusted with diamonds, pearls and emeralds and she wore a magnificent necklace of large rubies, garnets and diamonds whose facets flickered and glinted in the candlelight. It was on Katherine that Margaret's gaze now rested.

'I am always amazed how Queen Katherine manages to look so surprised when the King unmasks,' Margaret mused, 'she must know it is he as soon as he appears. No one else is as tall.'

Henry smiled. 'Everyone knows but we all join the Queen in the conspiracy.'

'Some more than others,' Margaret said cuttingly, staring hard at Mary Carey who was dancing with the King and flirting outrageously. 'A wife should behave with more decorum,' she added sanctimoniously. 'Have you noticed her sister?'

Henry shook his head. There were so many ladies dressed in white and gold and he had looked at them but briefly, to make certain that Mary Talbot wasn't one of them.

'Oh, very elegant and very full of herself, too. She speaks with a French accent just to impress people,' Margaret said spitefully.

'And does she?' Henry ventured. He disliked the petty jealousies of the girls at court.

Margaret raised her eyebrows. 'She doesn't impress me but quite obviously the Ambassador approves. It's sickening, a man of his age hanging on the every word of a chit of fifteen.'

'I hear she may not be at court for long. I think Sir Thomas is displeased with her.'

Margaret smiled happily at this news. 'Really? You think he may send her to Hever?'

Henry shrugged.

'Now tell me, Harry, what think you of Hal Norris? Do you think he favours me? I know you will answer truly.'

Henry smiled shyly. She was always teasing him like this. He would play her game, for her enjoyed the warmth of her attention, but he knew he had scant hope of a reward.

City of London

After Henry and Thomas had left to take part in the masque Will felt restless. Ever since he'd met Robert Aske he'd been in a state of heightened anticipation. He knew it was foolish: it would be some weeks before Captain Fanshaw returned and he was wasting his energies thinking solely of what profit he would make, but he decided it would only make him more ill at ease if he stayed here. The merry-making would go on well into the night. He would go down to the Pool of London. Taking his cloak and his short sword he left the palace and went down to the water stairs, leaving behind the huge windows blazing with light and the sounds of music and laughter drifting across the gardens.

As he waited for a lighter he debated whether he should first call on Robert Aske, and by the time the small boat had pulled into the side of the stone stairs, he'd decided he would.

His friend's lodgings were near the Inns of Court and after asking directions of the Watch, who were making their rounds, he found the house.

The door was opened by Aske himself. He wore no doublet and his shirt sleeves were rolled back, the fingers of his right hand stained a little with ink. He smiled. 'Will Chatton, what brings you here?'

'Impatience and restlessness,' Will answered. 'I wondered if you would come and share a tankard of ale with me, Robert? But if you are busy . . .'

'Come inside while I put on my doublet and cloak and then we shall take a walk.'

'My lord Cardinal is entertaining Their Majesties and the Imperial Ambassadors, which left me with little to do,' Will informed him as they walked. 'So, rather than stare at the wall wondering how long it will be before Captain Fanshaw returns and how much profit I shall make, or trying to concentrate on learning my letters, I thought I would visit you.'

Aske laughed good-naturedly. 'Then we will go to the Pool of London, mayhap the sight of all the ships will stop you fretting over your profits. The Waterman's Arms is as good a tavern as any.'

Before entering the tavern they leaned on the stone parapet as they had done the day Will had given all his savings to his friend. The wharf was quieter now for it was dark and there was little activity. Lanterns hanging from the bows and sterns of the ships threw small pools of light on to the black waters of the river and the cry of the Watch carried clearly.

'Given the tides and the winds, Will, I think the good captain might be back at the end of next week to put you out of your misery,' Robert said.

Will nodded, gladdened by the thought. Suddenly his attention was caught by a movement in the water below. 'There is something down there, Robert, in the water.'

Aske peered down. 'Rats, a dead dog or cat.'

'It's swimming so it's not dead. I swear it's a head. Someone is in the water!'

'Must have fallen in. Probably drunk.'

'Come on, Robert, we have to help,' Will cried, snatching up the lantern hanging at the top of the stone steps that led down to the water's edge.

'Over here! Swim to me! It's not far!' he yelled.

At last the figure reached the steps, clawing desperately to obtain a hold on the slimy green stones. Will reached out and with the help of Aske, who had joined him, they pulled the lad out.

'God's wounds! He stinks and is half dead,' Will cried.

'So would you be if you had been swimming in that sewer,' Robert replied as they half carried, half dragged the boy up the steps and laid him on the cobbles.

Will pulled open the neck of the loose, sodden garment the boy wore and he began to cough and splutter. They sat him up and Will pulled off the boy's tight-fitting cap.

They both stared in amazement as long dark hair, dripping with water, fell down over the boy's shoulders.

'By the Holy Virgin! It's a *girl!*' Will cried.

She stared up at them both with wild, terrified black eyes and struggled to rise, gasping something that was incomprehensible to them both.

'She's foreign,' Aske deduced.

Will nodded. 'And terrified. We can't just leave her here.'

'We'll try to make her understand we won't hurt her. Then I think we should take her to my lodgings and confront Mistress Brookes, my landlady, with our dilemma.'

With gestures and mimes they at last made her understand that they wanted to help her and finally got her to Aske's lodgings, after a journey which prompted a great deal of curiosity from passers-by.

'Poor wench. It's a wonder she didn't die,' Mistress Brookes commented as she bustled about getting blankets and hot wine. She was a stout, good-natured woman who treated her young lodger almost as a son.

The girl had calmed down considerably and Will thought she was beautiful. Her hair was blue-black and her skin the colour of a golden apple, her dark eyes almond-shaped and fringed with thick lashes. By means of gesticulations he managed to convey to her that his name was Will.

'Weel,' she repeated.

He nodded and pointed to her.

She smiled. 'Juana.'

'Spanish,' Aske pronounced. 'Though she looks more Moorish than any of the Spaniards I have seen. "Juana" in English is I think "Joanna". We will have to find someone who speaks the language to find out who she is and where she belongs.'

Will was perturbed. 'I know of no one.'

'But I do,' Mistress Brookes informed them. 'The pedlar, Benito. I will fetch him.'

She returned some fifteen minutes later accompanied by a small, swarthy man. 'I have explained everything to him. He will ask her what happened to her.'

The man sat beside her and began to speak in a language the like of which Will had never heard before. The girl became very excited and waved her hands about a great deal, then she clutched the little pedlar's arm and cried out, obviously in fear.

'What is it? Who is she and what is she afraid of?' Will demanded, troubled by her agitation.

'She is the step-daughter of Jewish parents. She is half-Moorish but was adopted by them when they found her abandoned as a small child. She swears she is Christian and her parents too professed to be Christian.' Benito shook his head sadly. 'But Spain today is not a good place to be either a Jew or a Moor. The Inquisitors took her parents away; she never saw them again. She was terrified and smuggled herself aboard a ship, and the rest you know. But she is afraid you will turn her over to the authorities and she will be sent back to Spain.'

Will dropped to his knees beside her and stared into the wide eyes. 'Tell her she need not fear. We will not let her be sent back to Spain. No harm will come to her. She is safe now.'

Benito relayed this and a smile lit up her face and she grasped Will's hands and broke into a torrent of words.

'I think we can assume she is happy to know that,' Aske laughed before becoming serious. 'But what are we to do with her?'

Mistress Brookes resolved the problem. 'She must stay here with me. She can help me with the chores for I am getting slow and my joints pain me at times.'

Benito conveyed this to the girl and she jumped up and threw her arms around the older woman's ample shoulders, babbling in Spanish.

'I will contribute to her upkeep,' Will offered, feeling it was the least he could do, though at the moment he had precious little extra money to spare.

'You will do no such thing, Master Chatton! 'Tis not seemly. She will work for her keep,' Mistress Brookes protested.

Will looked abashed. Having been the one to pull her from the river he felt an obligation to make sure she was safe and well cared for. Besides, she fascinated him. Her life so far had clearly not been easy. She was an orphan; in fact she had been orphaned twice. He thought of his father. She had lost her adopted parents in terrifying circumstances and had shown great courage in stowing away and taking her chances in the dark, filthy water of the Thames, not knowing what faced her when or if she got ashore. 'May I come and visit, Mistress Brookes?' he asked tentatively.

The woman smiled. 'You may, but only when I am present. She is young and I will have nothing ungodly taking place under my roof.'

Will smiled back. 'I am trustworthy and honourable, mistress,' he assured her, and he spoke no less than the truth.

Chapter Fifteen

‡

Greenwich Palace, London

MARY LOOKED VERY SMUG when she appeared in Anne's chamber the following morning. Anne was already dressed in a rather plain gown of black velvet, its square neckline bordered with silver lace, her matching hood edged with lace and seed pearls. She was sitting near the window which looked down into the courtyard, her Book of Hours in her lap.

'Why so serious? Is it not a beautiful morning?' Mary chided as she swept in, her pale blue satin skirt rustling over the floor.

Anne glanced out at the patch of sky that was visible above the palace roof and shrugged her shoulders elegantly. 'I suppose it is. But what has you looking so pleased with yourself?'

Mary arched her brows in surprise. 'Did you not see the King dancing with me last night? Not just for one dance either, but many.'

Anne frowned. 'I saw you flirting with him. Really, Mary, you should behave with more decorum or you will become the subject of vile gossip.'

'But he is the *King*! And he is the most handsome, the most *wonderful* man in the world and he favoured *me*! He said I reminded him of apple blossom, so pretty and delicate with my pink and white complexion.' Mary sighed at the recollection, her blue eyes sparkling.

'And I suppose he conveniently forgot that you are also a wife?'

Mary tossed her head dismissively. 'And what matters that?'

Anne stared at her speculatively. 'I thought you told me that William Carey pleases you? That you enjoy his lovemaking?'

'But he is not the King,' Mary replied, although she refused to meet her sister's gaze.

'And you are not the Queen,' Anne reminded her tartly, tiring of the conversation. 'Was that all you came to tell me?'

Mary looked downcast. 'No. Our lady mother has asked to see you.'

Anne stood up and laid the book on the window ledge. 'I have displeased her?'

Mary shrugged. 'She did not take me into her confidence, but she asked that you do not dawdle, for she has to attend the Queen.'

As she walked along the corridor towards her mother's chamber Anne smoothed down the folds of her skirt. She had enjoyed the masque. She danced with far more grace than many of the ladies present, including her sister, and she had not wanted for partners. She'd seen more than one admiring glance cast in her direction but she had not behaved in any way that her mother could complain of, so that could not be the reason for this summons.

A maid was adjusting Lady Boleyn's hood but upon seeing her elder daughter she waved the girl's ministrations aside.

Her mother's chamber was much bigger than her own and more comfortably furnished, as befitted her position as wife of the Comptroller of the King's Household. Anne stood quietly beside a carved cupboard on which were displayed plates and cups of silver-gilt, until the girl had departed.

'You wished to see me, Mother?' she said, her eyes downcast. Her hands, half hidden by the folds of her long sleeves, were demurely clasped together.

Lady Boleyn surveyed her elder daughter coldly. 'I did. Your father is greatly displeased with you, Anne.'

Anne looked up, her eyes full of surprise. 'Why, Mother? Did I not behave well last night?' She wondered vaguely what she had done wrong, especially in the light of Mary's behaviour.

'It is not your conduct last night that has caused his displeasure – and mine. It is your apparent refusal to agree to this match with James Butler for which your father has worked so assiduously. We both feel such behaviour is a great affront to our dignity and the respect you owe us.'

Anne bit her lip. Either Mary or George must have bruited about her comments; probably Mary for she was such an empty-headed chatterbox. She knew she must choose her next words carefully. 'For that I am truly sorry, Mother, I respect both you and my lord father greatly. My words were spoken carelessly but I thought they would be treated in confidence.'

'Obviously not!' Lady Boleyn snapped.

'It is not James Butler I have an objection to, my lady. I beg you to believe that. It is the fact that I shall have to live in Ireland which fills me with abhorrence after having spent most of my life at two of the most civilised courts in Europe.'

Lady Boleyn's expression hardened and anger filled her eyes. 'Indeed! So you think, Anne, that you have a choice in this? You think that you know better than your father, better than the King himself? Our sovereign lord has given much thought and consideration to this alliance and there are other more important issues involved than where and with whom *you* wish to live. We all have to make sacrifices in life, daughter.'

Anne thought of what George had said of the reasons behind this betrothal. To keep her Grandmother Boleyn and her father content and to secure the loyalty of the Irish chieftains to the Crown her feelings were to be sacrificed. She remained silent; her eyes downcast although she wanted to cry out that all her accomplishments, her education, would be wasted.

'Your father is so displeased that he has instructed that you are to leave at once for Hever, where you will remain until he sends for you.'

She managed to stifle the cry of protest that sprang to her lips, clasping her hands together so tightly that her knuckles became white. She had only just arrived at court, she was so excited by the prospect of the pursuits and entertainments life here offered and now . . . now she was to be banished to the Kent countryside. She nodded slowly, feeling hurt and bitterly disappointed and bruised that she was being gossiped about. She valued her reputation.

'Instruct Semmonet to supervise your packing and I do not

wish to hear any more words of complaint, Anne,' Lady Boleyn said firmly.

She was being dismissed. After curtsying with as much dignity as she could muster, Anne turned and left, keeping her head erect and her slim shoulders squared.

City of London

It was three days before Will managed to visit Mistress Brookes's house again. He had carefully counted what little money he had left and had decided that if he was careful, there was just enough to contribute to Joanna's keep for two weeks, despite the fact that Mistress Brookes had said it was 'unseemly'. He felt a strong sense of responsibility for her and he wanted to make sure that she had settled in. She had nothing, she didn't even speak the language and she'd fled her own country in terrifying circumstances. He remembered well how he'd felt when he'd left Redesdale and joined the Earl's household. Like him, she must have witnessed much unjustified evil. They both had memories that frightened and saddened them.

He didn't go via the river this time, that would save him sixpence on the whole journey. Instead he braved the noise, the stench and the rubbish of the London streets.

He knocked a little hesitantly on Mistress Brookes's door, wondering how he would be received.

Joanna herself opened the door, clad now in the plain dark grey wool dress and white apron of a servant. Her hair was confined beneath a white cap but her large dark eyes filled with delight as she recognised him.

'Will! I . . . I have . . . much happy . . .' She struggled with the words and fell silent, spreading her hands in a helpless gesture.

'I am happy to see you too, Joanna,' he said, smiling at her kindly.

She held the door open. 'Please, to come . . .'

Mistress Brookes appeared in the hallway behind her. 'Ah, it is you, Will Chatton. Come in. She is trying hard to learn English.'

Will was escorted into the kitchen where it was obvious that the preparation of a meal was in progress. 'I have come to see how she is faring and to offer you what little I can afford, mistress. I know you do not think it seemly but she will have need of clothes and . . . other things.'

Mistress Brookes shook her head firmly. 'Keep your money, lad. I have discovered that she can sew very well indeed. Her work is so fine I am sure folk will pay for it.'

Joanna was trying to grasp what was being said and when her benefactress picked up a shirt she had been mending she smiled and pointed to herself. 'Me. This . . . I do.'

Will smiled back at her. She looked much better; the hunted look had gone from her eyes and she seemed to be content and much more confident.

Mistress Brookes took her shawl from a peg on the wall and extracted a few coins from a small bag she took from inside a box. 'You may sit and try to talk to her for a little while, seeing as you've made the journey from York Place. I need to buy some fish for Master Aske's supper and I have just heard the cries of the fishwife.'

Will sat down opposite Joanna, feeling a little self-conscious. 'You are happy here, with Mistress Brookes?'

Her dark brows came together as she frowned, trying to understand him. 'I . . . like . . . Mistress . . .'

Will nodded. 'You are safe now, Joanna.'

She smiled at him. 'I . . . safe. *Gracias* . . . thank you, Will.'

Even in the sombre dress and cap she was beautiful, he thought, wondering how she would look in a dress and hood similar to the ones the girls at court wore. She would outshine them all, he mused.

'I see . . . you . . . again?' she asked, mouthing the words slowly.

'Would you like me to visit you each week, Joanna?'

She nodded for although she did not fully understand his question she realised by the tone of his voice and the look in his eyes that he felt concern for her and that pleased her. Not only had he rescued her from the filthy waters of the river, but he had found her a home too and instinctively she knew she could trust him. She liked him.

When Mistress Brookes returned Will got to his feet. 'I had better be getting back now. I have asked her if she would like me to visit her each week and I think she understood for she nodded. If you, too, are agreeable, mistress, I will call next week?'

The older woman nodded.

'It may not be the same day each week but I will come, I promise.'

Joanna saw him out, standing at the door waving until he turned into the next street. As Will made his way back he decided that when Captain Fanshaw returned he would buy her a little gift. Nothing too expensive or extravagant but a trinket, a keepsake, for she had nothing at all she could call her own. Even her clothes the generous Mistress Brookes had provided. He quickened his steps, feeling a warm glow of protectiveness for Joanna. It was the first time in his life he was able to be a true benefactor to someone other than his immediate family. It felt like an important step into the future.

In the weeks that followed Will visited as often as his duties would allow and Joanna began to look forward to these occasions and became more relaxed in his company. As her command of English improved he took her to visit the great churches and buildings in the city, slowly explaining their importance and history.

'I feel safe to come here with you, Will. I would have much fear to come . . . with myself,' she confided one afternoon as they stood in St Paul's churchyard.

'"By" myself,' he corrected, smiling down at her. 'I hope you will always feel safe with me, Joanna.'

She smiled back and nodded happily.

'And you are content to live with Mistress Brookes and to work at your sewing?' he asked, taking her arm as he guided her back towards the lane.

Again she nodded. 'Now I have a good life. We must go back now . . . yes? You must go to serve the Lord Henry?'

'Not for another hour. First I am going to escort you to Goldsmith's Row. It is where all the fine jewellers have their establishments – shops,' he amended, seeing her puzzled expression.

'Is it a place where the great lords and ladies . . . they buy gold?' she asked, thinking she would like to see such shops, even though she knew she would never be able to afford to buy anything.

'It is the place everyone goes to buy gold and silver and jewellery, if they can afford to,' Will replied, a sense of satisfaction filling him. He had chosen and paid for a small silver cross suspended on a fine silver chain which he intended to give her.

Joanna looked very apprehensive when they stopped outside the goldsmith's shop and Will pushed open the door and ushered her inside. 'I . . . I do not understand, Will? I . . . I have not money. I am a poor girl who works to pay Mistress Brookes that I might sleep and eat in her house.'

'I know that but I have a surprise for you, Joanna.'

She stood staring around, her dark eyes full of misgiving, as Will spoke to the man who appeared to be the owner. She watched as he took a small pouch from a drawer and passed it over to Will.

'She's a fine-looking lass, I have to say, lad,' he commented, smiling at Joanna.

Will nodded as he took out the cross and chain. 'This is for you, Joanna. I wanted to buy you something . . . special.'

Joanna's eyes widened in astonishment. 'You buy . . . this for me? But . . . but it is . . . so much, Will! I . . . I do not expect such a gift!'

He placed his hands on her shoulders, happiness and pride surging through him. 'I wanted to buy you this so that you will have something that belongs to you and you will know that I . . . care for you, Joanna,' he finished a bit awkwardly, fully aware of the goldsmith's presence.

Joanna nodded slowly as she indicated that he place it around her neck and fasten it securely. She would never take it off, she vowed to herself. It was the most expensive thing she had ever owned and even more precious was the fact that he had given it to her as a token of affection.

'I . . . I will wear it for always, I promise, because I . . . care too, Will,' she whispered shyly.

'Mayhap at some time in the future you will visit me again, Master Chatton? Perhaps when you have occasion to buy a ring?' the goldsmith smiled, winking at Will.

Will became flustered as he wondered if Joanna had understood the implications of the man's words. 'Maybe, maybe, but I don't want to embarrass the young maid by unseemly haste. We are . . . friends, that will suffice for now.'

Joanna pressed her fingertips against the little cross and smiled at Will, her eyes bright with unshed tears of happiness. She hadn't understood the goldsmith's words but her feelings for Will Chatton had deepened.

Chapter Sixteen

1523
City of London

'MISTRESS BROOKES, ARE YOU at home?' Will called as he entered the narrow hallway of the house. He had been calling here now to see Juana, or Joanna as he called her, for a year but he always took care to make sure the mistress of the house was at home. He had no desire to besmirch Joanna's reputation, she meant too much to him for that.

'Come in, Will Chatton, you'll find her where she always is. Seated by the window in the solar,' Beatrice Brookes called to him from the kitchen at the back of the house.

He smiled to himself. The minuscule room on the upper floor at the front of the house was really too small to be termed a 'solar' but it was where Joanna spent most of her days. She had quickly become a part of Mistress Brookes's household. She had learned English rapidly and had proved to be an expert needlewoman. So delicate was her work that all the local mercers bought it and she was kept busy and was well able to pay Mistress Brookes for her keep.

He went up the stairs and paused in the doorway, quietly watching her. A shaft of sunlight filtered in through the window and caught her long dark hair, giving it a sheen and the inky hue of the sky at midnight. Her skin glowed golden olive, accentuated by the colour of her pale russet gown. It was cut in the fashion favoured by the ladies at court but was not of brocade or velvet but plain worsted edged with black braid and he knew she had made it herself. Around her neck she wore the little cross he had bought her.

She suddenly sensed his presence and looked up, her dark eyes shining with surprise and delight. 'Will! I did not hear you. I did not expect you today.' She laid down the fine linen shirt she was embroidering and got up, smoothing down her skirt with small, dainty hands.

'Lord Henry has gone hawking with his friends so I have some time to spare,' he said as he took her hands and kissed her gently on the forehead. 'It's a fine morning, can you leave your work for an hour or so? I thought we could take a trip on the river.'

She nodded. 'I would very much like that, Will.'

They took a lighter and Will asked the boatman to take them upriver to York Place. She loved to wander with him in the gardens of the Cardinal's palace and admire the fine buildings, though he never took her inside.

They found a bench set against one of the walls of the garden and sat to enjoy the mild warmth of the spring sunshine. They had come here often over the months and he had told her of his boyhood in the North Country, of the death of his father and his entry into Lord Henry's service. She in turn had told him of her childhood in the beautiful city of Seville. She described the day the officers of the Inquisition had come and dragged away her parents. She had hidden for hours in a cupboard in the attic, too terrified to move, until at last she had crept away in the darkness and had made her way south, begging rides on passing carts whenever she could, until she had reached the port of Cadiz where she had stowed away on the ship that had brought her to London.

'Captain Fanshaw is due to return very soon, Joanna,' Will informed her. He had been gathering his courage for what he was about to tell her.

'That is good, Will, yes?'

He nodded, taking her hand and turning it over. Her thumb and forefinger bore the marks of the needle she plied all day and the sight strengthened his resolve. From the day he'd pulled her from the river she had fascinated him and he had come to realise that he no longer simply felt protective towards her. He loved her and would do so for the rest of his life.

He had been most fortunate in his trading. Captain Fanshaw was very honest and the agent had allowed him some credit on two cargoes so his profits had been more than expected. He had made enough money for them to set up a home of their own. Robert Aske, who continued to advise him on many things, had informed him that there was a small house for rent a short distance from that of Mistress Brookes. There would be little left over to purchase more cloth to trade but he consoled himself that he would soon accumulate more money and it would be a start.

'It is good, Joanna, for I shall rent a small house for us. I love you and I want to protect you and provide for you always. Will . . . will you marry me, Joanna?' His tone was gruff for he found the words hard.

Tears sparkled on her dark lashes as she reached across and gently touched his cheek. 'I will be so happy to marry you, Will. I love you so much that it is a pain inside me.'

He caught her in his arms and kissed her passionately. 'I want you with me always, Joanna.'

She clung to him tightly. 'Oh, Will! I would wed you this day I want you so much. I know it is wrong to love before the priest has given his blessing but I cannot help myself.'

The scent of her hair and the pressure of her body against him made him tremble with desire but he forced himself to draw away from her. 'No, Joanna. We will wait for the priest's blessing. It won't be long, I promise you. I will speak to Lord Henry this very day.'

'I do not understand. Why do you need to speak to Lord Henry?'

'He is my overlord; I must seek his permission, Joanna.'

'He will give it, yes?' she asked and he caught the note of doubt in her voice.

He smiled at her. 'Yes, I am certain he will give his permission.'

She kissed him on the cheek. 'Then all will be well.'

'All will be well, I promise,' he replied happily.

He would seek out Robert Aske and request him to under-take the rental agreement on his behalf for although his reading and writing had greatly improved he was not sufficiently familiar with such legalities.

The church did not permit weddings in Lent but as soon as Easter Day came he would marry her. She had no one whose permission he must obtain and he hoped Lord Henry would offer no objection. He was only a squire after all and Lord Henry could easily find someone to replace him, but he hoped he would be allowed to stay on in Lord Henry's service. He felt a deep sense of loyalty to his master and his position would provide the secure employment he would need as a married man. He was still too uncertain of his venture into trade to allow dreams of future wealth to influence him. Things were going well but his continued success was dependent on so many circumstances beyond his control. Besides, his master's time was taken up with the diversions of the court and his friends. His affairs would be of little account to Lord Henry.

Hever Castle, Kent

Anne pulled her heavy cloak more closely around her and shivered in the cold March wind as she walked slowly along the garden path that led back towards the castle. Although grandly styled a 'castle' Hever was little more than a fortified manor house set in the Kent countryside. She had always thought of it as home for this was where she had spent most of her time before she had gone to the Netherlands, but now she was bored and restless.

She had been sent here from court last spring on the instructions of her father and except for the occasional visit by George or her mother she knew little of what went on in London. The one thing she had heard was that the King's licentious gaze had fallen on Mary.

She found a sheltered spot out of the wind in an arbour and sat down on the bench under the leafless branches. George had paid a very brief visit a month ago. It had been one of those rare February days when weak sunlight had bathed the gardens, the air had been mild and faintly damp with a hint of freshly dug earth and the first green spikes of the daffodils had begun to appear. They had walked through the gardens, arm in arm. She had been delighted to see him and hear the news from court and he had been happy, he'd told her, to have a respite from the tenacious clutches of his wife.

'She is like a poisonous vine, twisting her noxious tendrils about me. Everywhere I go, she's there beside me, clinging and fawning on me, yet there is no sincerity in her. It sickens me, Anne.'

'At least you can escape. You can saddle your horse and ride away from her. I cannot do that. I am packed off here and left to . . . to expire of boredom!'

He'd laughed then. 'Would you sooner be at court and have the King lusting after you as he does little Mary?'

She'd frowned, remembering how her sister had flirted with the King at the masque at York Place. 'Mary? He wishes to bed Mary? He wishes to make her his mistress?'

He'd nodded. 'She of course is delighted by his attentions and they are encouraging her, Father and Uncle Thomas. They see a better way of gaining advancement for themselves than having to rely on William Carey, who has not done very well for either of them so far.'

Mary's attitude she had understood; she would think it a great honour. Mary had always been pretty but empty-headed. She would clap her hands and think herself inordinately fortunate to receive all the gifts King Henry would doubtless shower her with. 'And what of William Carey? He is happy to see his wife in the King's bed?'

George had shrugged. 'He has no say in the matter. He will be well rewarded for turning a blind eye.'

'She is a fool!' she'd retorted. 'Does she not value herself higher than that? The King's strumpet!'

George hadn't replied and she'd wondered if he too was encouraging her sister in this course for his own ends.

'There was something else I thought might interest you, sister.'

She'd looked up at him expectantly. 'And that is?'

'There appears to be something of a problem in settling the terms of your betrothal. In fact, from what I can ascertain, it seems certain that you will be spared marriage to James Butler.'

She'd clapped her hands in delight. 'Why did you not tell me this at first instead of gossiping about Mary?'

He'd grinned. 'I thought I would save the best piece of information until last.'

'Did Father tell you? Or was it Mother or Uncle Thomas?'

'No one "told" me, Anne. I obtained the information.'

'Then it may not be true? Oh, if you are lying to me, George, I shall never speak to you again!' she'd cried.

'Wait and see, Mistress Impatience,' he'd advised.

When he'd gone back she had waited for some news but there had been none and now she had begun to wonder if George had been misled.

The wind had a sharp penetrating edge and she shivered and got up, turning her steps towards the house again. If she had to remain here all summer she would go mad.

As she entered the courtyard her spirits rose for there were horses being led away towards the stables. She had heard no one approach but then she had been in the rose garden on the other side of the house to the drawbridge. She quickened her steps, wondering if it was George or her mother or maybe even her father. She hoped it was one of her parents for she was determined to plead with them that she be allowed to go back to London.

Semonnet met her at the door. She had accompanied her young charge from France although she liked neither the English weather nor the English food and customs. And, like her mistress, the countryside was less to her liking than the court. 'Mistress Anne. Come, change your gown. Your father has arrived and wishes to speak with you.'

'My father! Oh, I have a great wish to see him,' Anne exclaimed, running lightly up the stairs to her chamber where she quickly changed both her gown and hood. She was praying with all her heart that he had come with good news.

Sir Thomas was washing the dust of the road from his hands when she entered.

She dropped a deep curtsy. 'My lord, I am most happy to see you.'

'You are looking pale, daughter,' he remarked, pouring himself a goblet of wine.

'The air here does not agree with me.'

'Then you will no doubt take comfort from the news I bring,' he replied laconically.

She gazed at him expectantly, hoping he hadn't come just to inform her of the King's passion for Mary.

'Your sister has expressed a desire for your company, so

I have obtained a place for you at court. You will attend your former mistress, Queen Mary Tudor. You will accompany me back to London tomorrow.'

She was torn between the joy of returning to court and annoyance that it was at Mary's behest. Her sister must indeed be high in the King's favour for her to now hold such sway over their father. 'I thank you, Father. I shall serve Queen Mary well.'

He stared at her coldly. 'I trust you will and that you will not exhibit any more high-handed or wilful behaviour. Have your women pack your things and be ready to depart early for I cannot spare more time from my duties. The King has accorded me the honour of advancing me to Treasurer of the Household.'

She curtsied and bowed her head, a smile playing around the corners of her mouth. She felt relief and excitement rising in her but also speculation. So, already he was reaping the reward for Mary consenting to become the King's whore. How long would it last, she wondered? Long enough for him to get his hands on more titles, lands and wealth. Her father would be sure to draw the maximum profit from what rewards fortune and his own connivance had thrown his way.

York Place, London

Henry was tired when the hawking party returned for recently he had suffered another bout of the illness that had dogged him since childhood. He enjoyed the sport; the beauty of its flight when the hawk was released, its freedom and focus never failed to enthral him. As it soared upwards it was as though his spirit rose with it. He envied the purity of its existence as it fixed its attention on its prey, hovering and then dropping dramatically into the stoop. By comparison his own life was complex, aimless and entrammelled. But at the end of the hunt the bird must return to him, be hooded once more, brought back to the mews and tethered to its block by the heavy leather jesses. He felt a pang of sympathy for it. His hours of freedom too were brief, he must return to the court and the tedium, frustration and weariness. He did indeed enjoy hawking but the long hours in the saddle took their toll.

'I shall retire early tonight, Tom,' he confided to his friend as he changed.

'That would be wise, Harry, for we must rise early tomorrow. My lord Cardinal is to take his weekly Sunday trip to Greenwich,' Thomas Arundel reminded him.

Henry fastened his velvet doublet and adjusted the white lawn collar of his undershirt. Another day of idling away the time with vacuous girls like Margaret Fairfax and speculating whether Mary Carey had indeed become the King's latest mistress or if it was just talk. Rumours abounded at court. He'd heard George Boleyn commiserating with Jamie Butler that his marriage to his sister Anne would not now be forthcoming. Jamie hadn't seemed to mind at all.

He was about to follow Thomas down to the great hall when Will Chatton entered the chamber.

'You are back, Will.'

'I am, Lord Henry, and I wish to beg a favour of you.'

'What is it?' Henry asked, noticing Will seemed unusually tense.

'I wish to get married, my lord,' Will stated.

Henry was surprised. 'Married?'

Will nodded, still looking anxious and yet proud as well.

'You haven't been rolling a wench and leaving her in a delicate situation?'

Will flushed angrily. 'No, my lord. I have not. I love and respect her.'

Henry looked at him speculatively, wondering was it a serving girl here or someone he'd met beyond the walls of York Place. 'Where did you meet her?'

'I pulled her out of the river.'

'God's wounds! What was she doing in the river?'

Will explained how he had met Joanna and that he had been courting her for a year and that now he had enough to rent a small house.

Henry was aware Will Chatton had acquired money, due to the small success he had had in trade. In fact Will had lent him three crowns only last month.

'And she is half-Moorish. Is she comely?' Henry asked.

'I think she is beautiful, Lord Henry,' Will answered shyly.

Henry nodded. 'And you are sure her parents were Christian? If not, you can't marry her. No priest would perform the ceremony.' Henry didn't want Will to be hurt if the girl was not telling the truth.

'She assures me they were true converts; she herself attends Mass and Communion regularly. Both Mistress Brookes and Robert Aske say she is devout, so I have no reason to doubt her, my lord.'

Henry smiled. 'Then you have my permission, Will.' His smile vanished. 'I assume you will no longer wish to keep your position here?'

'Do you wish me to stay on, my lord?'

Henry nodded slowly. He would miss Will if he went. They had more or less grown up together and Will had been his most loyal servant. 'Yes. If it is what you also wish.'

Will was greatly relieved; he'd been praying he would not be dismissed. 'It is and thank you, my lord. Some would say it is not practical but we will not find it inconvenient. I will travel to the city when you do not require me.'

'You could find lodgings here. She will be your wife, you will not wish to be parted.'

Will shook his head. He had no desire at all to bring his beautiful Joanna here. There were far too many licentious youths and not just amongst the young lords. 'She would not feel comfortable here, Lord Henry.'

Henry smiled. 'You mean you wish to keep her to yourself, Will? I do not blame you for that but will you bring her here so I can meet her?'

'I will, my lord. Thank you for your generosity and consideration.'

As Henry went down the wide staircase he felt downhearted and irritable. In some ways Will Chatton was more fortunate than himself. He at least could choose the woman he wished to spend his life with. His squire could steer his own path in life, pursue his own destiny, something he could not do. In time he would become Earl of Northumberland and Warden of the Marches, which meant he must return north and deal with the constant skirmishes on the Border and the violence and lawlessness of the roaming bands of brigands. And it seemed there was to be no romance in his life. He would not know the love of a woman the way Will Chatton did.

Chapter Seventeen

Greenwich Palace, London

EVEN THOUGH SHE WAS weary from the journey Anne couldn't hide her joy at being back at Greenwich. As soon as she had dismounted she followed her father into the palace, along the corridor and up the wide staircase that led towards his chambers. It was a mild spring day and sunlight filled the room and her spirits rose still further as Lady Boleyn came forward to greet her, her hands outstretched, a smile of welcome on her face.

'Anne, we have been looking forward to your return.'

Anne curtsied and then took her mother's hands, thinking back to the last occasion on which she had seen her. Lady Boleyn's attitude then had been so different. 'And I am more than happy to be here, Mother. I seem to have been away for such a long time and I have missed the company and the diversions sorely. It is very quiet at Hever.'

'Your sister is most anxious to see you again but you must change your gown first, daughter,' Lady Boleyn instructed, frowning at the splashes of mud on Anne's cloak and skirts.

So, it was true, she thought. She was here at Mary's behest and it was obvious from her mother's attitude that she had no aversion to Mary's liaison with the King.

She washed the dust from her hands and face; it was all she had time to do, although she would have preferred to have washed herself all over for she felt dirty from the long ride. With the help of Semmonet she changed into a gown of emerald-green brocade shot with blue and, after brushing her hair, she placed the matching hood over it. Staring at her reflection in the polished steel mirror she touched the gold 'B' she wore around her neck and smiled wryly. Yes, she was now suitably attired to greet her sister: the King's strumpet.

Lady Boleyn escorted her to the Queen's chambers, which surprised her. 'I would not have thought to have seen Mary here, Mother,' she whispered as they entered the room and her mother sank into a deep curtsy. She immediately followed suit.

Queen Katherine was sitting with her ladies and they were all engaged in sewing shirts for the poor, whilst the Countess of Oxford was reading aloud a passage from the Life of St Augustine. Seated, and in her gown of black velvet trimmed with scarlet and gold, under which it was said she wore a hair shirt, Anne was struck by the change in the Queen. It was a year since she had last seen her and Katherine had aged. Her complexion was dull and sallow and there were lines of suffering and sadness etched deeply now on her face. She was thirty-seven and had failed to bear a living, healthy son despite so many pregnancies, pregnancies which had thickened her figure and seemed to have drained her of all vitality. But not, Anne thought, of her natural dignity.

Katherine laid aside her needle and signed that the Countess of Oxford should cease reading. She smiled kindly at the woman and girl who stood before her. 'Lady Boleyn, this I presume is your elder daughter, Anne?'

'It is, your grace. She is to attend Queen Mary whom she served in France,' Lady Boleyn replied, urging Anne to move a pace forward.

Anne did so, smiling and dropping another graceful curtsy.

Katherine nodded. 'You have spent a great deal of time away from your family, I hear, Mistress Anne, so it must please you to be reunited with them.'

'It does, your grace. I am most happy to be here and wish only to serve Queen Mary well,' Anne replied. Catching sight of her sister sitting watching her with a smirk on her face, she dropped her gaze, not wishing the Queen to think her insincere.

'But you will wish to spend some time with your sister?' Katherine turned towards Mary and although her eyes were cold her manner remained dignified and pleasant. 'Lady Carey, I give you leave to welcome your sister to our court.'

Mary rose and dutifully curtsied and, after thanking the Queen for her consideration, Anne followed her out.

As they walked through the ante-chambers where groups of courtiers lingered in the hope of obtaining some brief contact with the Queen, Anne was acutely aware of the glances cast in Mary's direction, but it was not until they reached Mary's chambers, now far grander than those she had previously occupied with her husband, that either girl spoke.

When the door was closed Mary impulsively hugged Anne.

'Oh, I am so glad you are here! I have missed you sorely. I begged Father to send for you.'

Anne laughed. 'I think not *too* sorely. I hear your time is spent in far more exalted company than mine.'

Mary blushed prettily and giggled and Anne thought she had changed little; she was still just a pretty, shallow, fifteen-year-old who thought of little but frivolity and self-indulgence. 'Oh, Anne, he is the most ardent and passionate lover! He adores me! He recites poetry to me; he gives me gifts. See . . . only yesterday he gave me this.' Mary touched the necklace that adorned her plump throat. It was a collar of gold filigree flowers set with sapphires, diamonds and pearls. The rich blue velvet of Mary's gown, cut very low across her plump white bosom, showed the stones off perfectly and Anne noted that her sister had abandoned the gable hood in favour of one in blue velvet in the French fashion. It suited Mary far better, she thought, framing her round face and showing off her corn-gold hair.

'It is indeed beautiful and very costly, Mary.' She smiled, helping herself to a cup of wine from the silver-gilt ewer on the table. Gold dishes filled with comfits, marchpane and nuts had been set out too.

'And he has promised that I shall have earrings and bracelets to match,' Mary enthused, crossing to the window and opening it wide. 'Oh, life is so . . . so pleasurable now, Anne.'

Anne sipped the wine. 'I am happy for you, Mary, but you do realise it won't last?'

Mary turned from the window, a look of consternation in her eyes. 'But he loves me. He has told me so on many occasions and I believe him and I love him, too. Who could not?'

Anne put down the cup and crossed and took her sister's hands in her own. 'Oh, Mary, don't be a fool! Of course he tells you he loves you, he may even think he does, but he won't put aside the Queen. She is his wife. Bessie Blount had to accept that and she bore him a son, which the Queen has tried and failed to do. He will tire of you as he tired of Bessie and that is something Queen Katherine knows well and it is why she ignores his . . . transgressions. Be happy while you can with his attentions and his gifts. Father and Uncle Norfolk will enjoy the advancement of the family which you can achieve: enjoy that too. But don't deceive yourself that he truly loves you. One day you must be content to be just Mary Carey again, no longer the King's mistress.'

Mary had pursed her lips and was looking mutinous so Anne kissed her gently on the cheek and smiled. 'I don't want you to get hurt, Mary, that is why I have spoken this way. Now, tell me everything that has happened while I have been away, all the gossip, all the rumours, who is betrothed and who is not. And tell me more about the King, your wonderful new lover.'

Mary's good humour was instantly restored and she began to regale her sister with details of the delights and entertainments the King had in store, once this present season of Lent was over.

York Place, London

Henry followed Thomas Arundel and the entourage that accompanied Wolsey through the gardens and down to the water stairs where the Cardinal's barge awaited. The sunlight that spring morning turned the ripples on the river to wavelets of gold that lapped around the carved and painted barge. The Cardinal's emblems and arms adorning the vessel were picked out in gold leaf and beneath a canopy of scarlet silk, cushions of velvet and gold brocade were set for His Eminence's comfort on the journey. Twelve oarsmen all wearing scarlet and black uniforms stood waiting, their oars held vertically upright. The river was crowded with craft of all sizes, many edging closer to get a better view of the Cardinal and his train.

Henry and the other young men boarded the second barge, which was not quite as sumptuous as their master's.

'No doubt we shall be able to gauge how high stands Lady Carey in the King's affections,' Thomas Arundel remarked as the barge slowly pulled away from the water stairs.

Henry didn't reply. He had grown tired of all the intrigues at court. All the gossip, the constant back-biting and malicious rumours he found distasteful and pointless. He had no interest at all in whether the King was still enamoured of Mary Carey, who, although pretty enough, was vain and vacuous and quite obviously unable to see how ruthlessly her family were exploiting her. It would be another day of waiting around in the royal apartments trying to find things to do to pass the time until they could return to York Place.

As the Cardinal greeted King Henry in the gallery which led to the presence chamber even the sight of the King did not elicit his usual feelings of awe and admiration. The King's clothes were always magnificent and today his short tunic of purple and cloth of gold was studded with diamonds and rubies and worked all over with silver thread. Over it he wore a sleeveless coat of purple velvet lined with ermine. Three heavy jewel-encrusted chains hung about his neck and every finger was adorned with rings set with huge gems.

He beamed at his Chief Minister and clapped him heartily on the shoulder. 'Greetings, Thomas! It is good to see you, though I warrant you bring me nothing but problems.'

'Nothing too ominous today, your grace,' the Cardinal replied smoothly, smiling confidently at the King.

The group of young men who had accompanied the Cardinal turned away as both men entered the chamber and then drifted, as usual, towards the Queen's chambers, seeking the company of the younger members of Queen Katherine and Queen Mary's ladies.

Henry sat on the broad, deep window seat in the outer chamber, which looked over the intricate and neatly kept knot gardens and the river. The rays of the sun streaming in through the window were warm and made patterns on the linenfold panelling of the room. He began toying half-heartedly with a lute, idly picking out the notes. He wondered what Will Chatton was doing now for he knew he had gone to see his Joanna. Would they be walking together beside the river, hand in hand and happy to be together again, making plans for their marriage and for their future life? Or would they be sitting in a small kitchen or chamber, alone and in each other's arms? He glanced around the room. Thankfully, Margaret Fairfax was flirting coyly with Hal Norris for he was in no mood for her innuendoes and games today. He returned to the lute.

As the door to the chamber opened he looked up. George Boleyn was leading a slim girl by the hand and suddenly Henry found all his languor had left him. He couldn't take his gaze off her. She had dark, elongated eyes fringed with thick sooty lashes. Her face was oval and her hair, which she wore set back from her face, was so dark it looked black. Her neck was long and slender and accentuated by a ribbon of black velvet worked with coloured stones, from which was suspended a gold letter B, her only ornament. She moved with infinite grace, seeming to glide across the floor. Her gown of deep rose silk with its long hanging sleeves was the most elegant he had ever seen on a girl, plain almost to the point of severity, but the cut and the way she carried it made it appear supremely elegant.

Tom Wyatt had gone to greet her, sweeping her an exaggerated bow and taking her hand and kissing it.

'I heard you had returned. I swear you will put every woman here to shame, Anne. Your time in France has not been wasted, you will be a most beautiful and greatly admired asset to Queen Mary's court. Your sister may well need to look to her popularity.'

She laughed and shook her head, her eyes dancing with merriment. 'I see you have not changed, Tom, your tongue still drips with honeyed words – and *non*! Mary has nothing to fear from me in that respect.'

Henry had never heard a voice so captivating: soft and resonant and with a definite French accent. He put down the lute and rose and moved towards George and his sister.

George grinned at him. 'This is my eldest sister, Anne. She has spent most of her life in the Netherlands and France and has just returned to court. Anne, this is Henry Percy, son and heir of the "Demon of the North", the Earl of Northumberland.'

Anne looked directly at him, her lips parting in a smile. He was a handsome enough young man with dark hair and large brown eyes in which she glimpsed the sensitivity of perhaps a poet. He was of middle height and slender, his complexion was pale and he seemed less brash and extrovert than his companions, most of whom she was acquainted with – albeit vaguely.

Henry managed to reply although his mouth had gone dry. Hal Norris and Tom Wyatt intervened and she turned away from him, leaving him rooted to the spot, staring after her. He had never felt like this in his life. He couldn't take his eyes off her as she laughed and joked with the young men who crowded around her, like insects drawn to a candle flame, all vying with each other for her attention. He was bewitched. She was beautiful; but no, it wasn't simply that. There was something magical about her. She was so *different*, so elegant and without that air of false, simpering gaiety that so many girls affected to attract attention.

At length he realised that Thomas Arundel was standing beside him. 'Like an exotic butterfly, is she not? And, I would wager, far more intelligent and versed than little sister Mary.'

With an effort Henry pulled himself together. 'Of course, she is Mary Carey's sister, but she is far . . . far more elegant and . . . and . . .' He couldn't find the right word.

'Sophisticated. I suppose that comes of being educated abroad and in royal schoolrooms and palaces,' Thomas supplied.

Henry nodded. 'And yet I do not think she is at all arrogant – just the opposite.'

'She is very sure of herself, very confident,' Thomas commented.

'I am glad . . . she has come to court,' Henry confided, his heart hammering in his chest.

Thomas looked at his friend speculatively. 'She was here last year, did you not see her then? She was one of the Fair Ladies in the Shrove Tuesday masque.'

Henry shook his head. How had he not noticed her? It seemed inconceivable that he had overlooked someone so fascinating.

'Then she angered her father by objecting to the match Sir Thomas had made for her with Jamie Butler, so she was banished to Hever in Kent.'

Henry frowned at this news, his spirits plummeting. 'Is she still betrothed to him?'

'No. Terms could not be agreed between the interested parties.'

Henry felt relief wash over him and he relaxed again.

'Sadly it looks as if our visit today is to be a short one. Here comes Master Cavendish,' Thomas informed him.

Henry turned to see Wolsey's secretary, George Cavendish, approaching. He was a serious young man in his twenties and dressed in a sombre black fustian gown.

'My lords, I am instructed to inform you that my lord Cardinal's business with the King is completed and so you must prepare to return to York Place,' he informed them gravely before moving towards the other young men.

Henry pushed his way to Anne's side. 'Mistress Boleyn, my lord Cardinal is preparing to depart and I must leave too. I . . . I hope we shall meet again soon.' Again he felt that surge of emotion rush through him as she turned her gaze towards him.

Anne held out her hand, smiling. She had enjoyed this brief encounter with the young men of Wolsey's court. 'I hope so too. Godspeed, Henry Percy.'

He took her long, slender white fingers and pressed them gently to his lips, feeling the hairs on the back of his neck rise. She had pronounced his name 'Henri' in the French fashion. Had she meant it to sound different – special – he wondered, or was it just her accent?

As he went about his duties throughout the day the echo of her voice haunted him. He became obsessed with the memory of her, recalling every detail of her appearance, the way she moved, her laughter, the way she had pronounced his name. That night he could not sleep and the next day he wandered in a daze, receiving a sharp rebuke from the Cardinal on one occasion. He sat for hours plucking at his lute, dreaming of her, composing poetry for her; and the days seemed to stretch into eternity as he waited impatiently for the Cardinal's next visit to the King's court.

Chapter Eighteen

———◆———

WILL NOTICED THE CHANGE in his master immediately, despite the fact that his mind was occupied with the thoughts of Joanna and their wedding. Gone was the air of boredom and despondency that had hung over Lord Henry for months. It had been replaced by what Will could only describe as a mood of constant reverie, and he realised that Henry was happier than he'd been for years. It had to be the result of his master meeting someone who had touched him deeply and he wondered who she was but refrained from asking that question. Lord Henry would no doubt tell him if he felt so inclined. It was not his place to ask such intimate things.

He had informed Joanna that Henry had given his consent to their marriage and that he had promised to take her to meet him.

She had looked horrified. 'Oh, Will! I will be so afraid. He is such a great nobleman . . . and . . . I . . . What will I say to him?'

He'd tried to reassure her. 'Call him "Lord Henry" and just speak to him as you would to me. He is very pleasant and considerate. There is really nothing to fear, Joanna.'

'Can we not wait until after the wedding?' she'd persisted, still unsure.

'I promised, Joanna. Perhaps he will come to the ceremony; he seems much happier of late. Maybe I should at least invite him?'

'Do you think he will come?' she'd asked hesitantly.

'I can ask. It seems only mannerly to do so.'

He took her to York Place two days later. She had dressed carefully in a gown of fine wool which she had recently finished making, and she had trimmed it with ribbon. Around her neck she wore the chain and the little silver cross Will had bought for her, which she treasured, and covered her hair with a hood with green ribbons.

'Do you think I look . . . suitable?' she'd asked.

He'd taken her hands and kissed her. 'You look beautiful.' In his eyes she outshone the brightest beauty the court could offer.

She'd gazed around in silent awe as he'd led her through the wide corridors and along the gallery flooded with sunlight by tall windows.

'This is like the palace of a great king,' she whispered to him almost reverently, looking up at the vast hammer beams of the roof of the great hall. Everything was painted in bright colours and the heraldic devices and shields carved into the beams were gilded. The floor was of green and white tiles and huge chests and cupboards, displaying dishes, bowls, ewers and cups of gold and silver-gilt, lined the walls.

'It is not wise to say so,' he'd replied quietly.

He found Henry with Thomas Arundel, who was trying to persuade his friend, without much success, to accompany him to watch a game of tennis about to be played by two of their companions.

Will bowed courteously to them both. 'Lord Thomas, Lord Henry, I have brought Mistress Olivarez as I promised.'

Joanna curtsied, keeping her eyes downcast, overawed by the rich apparel of the two young men standing before her.

Henry smiled at her. With her dark hair and eyes and her natural grace she reminded him of Anne Boleyn, although she was not as tall or as slim, nor had she any of Anne's air of supreme self-assurance. But there was a quiet dignity about the girl, he thought. He bowed formally. 'Mistress Olivarez, I congratulate you on your forthcoming marriage.'

Some of Joanna's acute nervousness left her and she smiled back. As Will had said, he was pleasant. 'I am most fortunate, Lord Henry, to have found such a man as Will Chatton.'

Henry gazed at Will who was standing holding her hand, looking at his future wife with unashamed pride and devotion. He understood exactly how his squire felt for if Mistress Anne would return the love that filled his heart for her he, too, would be consumed with happiness. 'I think it is Will who is the most fortunate one, mistress.'

'My felicitations to you both,' Thomas Arundel added, thinking that if Will Chatton had any sense he would not bring his wife to live with him here at York Place. In the right clothes she would be the equal of any of the girls at court.

Will nodded his thanks. 'Lord Henry, and Lord Thomas, Joanna and I would be pleased and honoured if you would attend the ceremony, but if your duties do not permit it we will be just as happy to simply have your blessing.'

'When is it to be, Will?' Henry asked, aware that it could not be until after Lent.

'Early on Easter Sunday morning, my lord. At the little church in the city where Joanna has attended Mass since she came to England. It will be a simple ceremony with just Mistress Brookes and Master Robert Aske as witnesses.'

Henry nodded but he was unsure. The Cardinal always paid his visit to the King on Sundays and he could not be excused, nor did he wish to pass up any opportunity of seeing Anne Boleyn. But he wondered if matters of state would be discussed on Easter Sunday. 'I cannot promise faithfully, Will, for I may have to attend my lord Cardinal when he goes to Greenwich or Whitehall.' He felt the colour rush to his cheeks as he thought of Anne. 'But I shall try to come.'

'We shall both try to be there, Will,' Thomas added.

'Thank you, my lords. Now, if you will excuse us, I have promised Joanna I will take her to Goldsmith's Row to choose a wedding band.' Joanna smiled up at Will, her dark eyes glowing with love and excitement at the prospect of choosing her wedding ring.

Henry watched them as they walked away, Joanna's hand resting on Will's arm, and he sighed longingly, thinking of Anne Boleyn.

'Take heart, Harry. Sunday will come soon enough,' Thomas said quietly, smiling at his friend.

Greenwich Palace, London

Henry found it almost impossible to match his steps to the sedate pace of the Cardinal and the rest of his companions as they walked from the water stairs towards the palace. He had been so restless all morning, his heart beating first quickly and then slowly, his anticipation at seeing her again so great that he had forgotten his bonnet and had had to run back to fetch it.

With his heart pounding and his hands trembling with the fear that for some reason she would not be here, he at last reached the Queen's chambers.

He scanned the groups of young men and girls anxiously. 'Thank God! Oh, thank God!' he murmured as he spotted her sitting beside Margaret Wyatt on one of the window seats. He greeted friends very briefly and went quickly to her.

'Mistress Boleyn . . .'

She looked up, her expression softening and she smiled at him, her bosom rising slightly. She had thought of him often in the past week. 'It has seemed so long since you were here last, my lord Percy.'

She had missed his company, Henry thought elatedly.

'Do you play?' she asked, indicating the beribboned lute in her hands.

'A little but I confess I am not very proficient.'

She held her head to one side as she looked up at him. 'Margaret and I have been composing some verses which I was trying to set to music. Would you like to hear them?'

Margaret Wyatt, an observant girl, quickly realised that her presence was superfluous. She excused herself and crossed to join another group.

Anne patted the vacant seat beside her and Henry sat down.

'I would indeed like to hear your composition, Mistress Boleyn.' The fact that he was now so close to her that he could smell the perfume of her hair and skin made him completely oblivious to everything and everyone else.

Anne smiled at him. He was very formal and seemed rather shy. 'Anne. You must call me Anne if we are to be friends.'

He could only nod and she began to sing a verse in French, softly but very sweetly. Her voice sounded as he'd imagined the voices of angels would sound: pure and clear.

'Did you like it?' she asked when she had finished.

'I . . . I thought it very beautiful and . . . touching, Anne,' he replied truthfully.

'Now you must play something for me.' She held out the instrument.

As he took it from her, their hands touched and for an instant an intense feeling of heady excitement shot through him. He could only gaze at her, his eyes speaking the thoughts he could not put into words. She held his gaze, her eyes large and luminous, until he felt he would lose himself in them. His hand tightened on hers and again he felt a surging force of joy rush through him.

'Henry . . .' she said, so softly that he could not even be sure she had spoken.

'I see it did not take you two long to become . . . acquainted!' The voice of Thomas Wyatt shattered the spell.

Henry dropped her hand. 'Mistress Boleyn has been singing to me the new verses she has composed,' he muttered, feeling suddenly bereft, infuriated by this intrusion.

'She is very skilled. She has been composing verses since she was a small and very precocious child,' Wyatt teased.

'Tom, you will not put me out of countenance with your banter,' she answered. 'I have known you too long.'

'I have known Anne since she was a young child; we frequently played together in those days – before she went abroad of course – and now since she has returned an accomplished and so elegant a lady, I have lost my heart completely to her.'

She tutted and shook her head. 'Shame on you, Tom. You are about to be wed and still you flirt and flatter innocent maids such as I.'

Wyatt leaned towards Henry. 'Beware, Harry, she will bewitch you,' he joked.

Henry felt her stiffen.

'Do not heed him, Henry. Sometimes he becomes a little too outrageous!'

Wyatt feigned a pained expression. 'I am wounded by your cruel words, mistress!'

Anne laughed. 'Go away, Tom! Practise your flattery on some other maid who will perhaps be foolish enough to believe you, for I know you too well.'

Wyatt laughed as he wandered away to find more congenial company.

'I . . . I did not know you were closely acquainted with him,' Henry said, feeling dejected. Wyatt's familiarity had upset him.

'You must not heed his words too much, Henry. His family are neighbours to us in Kent and I have known him since I was in the nursery. He is like a brother to me; I think of him as I do George.'

'But he declared he has lost his heart to you, Anne.'

Gently she placed her hand over his. He was, she realised, different from all the other young men at court, who flattered her shamelessly and flirted lavishly but who seldom spoke a word of truth or meant their protestations of affection. He was honest and sincere and sensitive and those qualities endeared him to her. 'It is but a game, Henry. Do you not realise that every young man here will swear undying love to whichever maid catches his eye that moment? But he does not mean it.'

'I would never swear undying love if I did not mean it, Anne,' he said simply, longing to take her in his arms and kiss her.

'I believe you. You are not the same as they, Henry. They are like silly peacocks with their fine clothes and loud cries, yet it is all outward show. I met so many like them in France. They are for the most part interested only in what positions and fortunes they can obtain for themselves. But you have a higher position than any of them and yet you do not behave as they do.'

He nodded, thinking that not only was she beautiful and so desirable, but astute too. 'I would not so demean myself or my family.'

'Tell me about your family, Henry. I know little of them, except that Harry Hotspur was famed in history as a most valiant knight.'

He smiled wryly at her. 'His fame seems always to overshadow me.' He began to tell her of his parents, his brothers and sisters, of the houses and castles in Northumberland, Yorkshire, Cumberland and Surrey and of the harsh climate of those northern counties. All too soon George Cavendish's appearance cut short their conversation.

'How long will it be before you come again to court, Henry?' she asked as he rose reluctantly to his feet.

'I do not know for sure but it might well be a week,' he replied dejectedly.

She held out her hand. 'Come back soon, Henry, please.'

He pressed her hand to his lips, wishing he could stay here with her for ever. Wishing he could tell her how he felt and that he was sure there would never be anyone else who could make him feel like this.

Chapter Nineteen

———— ✦ ————

ANNE SOUGHT OUT MARGARET Wyatt after dinner was over. It was useless to try to talk to Mary about anything; all she could think about was the King. Margaret had been at court for much longer than Mary had and, along with her brother, Anne had known her from infancy.

'It seems much quieter now that the Cardinal and his retinue have returned to York Place, does it not?' she commented as she found Margaret walking in the gardens, throwing a ball as exercise for one of the Queen's pet lap dogs.

Margaret laughed. 'You mean now that all those young popinjays have gone. Here, you foolish animal. Bring the ball back here to me, don't run off with it.' She gazed after the dog impatiently as it trotted away towards the knot garden, the ball in its mouth. 'Well, I am not going after him. We'll sit here and wait until either he tires of his silly game and decides to return or someone recognises him and brings him back to me.' She sat down on a stone seat that bordered the pathway, turning her face up to the warmth of the sun. The gardens were coming into full bloom now and it was pleasant to sit and admire them, rather than to get hot and flustered running after that errant creature.

Anne sat down beside her. 'So you think they are all popinjays, even Tom?'

Margaret smiled and nodded. 'Tom as well, though I know he is not the fool he pretends to be.' She was fond of her brother.

'What do you think of Henry Percy? He appears a little more bashful than most of them,' Anne asked nonchalantly, plucking a stem from the lavender bush growing beside the bench and crushing the fragrant leaves between her fingers.

Margaret turned and looked at her closely, her blue eyes twinkling. 'Ah, I thought you two seemed to be on good terms. He *is* quieter and more self-effacing. He plays well on the lute but his poetry leaves much to be desired when compared to Tom's. He tries hard though.' She paused. 'Why this sudden interest in him? I would not have thought he would have appealed to you. His health excludes him from most sporting activities, many of which I know you enjoy.'

Anne didn't reply immediately, but stared into the distance to where a fountain played, the sunlight dancing on the water trickling melodiously down its sides. She was choosing her words. 'I have become tired of young men who are interested only in courtly love. Even if it is the fashion to declare ardent passion to every woman – be she married or not – it is all so meaningless. I am weary of the contrivance, Margaret.' She paused again. 'I think Henry Percy is more sincere. Am I right or is that just a foolish whim?'

Margaret slowly shook her head. 'It is no foolish whim. He is very . . . transparent. He is just as you perceive him: truthful and honourable. He has little guile or malice in his nature and for that some would call him callow and foolish. Here he is like a lamb surrounded by a pack of wolves.'

Anne knew what Margaret meant although she would not have described him in such terms. Court was not the place for such worthy characteristics for it abounded with ambitious men and conniving women. Margaret's words confirmed the accuracy of her initial assessment of Henry Percy and it did not detract from her feelings for him, which she admitted to herself were growing deeper. She had not misread the look in his eyes as he'd briefly held her hand. It was such a pleasant change to meet someone whose affection seemed genuine. 'I think him kind and gentle; he has all the qualities of a true knight and he is handsome in an ethereal way.'

Margaret sighed. 'Perhaps he has too many knightly qualities for his own good. He is a sensitive youth and as I have mentioned his health is not robust.'

'Is he betrothed?' Anne asked, cautiously.

Margaret stood up, her attention distracted by the dog. 'At last, that silly animal has decided to return. Well, I shall not risk it running off again, it has had sufficient exercise for one day.' She bent and scooped up the ball of fluff, still with the toy in its mouth, and began to walk away down the path. 'I haven't heard that he is promised to anyone,' she called as she headed back towards the palace.

Anne stared after her, her mind on neither her friend nor the dog. She had come to a decision. She would encourage Henry Percy's attentions. She had liked him a great deal and could imagine that as she came to know him better the feelings she had for him would blossom into real affection. And, of course, he was heir to one of the greatest earldoms in the country, which would please her father. After incurring his displeasure over Jamie Butler that was important to her. It was not unheard of for people to marry for love. Her mistress, Mary Tudor, had married Charles Brandon for love and she was a royal princess and the Dowager Queen of France. Although she was as yet but plain 'Mistress Boleyn' she was of Howard blood. She was resolved not to be married off to someone like Jamie Butler or William Carey or to behave as her foolish sister was doing. Mary would have her brief moment of glory and then sink back into obscurity as mere Lady Carey, while she would perhaps become a countess, content with both her exalted position and her gentle, kind and poetic husband. Surely even her father could not find fault with Henry Percy's lineage, position or estates?

York Place, London

Again the days seemed to drag by interminably. Henry had won at dice and although his funds were again precariously low he had determined his winnings would be spent on a gift for Anne Boleyn. Thomas Arundel had accompanied him into the city where he'd commissioned a trinket to be made in Goldsmith's Row.

'Are you sure it is wise to spend so much, Harry? You have met her but twice,' Thomas asked, urging caution.

'I would spend four times as much if I could but afford it, Tom,' Henry replied, wishing that the gold pomander could be set with diamonds and rubies instead of garnets, that the design be more intricate, the metal more fully worked. 'I have your word it will be ready by Saturday?' he asked the goldsmith.

'You do, my lord,' he was assured.

He'd arranged to send Will Chatton to collect it and he raised the matter with him when he'd returned to York Place.

'I will go early on Saturday morning, Lord Henry,' Will promised, although it would mean he would not be able to visit Joanna until late that afternoon.

'You will take great care with it, Will? It is a . . . gift,' Henry asked earnestly. How he longed to see the smile of pleasure that was sure to light up Anne's face when he gave it to her.

'Indeed, my lord. It sounds a handsome gift.' Joanna had a pomander but it was made of crocheted silk decorated only with ribbon. Inside she had inserted an orange stuck with cloves, which helped to alleviate the worst of the smells for the weather was becoming warmer now and the city was noxious.

Henry smiled. 'It is for a lady.'

Will grinned back at him. 'I thought it might be, Lord Henry, for you seem so much happier of late.'

'I am. I shall confide in you, Will. I have met someone who makes me feel as you do about Mistress Olivarez.'

Will nodded. 'May I be permitted to know her name, my lord?'

'Mistress Anne Boleyn. She is the elder daughter of Sir Thomas and Lady Boleyn but her grandfather is the Duke of Norfolk. She is beautiful, Will, with dark eyes and hair and such grace. From the first moment I saw her I was entranced by her. I think she feels . . . affection for me too. We seemed to be drawn together.' He lowered his eyes, blushing, embarrassed to be confessing to a servant.

Will continued to smile but he felt a little uneasy, wondering if her morals were akin to her sister's. Mary Carey's affair with the King was the subject of common, often ribald, gossip.

Henry read his mind. 'She is not like her sister; they are different in every way.'

'Then I wish you only happiness, my lord. To find true love is a blessing beyond price, as I know well,' Will replied, hoping that Mistress Anne Boleyn would love Lord Henry as Joanna loved him. If that was so, he would be fortunate indeed.

Greenwich Palace, London

To Henry's chagrin the Cardinal chose to ride through the city to Greenwich that Sunday. It would be a much slower journey than by barge, he thought, and he was desperate to see Anne again and to give her the gold pomander. The Cardinal, resplendent in crimson satin, sat upon his grey and white mule, whose scarlet velvet trappings reached to the ground, while his wide-brimmed cardinal's hat and the Great Seal were carried on silk cushions before him. Henry, Thomas Arundel and the other pages of the Cardinal's household rode behind him. The procession seemed to wind its way through the streets at a snail's pace, Henry thought, consumed with impatience.

At the palace the officers of the King's household awaited them in their robes of state, bearing the white rods of their office as they conducted Wolsey to the gallery at the end of which was the King's presence chamber. At last Henry was free to make his way to the Queen's side of the palace. He had to stop himself from running, so great was his desire to see Anne, but finally he reached the chamber with Thomas Arundel panting at his side. Quickly he scanned the groups of courtiers and then despair swept over him.

'Tom, can you see her for I cannot?' he cried, clutching his friend's arm.

Thomas shook his head. 'No, but maybe she has been delayed by Queen Mary.'

Henry felt tears prick his eyes, so great was his disappointment. Had she just been flirting with him? Had he read more into a few words and gestures than was really there? Still clutching the gold pomander tightly he turned away and left the room. He could not bear to stay and make futile conversation with anyone else, not even Thomas.

He wandered miserably along the corridor which led to the chambers frequented by the older, more sedate ladies of Queen Katherine and the Duchess of Suffolk. Stopping and looking out of the leaded panes of the window which overlooked the gardens, he searched for her but there was no sign. Then, as he turned away, a door opened and she rushed out, holding up her skirts as she ran lightly towards him.

'Henry! Oh, Henry, Queen Mary detained me. I saw my lord Cardinal arrive and thought I should miss you!'

His heart thudded against his ribs as such a feeling of relief surged through him that momentarily he felt dizzy. 'Anne, I thought you were avoiding me. I thought you were only being kind last week or that perhaps you were just flirting.' He could hardly keep his voice steady.

Her hand went to her breast. 'I am wounded that you should think such things of me, Henry. Do you think me the same as the others?'

He instantly regretted his words and, reaching out, took her other hand. 'Forgive me. I was so . . . distressed, so . . . disappointed, for I have been longing all week to see you again.'

She smiled her forgiveness. 'And I you, and then . . . then I thought I should miss you and I would have been desolate thinking that I must wait for another seven interminable days before I would see you again.'

They were alone in the corridor and he longed to take her in his arms and kiss those soft lips that were slightly parted in a smile. 'Do you mean that?'

'Of course I do. I have found the days so long and a little dreary when you are not here.'

He pressed the pomander into her hand. 'I have brought you a trinket, as a token of my . . . affection.'

'A gift, for me?' She was surprised and touched and she examined the pomander carefully. 'It is beautiful, Henry. *Merci*, I shall treasure it always.' She reached up and kissed him gently on the cheek.

The perfume of her skin and hair, the soft caressing touch of her lips on his skin made him ache with desire and he cast convention to the wind and took her in his arms, kissing her forehead, her eyelids and at last her mouth.

She made no attempt to draw away from him, her arms sliding around his neck. It was not hard to submit to his embrace, in fact his kisses pleased her. He smelled of soap and leather and starched linen and the hair at the base of his neck was soft.

At last he reluctantly drew away from her, but he could not hide his love. It shone from his eyes and radiated from his face.

She looked down demurely. 'Henry, I do not wish you to think that I give my affections lightly. I would not have you think me—'

He couldn't stop the torrent of words that burst from him, his natural reticence forgotten. 'Anne, I hold you in the highest esteem, I would do nothing to besmirch your honour. I must say what is in my heart. I . . . love you. I have known it from the moment I first saw you. There will never be anyone else for me. You are my life and my dearest love.'

'We are barely acquainted, yet I feel as though I have known you all my life. I was drawn to you at first because you are so different from all the others. I admire your qualities and . . . and I have a great affection for you which I think will soon become love,' she said quietly, leaning her head against his shoulder, still with her arms around his neck. All she had said was true; she wasn't totally sure that she loved him – yet – but she did believe that love would come.

He held her tightly to him, full of joy. She hadn't scorned him; she hadn't said she loved him but she was being truthful about how she felt about him. 'I pray you will come to love me, Anne,' he whispered fervently.

'I too will pray for it, Harry, and I feel sure my prayers will be answered,' she replied and then drew away from him quickly for over his shoulder she had caught sight of two of the Queen's ladies, who had turned into the corridor.

Neither of them wanted to return to the Queen's chambers, so they walked in the gardens until it was clear from the increased activity that the Cardinal's visit was at an end.

She laid her hand on his arm. 'It will be so dull here now without you, Harry.'

He took her hand and kissed it. 'I pray that some important event will occur which will bring my lord Cardinal to court again before next week for now I cannot bear to be apart from you even for a day.'

'God speed, Harry. You will be in my thoughts and in my heart until we meet again.'

She watched him walk away down the path, a smile hovering on her lips. Happiness such as she had not experienced before spread through her.

Chapter Twenty

———◆———

'I HAVE TO SAY you are taking all the teasing remarkably well, Harry,' Thomas Arundel commented with admiration as he walked with his friend through the gardens of the palace towards the water stairs and the barge waiting to convey them to York Place. 'Though how you can ignore Francis Bryant's unmerciful mockery I can't conceive.'

It hadn't been long, Thomas thought, before it had become apparent to all their companions that Henry Percy and Anne Boleyn were in love, for they did not try to hide it and spent as much time as possible together.

Henry smiled, thinking of Anne's farewell kiss and her sweet words, which had brought him such joy. She had confided to him as they had walked together in these very gardens and not an hour since that she was sure she now loved him for she had never before known such happiness in anyone's presence and that she wished they could spend each day together. 'Her love gives me the heart and the spirit to ignore them, Tom. There are even times when I pity Francis.'

'Pity the "Vicar of Hell"?' Thomas exclaimed.

Henry nodded. 'He has never experienced the true and deep affection I have for Anne, he is shallow and self-absorbed. Let him mock: I'm sure his jibes are motivated by a secret jealousy, for have I not won the heart of the fairest maid at court? Nothing can mar the sheer joy I feel, Tom.'

Thomas nodded slowly. He had never seen his friend possessed of such confidence and happiness; the love of Mistress Boleyn had completely transformed Henry.

Even Mary Carey, still high in the King's favour with her thoughts on little but her own heady good fortune, finally noticed.

'It is being said that you are in love with Henry Percy, Anne,' she said as they walked from the chapel that Palm Sunday morning. Mary was wearing yet another sumptuous gown, heavily embroidered all over with silver thread. It was new, as was the rope of pearls around her neck, her sister noticed. Her own gown looked plain beside it.

'Is that so,' Anne replied quietly.

Mary's eyebrows rose. 'You surprise me, sister.'

'Why?' Anne asked.

Mary grimaced. 'He is so slight of bearing; he is wan and lacks any manly grace, unlike the King. Whenever I have spoken to him he appears tongue-tied and without wit and gaiety, and I have heard Francis Bryant mock his poetry. I would not have thought he would appeal to your tastes.'

Anne ignored Mary's comparison of Henry Percy to the King, for who could compare to such majesty? 'Francis Bryant mocks everyone's verses, even Tom Wyatt's, and I do not find

Harry tongue-tied or without wit. He has much about him that is very admirable,' she retorted.

'But he is such a *boy*!' Mary persisted.

'He will be twenty-one soon,' Anne shot back.

Mary looked at her archly. 'And you think to marry him?'

Anne shrugged carelessly. 'I have but recently come to court so I do not think of marriage.' She had no intention of telling Mary of her hopes of marrying him. Mary would think nothing of prattling such confidences to the King or to their father who was at present abroad. And although Harry professed his undying love, he had not yet asked her to marry him.

'Well, if he suits you, Anne, then you must please yourself.' Mary had ended the conversation abruptly, sighting the towering figure of the King coming towards them with a group of courtiers.

'Lady Carey and Mistress Boleyn!' King Henry beamed at them both as they sank into deep curtsies, Anne's by far the more graceful. 'You do put me in mind of the sun and the moon, one so golden and fair, and one so dark and pale, yet each possessing a beauty of their own.'

'Does not the moon but reflect the sun's light, your grace? Does it not draw its pale radiance from the glorious brightness of the other?' Anne replied, gazing up enquiringly at this giant of a man, almost dazzled by the precious gems and goldsmith's work encrusting his attire.

King Henry smiled at her. 'Well observed and aptly put, Mistress Boleyn. We could not have done better had we answered ourself.' He turned to Mary. 'Lady Carey, I would walk with you for a while, there is something I wish to ask of you.'

'I am honoured, your grace,' Mary simpered, her blue eyes full of adoration as the King took her hand and placed it on his arm.

Anne curtsied again and stood aside for them to pass, wondering how long Mary could hold the attention of a man like Henry Tudor, who, it was being whispered, was becoming increasingly worried and disappointed by his wife's failure to bear him a son.

Henry had managed to ascertain from George Cavendish that the Cardinal would be conducting no state business with the King on Easter Sunday but would of course be celebrating this special day in the ecclesiastical calendar with the King and Queen at Greenwich. The news pleased him greatly for it meant he could attend Will Chatton's wedding service and also be able to spend precious hours with Anne. He was even more delighted to learn from Cavendish that the affairs of state would therefore be undertaken on Tuesday and that my lord Cardinal would be staying at the palace overnight.

Will's forthcoming nuptials had made him think more deeply about his own future: one with Anne at his side. It was what he desired above all else. He would soon reach his majority and since that disastrous and now defunct betrothal to Mary Talbot there had been no further talk of a match for him. And, since her betrothal to James Butler had come to nothing, he could see no obstacles in their path. Though she was but 'Mistress Boleyn' Anne was of noble blood. Her mother was a Howard, a daughter of the Duke of Norfolk, and Sir Thomas Boleyn was kin to the Earls of Ormonde. Sir Thomas's star was rising rapidly now – though mainly through Mary's influence, it must be said, and that perhaps would not be viewed in a favourable light by his father? The Earl had no liking for Sir Thomas. Yet he wanted to please his father and Anne would more than grace the position of countess: she was so accomplished and learned, so intelligent, so elegant and witty. He felt sure that his father would welcome such a jewel as his daughter-in-law and be proud that his eldest son and heir had chosen a most suitable wife. What was there to stop him from asking her? Nothing that he could see and he determined that Tuesday would be the day to do it. If she agreed they would then be betrothed. Yes, they could make solemn vows to marry, a *de futuro* betrothal he thought it was called, it would be binding but they would need witnesses. He'd ask Tom Arundel and perhaps she would agree to accompany him to Will's wedding service? It was a thought that filled him with delight.

On Tuesday he sat as usual at a table with the Cardinal's pages and his eyes strayed throughout the meal to where she sat with the other maids. Their eyes met frequently and each time she smiled at him. He thought with pride that he had never seen her look so beautiful. Her gown was of gold-coloured silk embroidered with bronze thread, the long hanging sleeves lined with bronze silk and her hood, set back from her face, was of bronze silk trimmed with gold ribbon and tiny garnets. Around her neck she wore the gold chain he had given her and the gold 'B' suspended from a link of pearls. Each time he gazed at her he felt his heart swell almost to bursting.

After supper was over, Henry quickly detached her from the group she had been dining with.

'Anne, there is something of great importance I wish to ask you. Is there some chamber where we can speak privately?' His cheeks were flushed and his eyes bright with excitement and a little trepidation, although in his heart he knew she would not refuse him, for she swore she loved him.

Anne felt her heart begin to beat a little faster. This could only mean that he was going to ask for her hand in marriage and that thought filled her with joy. There were very few places here where they would have complete privacy.

'I cannot take you to my chamber for Semmonet and my maids will be there and it would not be considered proper.'

'I would do nothing to compromise your reputation, Anne,' Henry assured her.

She nodded and smiled. 'I know that, Harry. I have had a thought. There will be no one in the Queen's private chapel at this hour. Queen Katherine will not go there to pray until much later. But perhaps it would not be an appropriate place for what you wish to say . . .'

Henry took her hand and held it tightly. 'It would be the *most* appropriate place of all. Come, we will go there but we must have witnesses.'

She drew in her breath, her bosom rising slightly beneath the gold silk of her bodice, and she gazed into his eyes. 'Oh, Harry . . .' she breathed softly. Witnesses meant only one thing, that he was contemplating a *de futuro* betrothal now, this very night. A promise that they would marry in the near future, binding in the eyes of the Church. It would be an excellent match for her. She was sure she loved him and one day she would indeed become Countess of Northumberland: a circumstance that would surely please her father and her uncle. It would be a marriage that would be far superior in all respects to that of her sister and she would never betray Henry Percy as

Mary had betrayed her husband. She would be a loyal wife. She would be no man's mistress.

'I shall ask Thomas Arundel to accompany us . . .'

'And I shall ask Margaret Wyatt, she is discreet,' Anne added, her eyes shining with excitement.

As surreptitiously as they could, the little party of four made their way to the Queen's chapel. It was tiny, lit only by two candles and the sanctuary lamp, which cast a red glow upon the white cloth that covered the small altar. The walls were painted with scenes from the Passion and Crucifixion of Christ, but they were dim and obscure in the gloom. All four of them crossed themselves reverently and then Henry took Anne's hand and led her closer to the altar, followed by a somewhat mystified Margaret Wyatt and a decidedly uneasy Thomas Arundel.

As they reached the foot of the altar both Henry and Anne knelt and Henry took both her hands in his. 'Anne, I, Henry Percy, do swear in this holy place that I love you truly and ask for your hand in marriage.' Although his voice was low it didn't waver and he was filled with an all-consuming sense of love, happiness and devotion.

She gazed at him, her dark eyes glowing. 'And I, Anne Boleyn, do swear in this holy place that I shall be your true and loving wife.'

Henry turned to their companions, his pale features transformed by the force of his emotions. 'You are witness to these, our promises.'

Margaret stepped forward and kissed Anne gently on the cheek. She was happy for her. Only a blind fool could not have known that Henry Percy adored her.

Thomas nodded slowly, still unsure about the wisdom of his friend's impetuous actions.

Henry rose, drawing Anne to her feet also. 'Now we are betrothed, we will never be parted, Anne. I promise you we shall be happy.'

She leaned forward and kissed him softly on the lips. 'I am certain of it, Harry, and I shall endeavour to be a wife and a countess you will be proud of, this is a promise.'

A shiver ran through Thomas Arundel as they left, like someone treading on his grave, he thought. No doubt it was just the chilly air that pervaded the chapel.

Chapter Twenty-One

———◆———

City of London

DESPITE THE CEREMONIES OF Holy Week and his duties to Henry, Will's mind was fully occupied with his forth-coming marriage to Joanna. Robert Aske had secured for them the small house near Mistress Brookes's and they had furnished it, albeit very sparsely, and were both looking forward to spending their wedding night there. Joanna had chosen her wedding band and had been spending every moment she could spare on her wedding gown, which he was not allowed to see.

'You could wear a gown of sackcloth and you would still look beautiful, Joanna,' he'd told her as she hastily pushed him from her little solar where she'd been working on the dress.

'But I wish it to be a surprise, Will,' she'd replied emphatically.

Mistress Brookes had closed the door firmly behind him,

smiling as she'd ushered him down the stairs. 'I think you will be very surprised, Will. I warrant she will look as lovely as any lady of the Queen's court.'

'I am very lucky, mistress. I thank God on my knees every day that I pulled her from the water.'

'I shall miss her company but no doubt I shall see her frequently, especially when you are attending Lord Henry.'

Will had nodded. He hoped to be able to spend more time away from York Place in the future. Lord Henry seemed very preoccupied with Mistress Boleyn of late but he was glad his master was so happy with her.

He had been surprised and delighted when Henry had informed him on Maundy Thursday that both he and Thomas Arundel would attend his nuptials and had added that Mistress Boleyn would also accompany him.

'We will be greatly honoured by her presence, my lord,' Will had replied, secretly hoping that the elegantly dressed Anne would not outshine Joanna on her wedding day. He had taken more notice of Sir Thomas's elder daughter of late and he had to agree with Lord Henry that she was indeed beautiful.

Henry had looked flushed and excited and seemed to be trying to suppress something. 'Is there something else, Lord Henry?' Will had probed cautiously.

'I cannot bear to keep this joy confined inside me, Will. You will not be alone in becoming a husband for I have become betrothed to Mistress Anne. We made our vows to marry before witnesses in the Queen's chapel on Tuesday night. She is the love of my life!' Henry blurted out.

Will stared at him in astonishment for a second, then he

smiled broadly and extended his hand. 'Lord Henry, I wish you both great happiness.'

Henry shook his hand warmly, feeling there was a genuine bond between them now. 'So you see, Will, we shall be attending your nuptials as a betrothed couple who will soon be making vows such as you and Mistress Olivarez will make on Sunday morning.'

After Henry had gone to attend the Cardinal as he distributed the customary Maundy gifts to the poor, Will thought back to that day in the armoury at Wressle when his master had told him of his betrothal to Mary Talbot. Lord Henry had said then that a wife would be chosen for him and he began to wonder if the Earl would be content that his son had become betrothed to someone he had chosen himself. But Lord Henry loved her and had said she was of noble blood and his master would soon reach his majority, so surely the Earl would think him old enough and competent enough to make such a decision?

Easter Sunday dawned bright and sunny – if a little chilly at this early hour, Will thought as they made their way by river to the city. Lord Henry had insisted they all travel together in one of the barges the Earl kept at his London house, which had been brought along the river to York Place for the occasion. He had also informed Will that Mistress Boleyn would be waiting at the water stairs at Greenwich, accompanied by her chaperone Mademoiselle Semmonet.

'Master Aske will meet us at the church, Lord Henry,' Will informed his master 'and Mistress Brookes will accompany Joanna to church.'

'Are you not a little nervous, Will?' Thomas Arundel asked.

'I am, Lord Thomas. I cannot deny it and yet it is the happiest day of my life, for not only am I to be wed, and in the presence of such honoured company, but Captain Fanshaw has returned and I am richer by far than I was a week ago.' Will felt he could ask for nothing else in life now. He would have Joanna as his wife, they had a home of their own and his last cargo of cloth had brought him far more than he had expected. Enough, in fact, to send his mother and Thomas Tamford three gold crowns as a wedding gift, for after his last visit to York, Robert Aske had brought him the news that Mary Chatton was to become Mary Tamford. He had been greatly relieved that there was someone who would now care for his family for he did not foresee himself returning north for a long time.

Mistress Boleyn and her chaperone, a tall, thin and obviously annoyed Frenchwoman, were waiting at the water stairs. Will welcomed and thanked them both for extending him and his bride such an honour. That alleviated some of Semmonet's irritation at being obliged to accompany her mistress on a journey she felt was both inconvenient and demeaning, for ladies such as Anne did not attend the weddings of servants.

Will, his nervousness increasing the nearer the barge drew to the water stairs at Thames Street, had been relieved to see that Mistress Anne's cloak and gown were of plain velvet with little decoration. Her hood was also devoid of ornamentation, except for a band of narrow ribbon. She carried a small, velvet-covered prayer book and sat as close to Henry as decorum (in the person of Semmonet) would allow.

Anne smiled at Will. 'Harry has told me that Mistress

Olivarez is from Spain and is half-Moorish, and that she is very fair.'

'She is, mistress, and I think her beautiful,' Will replied, feeling a lump rising in his throat as they drew alongside the stone stairs. It was only a matter of minutes now before he would take Joanna's hand in his and swear before God to love and protect her for ever.

Robert Aske stood in the church porch, dressed in a doublet and breeches of grey broadcloth but with a short cloak of black velvet over them. Instead of the usual plain black felt hat he usually wore, a bonnet of black velvet adorned with a feather now covered his head. He smiled expansively as he bowed to Lord Henry and Lord Thomas and greeted Anne and Semmonet courteously.

'I think we should all go inside for the bride and Mistress Brookes will be arriving shortly and Father Mathew is getting anxious lest the Mass be delayed,' he urged.

It was a church Will had attended many times with Joanna and was not nearly as big or as richly decorated as the chapels at either York Place or Greenwich. Father Mathew, resplendent in his white satin Easter vestments, greeted them with relief and ushered them into the front pews, paying especial deference to Lord Henry and Lord Thomas.

Will clasped his hands tightly together for they were shaking a little.

'Be of good cheer, Will. They will soon be here,' Robert Aske whispered and Will nodded, swallowing hard.

A murmuring and a stir at the back of the church made him turn around and he caught his breath, his heart thumping wildly as he saw Joanna walking towards him with Mistress

Brookes. She looked radiant, he thought, almost bursting with love. Her gown was of fine wool in pale blue and around the square neckline and the edges of the sleeves she had embroidered in black thread a wide border of an intricate design of lover's knots, tiny flowers and leaves. Over her dark glossy hair, which fell loosely over her shoulders, was set a veil of white lace, held in place by a large comb in the Spanish fashion, and around her neck she wore her silver cross and chain. She looked so exotic she took his breath away and from the corner of his eye he caught a glimpse of Mistress Boleyn's nod of approval.

Father Mathew took both their hands and they bowed their heads as the sacrament that would bind them together for life commenced.

When the Mass was over Lord Henry, Lord Thomas and the ladies wished them both well and returned to the barge. Lord Henry had released Will from his duties for two days so Will and his bride, with Robert Aske and Mistress Brookes, returned to the older woman's house where a meal awaited them.

'I am relieved that their lordships had no wish to stay for I could not have provided a sufficiently goodly meal for them, nor dishes of fine quality to eat it off,' Beatrice Brookes said thankfully when they were safely back in her warm and newly swept kitchen.

'They must both attend my lord Cardinal, who is to spend the day with Their Majesties at Greenwich,' Will replied, pouring a cup of wine for his new wife.

'Lord Henry is very enamoured of Mistress Boleyn,' Robert Aske mused thoughtfully, helping himself to a leg of cold roast capon.

'I can understand why and I hope she returns his feelings. She has very . . . how to say . . . great style.' Joanna still occasionally struggled with some words.

'Sophisticated and accomplished,' Robert Aske supplied. 'She has spent many years abroad, I hear.'

Will cut a slice of roast capon for Joanna. 'He has asked her to marry him: they are betrothed and I think it will not be long before they are wed.'

Joanna smiled at him, her eyes shining. 'Then I hope they will be as happy as we are.'

Robert Aske looked grave.

'What's wrong, Robert?' Will asked.

'Does his father the Earl know of this betrothal?'

'I don't know. I don't think so, but Lord Henry is nearly twenty-one.'

Aske shook his head. 'There could be trouble ahead for them.'

'But neither is promised to anyone else.'

'Does King Henry know?' Aske persisted, more versed in the law and the customs of the nobility than Will.

'Why? Must King Henry also give his consent?' Will was now beginning to feel a little perturbed.

'When someone is of such a high rank as Lord Henry, His Majesty's permission must be obtained, as must the Earl's.'

'But surely King Henry cannot object?'

Robert Aske shrugged off his feelings of unease. 'Do not fret, Will. I can see no reason why the King should not give his consent. Now, let us drink a toast to Master and Mistress Chatton. God bless them with happiness, good health and, in time, fine children.'

Will raised his cup to Joanna. 'To Mistress Chatton, my wife, my dearest love and the future mother of my children.'

Joanna kissed him on the cheek, blushing. 'But not too soon do I wish to have these children, for I desire to spend some time with my husband.'

Chapter Twenty-Two

York Place, London

THEY HAD BEEN THE happiest two days he had ever spent, Will thought as he reluctantly kissed Joanna farewell on the Tuesday morning, leaving her standing at the door of their house waving to him, her dark eyes shining with love. He had promised he would spend as much time with her as was possible; he intended to ask Lord Henry if he could return to the city each night.

Ever since he had entered the Earl's service he had spent his days and nights in the company of other people, often hundreds of them, and it had been a little strange at first to share the three small rooms of their house with just Joanna. But it had been wonderful to be able to close the door and shut everyone else out. The kitchen, bedroom and tiny solar had become their own little world for two days and nights and during those two nights he had experienced an ecstasy he'd never even

221

imagined could exist. They had both been inexperienced and a little embarrassed at first and he had tried not to hurt her, but she was a passionate young woman and had quickly abandoned her inhibitions.

When he reached York Place he took the shortest route through the labyrinth of courtyards and corridors to the long gallery where he was sure he would find his master and his companions. He smiled to himself, knowing he would no doubt have to endure much in the way of innuendoes and jests concerning his newly married state, but that didn't worry him. He knew many of them would secretly envy him, particularly Lord Henry, and he wondered if his master had begun to formulate plans for his own marriage.

As he went up the wide staircase he was surprised to see that there were few people waiting in the gallery above, which was unusual.

'Is my lord Cardinal not here?' he asked of a manservant.

'He was summoned to the King's palace after breakfast but will return soon, before dinner, I am told.'

'And Lord Percy, Lord Arundel and the other gentlemen, they were with him?' Will probed, for it was not often that the Cardinal went to see the King so early in the day.

The man nodded and went about his duties and Will walked to the far end of the gallery where there was a wooden bench set beneath one of the bay windows. All he could do was wait until Wolsey returned, thinking ruefully that he could have spent more time at home with Joanna.

It was not long before he caught sight of the Cardinal's elaborately decorated barge draw up to the water stairs. His Eminence and his entourage disembarked and came slowly through the gardens and into the courtyard to enter the palace. Will got up and walked toward the top of the staircase to await Lord Henry's arrival.

The Cardinal's cold, reptilian gaze passed over him; Wolsey did not acknowledge his presence but made his way ponderously towards the privy chamber. Will could gauge nothing from the expression on his broad, coarse-featured, heavily jowled face. Lord Henry and Lord Thomas were in the middle of the group who followed the Cardinal and he stepped back to allow the foremost of them to pass.

As the Cardinal reached the door to the chamber he turned and beckoned to Lord Henry to come closer. Hooded eyes regarded the young man who approached him deferentially. Those eyes were filled with anger and scorn. 'I marvel not a little at your folly! That you have attempted to betroth yourself to a foolish girl at court, Anne Boleyn!' he said in loud, belligerent tones.

The conversations around Will faltered and died and Will could now see that Thomas Wolsey's face was flushed with anger. He shuddered involuntarily. The Cardinal's dark eyes reminded him of those of a snake about to strike at its prey.

Henry went pale at this sudden and unexpected attack but he was given no time to try to explain for Wolsey took a step towards him, raising his voice to a louder pitch. 'Do you not realise the position God has given you? After your father's death you will inherit one of the noblest earldoms in the kingdom. You should have obtained your father's consent in the matter.'

Inwardly Will groaned: Robert Aske had been right. But who had informed Wolsey of Lord Henry's betrothal?

'Moreover, and more importantly, you should have sought the King's consent and blessing. Had he agreed to give it, he would have ennobled you further,' Wolsey continued, glancing momentarily towards the group of silent and apprehensive young men to ensure everything he said was being clearly heard. 'Had you chosen in marriage a lady whose birth and estate matched your own, the King would have held you in high esteem and advanced you further. But now see what you have done! Through your wilfulness and arrogance in choosing such a one as neither the King nor your father will accept, you have not only offended your father but also your sovereign lord, who holds you in great affection and has great concern for your future and wellbeing.' Wolsey's voice rose yet again and spittle flecked the corners of his fleshy lips. 'Doubt not, I will send for your father, who when he arrives will either break this unadvised match or disinherit you for ever!'

Will heard the gasps of shock that came from Lord Henry's companions and he clenched his fists tightly, anger rising in him. What right had Wolsey, this son of a merchant, to berate and humiliate Lord Henry publicly like this? His eyes were fixed on his young master, whose face was now the colour of parchment and who was visibly cowed. What chance did someone of his lordship's temperament stand against this low-born bully? Then he remembered that this man had had the Earl himself imprisoned.

Wolsey had not finished. He wagged a short thick, fore-finger at Henry. 'Doubt not also that the King will complain of your actions to your father for His Grace has already intended Mistress Anne Boleyn be betrothed to another. This is a match in which the King has already invested much time and effort, a match almost concluded, though she did not know of it, but when she does I know she will be agreeable to it.'

Henry was shaking before this onslaught but he could not – would not – break his oath to Anne. He loved her to distraction, he had sworn before God he would marry her and he drew on every ounce of courage he could muster. He cleared his throat, praying he wouldn't stutter or stumble, that his voice wouldn't crack and break. 'Sir, I knew nothing of the King's intentions and I beg pardon for that fact,' he began slowly, relieved that his voice was steady. 'I consider I am of good years and am able to provide for a wife and so I thought I could choose a wife for myself and that my lord father would have been agreeable to my choice.' He took a deep breath. 'Though she is but a simple maid, a knight's daughter, she is of noble descent. Her mother is of the House of Howard, the noble blood of Norfolk, and her father is a descendant of the Earl of Ormonde, being one of that Earl's heirs general. I consider her to be a most suitable wife for me, even when I am become Earl of Northumberland. Therefore, I beseech your grace's favour and beg you to ask the King on my behalf for his consent and forgiveness of my ignorance of his involvement, for I cannot forsake her.'

Will wanted to cheer and to clap. Lord Henry had spoken well. He'd put his case clearly and with courage – courage that Will knew Lord Henry possessed but had seldom displayed so openly before.

Wolsey held up his hands in a gesture of shock and dismay, play acting to the silent and tense young men standing at the head of the stairs. 'Would you listen, sirs, to this wilful boy?' he called to them, before turning his attention again to Henry. 'I thought that when you heard of the King's intentions you would have the sense to relent!'

Henry swallowed hard but was determined, despite his fear and abject humiliation, not to be swayed. 'Your grace, I would but I . . . I *cannot*! I have promised before witnesses that I will marry her and I cannot in all faith and conscience break that promise.'

The Cardinal's face turned the colour of the scarlet robes he wore. 'Do you think that you know better than the King and I in this matter?' he roared.

Henry quailed visibly but clung tenaciously to the tattered shreds of his courage. 'No, but I cannot break my promise to her.'

Will, too, was shaking but with the anger that was consuming him. Why couldn't Lord Henry marry her? She was not betrothed to James Butler or anyone else.

The Cardinal was livid, his fleshy jowls quivering. 'Then I will send immediately to the North for your father; mayhap he can make you see sense. In the meantime I *forbid* you to see her or else suffer the King's wrath.'

He turned abruptly away and entered the chamber, slamming the door behind him so loudly that the sound echoed hollowly through the silent gallery.

Henry couldn't move. He was rooted to the ground with shock, his mouth so dry that swallowing was difficult. 'The King's wrath!' The words hammered in his head. Open defiance to King Henry meant the Tower – or worse. But why? Why did neither the King nor the Cardinal wish him to marry her? And surely it was not a treasonable offence to become betrothed without consent? He had begged pardon for that; he would continue to do so, on his knees before the King and his father, if necessary. She was not betrothed to anyone else; he knew nothing of this contract the Cardinal had spoken of. She loved him and he her and now . . . now he was forbidden to see her again. Despair was mingling with the humiliation and he began to tremble violently.

Will reached his side a few paces ahead of Thomas Arundel. 'Lord Henry, shall I escort you to your chamber?'

Henry looked at him blankly and did not move.

Thomas Arundel took his arm. 'Come away, Harry,' he urged.

'What am I to do, Tom? I cannot give her up,' Henry exclaimed.

Thomas shook his head. 'Come away from this accursed place, Harry.'

Like a man walking in his sleep, still shaking, Henry let Thomas and Will guide him to his chamber. Will was grateful that although he had been in the gallery and had seen and heard everything George Boleyn did not follow them. He poured both Lord Henry and Lord Thomas a cup of wine.

Henry didn't drink his. 'I am forbidden to see her. What can I do?' he pleaded. 'Sweet Virgin, what can I do? What will she think of me? I cannot bear her to think I have forsaken her, cast her aside . . .'

'How did the King come to hear of it, my lord?' Will asked, torn between anger at the way his master had been treated and pity for him.

Henry shook his head and at last took a sip of wine. 'I do not know.'

'Anyone at court could have mentioned it to him or to

Queen Katherine or Queen Mary,' Thomas replied, sipping his wine slowly. 'You know as well as I the gossip and the rumours that abound there. I know it was nothing I have said and I have faith in Margaret Wyatt's discretion.'

Will nodded his agreement.

'I swear I knew nothing of this betrothal that is in the King's mind and surely he, above all, must realise that an oath made in church, before witnesses, is sacred.'

'It seems strange that no one has heard of such plans for a match for her, beside the King and my lord Cardinal,' Thomas mused. He had his doubts that this promise of Harry's to marry Anne was binding. He'd been told that a *de futuro* was only recognised by the Church if the couple had intercourse before the marriage and he knew that Harry had not made love to Anne.

Henry was distraught with misery. 'What can I *do*? There must be something . . . some way . . .'

Thomas didn't answer and Henry looked at Will.

'Could I take a message to her, my lord?' Will suggested. 'Or if not to her directly, to Mistress Wyatt?'

Thomas looked dubious. 'It would not be easy for you to gain access to either of them, Will, not without Lord Henry.'

But Henry seized upon Will's suggestion. It seemed the only solution to his terrible dilemma. She may not even know that their future was at risk, she may even now be in ignorance of what had happened for he had not seen her that morning, although he had looked for her. Now, her absence seemed ominous. 'But he could try, Tom. I have to get word to her, Will,' he pleaded.

'I will go at once, Lord Henry. I will try to speak with Mistress Wyatt, even if I have to wait all day,' Will promised, praying that if he was late home, Joanna wouldn't be worried or upset.

'Would it not be better to send a message with George? It would not look amiss for her brother to visit her,' Thomas suggested, knowing Will could hang around the gardens, courtyards and ante-chambers for hours and possibly not even catch a glimpse of Margaret Wyatt, let alone Anne herself.

'Shall I seek him out, my lord?' Will asked, thinking that Lord Thomas's suggestion was indeed more sensible.

Henry nodded gratefully. 'I shall write to her for I do not trust George to convey my thoughts and . . . feelings as I would wish. He can be . . . flippant.'

Will hoped sincerely that George Boleyn would agree and would faithfully deliver Lord Henry's letter. He might view it as too dangerous an undertaking in light of both the King and the Cardinal's wrath.

After searching the gallery, great hall and the watching chamber, Will went quickly across the courtyard and into the gardens where he at last found George Boleyn, staring down at the carp swimming in the ornamental pond.

'Sire, I have been searching for you. My master, Lord Henry, asked me to seek you out. He begs that you will take a letter to Mistress Anne. He is distraught that he cannot see her and does not wish her to think ill of him.'

George continued to watch the fish, pondering the matter, but after a few seconds he turned to Will. 'I do not wonder that he is distraught and I will take his letter to my sister. He is in his chamber?'

Will nodded and they walked quickly away towards the courtyard.

George waited silently whilst Henry wrote to her, telling her of what had happened and of his feelings for her and the fact that he intended to go on pleading their cause. George had been shocked by the Cardinal's humiliating treatment of Henry; Wolsey's scathing words should have been uttered in private. Nor had he seen Anne on the visit to the palace and now wondered was this the reason why? He also feared his poisonous wife had been spreading gossip, for she had little love for Anne. Or had it been that empty-headed chatterbox sister of his, Mary?

Henry handed him the note, which he had sealed. 'Beg her not to despair, George. I cannot forsake her and when my lord father arrives I shall plead with him for his consent.'

George nodded but he doubted Henry would get any support from the Earl. Henry Algernon Percy was of the old nobility who heartily disliked and mistrusted the 'new' men like his father. The Earl would view her as more Boleyn than Howard and therefore of little account or estate. And he doubted the Earl would cross Wolsey again after his imprisonment in the Fleet. He could not see how Henry's pleadings would find any favour at all. How would Anne take the news? He'd been rather astonished that she seemed to have a real affection for Henry. If she could have brought this match off she would have done well for herself: Anne, Countess of Northumberland, and all the status, wealth and estates of the Percys that went with it. A pity it was unlikely to come about.

After George had departed Henry began to pace the chamber, unable to sit and wait passively for his friend's return with news of Anne. The events had shaken him to the core but as the minutes dragged by he began to realise that it wasn't just shock and despair that were making him feel so depressed and low. The ache in his bones had returned, reminding him that the shaking and fever of the ague that plagued him was upon him again. Frustration was added to his misery. Now when he needed all his strength to try to find a means to resolve the situation he could not be laid low by illness. He *would* not succumb to it, he resolved, he would fight it. This time he *had* to fight it.

Chapter Twenty-Three

Greenwich Palace, London

ANNE WAS IN HER sister's chambers where her father had left her. Mary was walking in the gardens with the King and Anne stood staring at the distant couple who walked ahead of the small group of courtiers, looking like exotic birds in their brightly coloured silks, satins and velvets. The jewels on the King's clothes and bonnet and around her sister's hood and neck flashed in the sunlight like rainbow fire. Anne's eyes were dull, her face a mask of disappointment, anger and hurt. Her nails dug into the stonework of the mullioned window, her fingers curled over the painted windowsill, as she watched her sister laugh coquettishly at something the King had said. Had it been Mary who had whispered into his ear about her betrothal to Henry or had it been sly, jealous, whey-faced Jane Boleyn or one of the many others here who disliked and envied her whilst pretending friendship?

Sir Thomas had left her with no illusions at all about her prospect of ever becoming the wife of Henry Percy. The King and the Cardinal forbade it and he had been furious when, on his return, he had been informed of her conduct. He had no wish to displease either the King or the Cardinal and both had expressed more than just concern.

'Your lady mother has been remiss in her conduct to allow this . . . this illicit dalliance to take place beneath her nose!' he had snapped at her.

She had wanted to cry out that she had done nothing more than pledge she would become Henry Percy's wife and in time Countess of Northumberland, which she'd been certain would please him and which, beside Mary's behaviour, seemed positively virtuous, but she had bitten back the words. She didn't wish to increase his anger. She was bitterly hurt and disappointed by both his attitude and the fact that Harry Percy, with whom she felt she would have been happy, had been cruelly torn from her. But despite her emotions she had always been a dutiful daughter and so she had uttered no words of anger nor had she pleaded with her father.

She didn't turn when George came into the room. 'I require nothing, leave me alone,' she said sharply, a catch in her voice, thinking it was Semmonet. 'Can I not have an *hour's* peace, please?'

'So, they've told you,' George said flatly, taking off his bonnet and throwing it carelessly on top of a press.

She turned to face him and suddenly her eyes blazed. 'Was it you? Did you go running to them with tales about Harry and me?'

He shook his head. 'No, Anne, but I suspect my dear wife

Jane might have done, though she will swear she did not.'

Her anger died and she sat down on a damask-covered stool before the empty fireplace, looking pale and dejected. 'Father told me it . . . it cannot be. He said that Harry should have obtained the consent of the King and his father first, but why? Why George? There are no pre-contracts, I am of little importance and Harry is of age. It would have been an excellent marriage for me and we would have been happy. I would have been content to be Harry's wife. Why is Father siding with the King and the Cardinal?'

George smiled at her sadly. 'You know why, Anne. Father will never disagree with either of them; he is too cautious and too mindful of his position and his hopes of future ennoblements and wealth. And Harry *is* important. Too rich a prize for a daughter of the lowly *Sir* Thomas Boleyn. Father may be making himself useful to the King but he is, nonetheless, a descendant of Norfolk tenant farmers from Salle. It was Harry's duty to gain permission first; he should have known that.'

She brushed this aside and stood up to pace the floor, her long skirts rustling against the rush matting. 'But what matters it to the King? What matters it to the Cardinal?'

'His grace is likely to think his supreme majesty and dignity have been sorely affronted, and you know how seriously our sovereign lord views that. As for the unholy Cardinal' – George shrugged – 'who knows what plans are fomenting in that mind of his?'

Anne stopped pacing and her stricken expression softened. 'What of Harry?'

George shook his head, remembering the scene a few hours earlier. 'My lord Cardinal upbraided him vehemently in front of us all as if he were berating a mere scullion caught stealing. I pitied him, Anne, but he stood up to the Cardinal's wrath. He swore he could not in all faith and conscience break his oath to you.'

She looked at him, a flash of hope in her eyes. 'So all is not entirely lost?'

He shook his head. 'I fear it is. The Earl has been sent for to talk sense into Harry and I have little confidence that he can stand out against all of them. He is forbidden to see you again, Wolsey commanded, or he will suffer the King's wrath.'

She turned back to the window, her hands clenched tightly together, impotent rage filling her at Wolsey's arrogant dictate. The whispers were true; it was Wolsey and not the King who ruled this country, she fumed. She hated him; he had far too much power and now he had lost her the illustrious marriage that had been within her grasp. 'My lord Cardinal has risen high, but I swear to God, George, that if an opportunity arises to hurt him, I shall seize it with both hands.'

He went to her and placed his hands on her slim shoulders and realised she was trembling with the force of her emotions. 'You are just a girl of sixteen, Anne. You cannot fight the King, the Cardinal, Father and my lord of Northumberland. You have no choice but to submit. I have brought you a letter, from Harry.'

She turned towards him, her lips parted in a sad smile, tears sparkling on her dark lashes. 'Poor Harry. I did love him, George.'

He smiled back and kissed her on the forehead. 'But it was the title "Countess" you coveted more. I know you too well, Anne, for we are alike.'

He poured himself a large cup of wine from the ewer on the table and drank it slowly as he watched her read Harry's letter. Perhaps they would have been happy had they been left alone. Harry Percy would have striven hard to please Anne. He was good-natured, generous, honest and loyal, which was more than could be said for his own life companion, he thought bitterly.

'Will you keep it?' he asked as she folded the letter up.

She shook her head slowly. 'What would be the point? It would only remind me of how I feel now.'

'What did Father say?'

She frowned. 'That I am to go back to Hever – today! Semmonet is packing. I am banished to the country in disgrace, yet again. Will you come and visit me, George, please? I shall be so lonely and I shall miss Harry so much too. He is so different from the rest of you. He is not shallow or full of self-importance or so blatantly insincere . . . I . . . I loved those things most about him. What will happen to him now?'

'I don't know, Anne, that is the truth. Remain at York Place, I suppose. But I will visit you at Hever as often as I can, I promise.' He felt sorry for her; she had suffered a crushing blow and she was too young and full of life and vivacity to be buried in the Kent countryside once again.

York Place, London

For the next three days Henry went about his duties almost in silence, valiantly fighting the illness which threatened to overwhelm him. He could not stop himself from thinking about her. He went over every word George had said, of how she had looked, what she had said, and the stark fact that she had already been sent back to Hever. He clung desperately to his hope that he would see her again and that they would be properly married. That somehow he could persuade his father to sway the Cardinal and make the King relent. He couldn't lose her – he *couldn't*. If he did his life would be without all meaning or purpose. Surely his father would help him?

He ate virtually nothing; he slept little at night, tossing and turning in his restless anguish.

Will tried to bolster his spirits and pleaded with him to take more care of his health. He had never seen Lord Henry look so distressed. 'I beg you, my lord, you must eat. You will need all your strength for what lies ahead of you. If you have any hope of standing firm in your resolve to marry Mistress Anne, you must eat,' he'd implored. Henry had tried but food made him nauseous.

Thomas Arundel too had tried and failed. He was dismayed by what Henry's Father Confessor had pointed out to him the day after Anne had left. Apparently the *de futuro* contract was invalid because there had been no consummation.

'I did not realise, Tom,' Harry had said brokenly. 'I would do nothing to besmirch her reputation, I love her too much, you know that, but had I known . . .'

'How could you, Harry? Why would we be so well versed in canon law?' Thomas had replied sympathetically.

'But it makes the case even more hopeless. Our vows were *not* binding and the Cardinal knows that and he will inform my father of the fact. What hope do I have, Tom, of ever seeing her again?'

'We can only pray that in time they may relent, Harry,'

Thomas had replied, but he didn't have much faith in his words.

It was Will who saw the Earl arrive. As the group of horsemen clattered into the courtyard, the liveries of the marcher men travel-stained, their faces streaked with dust and sweat, he stopped and watched the Earl dismount, his black velvet cloak and bonnet as grimy as those of his retinue, his expression grim. The Earl made straight for the door that led to the corridor and staircase to the long gallery and Will realised he was going to speak to the Cardinal before he spoke to Henry. He went in search of his master, his apprehension building.

'Lord Henry, your father has just arrived,' Will announced, finding Henry staring aimlessly across the gardens to the river.

A shiver ran through Henry as he turned towards Will. 'I must speak with him, Will, urgently. I must explain—'

'He has gone straight to my lord Cardinal's chambers, Lord Henry.'

Henry felt his fear and despair deepen, knowing how Wolsey would present the facts to the Earl, knowing of his father's fear of Wolsey's power. He still had to *try* to convey his side of it: his feelings and his hopes and his desire to please the Earl. 'I shall go to my lord Cardinal's ante-chamber to await him.'

Will followed him, praying that the forthcoming meeting between the Earl and his son wouldn't be as painful for Lord Henry as that terrible interview with the Cardinal had proved.

There were always people in the long gallery: pages, priests, visitors, servants going about their chores, and Henry hesitated as he reached the head of the staircase.

'Perhaps we should wait further down, Lord Henry,' Will suggested, indicating an area that seemed less busy. His master's face was deathly pale and there were beads of perspiration on his top lip. Will thought he looked ill and hoped they wouldn't have long to wait. 'Shall I fetch you some wine, my lord?'

Henry shook his head, leaning on the stone windowsill for support and feeling a little dizzy. It was lack of food, he thought, for he had eaten only a small piece of bread at breakfast. It would pass.

For the most part they were ignored and Will was relieved; he could see Lord Henry had no wish to engage in conversation with anyone. When the door to Thomas Wolsey's chambers at last opened he looked up and saw the Earl striding purposefully along the gallery towards them. As he reached the head of the staircase he stopped and looked around, then he caught sight of his son.

Will urged Lord Henry to go to him, murmuring encouragement as though to a reticent child, and Henry's hand slid from the windowsill and he took two steps forward. So much – his entire future – rested on these next few minutes but he felt weak and ill.

Will looked at the Earl's face and his heart plummeted like a stone. Henry was not going to be spared.

'Henry! You have always been an arrogant, unthrifty waster and now what have you done?' the Earl shouted, not caring that everyone was staring. 'Without consulting or obtaining the consent of either myself or your sovereign lord the King, you have betrothed yourself to a foolish girl of little estate.' He strode towards his son, anger suffusing his cheeks. 'Have you no thought for your position? No care for the House of Percy? No care for the wishes of myself, the Cardinal or your King? Are you determined to ruin us all?'

Wolsey had not minced his words on this subject and the Earl was fearful for his liberty, his position and estates once more. And his health was not as good as it once was; age was creeping up on him. He could ill afford a disaster such as that engendered by his own son.

Will could see Henry wilting beneath this attack and he wished there was something he could do or say on his master's behalf but he was impotent, a mere servant.

'Are you determined to bring down the King's righteous anger upon our heads? Son, if you persist in this wilful, arrogant, selfish behaviour you will be the last Earl of this house! I will disinherit you! I thank God I have Thomas and Ingram who I trust will prove to be more suitable than you!'

Henry couldn't speak; he felt himself sway as the import of his father's words hit him but the Earl had turned away from him and was gesturing to the people who stood around watching and listening avidly.

'Now, good masters and gentlemen, when I am dead remember how I had to take this fool boy to task over the trouble he has caused.' His gaze alighted on Will Chatton. 'But, in the meantime I ask you to act as his friends and persuade him to obey both myself and the King.' He turned back to Henry. 'Go about your duties and heed my lord Cardinal's instructions regarding Mistress Boleyn.' He lowered his voice almost to a whisper: 'Or we will both end our days in the Tower or on the scaffold!'

Will watched the Earl descend the stairs. He realised it was the end of all Lord Henry's hopes but he was more concerned about his master's present state of health. He seemed on the verge of collapse and he caught him by the shoulder as Henry staggered.

'Lord Henry, you are ill?' Will cried, seeing the sheen of sweat glistening on Henry's face and feeling his body trembling.

'I . . . I fear am losing . . . all . . . control.' Henry was fighting down waves of nausea and the grey fog that was threatening to envelop him.

'Master Norris! Lord Thomas! I have need of you,' Will called to the two young men who were approaching but who had missed Henry's encounter with his father.

'God's wounds! Harry, what ails you?' Thomas Arundel cried as he and Will and Norris supported Henry.

'I fear he has a fever, Lord Thomas,' Will said grimly, 'but it has not helped that the Earl has threatened to disinherit him, if Lord Henry persists in defying him.'

'Sweet Mother of God! Have they no pity?' Thomas replied, shocked.

Hal Norris looked concerned. 'It would be best to get him away from here, to his chamber, and I will send for a physician for I think more ails him than his father's threats.'

When the physician came he bled Henry, who was now burning with fever, delirious, crying out that he would not forsake Anne, that he would ride to Hever and rescue her and take her to Alnwick and that if it be necessary, he would raise the men of Northumberland to defend them both.

'Sweet Jesu! Has he lost his reason?' Will asked the physician fearfully. Such wild threats as his master was making were dangerous.

The man shook his head, looking thoughtful. 'Little credence should be given to his ravings, it is but the fever that is affecting his brain. It will no doubt pass when the fever abates.'

Thomas Arundel and Hal Norris exchanged glances. Wolsey had spies everywhere and no doubt these ravings of Henry's regarding Anne would be relayed back to him. Thomas hoped his fever-torn friend wasn't digging his own grave.

Chapter Twenty-Four

Thomas Wolsey clasped his hands together over the scarlet silk robes that did little to disguise the paunch of his stomach and nodded slowly, deliberating on everything the man who stood before him had said. The walls of the chamber were hung with rich tapestries. Large intricately carved cupboards were placed around the room, displaying gold and silver plate and the symbols of his office. On the desk before him lay rolls of parchment and the Great Seal of England, all of which served to impress upon lesser beings his wealth and power.

If what he had just been told was true then the matter would need some serious consideration. He did not doubt the man's words for he'd proved very useful to him in the past, but he would have preferred that the information had been brought to him much sooner. Three days had now passed since young Percy had fallen ill and the Earl had already left for his castle at Wressle. His informant was of course only a servant, but these young lords were frequently careless in their speech before such people, thinking them little better than dumb animals; a folly born of arrogance, of course, but it often served his purposes well.

He leaned forward and drew a roll of parchment towards him, an indication that the interview was at an end. 'You may go. You will be rewarded for the information you have gleaned. Master Cavendish will attend to it.'

'Your grace is most generous,' the man replied humbly, bowing low before he left the room.

The Cardinal stared at the document before him and then pushed it to one side. Should any credence be given to the ravings of a fever-ridden boy? he mused. But what if this fever apparently consuming Henry Percy were but a pretence, an elaborate subterfuge? Even if it were not the lad had some loyal people around him who might be willing to ride secretly to Hever carrying messages from him to Mistress Boleyn. And, when he had sufficiently recovered, did he indeed plan to ride to Hever himself to persuade the girl to accompany him to one of the Percy castles in the North Country? He doubted she would need much urging to agree to become Lady Percy; she would be a very willing accomplice. As for the lad's threat of raising the men of Northumberland – that certainly could not be taken lightly, even if it was merely the product of a fever-afflicted mind. The whole affair must be brought to a rapid and satisfactory conclusion.

He would have to move swiftly now. Young Percy would have to be sent north as soon as possible, regardless of the state of his health. His father could then watch him closely; he doubted the Earl would countenance any further defiance or resistance to the commands of either himself or the King. He had made very clear to my lord of Northumberland the consequences of such actions.

He toyed for a moment with the large gold and ruby ring he wore, then he reached for the silver inkpot, quill and a blank sheet of parchment. Henry Percy would be sent north as General Warden of the Marches, the position's present incumbent being the Earl of Surrey. He was sure Surrey would offer no objection; it was an unenviable post in a bleak and hostile part of the country. The sooner the troublesome boy was safely north of the Humber the better. And he would urge the Earl to undertake speedy negotiations to bring about a suitable marriage for his son and heir.

His letters containing detailed instructions complete, he called his secretary to him. 'Master Cavendish, I would ask that this missive be sent with all haste to my lord of Surrey in the North, and that you deliver this one yourself to Lord Henry Percy.'

Cavendish nodded. He was aware that the Cardinal knew the young man was gravely ill, but it was not his place to question the motives or the orders of Thomas Wolsey.

City of London

Will made his way through the dark, narrow streets of the city towards Mistress Brookes's house. He was deep in thought, his cloak wrapped tightly around him, one hand on the short sword at his waist. He had been very late home the day Lord Henry had collapsed and Joanna had been so worried that something terrible had befallen him that he'd found her in tears. After he'd calmed her and had explained the situation she had again wept, but this time for Lord Henry and Mistress Anne.

'Lord Henry loved her so much, Will. I could see it in his eyes on our wedding day, even though I did wonder did she love him as deeply. She appeared a little . . . reserved but, oh, it is so cruel to part them! It is a *wicked* thing that they have done! God will punish them all!'

He'd held her and kissed the tears from her cheeks. 'Hush, Joanna. You must not speak like that of either the King or the Cardinal or the Earl. It is dangerous.'

Anger had flashed in her dark eyes. 'I do not care! I say they are bad men and God will surely punish them.'

He'd stroked her cheek. 'But *I* care about you, I want no harm to come to you. I agree with you that it is cruel, but while we may think such things we must never say them.'

He'd confided in her his deep concern for Lord Henry's health, his life even, and she had reluctantly agreed with him that until there was some improvement in his lordship's condition he must stay at York Place. He had not been happy for her to be in the house alone at night and so she had agreed to stay with Mistress Brookes. He was torn between his responsibility and love for her and his loyalty and concern for his young master.

He found Mistress Brookes and Joanna about to serve supper. Robert Aske was also seated at the table, his expression as sombre as his plain black doublet.

Joanna embraced Will and kissed him on the cheek. 'I am so glad you have come, Will. Now you must eat with us.'

He nodded for he had not eaten since early that morning. 'I cannot stay long. I promised Lord Thomas I would be back before ten o'clock but I had to make sure that you are safe and well.'

'And I am both so now you must eat, my husband,' Joanna urged, gently pushing him down in the chair beside hers.

'How is Lord Henry? Is there any improvement?' Robert Aske enquired. He knew the young man frequently suffered ill health but wondered whether this latest bout had been induced by shock, grief and humiliation.

'A little but not much. We still fear for him. He sleeps but even when he does he is restless and greatly agitated. But at least he has stopped his ravings.'

Mistress Brookes, her brow creased in a worried frown beneath her white cap, tutted sympathetically as she served the thick beef pottage and bread.

Joanna laid her hand on Will's arm. 'I have been thinking all the day of some way in which I can help, and I have made up my mind that I will go back with you and help you to tend Lord Henry.'

Will smiled at her but shook his head. 'You are kind and thoughtful, Joanna, and it is generous of you, my love, but . . .'

She frowned. 'But? It is not, as you say, "seemly"? Do not forget that I am no longer a maid, Will. I am now a married woman.'

He squeezed her hand. 'I know, it is not that. But . . .' He paused again. 'You are like her: dark hair, dark eyes . . . beautiful. He might think in his troubled mind that . . .'

Joanna understood but she was disappointed for she had hoped to spend more time with Will as well as be of some assistance. 'That I am she?'

Will nodded.

Joanna sighed sadly. 'This I understand.'

Robert Aske looked questioningly at Will. 'What is to happen to him when he recovers and I pray God he does quickly?' He had been shocked when Joanna had told him of Lord Henry's treatment at the hands of both the Cardinal and the Earl. He had doubted the wisdom of Henry Percy's conduct in the manner of his betrothal, but he had not expected the matter to have been so publicly addressed, or his lordship so scathingly and soundly berated before the Cardinal's household.

Will shook his head. 'I do not know, Robert. It would be cruel and humiliating to keep him at York Place in attendance on Wolsey, having to accompany my lord Cardinal to court where he recently spent so many happy hours with Mistress Anne. It would be just as cruel to banish him but I think it will be a good while before he is able either to resume his duties or undertake any journey. We must wait and see and pray God he improves.'

Mistress Brookes placed the joint of mutton in front of Robert Aske and indicated that he should carve. 'Time will heal both his body and his heart. Young hearts mend quickly and I feel sure that this sickness was upon him before his father arrived. I will pray to the Blessed Virgin that his sufferings of body, mind and spirit will soon be over.'

Aske nodded. 'We would all agree with that, mistress.' He turned to Will. 'And if there is any way I can be of assistance, please tell me.'

Will thanked him but as he ate his supper he wondered if there was anything anyone could do to ease Lord Henry's suffering or mend his shattered heart.

York Place, London

Henry tossed restlessly in the bed on sheets damp and stained with sweat, crumpled by his constant movements. In the brief moments when he was lucid he felt weak and consumed by an overwhelming sense of despair. He was deeply shocked that his father had threatened to disinherit him but he cared little for the public humiliation inflicted by both the Cardinal and his father. It was as nothing compared to the loss of the girl whose love was the only thing he really cared about. He would never love anyone else the way he loved Anne, he was certain of that. If he could only see her again, even for a few brief moments . . . that was all he would ask of God. Just to hold her in his arms once more, to kiss her and beg her forgiveness for breaking his sacred promise to marry her. His God must surely understand the torment and guilt he endured because of that betrayal?

Then the fever would return, searing his flesh, causing the sweat to break out on his body and driving away all rational thoughts from his mind. Occasionally he slept but even then he was not at peace. There were times when he awoke to find the chamber in darkness, lit only by the flickering flame of a candle, the embers of the fire giving little light but adding to the suffocating heat in the room. Then Will Chatton, Tom Arundel or Hal Norris would be bending over him, their expressions grave and concerned as they coaxed him to drink some wine. But it made him nauseous and he would retch horribly. And the fog would descend again and fire would surge through his body. In his fevered mind he begged God to take away the suffering, at others he asked only to die.

Thomas Arundel had summoned the physician yet again for he feared for his friend.

'Has the fever broken?' the man asked sharply, looking irritated at this summons so late in the evening.

Thomas shook his head. 'No, and he has become delirious again.'

'I will bleed him.' He stiffened suddenly. 'Who opened the window?' he demanded.

'I did. The chamber is stifling, the air noxious and he appeared to be gasping for breath,' Thomas informed him. It was the truth and Harry's breathing had become less laboured once the fresh air had started to filter in.

'Close it at once, my lord! All air is dangerous but none more so than at night.'

Thomas did as he was bid and then stood watching as the physician placed the bowl under Harry's arm and produced a sharp scalpel, the blade of which was stained brown with dried blood.

'He is no better then?' Will asked quietly as he entered the chamber and went to stand beside Thomas.

'He was calling out for her, begging her to come to him. I could not calm him so I called the physician.'

Will nodded slowly, watching his lordship's blood draining into the bowl. 'I pray it will pass soon, Lord Thomas. He is already so weak that he can ill afford to lose more blood.'

Thomas nodded miserably. There seemed little else the physician could do to help Harry.

'I will stay with him now, my lord. You must get some rest, you have your duties to attend to,' Will urged as the physician left.

Thomas nodded. He was exhausted but the Cardinal would still expect him to be at Mass at six next morning.

When the physician had gone Will gently lifted his master higher on the pillows and pulled the sheet and the green and gold damask coverlet up around him. Lord Henry was deathly pale, his eyes seemed to have sunk even further back in his head and his lips were bloodless, but at least he appeared calmer, his breathing was shallow but regular and there was only a light sheen of perspiration on his forehead. Will prayed that whatever it was that had laid Lord Henry so low would soon pass for, like Mistress Brookes and Hal Norris, he was certain that it was a real illness and not just the heartbreak of being so abruptly and irrevocably parted from Mistress Anne Boleyn. He prayed too that Mistress Brookes was right, that time would heal his master's body and spirit.

Chapter Twenty-Five

⬦

WILL WAS WAKENED EARLY next morning by Thomas Arundel who had called on his way to Mass. Dawn was just breaking and the faint light seeping slowly through the casement window revealed the disorder in the chamber. The ashes of the fire were cold and grey in the hearth, a pool of wax surrounded the burned-out candle, stained damp cloths and the small bowl, half full of congealed blood, stood on top of a press.

Will rose stiffly from the truckle bed on which he'd only a bare hour ago lain down, rubbing the sleep from his eyes. 'He has slept easily these past three hours, Lord Thomas.'

'Praise be to God! Do you think he is over the worst of it at last, Will?' Thomas looked down at his friend, concern mingling with relief in his eyes. He hadn't slept well himself but Harry did look better. He was still very pale – his skin the colour of candle wax – and he looked gaunt and drawn, but he was breathing more deeply and evenly. There was no sign of the fever or the profuse sweating and agitation that accompanied it.

'We can only hope and pray, Lord Thomas, that it will not reoccur as it has done before.'

Thomas Arundel nodded slowly. 'I must attend my lord Cardinal at Mass but once it is over and there is nothing pressing to attend to, I will return, and you must take some time now to eat and drink.'

Will smiled tiredly. 'Not until you return, my lord. I fear to leave him unattended.' He looked around the untidy room, the air of which was heavy and saturated with the odours of sweat, blood, wood smoke, candle grease and soiled linen. 'There is plenty to keep me occupied while I watch him.'

Thomas Arundel crossed to the door and moved a carved wooden screen that stood beside it, placing it beside Henry's bed. 'For the love of the Almighty, Will, open the window! I am aware of the good physician's fear of fresh air but this chamber is like a fetid cell. I am certain that is more detrimental to Harry's health and wellbeing than clean air. The screen will protect him from any cold draughts.'

Will did as he was bid, taking in gulps of the still slightly damp and chilly air. He would not leave it open for long, but just time enough to dispel the sour odours of the sickroom. How he longed to see his master back in the world of light, free from the shadows of illness and fear.

Henry stirred in his sleep and slowly opened his eyes. His field of vision seemed to be obscured by a dark panel or was it a door? He was confused. Where was he? He felt light-headed and weak and a little cold. As he breathed in he realised the air was fresher and cleaner and he discerned movement beyond the screen, for such it must be for if it were a door he would be unable to hear or sense anything. 'Tom? Will?' he called tentatively.

He heard the scraping of a metal latch against stone and then the screen was pulled back and a brilliant shaft of sunlight dazzled him.

'Lord Henry, you are awake. You have slept peacefully these past four hours with no sign of feverishness.' Will was relieved to see that his young master was calm and lucid.

'I am . . . exhausted and chilled, Will.'

Will instantly regretted leaving the window open for so long. 'I will bring another coverlet, my lord, and build up the fire. Can you take a little wine?'

Henry shook his head; even the thought of it made him feel sick. 'I just want to sleep,' he murmured, closing his eyes again. It had been an effort to keep them open for his eyelids felt as though they had lead weights on them.

Will brought another coverlet and tucked it securely around his master and then rekindled the fire, placing more logs on it until the room was once again warm and stuffy.

When Thomas Arundel returned he insisted that Will go and take some breakfast, promising he would sit with Henry. He was relieved that his friend appeared to be on the way to recovery although he surmised that it would be a long road and one strewn with many moments of pain. But he would do all in his power to help.

Will was glad to leave the stifling chamber and walk across the courtyard towards the kitchens for it was a fine early summer morning, the sun was warm on his back and the sound of birdsong resonated around him. The hour for breakfast was long over so it was no use him going to the great hall, he deduced. He breathed deeply; the air was filled with the perfume of the early flowers in the gardens and the tang of the river wafted in on the breeze. He was tired and hungry but much easier in his mind than he had been since Lord Henry's collapse. Perhaps at some time during the day he could find time to go home to Joanna. He hoped so. He also hoped that if his master's health improved life could take on a semblance of normality, at least for himself. He knew that there stretched ahead of him days and weeks of caring for Henry. His master's constitution had not been strong even before this illness had afflicted him, and then there was the loss of Mistress Anne. He had to strive to come to terms with that and it would not be easy. He hoped the Cardinal would not insist on Lord Henry returning to his duties before he was well enough in both body and spirit to do so, but his dislike and mistrust of Thomas Wolsey had deepened. The Cardinal cared little for the wellbeing, desires or feelings of anyone other than himself and the King; the events of these past few days had shown him that.

City of London

Joanna was delighted both to see him and to hear of Lord Henry's progress when Will arrived home late that afternoon, looking weary but relieved. 'I am so happy that the sickness has left him,' she cried, putting down the shirt she had been working on and throwing her arms around his neck.

Will kissed her and held her close, drinking in the scent of the lavender water with which she had recently taken to rinsing her long dark hair. 'He has slept much of the day but it is for the best. Maybe he will take a little food later.'

She reached up and gently traced the lines on his forehead, etched by days and nights of worry and lack of sleep. 'And you too are tired and must have food. I will fetch something for you now.'

He sat and watched her as she prepared a platter of cold meats and cheeses, a white apron tied over her rose-pink gown, its long sleeves turned back, her hair covered by a matching hood. It was a colour that suited her well, he thought. She seemed to grow lovelier each day and he had missed her, he mused, feeling a deep sense of contentment creep over him. He was so fortunate to have her as his wife; he couldn't envisage his life without her now. Sadly he contrasted his position to Lord Henry's. His master was possessed of far greater wealth and held an esteemed and important position, but whereas he, Will, enjoyed robust health, happiness with Joanna and a small amount of good fortune from his involvement in trade, Lord Henry's health was poor, he was not free to make choices or decisions for himself and a future with the woman he loved deeply was no longer possible. Indeed, he thought as Joanna set the meal before him and poured him a tankard of ale, he possessed riches others had no hope of, and for that he thanked the Lord.

York Place, London

Dusk was falling as Will stepped from the lighter and went up the water stairs and into the gardens of the palace. The air was heavy now with the perfume of roses and honeysuckle and he smiled to himself: God willing tomorrow night he might be able to go home and spend the night with Joanna in his own comfortable bed.

As he reached Lord Henry's chamber he observed George Cavendish leaving it. He was a serious young man, always dressed soberly in a long black gown with a plain white collar, a simple unadorned cap over his dark hair.

'Good evening, Master Cavendish,' he greeted him pleasantly. 'I trust you found Lord Henry much improved?'

Cavendish nodded. 'Thankfully I did, Master Chatton.'

Will was about to enquire if Lord Thomas was still with his master but Cavendish had moved on along the corridor, heading for the staircase.

The heat in the chamber hit him forcefully, causing him to pause for a second. 'Lord Thomas, I have just seen Master Cavendish. Had my lord Cardinal sent him to enquire after Lord Henry's health?'

As Thomas Arundel turned away from the bedside Will could see that his master's eyes were closed. A folded parchment lay discarded on the coverlet. He also observed that Lord Thomas was furious, his cheeks flushed, his eyes bright with fury.

'No, he did not! He came to deliver a letter. Wolsey's letter containing his monstrous *commands*!'

Will went cold. 'What commands, my lord?'

Thomas snatched up the parchment from the bed and thrust it at Will, fully cognisant of the fact that Harry's squire was now literate. 'Read it. By God's blood, the man is inhuman!'

Will quickly scanned the lines of neat, flowing script and utter disbelief surged through him. 'Sweet Jesu! This can't be true! Lord Henry is too ill and weak to travel so soon and so far, surely the Cardinal knows that?'

'Indeed he does but he obviously cares little that the journey might kill Harry! And he calls himself a man of God!' Thomas fulminated.

Will's anger and outrage were increasing. 'Lord Thomas, I grew up in the border country and I know full well the harshness of its climate and the violent, lawless nature of the men who live there – my poor father, God have mercy on his soul, was murdered by them. Lord Henry is not marcher reared as are his brothers, he is ill fitted to take up the position of General Warden of the Marches. Is not my lord of Surrey the present Warden?'

'Cavendish told us that word has been sent to Surrey informing him of this change. It is an act of pure malice and vindictiveness on Wolsey's part,' Thomas replied bitterly. Will Chatton was absolutely right. Harry was unprepared for such a post whereas Surrey was a veteran with years of experience in warfare and not just on the Border.

Will nodded his agreement, filled with a sense of silent fury and impotence. This seemed to him nothing less than an act of vicious spite. Even had Lord Henry been in the best of health he was too young and inexperienced and he abhorred the violence of border warfare. He had spent these last years at court, enjoying music, poetry, masques and hawking expeditions in the company of his friends. The cold and the dampness of the northern counties would damage his health and he was still suffering over his lost love. Fighting down his emotions he made a decision. He crossed to the bed and looked down at his master.

'Lord Henry, I will beg an audience with the Cardinal and impress upon him that you are too ill to travel. I will ask the physician who has attended you to accompany me.'

Henry opened his eyes and tried to smile, grateful for Will's loyalty and his attempt to intercede. 'I thank you, Will, but it would be to no avail. I must do as he instructs me. I cannot refuse.' He was trying to dismiss from his mind the implications of Wolscy's commands and the despair that filled him. He was aware that he was too weak to undertake such a journey but he had no choice. The alternative would be confinement in the Tower on a trumped-up charge, such as the one that had sent his father to the Fleet.

Will turned to Thomas Arundel, acute anxiety evident in his eyes. 'Lord Thomas, he can barely stand, let alone ride!'

Thomas gnawed at his lip. 'I know that but what can be done? You read it, there is no question of dissent, you must be ready to leave the day after tomorrow.'

For the first time Will thought of Joanna and he frowned. He could not leave his master to endure such a journey with only a handful of servants to accompany him and yet he could not, *would* not leave Joanna in London. He would take her with him for he had little idea of how long he would be away. With blinding clarity and a growing hatred he realised that this cruel decision of the Cardinal's had put an end to his hopes and plans for the immediate future. He must now leave the first home they had so recently set up together and take his beloved wife north.

Chapter Twenty-Six

City of London

JOANNA WAS CONFUSED AND upset when early the following morning Will arrived and told her what had happened.

'But why do they do this to Lord Henry? Has he not suffered much already? And why must we leave too? We are happy here. I was so glad that he is improving and that you can come home to me again,' she cried, tears of disappointment and apprehension sparkling on her dark lashes as she recalled the details of his childhood and his descriptions of the bleak, wild country he had left behind.

Will took her in his arms. 'I do not expect you to understand, Joanna, I do not fully understand myself why Lord Henry is being treated this way. It seems we are all helpless pawns in the hands of a powerful and malicious man, but I cannot abandon his lordship, my love. I owe him my loyalty, my service, my protection. He is more than just my master, I am indebted to him for so many things. He has been my benefactor, my companion and, I hope, my friend.' He kissed her forehead. 'If I had not come to London with him – and he did not need to bring me – I would never have met and found such joy with you. I love you so much, Joanna, you know that, and I will never desert you, but he is sick and weak, he may even die on this long and hazardous journey.'

He felt some of the tension go out of her and she nodded slowly. 'What you say is true, Will, and I . . . I will go with you. I love you too much, my husband, to be parted from you.'

He kissed her tenderly and she clung to him. 'I shall pack our things and I must go and bid farewell to Mistress Brookes,' she said sadly, looking around the small, neat room, her first real home since she had left Spain.

'And I have now to go to the Inns of Court and seek out Master Aske for time is pressing.'

Again she nodded, knowing he had to put his affairs in order and wondering what lay ahead for them both and for Lord Henry, for their futures seemed to be bound together.

'We will be safe, Joanna, I promise. We will stay with the good monks each night on our way north and then I will take you to my mother's house, if you do not wish to stay at the castle. It is not far away and you will have Meggie for company, she is just a few years younger than you.'

She managed a sad little smile. 'I will be happy to meet your family at last, Will.'

'They are *our* family, Joanna,' he impressed upon her.

Will escorted her to Beatrice Brookes's house, bade the woman farewell, and then made his way through the narrow and increasingly malodorous streets to the Inns of Court and asked directions to Robert Aske's chambers.

He found his friend seated at a desk in a small, rather cramped room, surrounded by papers, books and documents.

'Will! What is it that brings you here?' Robert enquired, getting to his feet. Something must be wrong.

Briefly Will informed him of the events of the past hours and Aske shook his head. 'Is Wolsey trying to kill him?' he said bluntly.

'I pray not, Robert, but I cannot leave him. I have come to beg you to look to my affairs until such time as I can make more formal arrangements with both Master Hinch and Captain Fanshaw.'

'I will be happy to do so, Will, but I am going north myself. I have business to attend to but I will not remain there long, a day or two at most. I will send word today to Master Hinch to inform him of our intentions; he will attend to any pressing matters until I return. I will ride with you and Lord Henry.'

'I will be glad of your company, Robert, for it is going to be a long and arduous journey. I'm not even sure how well Joanna rides and I must obtain a suitable horse for her.'

'How many will be in the company?'

'Lord Henry, myself and Joanna, two grooms, three servants and Lord Henry's own men-at-arms.'

'Marcher men?' Aske probed.

Will nodded. The roads often proved dangerous with thieves and outlaws lying in wait for the unwary traveller, but accompanied by the hardened, burly soldiers in their Percy livery, he doubted they would be molested.

'I will be at York Place by eight o'clock tomorrow morning,' Aske stated, shaking Will's hand as he showed him out.

Will strode quickly away. His next task was to find a suitable horse and a saddle and bridle for Joanna and he had little time. He had promised Lord Henry and Lord Thomas he would be back before suppertime, accompanied by his wife.

York Place, London

Henry had forced himself to get up, although he had to cling to the post of the bed as dizziness swept over him. Gradually it had passed and he had dressed slowly, even this small exertion proving exhausting. He knew he must eat for he had to try to regain some strength for the journey and he managed to keep down some bread and a little cold mutton. After that he had sat and laboriously written another note to Anne. His heart was heavy as he again declared his undying love for her and begged her forgiveness for his broken promises. Inside he felt cold and dead, dreading both the forthcoming journey and a future that stretched bleakly ahead of him. He disliked the cold climate of the North, the starkness of the countryside, the chill mists and often incessant rain. He did not enjoy the company and pursuits of his brothers and he knew he would find little favour with his father. He hated the bloody violence of the Borders and the lawlessness and treachery that would soon be his lot to try to curtail. However, ill and heart-sore though he was, he had never lacked the courage to do his duty. He would fulfil his position of Warden to the best of his ability.

He looked up as Thomas Arundel came in, bearing a silver ewer. 'Is that to bolster my spirits or aid my recovery, Tom?'

'Both, Harry. It is the best Burgundy I could find.' He poured two goblets and handed one to his friend. 'You have found the strength to write?'

Henry nodded, taking a few sips of the wine. 'Will you ask George Boleyn to . . . ?'

'I'll take it myself, Harry,' Thomas promised, 'though it would be prudent for me to wait a while before I ride to Kent. I do not wish to find myself in my lord Cardinal's disfavour and banished to Arundel.'

'I want her to know that I . . . I shall never forget her or stop loving her, even though I am exiled in the North.'

'I will miss you sorely, Harry,' Thomas said truthfully.

'And I you, Tom. You have proved a true and loyal friend. Promise you will write to me with such news as you think may be of interest to me.'

'Indeed, but you will surely come to London at some time in the future? You will not be expected to remain in such a desolate place for ever.'

Henry shrugged. 'I pray God I may find favour again at court but I do not expect it to be soon, Tom.'

Thomas looked downcast. In his opinion Harry had done little to deserve the treatment that had been meted out to him. 'At least I know you have a true and loyal servant to accompany you: Will Chatton.'

Henry took another sip of wine. 'Will *is* loyal and steadfast but he too has responsibilities now: a wife and his trading. He may not wish to stay in my service for ever and if his ventures are successful he will have the means to leave me.'

Thomas considered his words. Will Chatton had been Harry's squire since they were both eleven years of age: they had grown up together, but now they were men and their paths might well part in the future. He hoped it would not come too soon, however, for Harry badly needed someone with him to bolster his spirits.

Godmanchester, Near Huntingdon, Cambridgeshire

They had left London early yesterday morning and had ridden north but their pace had been slowed by Lord Henry's weakness and Joanna's inexperience as a rider. Will looked across at her and gave an encouraging smile; she was clinging tightly to both the reins and the mane of the steady little palfrey he'd found for her, obviously still afraid of falling. They had stayed overnight at a small monastery and she had complained that she ached all over and this morning she was sore and stiff. The friars had been hospitable, bringing them water to wash and ale to quench their thirsts and they had dined in the refectory with them, sharing their simple meal.

At least the weather this morning was fine, he thought, although he realised that by midday the sun would be uncomfortably hot, but it was infinitely better than riding in the rain which would have turned the road to a muddy track and soaked into their clothes. However, now the dust was rising up in a cloud from the rutted road to lie thick on their clothes and skin and both men and beasts were being tormented by flies. When they reached the first inn he determined they would stop for, turning in his saddle, he saw that Lord Henry looked close to exhaustion already.

Robert Aske urged his mount forward until he was beside

Will. 'If we go much further I fear he will fall from the saddle in a faint. He can barely remain upright,' he said quietly.

'There is a village ahead, it must have an inn or a church or somewhere he can rest.' Will wiped the dust from his lips with the back of his hand. 'We may have to stay here for the rest of the day, at least until late afternoon when it will become cooler. It is going to take us far longer to reach Wressle than I had anticipated, Robert. Perhaps you should ride on ahead for you have matters to attend to.'

Aske shook his head. 'No, they will wait. I will not leave you to take care of both his lordship and Joanna, for I fear she is not at all at ease and may take a fall.'

'I pray not, Robert. The palfrey is sure-footed and thank God the road is dry – too dry for much comfort.'

His companion smiled grimly. 'Travelling is always a necessary evil.'

When they reached the village Will found, to his consternation, that although there was indeed an inn it was a very poor hostelry. The landlord, however, informed him that there was a manor house but a mile distant. Will thanked him and went to Henry's side.

'My lord, this place is not fit to house a dog but there is a manor house a short ride away. Will you be able to endure the additional discomfort?'

Henry nodded although he seriously doubted he could. During the last few miles waves of nausea and dizziness had been washing over him and it was only by sheer willpower that he had managed to stay in the saddle, one hand clamped firmly on the pommel, the other holding the reins so tightly his fingers were stiff. Yesterday, as he'd sunk thankfully on to the narrow bed the friars had provided, he'd wondered how he had managed to survive a day in the saddle at all.

Will handed the reins of his own mount to Robert Aske and led his master's horse on down the lane.

It was a small brick-built house with a courtyard in front and barns and stables at the back, and upon seeing the liveried men-at-arms and the richness of Henry's dusty clothes, the squire hurried out to greet them.

'Sir, we are travelling north to York but my lord Henry Percy, son of the Earl of Northumberland, is recovering from a fever and is unable to go further. We seek rest and shelter.'

The man's eyes widened with shock as he realised the importance of his visitor. He was a plain country gentleman but he quickly recovered his composure and bowed deeply. 'My lord, I will be honoured to be of assistance. You are most welcome in my humble house.' He turned and called loudly for his wife and servants all of whom came rushing out.

Will almost lifted Henry from the saddle and Henry's legs buckled beneath him. One of the men-at-arms came instantly to assist Will while Robert Aske helped Joanna dismount.

Squire Blake's small, portly but redoubtable wife bustled around, directing one of her maids to go quickly and change the linen in the largest bedroom, another to draw water and find towels, a third to go to the kitchen and prepare food and drink and she then led the small party towards the house.

Aske caught Squire Blake's arm. 'Sir, as you can see, Lord Henry is too weak to ride, can you procure a litter and another horse?'

'Certainly, you are welcome to take one of my animals and I

shall instruct a carpenter to construct a litter to carry his lordship, but you must all rest here tonight.'

'On his lordship's behalf, I thank you most kindly for your hospitality and you shall not suffer financially for the provision of the litter and the horse.'

Squire Blake nodded but looked perturbed. 'Would it not have been better to have delayed his lordship's journey until he was stronger?'

Aske nodded. 'It would but it was upon the direct command of my lord Cardinal – Thomas Wolsey – that he was forced to undertake it now,' he said grimly, 'and it is the intention of both myself and his squire, Master Chatton, to ensure that he does not die from the rigours of it.'

Squire Blake's florid complexion paled a little. Rumours had reached even this rural village of Thomas Wolsey's increasing power and now he realised that they were more than just idle gossip. The boy was the son of a great Earl yet he had been forced to take to the road when it was obvious he was gravely ill. He shivered as he followed Robert Aske into the house, despite the fact that the heat of the day had caused beads of sweat to form on his forehead.

Chapter Twenty-Seven

❖

1525
Hever Castle, Kent

Anne glanced around the courtyard at the flurry of activity that surrounded her. Grooms were making final checks to girths and stirrup leathers and two maids were hurrying across towards them bearing the last small items of luggage that had been overlooked. The slight commotion added to her relief and pleasure that she was at last leaving Hever and returning to court. The sun was warm on her face and its rays caught the metalwork on saddles and bridles making it gleam like silver-gilt. The two years she had been forced to remain here had seemed interminably long and dreary, especially the short, cold, dark days of winter and there had been times when she had despaired of ever being allowed to leave, of ever being summoned to court again.

'You are ready, Anne?' George asked, smiling at her and

thinking that already the air of despondency that had clung to her had vanished. Each time he had managed to visit her his fears for her wellbeing had deepened and he had urged his father to reconsider. She was too young and vivacious, too great an asset to the family to be buried in the country for ever, he had insisted, and finally his persuasion had at last succeeded.

'I am more than ready, George, for I feel like a caged bird that has been set free,' Anne laughed. Her reply incurred a grim look of censure from Sir Thomas, which made her cast her eyes down demurely but her heart was still beating rapidly. Oh, how she had missed the entertainments, the gossip, the intrigue and the company of her friends.

The first months of her banishment had been so miserable, she thought as the small party at last set off led by her father and brother. She had missed Harry Percy so much and had wondered how he was faring. Was he as miserable at Alnwick or Wressle or at whichever of his father's castles he was now forced to reside in as she was? She had heard that he had been sent back north. Would she ever see him again? she had wondered sadly. She feared not.

The fields and open heathland stretched out now before her and she urged her palfrey into a canter to keep pace with her father and George. She rode well and enjoyed it but the thought that every passing mile was taking her closer to London increased her pleasure. It was so good to once again be riding towards the capital, she thought; she felt happy, animated, even excited again, feelings she had not experienced for so long. As the weeks at Hever had passed her feelings of loss and regret had gradually diminished to be replaced by restlessness and frustration induced by the tedium of daily life.

She heard little of what was happening in London. George had written the occasional brief note and had visited infrequently. From her parents and Mary there had been no communication at all.

They had been dark days and she knew they had changed her. She felt she had grown up. How naive she had been to think that she could follow where her heart led. Well, she was no longer that girl. Perhaps she had become a little cynical too, she now mused, but was that such a bad thing? Her experiences had taught her that it was unwise to totally trust her emotions. She would not let her heart rule her head again and she had resolved to put the past firmly behind her and look with optimism to the future. She had also vowed that if she was ever allowed to return to court she would not make another mistake.

She was distracted from her thoughts by a shout from George, who was pointing to a small village just visible in the distance.

'There will be an inn ahead, Anne. Is it your wish that we stop and take such refreshments as they can provide?' he called to her.

She laughed and shook her head vehemently. 'No, let us ride on. We will find better fare when we reach London and I have spent too long in the countryside,' she called back. She had no wish to linger for a single moment at a rustic inn when a new life at court now stretched before her. A life she would embrace readily.

1526
Warkworth Castle, Northumberland

Henry stared aimlessly out of the window; a lethargy had possessed him these last three years which he seemed incapable of overcoming and at times he found it hard to marshal his thoughts and concentrate on even simple matters. Ever since he'd returned from London his health had been poor and in the cold and damp of this northern climate the illness which had laid him low on his banishment from court frequently returned.

He remembered little of that journey three years ago; he'd lapsed in and out of consciousness for most of it, but he realised that had it not been for the ministrations of both Will Chatton and Robert Aske he might well have died. He'd learned from Will that it had been Aske who had procured and reimbursed the squire at Godmanchester for the litter and he was indebted to the young lawyer for his consideration. It had been many months before he had felt able to resume what could be deemed his 'duties'. Indeed it was only due to his mother's assiduous care for his health that he could do so at all.

Less than a mile away across the fields was the coast and he watched as the October wind drove the grey angry waves against the shore where they broke, throwing white plumes of spray into the air. He shivered involuntarily; winter was approaching and these autumn gales were the harbingers of the maladies that lay ahead of him.

The two large arched windows, set above the dais in the great hall, were in the great tower where he had chosen to reside. It was quieter than the chambers in the hall range where his parents had their apartments. That was close to the gate-house and the Carrickfergus Tower and the constant activity of a household of over two hundred people that accompanied everyday life at Warkworth. Like Alnwick it was built of sand-stone and impregnable, set on a high spur of land overlooking the River Coquet, surrounded by a moat, approachable only on one side and through its massive and heavily fortified gatehouse. Like Alnwick he found it bleak, chill and draughty. He drew his fur-lined cape closer to him and turned away, making his way towards the narrow stone stairway cut into the wall which led down into the hall below. From there he could enter the chapel, which would be deserted at this time of day, and pray for the strength he knew he would require to face the forth-coming interview with his father.

He descended the stairs and was crossing towards the chapel door when he caught sight of his squire approaching. He could not recall this one's name. There were many in his father's household, but since Will Chatton had left his service two years ago he had little affinity with any of them, he thought ruefully. Will was a father now for Joanna had given birth to a healthy boy a year ago. Will's fortune from trade had increased; he had become a successful merchant trading in many commodities and had moved his little family to Beverley where he had purchased a house in the shadow of the minster. He missed him sorely for Will had been more than a servant to him; he had no other close companions and for his brothers he had little time or patience. It had been with some reluctance that his former squire had left his service but Will had promised to return should he have urgent need of him in the future.

'Lord Henry, this has arrived from London, it is addressed

to you,' the youth informed him, handing over the parchment.

Henry nodded his thanks as he took it from him but made no attempt to break the seal and open it. He would read it in the privacy of the chapel for the seal bore the arms of Arundel; it was from Tom. He smiled wryly, Tom had kept his promise and wrote as frequently as time and his duties permitted.

Even within the chapel the whistling of the wind could be heard as it buffeted the thick stone walls and battlements. Henry crossed himself and genuflected devoutly before the altar before settling himself in a carved pew and breaking the seal on the missive. Slowly he read the lines of flowing script, learning that there was something new being whispered about at court and that it was making the usual intrigues dull by comparison. The King was greatly concerned about his lack of a male heir, a *legitimate* male heir and was having serious doubts about the validity of his marriage to Queen Katherine. So concerned was their sovereign lord that my lord Cardinal was undertaking to enquire into the matter at the highest ecclesiastical level. Tom wrote that these concerns stemmed from the old and well-known fact that Katherine had been wed first to Henry's older brother Arthur, who had died. The Queen had always sworn that that brief marriage had never been consummated but now it appeared that the King was doubting her word.

This news was not of any great moment, although he admitted that for every duke, earl and nobleman in the country the matter of a male heir was of importance and greatly so indeed for Henry Tudor. Tom wrote that it would be of interest to see how and if the 'King's Great Matter' as it was being called, progressed; Henry wondered idly would it in fact progress at all. Ecclesiastical investigations of this kind were notoriously slow moving, more so when two monarchs – one of whom was the aunt of the Holy Roman Emperor – and many miles in distance were involved.

He laid the letter aside as he pondered his own future. He knew the Cardinal corresponded with his father on many subjects and that one of them was his own marriage. It had been under discussion for months now: discussions in which he was allowed no part at all. He shivered as he always did when he thought of Thomas Wolsey. The Cardinal's influence had not diminished, and that King Henry apparently required his assistance in dealing with Rome, Wolsey's position would be unassailable. It was little wonder his father was reluctant to alienate the great Cardinal in any way at all.

Henry leaned against the carved back of the pew and stared morosely at the stained-glass windows above the altar. The light filtering through them threw small dull pools of red, blue, green and gold on to the pale wood of the floor. He picked up the letter again. Tom wrote that there was another piece of news which he felt he should in all conscience impart, else Henry hear of it from another source, but which he hoped would not cause his good friend to be downcast. It concerned Mistress Anne Boleyn.

Henry sat up, his hands trembling a little. There had been no news of her for so long but he had not forgotten her. He loved her as much now as he'd done when they had been parted. The betrothal Wolsey had said the King had intended for her had come to nothing and he wondered if it had been a mere fabrication on the Cardinal's part. Then last May Tom had written to inform him that she had returned to court. He'd instantly written begging his old friend to tell him of how she was faring but so far he had learned very little.

He read slowly; any news concerning her was of far more importance to him than anything the King might be undertaking, but as he read the trembling of his hands increased. It appeared that she was the latest object of the King's desires. He was plying her with costly gifts, Tom wrote, he was always seeking her company and had apparently ended his liaison with her sister Mary. Henry paled, a dart of anger stabbed him and the bile rose in his throat. She was so young, not yet twenty, and Henry Tudor was in his thirty-sixth year, but he was the *King*. What hope had she of holding out against him and thereby risking his wrath? Her family would encourage her to entice the King for their own advancement, for had they not blatantly encouraged Mary? Thomas Boleyn was an ambitious man, as was her brother George.

He let the parchment fall into his lap and beads of clammy perspiration broke out on his forehead. He had no desire to learn more of this. He had no wish to dwell on the hideous thought of Anne, young, vivacious and alluring, in the King's embrace. That thought tormented his very soul but he was unable to stop himself from learning more. He picked the letter up and resumed reading, then he uttered a sharp cry as he read Tom's next sentences. She was indeed holding the King at arm's length. Tom wrote that she was doing it with great subtlety and charm but with an underlying determination. It was whispered that she had told him his wife she could not be, and his mistress she would never contemplate becoming, but that such was the King's ardour that this had not angered him, it appeared only to have increased his desire for her.

Henry laid the letter aside, his emotions in turmoil. Did she still think of him and the love they had shared? Did she still love him? Was this her reason for denying the King? He hardly dared to hope but prayed it was. Yet how long could she continue to charm the King before his impatience and lust turned to anger? What would happen to her then? He'd abandoned all hope of ever seeing her again but what did the future hold for her? he wondered. Would she be banished again to Hever? Would she be married off to some minor nobleman as her sister had been?

It was some minutes before he realised he was no longer alone.

'Lord Henry, the Earl is growing impatient and has sent me to find you,' his squire informed him gravely. In fact the Earl was more than 'impatient' and his words had been blunt and forceful.

Henry reluctantly stood, rolling up the parchment once more and trying to dispel all thoughts of Anne from his mind. He had forgotten his appointment with his father, which did not bode well for these days the Earl's temper had become ever shorter as his health increasingly failed.

He hastily crossed the bailey, skirting the half-completed collegiate church in the centre which had little hope of ever being finished now that money was scarce, and entered the Little Stair Tower, which gave direct access to the Earl's private apartments.

Henry Algernon was seated before the fire in the withdrawing chamber, huddled in a gown of black velvet lined with sable fur over his green and black velvet doublet. As the Earl turned Henry noted, as he always did, how his father's appearance of late had changed. The Earl seemed to have shrunk, his hair was thinning and grey, his flesh hung loosely and there were lines of pain and anxiety etched more deeply on his face. Henry was aware that the debts were mounting but apart from that he had no clear insight into his father's finances.

'God's wounds! It is grossly churlish of you to be so dilatory, Henry, that I must send a servant to remind you that I expressly commanded you to attend me at two o'clock.'

'I beg your forgiveness, sire. I was in the chapel,' Henry replied respectfully.

'Think not that your devotion to your prayers excuses you or finds favour with me,' the Earl snapped. The boy was forever idling in the chapel and it irritated him. He considered himself a devout man and attended his religious duties assiduously but there were temporal duties which also demanded time and attention and his son seemed for the most part incapable of realising what was expected of him both in the matters of the estate and his position as Warden of the Marches. Due to Henry's health and inexperience old Surrey still maintained control of Wardenship duties and he oversaw Henry's progress in any undertaking closely. He feared however that Henry was neither an apt nor enthusiastic pupil.

Henry didn't reply but waited for his father to speak. Anything he said would, he knew from experience, only increase the Earl's irritation.

'You are aware that my lord Cardinal is greatly concerned that a suitable marriage be contracted for you.' The Earl indicated the pile of documents set out on the table before him. 'We have both been working diligently towards that end since that misguided dalliance and your return from court.'

Henry felt the blood rush to his cheeks, remembering the public humiliations he'd suffered at the hands of both his father and Wolsey, but he nodded his agreement.

'It has at last been decided that you will marry the Lady Mary Talbot when negotiations with my lord of Shrewsbury are completed satisfactorily. You are both now of age.'

Henry stared at him in silent horror, shock and revulsion robbing him of speech. He had given little thought or care to whom he was to be married – until this moment. There had to be a marriage, there had to be an heir to the Earldom of Northumberland but . . . *Mary Talbot!* He had disliked her and she in turn had despised him. They had quarrelled incessantly and he had been greatly relieved when the betrothal had been broken off and she had returned home to her father.

'Have you nothing to say, Henry?' the Earl demanded testily.

Henry swallowed hard. 'My lord, I beg of you . . . That lady bears only . . . malice towards me and I . . . I have no liking for her.'

The Earl got to his feet slowly, leaning heavily on a carved cane and wincing. 'You were but children then. Now you are both of age and I trust have the sense to be aware of your responsibilities. The Lady Mary is mindful of her father's wishes and of the time and effort my lord Cardinal has spent in bringing this matter to a satisfactory conclusion.'

'I doubt not that that is the case, sire, but . . .'

The Earl glared at his eldest son. 'There will be no prevarication, Henry! Do you wish to subject us both to my lord Cardinal's displeasure again? Do you wish the King to think

you ungrateful, resentful and even rebellious? When the con-
tractual arrangements have been completed you will marry the
Lady Mary.'

Henry bowed his head so his father would not see the anger
in his eyes. Wolsey was not content with parting him from
Anne, humiliating and banishing him. In this choice of a wife it
was obvious that the Cardinal's malevolence was to continue,
causing him more pain and unhappiness – yet what could
he do?

The Earl had resumed his seat; the interview was at an end
and so Henry left. He would seek out his mother and plead
with her to mediate with his father on his behalf.

Chapter Twenty-Eight

———•◦◦•———

THE COUNTESS HAD BEEN expecting the visit from her eldest son. She was fully aware of his feelings towards Mary Talbot and knew he would view marriage to her with deep aversion, although she also knew he had little choice in the matter. She was seated in her solar with her ladies when Henry arrived; instantly she dismissed her women and indicated that he should sit. After kissing her hand in greeting he selected a brocade-covered faldstool close to the carved stone fireplace.

The news had chilled him to the bone and he sat as close to the leaping flames as was prudent. The chamber was warm and smelled sweetly of the herbs that had been strewn on the rushes covering the floor and cast upon the fire. The heavy tapestries that covered the walls kept out the worst draughts and their bright colours lent the room a cheerful ambience, but Henry noticed none of these comforts.

'I assume from your countenance that your father has informed you of the lord Cardinal's decision,' she said quietly, thinking how drawn and dejected he looked. She could remember as if it were yesterday the shock she'd received when he'd arrived home from court. She had gone out into the courtyard to greet the small party and was horrified to see her son lying on a litter, semi-conscious. He had become so emaciated that she had been certain he could not stand and his face beneath the dust and grime that covered them all was deathly pale, his lips dry and cracked. Despite the fact that the day had been warm and he had been covered by a rough blanket he had been shivering uncontrollably. After but a few seconds she had realised that he was utterly disorientated. He had not known who she was or that he was home and she had feared he would not live for much longer. He'd come home broken in both body and spirit and she had overseen his long and arduous recovery with the greatest care. She sighed heavily; she was beset with many anxieties of late and was beginning to feel the weight of the years upon her. Beneath her green velvet and gold lace hood her hair was now grey, her complexion was dull and each day there seemed to be more lines at the corners of her eyes. On her hands, carefully folded into the wide sleeves of her forest-green gown, were dark spots that had come with increasing age.

'My lady mother, I . . . I cannot contemplate marriage with the Lady Mary. I beg of you to speak to my lord father, to intercede . . .'

'Henry, do you think that I have not already done so? I know of your incompatibility, your . . . animosity . . . towards the Lady Mary but I fear there is nothing I can say or do to change the course of events.' Her grey eyes hardened. 'It is the will of the Cardinal – and therefore that of our sovereign lord the King.'

Henry looked at her pleadingly. 'Why does Thomas Wolsey continue to torment me thus?'

His mother's lips tightened. 'Why does he continue to torment *us*, Henry? Because he is of low birth but has risen to great heights. No matter how powerful and wealthy he is, he cannot forget that fact. And he is fully aware of the scornful mistrust with which the old and noble families of the realm view him. He seeks every opportunity to heap humiliations upon our heads.'

Henry could only nod in agreement, feeling suddenly very weary. 'So there is nothing that can be done?'

The Countess rose and crossed to his side, her heart heavy at this latest indignity to be inflicted upon her eldest son and he so ill equipped to deal with it. She laid a hand on his shoulder. 'Henry, age is coming quickly upon your father and bringing with it many worries and failing health. I fear the debts that have been incurred are weighing too heavily upon him, and I beg of you, do not add to his increasing burdens by refusing to countenance this marriage to the Lady Mary.' Her voice was uncharacteristically pleading and her desperation shocked her son.

'You know I would do nothing to anger him or to bring down the King's displeasure upon him, but . . .'

The Countess could see in his dark eyes the conflicting emotions: respect and concern for his father, deep affection for his mother and despair at the future descending on him. She tried to bolster his spirits. 'It is many years since you have seen the Lady Mary, Henry. She was little more than a child then and of an age where childish emotions and those of a young woman are in daily and sometimes hourly conflict. You may now find her much changed. She may be more accomplished, more graceful and of a more... amiable... disposition. Perhaps you will become amenable to her; in time there could even be affection between you. Let us wait and see how the matter progresses for, as you are aware, my lord of Shrewsbury drives a hard bargain and can be stubborn.'

Henry nodded, praying that she was right that the negotiations would be prolonged and perhaps not come to fruition at all. He doubted that Mary Talbot had changed or that there would ever be any affection between them.

His mother resumed her seat. There was nothing more she could say or do to help. She glanced towards the window to where the pale autumn sun had broken through the ragged clouds. 'The weather is clearing, would not some time spent with your falcons benefit you, Henry?'

He followed her gaze, aware she was trying to lighten his spirits. He smiled at her. 'Perhaps I shall go down to the mews to see how they fare. If the wind has abated I shall ride out.'

She nodded, relieved.

Norham Castle, Northumberland

Henry reluctantly left Warkworth two days later. He was obliged to preside over a Warden Court at Norham for his two most trusted lieutenants, Sir Thomas Tempest and Sir Roger Lassells, had recently rounded up the brigands who had been terrorising the people in that area. The wagons had left the previous day although Henry had informed his mother that he intended to stay only one night at Norham. The Countess had agreed that was sensible, knowing that the castle was in a poor state of repair.

After a long hard ride Henry and his escort of retainers crossed the drawbridge and entered the castle at the West Gate. He immediately became aware of the activity in the inner ward and squared his shoulders. He did not take any pleasure in these courts but as Lord Warden it was his duty to preside, judge and pass sentence upon the offenders.

He dismounted stiffly and drew his cloak more tightly about his body. It was a bleak day heavy with autumnal damp and mist and the obvious dilapidation of the buildings was apparent. He would find little in the way of comfort here, he mused, save that which had been brought from Warkworth.

Sir Thomas Tempest ushered him into the great hall and towards the chair that had been set upon the dais beneath the canopy of estate. The room was already thronged with people. 'Is it your wish, my lord, that the prisoners be brought before you now or do you wish to rest and take some refreshement after your journey?'

Henry shook his head. He liked and respected Sir Thomas, who was in his thirties, tall and muscular and a hardened veteran of border warfare. 'I shall take some wine, that is all, Sir Thomas, thank you. I would have this court over with speedily for I intend to return to Warkworth on the morrow.'

The wine was brought and the proceedings were formally opened. Henry stared stonily at the brigands who were brought one by one before him. They were all hard, brutal men for whom he felt no pity. Their names were familiar to him now for their families seemed to be permanently engaged in the pernicious practice of reiving; many of their kin had been brought before him on previous occasions: Robinsons, Rawes, Andersons, Shaftoes and Hoghtons. Their crimes were read out and witnesses called to give testimony. He listened in grim silence to their perjurious words of defence and then pronounced each verdict.

'Guilty of March Treason,' he stated coldly, the penalty for which was death, either by hanging or beheading, although he determined to be on his way back to Warkworth when the executions were carried out.

He was relieved when the last case was brought before him. He was cold, hungry, weary and sickened by the seemingly neverending list of their barbaric crimes.

'Nicholas Clarke, accused of stealing and butchering a sheep, the property of one William Wakeham, farmer,' Sir Thomas read out.

Henry nodded as a young man of an age with himself was brought before him. He was very poorly dressed, unlike some of the men on whom he had already passed sentence. His tunic and breeches were of dirty, torn homespun, but he had none of their sullen defiance and he was obviously very afraid.

'What say you to the charge laid against you?' Henry demanded quietly, leaning slightly forward in his chair.

The young man fell to his knees, snatching off a grubby woollen cap. 'My lord, the animal was already dead. I found it lying beneath a hedge; it was barely more than a lamb and had been killed by some other animal. I swear to you, my lord, that I did not steal and butcher it.'

'There was no witness to the fact that the animal was already dead?' Henry asked.

'No, my lord, I fear not. I . . . I saw it there and . . . the bairns are starving. We . . . we buried the youngest a week since. I am a poor man, sire, poorer still after what little I had was taken from me by that same Richard Shaftoe who stood trial this day.'

Henry's expression changed. 'You have suffered at that brigand's hands?'

Clarke nodded. 'I have nothing left, sire, I swear! He took everything! I took the animal for meat to help feed my wife and the bairns we have left.'

'How many children are there?'

'Two, my lord, and they needed food and I . . . I had nothing! I could do nothing . . .' His voice cracked with emotion.

Henry nodded; it was not an unfamiliar tale. It reminded him forcibly of the plight of Will Chatton and his family after the reivers had descended upon their small farm. Having just seen how little remorse Richard Shaftoe had shown for his crimes, Henry tended to believe Clarke. The man had not been called as a witness against Shaftoe because he himself was on trial. It seemed only too likely that he had not set out to steal the sheep; he had seen an opportunity to keep his wife and children from dying of starvation and seized it. Henry had witnessed so much petty larceny in the palaces of London – expensive trinkets taken and slipped into the pockets of those who could well afford to pay for them and no case ever brought against them – yet Nicholas Clarke was on trial for his life for the 'crime' of trying to prevent his family from dying.

Henry turned to his lieutenant. 'Sir Thomas, is the man Wakeham present?'

'He is, my lord,' Sir Thomas replied, pointing to a stout middle-aged farmer and indicating that he step forward.

'Master Wakeham, you brought this charge, what evidence have you?' Henry demanded.

'My lord, one of my lads came upon him carrying the carcass of the animal on his shoulders. He knew it belonged to me by my mark on its rump and knew that Clarke owned no such beast. He brought the news to me and when I went to Clarke's cottage I found him in the act of butchering it.'

Henry leaned back in the chair. 'So, Master Wakeham, you have no evidence that the accused deliberately stole and killed the animal, only that he was caught making off with the carcass?'

The farmer, his florid complexion deepening a shade, looked obdurate. 'My lord, I found him butchering it and sheep-stealing is a heinous crime,' he said stubbornly.

'It is, if indeed that was the case, but I am inclined in this instance to show leniency for there is grave doubt in my mind that the animal was alive when the accused came upon it.' Henry directed his attention to the younger man. 'Nicholas Clarke, I believe you, but in law the animal, even though dead, was not your property and you had no right to carry away its carcass. However, I am mindful of your circumstances and your motive and therefore I shall not exact the prescribed punishment. Instead you will pay Master Wakeham in kind for the beast. You will labour for him at whatever tasks he demands, without payment, for a period of two weeks. That is my judgement, these proceedings are now at an end and the court concluded,' he stated firmly.

There was silence in the hall for a few seconds as Henry rose, then the murmuring began. He ignored it and turned to Sir Thomas, who was looking rather bemused. 'Bring the man Clarke to me, Sir Thomas, when this assembly has dispersed.'

The older man nodded. It was rare that a case of sheep-stealing ended thus and yet he could understand Lord Henry's decision. The evidence against Clarke had been hearsay and inconclusive and therefore his lordship was right not to demand that the man pay with his life.

Henry had finished his meagre meal and was endeavouring to warm himself by the spluttering fire that burned in the hearth when Sir Thomas entered his chamber, followed by Nicholas Clarke.

'The man Clarke, my lord,' Sir Thomas announced.

Again the young man fell to his knees before Henry. 'My lord, I thank thee with all my heart for your mercy!'

'I could not in all conscience sentence you to death upon such evidence. Pray arise.'

'My lord, you are a noble and merciful Warden,' Clarke continued, getting to his feet.

Henry waved him into silence. 'You will labour willingly and freely for Master Wakeham for two weeks?'

'I will, my lord, I thank you.'

Henry nodded. 'After that arrangements will be made to transport you and your family to Alnwick, where employment will be found for you in my father the Earl's household. Have you any skill other than husbandry?'

If Sir Thomas looked surprised at this announcement, the young man was completely overcome by his good fortune. He broke down, falling yet again to his knees.

'Master Clarke, I beg you to compose yourself,' Henry said quietly. All he was offering was a safe but very minor position as a common labourer in the gardens or stable block for it would have been pointless to have spared the man and then left him and his family to starve over the winter months.

'I . . . I have not, my lord, but my wife . . . she is skilled in weaving rushes into baskets and matting.'

Henry nodded. 'Items which are always of use in any household. Go now and tell your goodwife that her skill and fortitude will be rewarded.'

'May the Good Lord bless and preserve you for your charity and mercy, my lord. We will offer prayers for you each and every day, I swear!'

Henry managed a smile. He would need their prayers for the prospect of marriage to Mary Talbot and his life thereafter looked increasingly bleak.

Beverley, Yorkshire

Did he really own the two-storeyed, half-timbered house in the narrow lane in the shadow of the great minster? Will thought as he came within sight of home that October evening. The fact never ceased to amaze him, nor that he was now a respected merchant and the burghers and members of the town's guilds greeted him cordially. His clothes were of good quality although of sober cut, his boots and gauntlets of leather, as were the saddle and trappings of his horse. He was able to provide a fine home and a secure future for Joanna and his son, Edward. Joanna now had two servants to help her in the house and a woman who did the laundering.

His sister Meg had come to live with them last year, at Joanna's request, for Meg was now just eighteen and Joanna had said she would be better able to find a good husband in a town such as Beverley than in a small village like Lund. His brother had recently married and now lived and worked a few miles from Lund. John's wife's family were farmers and as they had no sons had welcomed his brother. John and his wife had been delighted with the sum he had sent as a wedding gift. He was able to make sure his mother and Thomas Tamford lived in comfort in their advancing years. Indeed fate had smiled on him but he never forgot that it was due in the main to his time with Lord Henry and his chance meeting with Robert Aske.

He gave his horse into the charge of his groom, who led it away to be stabled, crossed the narrow yard and let himself in through the back door of the house.

'Will, we did not expect you home this early, supper is not ready,' Meg greeted him, smiling. She had grown into a pretty, slender girl with glossy brown hair confined beneath her hood, clear grey eyes and a fresh complexion. She had benefited greatly from Joanna's influence and example in her manners, speech and dress, Will mused. The gown that matched her hood was stylish and the colour suited her. He doubted it would be long before he would be asked for her hand in marriage for she had suitors aplenty amongst the sons of Beverley's merchants.

'My business with Master Hartley was concluded speedily and then I met Master Aske who had news from London, news I would like to discuss with Joanna. Where is she, Meg?'

Meg put down the dish she was holding; she liked to supervise young Amy in the kitchen to allow Joanna to spend more time with little Edward. 'Where she always is at this hour, Will. Upstairs with Edward.'

Will removed his cloak and hat and went up to find his wife. The small solar was immediately above the kitchen, the window overlooking the street, and he always felt a sense of pride and satisfaction when he entered it. The furniture was of solid dark oak and heavily carved, there were painted cloths on the walls and a good fire burned in the hearth. The polished pewter plate and jugs set out on the table and cupboard reflected the firelight and the rush matting on the floor was clean for Joanna insisted it was changed regularly. He felt the familiar surge of happiness as his gaze rested on his wife, who was kneeling on the floor holding his son's little arms as he attempted to take a step towards her. She was more beautiful now than when he'd first set eyes on her, he thought. Her skin seemed to glow and her cheeks were flushed with the heat from the fire. Her gown was finer than anything she had owned when they were first married and around her neck she wore a gold chain suspended from which was a river pearl. He'd given it to her when his son had been born.

'Is he not a little young to be trying to walk?' he asked, smiling.

'Will! How you startled me, I did not hear you arrive,' Joanna cried, catching up the child and getting to her feet.

'And how has this little man been today? Not too fractious, I hope.'

The child struggled to be set down and so Joanna sat him on the floor, handing him a carved ivory rattle before she kissed Will. 'No, but I think his teeth are a little painful. Meg went to the apothecary for some oil of cloves and he is happier now.' She sat down in a chair beside him. 'Your business with Master Hartley, it went well?'

'Very well indeed. We agreed a good price for the wine that arrived in Hull last week. I have every hope of being able to provide Meg with a good dowry, one that many a merchant's son will find attractive.'

Joanna nodded her agreement. 'We will find a good man for her, Will. One who is kind and generous and then she will be as happy as we are.'

Will smiled and took her hand. 'When I left Master Hartley, I chanced to meet Master Aske, Joanna.'

'Robert? Where are your manners, Will? Did you not think to bring him home with you for supper? We have not seen him for many months.'

Will nodded. 'I did but he was on his way to York and did not wish to linger. He had news from London.'

Joanna raised her eyebrows questioningly. Any news from London was of interest to her although by the time it reached them it was often weeks old. She had missed the bustling city when she'd first come north with Will and Lord Henry but now she preferred the quieter pace of life in the small market town and the bluntness of speech, openness and fair dealing of the people of the North.

'It concerns Mistress Anne Boleyn.'

'She is well?' Joanna had never forgotten the vivacious dark-haired girl who had attended her wedding with Lord Henry and Lord Arundel or of how cruelly she and Lord Henry had been parted.

'So it would appear. She has returned to court and it seems that she has captured the attention and, er . . . affections of the King himself. Robert told me she is always at his side, that now she has many fine gowns and jewels and that he showers her with costly gifts.'

Joanna's dark eyes narrowed a little. 'You mean he seeks to

take her to his bed as he did her sister?'

Will nodded.

'Has she forgotten Lord Henry?' she asked quietly.

He shrugged. 'I don't know, Joanna. Maybe she has; she is older now and perhaps she realises she will never see him again.'

'I did doubt that she loved him as much as he loved her. And she is happy to have the King's . . . affection?'

'Robert says she is holding him off but that there is great speculation at court as to how long and to what purpose. He said it is reported that she has told him she will not be his mistress but her family is an ambitious one; they will try to persuade her to submit to the King so they will become richer and more powerful.'

Joanna shook her head. 'That is wrong and shameful, Will. Would you encourage Meg to do such a thing so you could increase your wealth?'

'Of course not, but we are simple people. It is how advancement has always been obtained by such as Sir Thomas Boleyn.' He paused. 'Robert had more news.'

'Of Mistress Anne?'

Will shook his head. 'Concerning the King and Queen.'

Joanna frowned, wondering how Queen Katherine felt about her husband's obvious interest and intentions towards Anne Boleyn. She would never stand quietly by if Will treated her in such a way, but had not that poor lady had to 'turn a blind eye', as the people of the North termed it, to the King's other affairs?

Her frown deepened and her anger increased as Will explained to her the 'King's Great Matter'.

'But he has an heir! The Princess Mary is his legitimate child.'

Patiently Will explained why the King feared what would happen if Mary became Queen. That a woman was not strong enough or competent to rule the country alone, that she would have to marry a foreign prince, which was not what King Henry or the people of England desired at all.

'But Queen Katherine may yet have a son,' Joanne argued.

'He does not think so. She is older than the King and is approaching the age when she will be unable to conceive.'

Joanna shook her head sadly. 'So he now seeks to put her aside, poor lady.'

'It is for His Holiness the Pope to decide. Who knows what will happen.'

Suddenly Joanna looked concerned. 'If Robert has heard all of this news, particularly the talk of Mistress Anne and the King, many people in London must know. Lord Henry must also have heard. Oh, Will, how will he feel when he learns of the King's intentions towards Anne? He was so heartbroken and ill when he was forced to leave her.'

Will nodded slowly; he had been wondering this himself. He hadn't seen his former master for two years but he had made it his business to find out how Lord Henry was faring. He'd been reluctant to leave his service but after they had reached Wressle the Countess and her servants had taken over his lordship's care, and as his master had slowly recovered, he'd realised that there was little he could do to help him or to lift the lethargy that held him so deeply in its grip.

'Would you not wish to visit him?' Joanna asked, although she was not happy when he was away from home and was fearful of the reported unrest and violence of the border country.

Will considered it. 'I promised him I would go to him if ever he had urgent need of me but I doubt there is much I can say that would help in this instance. But I shall write to him and see if he wishes me to visit when I next call upon Mam and Thomas. I would willingly ride from York to Alnwick or Warkworth if he wanted me to.'

'If he wishes to see you, Will, I shall not complain of your being away from home for a few more days,' Joanna informed him as she bent to pick up little Edward, who had crawled too close to the fire for his own safety.

Chapter Twenty-Nine

1527
Beverley, Yorkshire

WILL HAD NOT RECEIVED a summons from Lord Henry in reply to his letter. Henry had written thanking him for his concern but begging him not to inconvenience himself by making the arduous journey north for he was about to set out for the castle at Norham again to preside over a Warden Court, to try and sentence the outlaws who had been responsible for the latest instances of reiving in the border country. It was his duty, Henry had written, as Warden of the Eastern Marches, the position he had now taken sole charge of. He had made no mention of Anne Boleyn, the King or Queen Katherine and Will had assumed that he found it too painful a subject to comment on. He himself had made only a passing reference in that letter to the news from London.

Will had wondered at the time how his former master would

cope with the rigours of winter on the Border and the task in hand, given his abhorrence of violence of any kind, but he had heard that Lord Henry had sentenced five to be beheaded for March Treason and five more to be hanged for their crimes before he had returned to Alnwick, so it appeared that he was well able to fulfil his duties no matter how personally distasteful he found them. Will had always respected and admired Lord Henry's quiet courage and deeply held sense of justice.

He recalled that news as he rode home in the warm twilight of the May evening. He had not had word from Lord Henry for many months but he knew his former master was well for Robert Aske had been engaged as his secretary and visited him on his frequent trips north, advising him on certain legal matters. Will had been rather astonished to learn from Robert that he was a cousin of the Earl of Cumberland, which was one of the reasons why Lord Henry had engaged him. In all the years he had known Robert the fact that he was so well connected had never been mentioned. Indeed it was only when he'd congratulated his friend on his appointment that Robert had enlightened him.

It was the young lawyer who had told him that the proposed marriage of Lord Henry to Mary Talbot had been recently revived. Perturbed, Will had reluctantly told himself that there was nothing he could do and that the affairs of such great men as the Earl and his son should be of no concern to a humble merchant like himself. But still, he felt his old master would be far from happy.

When he arrived at the house Joanna greeted him with a kiss as she always did but he could see from her expression that something was troubling her.

'Is Edward well? You look anxious.'

She nodded. 'He is well but a letter has arrived from Lord Henry, Will. A messenger brought it this afternoon and he told me that his lordship is on his way to Topcliffe, that he left Alnwick in great haste. Something must be very wrong, I fear.'

Will quickly broke the seal and scanned the lines. 'You are right, my love. The Earl is dying; by now he may even have taken his last breath. I must go at once to Topcliffe. Lord Henry has not asked me to but . . . but I feel he will have need of some support at this time.'

Joanna embraced him, her dark eyes full of concern. 'Of course you must go to him, Will.'

Will held her close for a few seconds. 'This means that Lord Henry will now become Earl of Northumberland, Joanna, and his responsibilities will be greatly increased.'

She nodded. 'And he is but a young man for such burdens, twenty-five as you are. Amy will prepare you food and wine for the journey. I shall go and speak to her at once.'

Will released her and went to pack the things he would need for the journey. He would go first to Thirsk and then on to Topcliffe. He would not be away from home for very long, he surmised, for the Earl would surely be brought to Beverley and buried in the minster as his forefathers had been.

It was almost dark when he left and as she bade him farewell Joanna could not hide her concern that he would be riding through the night. 'Take great care, Will, please. I shall not rest easy until you are home again.'

'I promise I shall, Joanna. With luck I should reach Thirsk by midday tomorrow. I will rest there and then go on to

Topcliffe. God willing, I shall be with Lord Henry by evening.'

She watched him lead his horse to the end of the lane and then swing himself up into the saddle and urge the animal into a trot. She turned to Meg, who stood at the door with her. 'We must pray that no harm will come to him, Meg. Lord Henry may have need of his support and comfort but so do I . . . I could not bear to lose him.'

Meg nodded as she put her arm around her sister-in-law. 'Don't worry, Joanna. He will do nothing foolhardy. He is still a marcher man at heart.'

Topcliffe Castle, Yorkshire

It was still warm and the road was dusty; the sun was a huge ball of orange fire as it sank slowly in the sky. Will's clothes were travel-stained, his lips dry and his eyes stinging from the dust as he at last rode into the courtyard at Topcliffe. He was weary for he'd ridden hard on the fifty miles to Thirsk and had stopped at an inn there for only a few hours, to rest and water his horse and to take food and ale himself.

It was obvious from all the activity in the courtyard that Lord Henry had arrived. Wagons and carts were still being unloaded, grooms were leading sweating mules and horses away towards the stables and servants were darting in and out, carrying a variety of articles from food to furnishings. He caught the arm of a passing groom.

'Lord Henry is here?'

'Since after noon, he is in his chambers. Who are you and what business have you with his lordship?' the lad asked bluntly, peering at Will suspiciously.

'I am Will Chatton, I was his lordship's squire for many years and my business is of no concern to you. Take the mare to the stables and tend her well; we have been on the road since yesterday evening.'

The lad's expression softened and he became respectful as he took the reins from Will. The story of the young, illiterate son of a poor border farmer who had become Lord Henry's squire and had been with him at court in London, and then subsequently risen to become a wealthy merchant in Beverley was well known. It was an almost unheard-of achievement.

As Will was unfamiliar with Topcliffe he first obtained directions from a steward he found in the great hall and then walked briskly up the carved oak staircase to the upper floor. The passageway, lined with oak panelling, was illuminated by candles in sconces attached to the wall. Its ceiling was painted and at the end was an archway into which was set a door of old and darkened oak. He paused and then knocked sharply; he was ushered inside – after giving his name – by a young man he did not know.

'Lord Henry, I came as quickly as I could. Is there ... news?'

Henry rose from the chair beside the fireplace and Will was taken aback by the change in him. He was thinner and paler, his dark eyes seemed to have sunk and he looked older than his twenty-five years, yet there was an air of what Will could only describe as authority about him.

Henry crossed and clapped him warmly on the shoulder. It surprised him how relieved he felt to see his former squire again. 'Will, I wrote only to inform you. I did not expect you to make the journey here but I confess I am glad to see you

301

again.' Then he frowned. 'The news is . . . distressing I fear. My father is dead. In these last years his strength had failed greatly, and the illness came upon him suddenly two days ago at Wressle.'

'I am sorry to hear it, Lord Henry, it is a bitter blow. Even after all these years I still feel great sadness at the loss of my own father.'

Henry nodded, remembering that night so long ago when he'd ridden at the Earl's side into the valley of Redesdale. How strong and commanding his father had been then and how changed he had become of late, he thought. Reclusive, beset by worry and illness, his temper and memory bitter and short. 'I am now become Sixth Earl of Northumberland and all that title brings with it, Will. And I fear that includes a great many things of which I have scant knowledge or experience, for my father did not see fit to take me into his confidence. The accounts and entailments of the lands and establishments we hold, besides the care and estate of my lady mother, my sister Lady Maud and of course my brothers . . .'

Will nodded. There had never been much affection between Henry and his brothers. Thomas had always been openly envious of Henry's position and now that he had inherited the title and Thomas would be beholden to him for everything, that jealousy was likely to increase. 'Lord Thomas and Lord Ingram are . . . ?' Will hesitated, hoping they were not here.

'At Wressle,' Henry informed him curtly, 'with my mother and sister. Lady Margaret and her husband the Earl of Cumberland are travelling there. My duties as Lord Warden kept me at Alnwick else I would also have been at Wressle. It saddens me greatly that I could not be there with him in his last hours or comfort my mother in her grief.'

'If it pleases you, my lord, I shall remain with you until the funeral. I trust your father is to be buried in Beverley Minster?'

Henry nodded. 'It is the custom within the family and I shall be happy for you to accompany me, but will not your affairs suffer in your absence? It will take time to organise my father's funeral.'

'My lord, I have friends amongst the good burghers of Beverley who will see to any outstanding affairs should it become necessary,' Will assured him firmly.

Henry nodded slowly. 'Then now you must have food and rest for I warrant you have had little of either. Maynard, my Steward of the Household, will see that your needs are attended to.'

Will thanked him and left to seek out Maynard and much-needed sustenance, water to wash away the dust of the roads and a bed for the night. There might be little he could in fact do but he was determined to try to assist the new Earl as much as he could, even if by just being at his side and offering companionship.

Henry resumed his seat and stared wearily into the flames. His life was about to change and tomorrow the full weight of his inheritance would descend upon his shoulders. He was now responsible for the welfare and support of not only his family, but also of the hundreds of people in his household, the many thousands of tenants on his estates, for the upkeep of all his castles and houses and the maintenance of law and order on the Border – and all when he had no clear and precise idea of his financial situation.

He stood up and poured wine from a silver jug into a goblet and drank deeply. To face whatever tomorrow would bring tonight he needed to sleep soundly. He prayed that his health, stamina and courage would not fail him. He felt far older than his twenty-five years.

Chapter Thirty

IT WAS MID AFTERNOON the following day before Will saw Henry again. He was aware that a messenger by the name of Ambrose had arrived that morning for he'd been crossing the courtyard at the time. He'd instantly recognised the Cardinal's livery and had watched with foreboding as, with a show of arrogant self-importance, Ambrose announced that he had letters for the Earl from Cardinal Wolsey and demanded he be taken to his lordship immediately.

Will found the new Earl pacing the floor of his private chamber, greatly agitated.

'Your lordship, what has happened? Has it to do with the arrival of that man Ambrose?' Will asked bluntly.

Henry stopped pacing and thrust the sheet of parchment he was clutching towards Will. His dark eyes were bright with anger, his hands shook and his expression was hard. 'Read it, Will!' he commanded.

In all the years he had known Lord Henry Will had never

seen him so furious. He scanned the lines quickly and then stopped, unable to believe what he had just read. Slowly he read the letter in its entirety and then handed it back as waves of pity and outrage surged through him.

'My lord, this . . . this . . . is *monstrous*! What right has he to forbid you to attend your own father's funeral? What right has this . . . this low-born son of a merchant to order you, one of the greatest earls in the kingdom, to take no part in the arrangements?'

Henry threw the parchment on the table and resumed pacing the floor. 'He has no right, no right at all, but he seeks to further humiliate me because he cannot forget that I once sought to marry without his consent!' he cried bitterly.

'My lord, you must refuse to obey him! It is within your power to defy him. No common man would tolerate such heartless, arrogant interference and no common man would think the worse of you for doing so. When this . . . this outrageous insult becomes known they will applaud and support you.' Will shook with the force of anger that possessed him. 'He has become so proud, so . . . besotted by his power and what he perceives to be his own greatness that he has forgotten that the men of the North will flock to the banner of the House of Percy. I myself will go out and rally them to your cause, my lord. I beseech you to defy him, to stand firm against him. He *cannot* treat you like this!'

'He *can*, Will, because he has such influence over the King. He can persuade the King to agree with him in these demands, and to defy the King is treason.'

'If King Henry is even aware of Wolsey's instructions to you,' Will retorted. 'Write to the King himself, my lord, I beg you.'

For an instant Henry was tempted by Will's words but slowly he shook his head and slumped down in the chair beside the table, his anger diminishing as he remembered the other letters of instruction that lay before him on the table. 'I . . . I cannot, Will. I am certain that the King knows of this. I am sure that my lord Cardinal has informed him of *all* the matters concerning my father's demise.'

Will shook his head in disbelief but Henry handed him a sheaf of papers and indicated he should read them.

'You are a merchant, you have a good grasp of figures. When you read these you will understand why I have no alternative but to submit to the Cardinal's demands,' Henry said.

One by one Will read them slowly and he felt his anger give way to incredulity. The debts Henry's father had left almost defied belief. Seven thousand pounds was owed to private individuals, mainly merchants, but the debt to the Exchequer totalled over ten thousand pounds: in all the enormous sum of *seventeen* thousand pounds. He went over the figures again carefully. As far as he could see there was only the paltry sum of fourteen pounds left with which to pay for the funeral. In addition Wolsey had informed his lordship that he had instructed his brother-in-law, the Earl of Cumberland, to take charge of the funeral and act as executor of the estate and that when the maintenance of the Dowager Countess and her unmarried children had been attended to, the Cardinal would himself oversee the Earl's expenses.

'My lord, it is hard to conceive that . . . that so much is owed.'

Henry nodded dejectedly, his anger now spent. 'I was not fully aware how matters stood.'

Will was still dazed at the mountainous debt. 'What is to be done?'

'I have no choice but to pledge the plate from Wressle, Leckinfield and here to the monks at St Mary's in York to pay for the funeral. After that I must find some means to pay off the debt to the Exchequer,' Henry replied, although he had no idea how he was ever to accomplish this.

'If there is anything I can do to help . . . I have some gold put aside . . .' Will offered. His small hoard was but a drop in the ocean compared to Henry's debts but he was willing to part with it if need be. Now he was beginning to understand why the Earl was utterly powerless to defy the Cardinal. He was little more than a pauper beholden to the State for everything from the roof over his head to the food on his table and the clothes on his back. Never had a father left such a terrible legacy to his son.

Henry smiled but shook his head. 'I thank you for your offer, Will, but I fear what gold you have would not alleviate the situation I find myself in.'

'It is an *impossible* situation, my lord,' Will agreed. How, with such vast estates, revenues and resources at his disposal, had the deceased Earl managed to succeed in virtually ruining his son and heir?

'And one which is likely to grow worse, I suspect. As he states, my lord Cardinal intends to supervise my expenditure and accounts personally and I fear that does not bode well for my future dealing with him.'

'My lord, I would urge you to take care in any dealings you have with him; he employs a great many spies. Ambrose is almost certainly one of them and there could already be others in your household who are in his pay. The lowliest of servants report back to him.' Will had become aware of Wolsey's network of informers during the time he'd spent in London with his lordship. On one occasion he'd overheard Markham, a minor servant of the Boleyns, reporting to the Cardinal's secretary a conversation that had taken place between Sir Thomas and Hal Norris.

'I shall be watchful, I promise,' Henry agreed, frowning. He shivered involuntarily as he thought of the extent of Wolsey's power and his own dire predicament. 'No doubt once the period of mourning is over there will be demands that my marriage be speedily contracted.'

Will had forgotten that in the light of the current terrible situation. 'I did hear that it was to be to the Lady Mary Talbot.'

Henry managed a bitter smile. 'Mayhap that lady has improved in both appearance and demeanour,' he said quietly as if to himself.

Will didn't reply. He felt heartily sorry for the young Earl.

Henry's emotions had been lacerated by the day's events and now he felt cold and exhausted. 'I shall await the arrival of my lord of Cumberland and then I shall travel north, to my castle at Prudhoe. There is no need for you to remain here, Will. Return to your family and your affairs of trade. Joanna and your son are well? Forgive me for not enquiring after their welfare before this.'

'That is of small matter, my lord, and they are both well,' Will replied amiably. However, he had no wish to leave his former master without companionship in the present circumstances. 'If it pleases you I shall remain until you depart for Prudhoe, then I shall return home.'

'Thank you, Will. I shall have need of a . . . friend,' Henry replied, thinking back to the times when as young boys they had gone hawking together, ignorant of what the future held for them both, watching, spellbound, the falcon's stoop. Today he felt more akin to its hapless prey, frozen in the face of irresistible power.

Henry Clifford, Earl of Cumberland, arrived with a small entourage two days later and as they were ushered into the young Earl's chambers, Will recognised Brian Higden, a servant of Wolsey and, William Worme, the chief steward from Wressle, a small, dark-haired man with features Will thought resembled those of a weasel. He had little liking for either. Quietly Will withdrew to the back of the chamber where he could observe and listen without drawing too much attention to himself.

'Greetings, Henry. My condolences upon your father's death.' Henry Clifford, a tall, well-built man in his mid thirties and the first earl of his line, was cordial.

'I thank you, brother-in-law. How fares my sister, Lady Margaret, and my lady mother?'

'Both are well but much grieved by their loss. You have received my lord Cardinal's instructions?'

Henry indicated that Clifford be seated and duly handed over the letters, after instructing that wine and ale be brought and served.

'It is indeed a sorry state of affairs, Henry, but we are here to see that the Cardinal's instructions are carried out to the letter. I have spoken at some length to the Dowager Countess and to your brothers and it is agreed that after the funeral, which will take place in two weeks, they will return with me and reside in Cumberland until my lord Cardinal's pleasure concerning them is known.'

Henry could only nod his assent.

Will stood with his back to the wall as the discussion continued, watching both Higden and Worme closely. Every word of this conversation would be reported back to Wolsey and he was relieved that his former master was saying very little and giving away nothing as to his true feelings. Although Worme was the steward at Wressle Will was almost certain he was in Wolsey's pay and he despised the man for his treachery.

Clifford did not stay long at Topcliffe but departed the following morning. Henry went down to the courtyard to bid him farewell, relieved but still angered by the injustice of the situation. 'I wish you a safe journey, my lord, and tell my lady mother of my deep regret that I am unable to pay my respects to her.'

'I will make sure she is in possession of all the facts, Henry,' Clifford promised. 'There is much to discuss with the Dowager Countess. Farewell.'

Henry watched them ride out and as he turned away he smiled ruefully at Will, who had also been watching the group's departure. 'I cannot say I am sorry to see them leave.'

Will nodded his agreement. He was glad the visit was at an end and that Worme and Higden had left with the Earl of Cumberland. Now his lordship could journey to Prudhoe and he could return home. He had no stomach for the intrigues and machinations of the Cardinal and his spies.

Chapter Thirty-One

Hever Castle, Kent

EVEN THOUGH THE ARBOUR'S shade was deep she could feel the heat of the sun on her back as its rays penetrated the patterned foliage. Her hood was uncomfortably heavy; she wished she could remove it and expose her neck and shoulders to the cooler air.

She folded the letter and stared out across the rose garden. In the strong July sunlight the blooms were numerous and full blown, their perfume filling the still, bright air. Mingled with their scent was that of lavender and rosemary and the bees were industriously hovering amongst the bushes, their droning virtually the only discernible sound. She closed her eyes, thankful for once for the tranquillity which surrounded her – a far cry from the constant chatter and activity of court.

She had come home to Hever expressly for a brief respite. It was a tactic she had used before when Henry Tudor's impatient ardour became too passionate. She needed time to gather her thoughts and resolve, for the game she was playing demanded all her tenacity, shrewdness and strength of character and the stakes were giddily high. If she played skilfully and successfully the prize would be the Consort's crown. Once she would have been content to have become Countess of Northumberland, she mused. Had she loved Harry Percy then? She believed so. He had come into his inheritance now his father had died, but she'd recently heard he was deeply in debt. There would be no costly gowns or gifts for his Countess when he eventually married, she surmised, whereas she was possessed of jewels and a wardrobe the equal of the Queen's own, although infinitely more fashionable and stylish. Katherine frequently wore crimson and purple at the same time, colours which, in Anne's opinion, clashed violently and did little to enhance the Queen's sallow complexion.

When she had agreed to marry Harry Percy she had been very young and new to court, and though she had loved him she now thought those feelings had been a passing flight of fancy, possibly engendered by the opportunity to become a countess and thereby gain her father's approval. To prove herself more astute than Mary. Mary had finally fallen from favour and had now been cast aside just as she had told Mary she would be, as had the King's other women. Poor Harry, to be banished to the cold, inhospitable North and its state of constant violent turmoil and to what would appear a life of penury. How he must hate it.

She turned her thoughts to her own predicament. She had caught the King's attention and that fact had at first astonished, excited and amused her a little. She had been flattered by his attentions – for who would not be? He was handsome, highly intelligent and learned, athletic, all-powerful and inspired awe in everyone. Indeed he was veritably God-like. She had completely captivated him; he constantly sought her company and showered her with gifts; it was a heady experience and one that had regained her father's approval. But when she had become aware that Henry was seriously questioning the validity of his marriage to Katherine and was desperate for a male heir she had begun to realise the opportunity and power that his desire for her might afford her. All her life she had sought to please her family, had been prepared to submit to be used as a pawn in the game so many noblemen played. She could now see before her a way to shape her own destiny, something few women of her station in life ever achieved, and she had the will, the intelligence, the education and the experience to succeed. She had resolved that she would not follow in her sister's footsteps. She would not yield to Henry's desires, she would not become his mistress – for what was to be gained by that? No, she had decided to aim for the ultimate prize. And why not? Had she not been brought up with princesses and archduchesses in the palaces of Europe? Was not her uncle the Duke of Norfolk, one of the most influential men in the country? Was she not more graceful, elegant and accomplished than any other lady either at court or indeed in the entire realm? Henry had already determined to put Katherine aside so why should she not become his new Queen? She was not a foreigner who might try to influence the King in matters of policy but an Englishwoman with the interests of his subjects at heart. And she was young and healthy. She could give him sons, something Katherine had failed to do, and he desperately needed a legitimate son and heir for the stability of the Crown.

She leaned against the cool stone back of the seat and reread his letter, delivered only an hour ago. She smiled; he hated being apart from her. With Henry absence did indeed make the heart grow fonder. 'Give yourself up, body and soul, to me,' he wrote. 'I wish myself at this time private with you,' he continued, and begged her to return with all possible speed. She folded the parchment again, smoothing it gently with her long, slim fingers. She would *not* give herself up 'body and soul' until she was certain her goal was within her grasp: the security of marriage and the crown. But it was nearer now than it had been six months ago, she thought with a degree of satisfaction.

Only last month Henry had told his wife bluntly that they must separate and that he had sent to Rome for an annulment because she had been his brother's wife. Anne frowned; of course it had been a disastrous setback that the Emperor Charles's troops had sacked Rome and imprisoned the Pope, but Henry had sent Wolsey to France to seek King Francis's help to restore Pope Clement and obtain the annulment. Henry had assured her that it would not be long now before the matter was resolved.

Her deliberations were interrupted by the sound of voices and dogs barking. Reluctantly she rose, smoothing down the satin skirt of her gown, tucking a stray wisp of dark hair under her pearl- and diamond-encrusted hood. She had reached the pathway between the rose beds when she observed her brother approaching. She smiled with genuine pleasure. The King was on his summer progress with the Queen and was at Beaulieu, but her brother was no longer a Groom of the Chamber and had not been required to accompany them.

'So, you have retreated again, Anne. You are becoming quite the anchoress. Surely you are not about to trade masters?' George greeted her, kissing her affectionately on the cheek.

She laughed at his audacity. 'Oh, have no fear, George, my resolve to serve my temporal lord does not falter. But I find it both prudent and restful to spend some time alone.'

George's smile was full of admiration and pride. There was no one more attractive, vivacious or as richly attired at court than Anne; there was no one more ambitious either, except perhaps himself, he thought. Thanks to her influence their father was no longer plain Sir Thomas Boleyn but Viscount Rochford. Anne was the star on which the fortune of the Boleyns was ascending – if both she and her family could outwit that sly old toad Wolsey.

She tucked her hand through his arm as they walked back towards the castle. 'My lord Cardinal has at last departed for France, I hear.'

George nodded. 'I wonder how he will fare with Francis, who is no fool.'

'Well, I hope, for neither has he any love for the Emperor Charles,' she replied sharply. 'It is to be hoped that the Cardinal can readily obtain his support for the King grows more impatient each day, as do I.'

George frowned as he pushed his gold and black brocade bonnet back from his forehead. 'Would that Wolsey's help were not required in this matter. Do not forget that both Father and I were dispatched ignominiously from court under my lord Cardinal's Eltham Ordinances.'

Anne nodded her agreement. Wolsey had undertaken to reform the royal household which, he had persuaded the King, had grown too large and had become too expensive. The numbers of courtiers and their retinues of servants had to be greatly reduced for the sake of 'economy', Wolsey had declared. William Compton, Francis Bryan and Nicholas Carew – all relations or friends of the Boleyns – had also had to leave, but it was obvious to anyone of even slight intelligence that the Cardinal was removing from court a faction over which he could exercise little power. 'I have not forgotten,' she replied firmly.

'The Cardinal is no friend of ours, he mistrusts and hates us,' George reminded her.

Anne's expression hardened and her dark eyes were filled with bitterness. 'He has always despised and scorned me, George. I do not forget that he once termed me "a foolish girl of little estate". Such an insult will never leave me. But, unfortunately, we need his help to obtain the annulment. Without that nothing can be accomplished.'

George looked down at her and smiled wryly. 'You have not forgotten Harry Percy entirely then, Anne?'

Her dark eyes held his gaze steadily. No, she had not forgotten Harry Percy entirely but the past was behind her now, it was the future that demanded all her attention. 'I have not forgotten the hurt and humiliation the Cardinal heaped upon us both and for no good cause other than to serve his own devices. Anger is as powerful an emotion as love and endures, I think, longer.'

George looked away and they walked in silence until they reached the gate that led into the courtyard. He would go to pay his respects to his mother but first he had a piece of news to impart to Anne.

'You have heard that he is to be married?'

'Harry Percy?'

He nodded. 'To Shrewsbury's youngest daughter, Mary Talbot, to whom he was betrothed years ago. But I also heard she brings him no dowry and he is in sore need of money for they say his father's debts have reduced him to a state of insolvency. My lord Cardinal is now to oversee the accounts and will keep a tight grip on the purse strings. I fear it is a poor and empty title the Lady Mary has aspired to. One wonders how she views her predicament, but as her father has proved so parsimonious, she can hardly complain. There are many who would refuse to take her without a dowry for it is well known that Shrewsbury is an affluent man.'

Anne didn't reply. She barely knew Mary Talbot for my lord of Shrewsbury's daughter had rarely been at court, but she remembered a plain, badly dressed girl with few accomplishments and now, it seemed, no dowry either, which she must find humbling. She had not known that Harry had once been betrothed to her.

'Why was the betrothal broken off?' she asked her brother. George had been at court for many years and knew all the gossip.

George shrugged. 'Mayhap the Lords Shrewsbury and Northumberland could not agree upon the conditions. Mayhap even then Shrewsbury was proving obdurate in the matter of the dowry. Mayhap the couple had a great aversion to each other, who knows?' he replied, thinking bitterly of the 'great aversion' he had for his own wife Jane.

Poor Harry, Anne thought, how their paths had diverged. He had been a quiet, sensitive, honourable and generous young man. Far less worldly-wise and cynical than George. He had obviously been coerced into marrying the dull and dowerless Mary Talbot, while she . . . she would do all in her power to marry the King of England, who adored her. And she knew now, far from being a foolish girl of little estate, her powers were considerable indeed.

Chapter Thirty-Two

Wressle Castle, Yorkshire

HENRY LEANED BACK IN the chair and stared up at the gilded ceiling of the library. It was still his favourite room in the castle and in it, surrounded by the books and illuminated manuscripts his father had amassed, he always found a measure of peace and serenity of spirit. He had sore need of a few hours' respite in this sanctuary today, he thought. The bright sunlight streaming in through the two windows set either side of the circular chamber played upon the wall tapestries, deepening their vivid colours. Dust motes caught in the rays of light danced as they descended slowly to the ground from where the faint aroma of sweet herbs drifted upwards.

He was restless, uneasy both in mind and spirit as he rose and crossed to a window. The early-morning mist that had covered the fields and parkland had been burned off by the intensifying strength of the sun and now a heat haze shimmered over the distant river and its water meadows.

He turned away, plucking nervously at the lace that edged the lawn cuff of his shirt sleeve. Over the embroidered under-shirt he wore a doublet of dark blue velvet trimmed with silver lace, which he was finding increasingly uncomfortable in the warmth of the day. The short sleeveless surcoat and bonnet that matched – a silver filigree brooch anchoring the white plumes – lay on the table beside the empty fireplace. His clothes were not new. Even though this, his wedding day, warranted a new and splendid outfit, there was insufficient money for such things these days.

He was loath to leave the room even though he realised that the minutes were slipping quickly away. George Talbot, Earl of Shrewsbury, had arrived yesterday with the bride and her sister Lady Elizabeth Dacre, but he had no wish to spend longer in their company than was necessary, at least not before the ceremony. He fingered the jewelled dagger he wore at his waist and frowned. Lady Mary Talbot had not improved either in looks or nature as both his mother and he himself had hoped. She was of small stature but had gained in weight. She could still only be described as plain and the pale grey eyes, fringed by those insipid fair lashes, had regarded him with the same cold hostility when he'd welcomed her again to Wressle. Her reply had been curt and lacking entirely in warmth. It was quite obvious that she had as little stomach for this match as he had. He sighed heavily, wondering what her reaction would be when she learned of the pittance the Cardinal was allowing them both to live on; she would have very little to spend on her wardrobe, or anything else for that matter.

The ceremony itself was to be a quiet one in the chapel here at Wressle, with a meal afterwards for such family and friends who were to attend. There would be no sumptuous banquet with jugglers, jesters and musicians to entertain the guests, although this did not greatly concern him. What was causing him embarrassment and shame was the fact that his wedding would not be celebrated in the manner to which his tenants and the local people had become accustomed. There would be no largesse distributed to the poor, no sheep and oxen slaughtered and roasted on spits, no ale and wine freely distributed as there had been when his father, his grandfather and all his forebears had been married. The Cardinal had forbidden such extravagance. In vain he had written pleading for the necessary funds but his pleas had fallen on deaf ears. It was to be so miserly a wedding that a wealthy merchant would have cause to sneer and that was a further public humiliation he must bear.

A squire entered the room, looking a little apprehensive. 'My lord, your guests are assembling in the chapel and your lady mother has sent me to urge you to go down to greet them.'

Henry nodded. His mother, his sister Maud and his brothers had also arrived yesterday. He must put aside his reticence and at least try to show some enthusiasm for the occasion, although he was beginning to panic. He was about to take solemn vows that would bind him for life to a woman he did not love and for whom he had very little liking and there was no way he could avoid it.

He had slept little the previous night, his thoughts turning again and again to the woman he still could not forget: Anne Boleyn. How he wished it was Anne with her dark beauty, her vivacity and wit, her love of music and poetry, her grace and her elegance who was to be his bride. How utterly different she was to the woman who was to become his wife. He had struggled in vain to obliterate the memory of the precious hours they had spent together. He had lost her that day when the Cardinal had so publicly parted them and when the sun set again this evening she would be lost to him for ever. Mary Talbot would be his lawful wife. Trying desperately to control his emotions he picked up his surcoat and bonnet and followed the lad out.

The chapel was cool for it was on the north side of the castle. Its walls were shaded and their thickness kept out the fierce heat of the July sun. It was hung with tapestries depicting religious scenes and the light filtering through the stained-glass windows made rich patterns on the white lace altar cloth. On either side of the altar, resting on angel corbels, stood painted plaster statues of the Virgin and St Cuthbert. In addition to the daylight the chapel was further illuminated by the candles in their tall silver mounts on the altar. Despite the cooler air Henry shivered. His nemesis was drawing ever closer.

The members of his family who had desired and been permitted by the Cardinal to attend were already seated in the richly carved oak pews at the front of the chapel; his mother, his sister Maud and his brothers. His sister Margaret and her husband Henry Clifford, his Uncles William and Jocelyn were absent. A few of the senior household servants stood silently and respectfully at the back of the chapel but as he caught sight of Will Chatton and his wife Joanna he smiled with genuine relief. He had invited Will, who had written back stating that he refused to seek Wolsey's permission to attend the Earl's wedding. He was merely a former servant and would pay all expenses incurred out of his own pocket and so the Cardinal could raise little objection.

Henry strode over to greet them. 'Will, it is good to see you again. I have a need of a friendly face about me this day for Lord Arundel could not be spared from his duties to attend.'

Will smiled back after casting a quick glance at Lord Thomas and Lord Ingram, both of whom were looking sullen and discontented. 'My lord, we are both honoured to be here.'

'Mistress Chatton, you are well? How fares your son?' Henry enquired politely but a little tremulously. The sight of Will's half-Moorish wife with her dark, elongated eyes fringed with sooty lashes and blue-black hair just visible beneath her hood had brought a sudden image of Anne hurtling into his mind.

Joanna managed to smile. She was feeling a little overawed by both the surroundings and the high rank of the wedding party. 'Edward is a fine, healthy boy of two, my lord. We are blessed indeed.'

'You have brought the child with you?' Henry enquired, vaguely wondering if the boy favoured Will or his dark-haired, beautiful mother.

She shook her head. 'We deemed it best to leave him in the care of Will's sister Meg . . . Margaret,' she amended. 'And of course the maids will assist her to care for him. He gives little trouble.'

Before Henry could engage Will in further conversation the bridal party arrived at the door of the chapel and with a word of regret Henry turned away and made his way to the foot of the altar steps where the priests awaited. He tried to concentrate his thoughts on the sanctity of the occasion as Lord Shrewsbury and his daughter took their places beside him, Lady Elizabeth Dacre behind them. He prayed that his responses would be clear, calm and steady. That he would not display by his demeanour or mannerisms the despair he felt. If this was to be the destiny Almighty God had chosen for him then it was his duty to accept it with as much dignity and courage as he could muster.

Joanna slipped her hand into Will's as the priest intoned the opening prayers of the Mass. Will had explained to her why the Earl must wed the Lady Mary but she also knew that he was not entering into this marriage happily or willingly and she felt a great sadness for him. She remembered how joyous had been the day when she had married Will. How much in love, too, Lord Henry had been that day. How different the Lady Mary was to Mistress Anne, she thought. This lady who was to become Countess of Northumberland was small, plump, insipidly plain and was not stylishly dressed at all. Her mouse-brown hair was confined beneath a heavy gable hood of saffron velvet, with lappets of black velvet: colours that did not suit her complexion. Her gown of matching velvet over an ivory satin underskirt was trimmed with gold lace which was of so similar a hue that it did nothing to enhance or embellish its style. Around her neck she wore a necklace of gold and garnet stones. Next to Mistress Anne, Lady Mary would be as a sparrow beside a peacock, she thought. Indeed her own gown and hood were more becoming than the bride's.

Will's thoughts were not on the attire of the bride but on her demeanour. She looked dour, resentful and uncomfortable and he suspected that she too was far from happy with the man she was about to take as her husband. All he could do was pray that in time the Earl and his Countess could find some small measure of affection for he knew his former master would

never love his wife. Henry Percy's heart belonged to Anne
Boleyn.

'Who *is* that lady, my lord husband?' Countess Mary demanded
of Henry as they sat at the table on its raised dais in the great
hall of the castle. This day was proving to be one of the worst
in her life. She had never wanted to marry Henry Percy and
now instead of being fêted as her status demanded she had been
subjected to sparsely furnished chambers, plain food and
inferior wine. Instead of the auspicious wedding attended by
hundreds of guests from all the noble families of the North,
there had been a simple Mass in the small chapel attended by
barely a dozen people. Instead of a lavish banquet, there was
this modest meal. Nor would largesse be given out at the castle
gates, no feast and entertainment be provided for the tenants
and townsfolk. She had married a pauper and as her father had
flatly refused to provide her with a dowry of any sort she could
not complain and that added to her burning shame and resentment. Throughout the meal her new husband had virtually
ignored her, his attention seemed to be entirely focused upon
another woman – a guest – and the fact increased her annoyance.

'She is Mistress Joanna Chatton, the wife of my former
squire. You must remember Will; he was with me for all the
years of my youth. He is now a merchant in Beverley and
has amassed a considerable fortune, so I understand,' Henry
replied, after drinking deeply of his wine. It was the longest
speech he had made to her during the entire meal.

'Indeed, I do remember him,' the Countess replied curtly.
She had had no liking for Will Chatton then, thinking him too

familiar with his master. She cast her husband a surreptitious glance from beneath her pale lashes, still curious to know why Mistress Chatton seemed to fascinate him so. 'She is very comely.'

Henry nodded, signalling that his goblet be refilled. He was drinking too much, but he was beyond caring. 'She fled from Spain where she had lived for most of her life, aboard a ship, disguised as a boy. She swam ashore and Will dragged her from the river in the Pool of London. She was on the point of drowning.'

Mary shuddered at the thought of swimming in the foul waters of the Thames as she directed her gaze at Joanna. It galled her that the young woman was more richly dressed than herself and she a countess. Joanna Chatton's gown was cut in the French style and was of pale blue and silver brocade, trimmed with silver lace. The French hood she wore was of the same material and bordered with tiny seed pearls; her earrings were of silver filigree set with pearls as was the necklace she wore around her slender throat, her large, dark, expressive eyes and glossy blue-black hair gave her an air of mystery and exoticism. As she watched Joanna threw back her head and laughed at something her husband had said and Mary was suddenly reminded of a girl she had seen on the few occasions she had been at court: Mistress Anne Boleyn.

Her pale cheeks flushed with anger and jealousy. So that was why Henry seemed unable to take his eyes off Will Chatton's wife. She was fully aware that some years ago he had made a foolish exhibition of himself over Anne Boleyn and it was now obvious that his passion for her had not diminished. Waves of humiliation washed over her. He must even now be thinking of her. Was he in truth comparing her, his wife, to that . . . that nobody? That daughter of a conniving, grasping, arrogant man who came from mere merchant stock? That granddaughter of a Norfolk tradesman? On the rare occasions when she had spoken to *Mistress* Anne she had found her dismissive and condescending. It was as if *she* were the daughter of an earl and herself little more than a simple maid without title or estate. Those dark, elongated eyes – so like those of Joanna Chatton – had swept appraisingly over her and in them there had been pity mixed with contempt. She did not think Anne Boleyn attractive, witty or clever. In her opinion she was self-absorbed, arrogant and as cunning as a vixen.

She sipped her wine, glancing again at her husband. How did he feel now that the woman he had so foolishly loved had supplanted her sister in the King's affections and maybe even his bed? A shudder of distaste ran through her. This night she must share the same bed as Henry Percy and she found the idea utterly repugnant. It had been impressed upon her that it was her duty to submit to him and bear him children – heirs – but she could barely stomach the thought of it. She took a deeper draught of her wine. This day and the prospect of the ensuing night were proving to be little better than hateful.

Chapter Thirty-Three

<hr />

1528
Norham Castle, Northumberland

NEVER HAD HE FELT so cold, Will thought as he climbed the spiral stone staircase in the Great Tower that led from the vaulted undercroft right up to the battlements where cannons were positioned, their muzzles pointing toward the none-too-distant border with Scotland.

Norham was built at the top of a steep cliff overlooking the River Tweed with a deep ravine on its east side, an excellent position to withstand the forays of border warfare but not the elements. Had he known the castle was in such a poor state of repair he would never have brought his family to stay here but the Earl had invited them to join the Christmas and New Year celebrations, although they had been but a pale shadow of those he remembered from his youth at Alnwick and Wressle when the old Earl had been alive.

All revenues from the Earl's vast estates were still going straight to the Exchequer; there was no money for lavish feasts. By making discreet enquiries accompanied by the exchange of some coins, Will had learned that the Cardinal had instructed that the Earl and Countess were to have paid to them the sum of six shillings and ten pence a week each, little more than an insult considering their position. Out of this the four personal servants they were permitted to wait upon them had to be paid one shilling and sixpence each. The Countess was allowed an insulting forty pounds a year for her wardrobe and jewels. He spent more than that on Joanna and Edward and if Meg's clothes and trinkets were added it would amount to treble the pittance Mary Percy received. Because they were forced to suffer such penury, he had quietly and surreptitiously arranged with the Steward of the Household to pay for his family's board and lodgings himself but he had not humiliated his former master by disclosing this. He had also brought gifts for the Earl and his wife.

Even though he wore a thick woollen shirt beneath his heavy worsted doublet and a cape of felted wool, he felt chilled to the marrow. This winter was one of the harshest he'd ever known, one of the worst in living memory and not only in the north. In London the Thames had frozen to such a degree that Frost Fairs had been held upon it and people had strapped skates made of bone to their feet and skated from one bank to the other. Even the King had ridden his horse across to the opposite bank and back. Despite the fact that Will had paid for extra logs to be brought so the fire in their chamber burned fiercely day and night, the room was never really warm. The stone walls seemed to have trapped the intense cold.

As he finally reached the door that led into the great hall the icy draught from the battlements that seeped down the narrow funnel of the stairway caught the back of his neck and he shivered, wondering why the Earl had summoned him at this late hour. Supper was long over; Joanna had wrapped Edward tightly in thick woollen blankets and settled him in his truckle bed, covering him with a rug of sheepskin. He'd left her, with Meg for company, sitting huddled before the hearth sipping hot spiced wine.

Henry was standing before the enormous stone hearth wrapped in a thick, fur-lined cape, a manservant by his side assiduously attending the fire. Will noticed instantly that he looked far from well. Although he was shivering there were beads of perspiration on his forehead; as well as feverish he looked angry and anxious. A group of three men were standing beside him, their expressions grim; Will recognised one of them as Sir Roger Lassells, the Earl's senior captain. Lassells nodded curtly in recognition before turning away and drawing his companions towards the round-headed window embrasure.

'My lord, you are sick?' Will queried.

Henry nodded. 'I fear it is my old illness that has returned, Will, but it does not surprise me given the weather and the poor condition of these lodgings. I swear there is not a single room that is comfortable or dry for the roof appears to be incapable of keeping out the rain. But all that is of little matter at the moment.'

Will silently agreed with him about the decrepitude of their housings. There had been heavy rain and gales during the last two days and Joanna and Meg had had to resort to the use of buckets to catch the water that dripped from the leaking roof.

Part of this Great Tower had been brought down by Scots cannon fire fifteen years ago when the castle had been besieged. Repairs had been carried out urgently after the Battle of Flodden by the victorious Earl of Surrey, but they had not been enough to withstand either the harshness of the climate or the passage of time. 'There is news of more trouble, my lord?' he asked.

'Sir Roger here has come with great haste to inform me that violence has again occurred this day, led by that blackguard William Charleton of Shottington. This time they descended on Woolington, murdered any who opposed them and stripped the village as clean as a dog strips a bone. They drove off all the villagers' beasts before them.' Henry could not keep the anger from his voice at this act of unprovoked barbarity on defenceless men and women. 'And to add to their cowardly crimes they have carried off the priest for ransom.' Henry could not contain his outrage at the news, flushing unhealthily as he spoke. 'God's wounds! I will not tolerate such criminal flouting of the King's laws! As Lord Warden I am determined to see that they are pursued, captured and brought as prisoners to me. There has been so much rain of late that the South Tyne will be too swollen to cross except at Haydon Bridge, and I have sent instructions that the bridge be locked fast against them. They will be forced to turn back.'

There flashed through Will's mind the memory of that winter's day when as a terrified boy of eleven he had tried to defend his father from such blackguards. 'My lord, Thomas Errington, one of your tenants here, has many sleuth-hounds. They can be used to track down these brigands.'

Henry nodded. 'It will be done. Charleton, Lysle, Hedley,

Crawshawe, Armstrong and all those who ride with them will find no sanctuary this side of the border. This time they cannot escape into Scotland and throw themselves on Angus's mercy. I swear by God's blood that they will be caught and tried and beheaded for March Treason!' Henry was now shivering violently and a sheen of sweat glistened on his drawn features. It was obvious that he was near to collapse.

'My lord, you cannot ride out this night and in such weather. You must rest,' Will urged as Henry beckoned Roger Lassells to him.

'Sir Roger, as you see my old illness is upon me, but seek out Thomas Errington; he has hounds and will help you to track down Charleton. Take a troop and ride with all haste towards Hexham for Haydon Bridge will be secured. They cannot cross the river.' Henry wiped the perspiration from his face with the back of his hand. 'I swear by the tears of the Virgin that I will set Charleton's head on a spike at the gates of Newcastle for the crimes he has committed this day!'

Lassells nodded grimly and, summoning his companions, hastened away.

'My lord, let me fetch one of Joanna's herbal potions and then escort you to your chamber before the fever overwhelms you,' Will begged. In the past he would eagerly have joined Lassells and the Earl's marcher men in hunting down the outlaws but Henry was ill and he would not leave him or his own family in this cold, inhospitable castle with little protection against others who may seek to follow Charleton's murderous example.

Joanna was very concerned when Will told her of both the Earl's illness and of the violence that had been perpetrated that day. Her dark brows rushed together in a frown and she laid a hand on Will's arm.

'You must see that Lord Henry is attended well by his servants and a physician sent for if needs be.' She paused to delve into the travelling trunk for the potion, and then asked anxiously: 'But are we safe here, Will? I fear for Edward and for Meg.'

Will tried to smile reassuringly. 'Norham is still a formidable fortress and the likes of Charleton and his reivers will be too concerned for their own freedom and safety to come anywhere near here. They will be searching for a place to cross the river and ride north for the border.'

She still looked uneasy and Meg had gone pale, she too recalling the terrible day the reivers had come to her childhood home.

Will put his arm around his wife. 'As soon as these outlaws have been captured and his lordship is feeling stronger, I promise we will go home to Beverley.'

Joanna nodded. How she longed for her warm, comfortable, neat house. Life in the affluent little market town further south was so much more civilised. 'Thank you, but go now and see what assistance and comfort you can give to his lordship.'

Countess Mary sat shivering in the dismal withdrawing chamber listening to the wind hurling the hail and sleet against its stone walls. The inferior tallow candles flickered erratically in the many draughts the tapestries and painted cloths failed to suppress. The fire would not draw properly and therefore gave little heat. Most probably the chimney was blocked. This was the worst place in which she had ever had the misfortune to reside, the worst place in which any lady of her rank had ever been forced to dwell, she thought venomously. The rain that dripped through the roof made the furnishings musty, the food when it arrived at the high table in the great hall was lukewarm and of mediocre quality, the wine often sour. The logs provided for the fire were either green or damp or both and so the heat they produced was too feeble to alleviate the bitter chill which had seeped deep into her bones. Was there ever a lady forced to endure such tribulations, she seethed as Will Chatton, aided by a manservant, helped the Earl into the chamber.

'My lady, his lordship is stricken with his old illness, I fear,' Will informed her.

'Yet again,' Mary replied curtly. Henry always seemed to be ailing. ''Tis not to be wondered at when he insists on residing in this . . . this . . . hovel!'

Will did not reply; there would be little or no sympathy for his lordship from his wife, that much was obvious. He helped Henry towards the heavily curtained bed, instructing the servant to build up the fire and place bed-warming stones in it.

'There is little point in that, Master Chatton. I fear the wood is green and the heat so poor that it will have little effect upon them.'

'My lady, this chamber is as cold as a church vault. Is there not sufficient dry kindling to provide a good fire?' Will could see that the Countess too was shivering despite the fur lining of her cloak, and that her hands were blue with the cold.

Mary shrugged. 'It appears not. It is a wonder that we are not all struck down with the ague.'

'Indeed, my lady, I agree wholeheartedly with you but I shall do whatever I can to make his lordship comfortable.' He felt sorry for her; she looked sick at heart and should not be subjected to such poor living conditions, but many of the border castles were in a similar state and as Lord Warden the Earl was obliged to reside in them. He certainly did not have the funds to repair them. 'I would urge you, Countess, for your own health, to seek refuge for a while with my wife and sister in our chamber for there is a goodly fire, fewer leaks and hot spiced wine.'

Mary didn't reply, thinking bitterly that things were very amiss when Will Chatton and his family had more comforts than she herself. But the prospect of sitting shivering in here while Henry tossed and raved in the grip of the fever was intolerable, so gathering her cloak closely around her, she left, closing the door quietly behind her.

Joanna was startled when the Countess entered the room and both she and Meg rose quickly to greet her deferentially.

'Your husband suggested that I take refuge here with you, Mistress Chatton, while he attends to the needs of the Earl,' Mary informed her flatly, surreptitiously glancing around and noting that the room was far warmer, brighter and more comfortable than her own. The rushes on the floor were clean, the fire in the hearth roared up the chimney and the wall hangings were illuminated by the light of a dozen more candles than burned in her chamber, and they were of beeswax. Joanna had prudently brought her own bedding, tapestries, plate, candlesticks and candles with her for Will had been uncertain as to what would be provided for them at Norham.

'My lady, you are most welcome. Please be seated,' Joanna urged and then, noticing that the Countess was shivering, she took one of her own heavy cloaks from a press and placed it around her shoulders. 'My lady, you are so cold. Meg – Margaret, my sister-in-law, will make you a drink to warm you.'

'I thank you, mistress. This residence is in such a state of decay and is so cold that even the vermin have deserted it for somewhere that offers better shelter!' Mary did not try to conceal her contempt and anger at the conditions she was forced to endure.

'I too had noticed that, my lady. In Beverley I keep a couple of cats about the house and yard, which helps to limit their activities,' she informed the Countess.

'Indeed and does that curtail their incursions?' Mary asked without much interest.

'To a great extent. At least it stops them from devouring the food in the kitchen and ruining the linen and furnishings,' Joanna replied, adding more logs to the fire.

Mary stretched out her numbed fingers to the blaze and watched as Meg took the poker that she had a few minutes earlier plunged into the fire and dip its red-hot metal tip into a goblet of wine, which hissed, steamed and gave off the rich aroma of cloves and cinnamon.

'Drink this, my lady, it will warm you,' Meg urged, handing her the goblet.

Mary cupped her cold hands around it and felt her fingers begin to thaw as she sipped. 'You will return to Beverley in the near future, I assume, Mistress Chatton?'

Joanna nodded. 'As soon as my husband feels he is able to leave his lordship and those responsible for the terrible crimes committed this day at Woolington have been caught.'

'You are most fortunate in that, mistress. This border

country is an ungodly place. These men who call themselves reivers or moss troopers are all common thieves, brigands and murderers, no matter that some of them style themselves as gentlemen and even knights; and the castles in which I am expected to reside have few comforts, as you can plainly see. Is it small wonder that my lord husband is always troubled and ill?'

'He is a good man, my lady. His health is poor yet he does not shirk his duty, despite the harshness and discomfort and his hatred of all violence.'

Mary didn't comment but continued to sip her wine. 'You have a son, I hear, Mistress Chatton.'

Joanna nodded and crossed to where Edward lay asleep, just his dark curls visible beneath the sheepskin coverlet. 'I will feel easier in my mind when I have him safely at home in Beverley. I fear the cold and dampness here is not good for him. I shall take him into the bed with myself and Will later, that way he will share our warmth and not freeze during the night.'

Mary looked puzzled but then she shrugged; she knew little of the customs of the common people. If she ever had a child it would be cared for by a nurse in separate chambers, but the prospect seemed a distant one for on the occasions when Henry came to her bed, compelled, she knew, only by his profound sense of duty, she offered him neither encouragement nor any token of affection. It was her own duty to submit to him, to provide him with an heir, but there was nothing to say she must obtain any pleasure from it. Pleasure, she reflected wretchedly, was not to be got from a marriage as bleak as the northern wastes that surrounded her.

* * *

338

Charleton, Lysle and their companions, after a short, bloody fight with Lassells at Haydon Bridge, managed to escape and cross the border into Scotland but were forced to return to Northumberland and were subsequently arrested and taken to Alnwick.

Henry, slowly recovering from his bout of illness and the rigours of Norham, presided over their trial in the great hall. His anger at the crimes they had committed had not diminished, even though the priest they had kidnapped for ransom had been released. He showed little surprise that they made no attempt to deny the charges against them, which were read out by Sir Roger, who was nursing a wound in his arm inflicted during the fight at Haydon Bridge.

'How do you and your followers answer these charges, Master Charleton?' Henry demanded.

'My lord, we offer no defence,' Charleton replied defiantly. He was a burly man of middle height and years, decently dressed in a doublet of black broadcloth. His left cheek bore an old jagged scar, testament to his violent past. 'And men usually address me as Sir William,' he added arrogantly.

'*I* do not for a common brigand has no legal right to such a title. A true knight has high moral standards, you, *Master* Charleton, are devoid of both morals and humanity for I have heard that if men do not address you as "sir" you cut out their tongues!' Henry replied, his voice cold with suppressed anger. 'You will all suffer the penalty for flouting the King's laws. I find you all guilty of March Treason. William Lysle, Thomas Hedley, Robert Crawshawe, Richard Armstrong, Humphrey Lysle, you will all be executed for your crimes. You, *Master* William Charleton, will be beheaded and your head placed on a spike at the gates of Newcastle as a warning to those who would think to follow your example.' He turned to Sir Roger. 'Have them taken away and placed in the dungeon beneath the North Tower to await the King's justice.'

Sir Roger signalled the men-at-arms to remove the prisoners and then he handed Henry a goblet of wine, nodding grimly. 'Northumberland will be a safer place for their deaths,' he said, his growing admiration for the young Warden evident in his tone.

'I hope so, Sir Roger, but I have my doubts,' Henry replied.

'You will remain to see the sentences carried out, my lord?'

Henry drank deeply and then shook his head. 'No, I shall return to Wressle. There has been enough bloodshed these past weeks. I have no desire to witness more.'

Chapter Thirty-Four

Wressle Castle, Yorkshire

A S HENRY BROKE THE seal on the Cardinal's letter he could not help but permit himself a cynical smile. Ever since William Charleton, four of his followers and Sir William Lysle of Felton had been tried and found guilty of March Treason, then executed at the King's command, Wolsey's attitude to him had changed.

He was still living in straitened circumstances; he was still paying his father's debts, but since he had furiously imprisoned the treacherous William Worme in the Auditor's Tower at Alnwick for defrauding both himself and the Exchequer things had improved a little. He was aware that he was still surrounded by Wolsey's spies. He even suspected his wife of being in the Cardinal's pay, something she stoutly refuted and over which – amongst other things – they quarrelled frequently.

It had been the plight of Lysle's eldest son, thirteen-year-old Humphrey, that had caused him to write to the Cardinal. He had begged him to ask for clemency from the King for the boy. Humphrey had been found guilty with his father and sentenced to death but Henry had been unable to bring himself to make the lad pay such a terrible price for his doubtful filial loyalty and foolishness.

He frowned as he scanned the lines of elaborate script. Wolsey's response was ponderous; he always used ten words where two would have sufficed. At last he laid the parchment down on the desk. Humphrey Lysle's sentence had been commuted to imprisonment in the Tower of London, although the length of his incarceration was not mentioned. His father's lands and goods had been confiscated and were now held by the King, but at least the boy still had his life.

He read the Cardinal's final paragraph again and emotions he had held for so long in check surged through him. Wolsey had commanded that he go to London, to enlighten the King as to the true state of law and order on the Border. Once such a command would have filled him with relief that he was no longer under the displeasure of either the King or the Cardinal. He would have been filled with eager anticipation at seeing his friends once again, mingling with statesmen and courtiers in the splendour of the royal palaces but most of all at the prospect of seeing the woman he had never stopped loving: Anne Boleyn.

He folded the parchment and stood up and crossed to the window. Mist shrouded the parkland and distant water meadows of the Derwent, but the pale October sunlight picked out the vivid colours of the turning leaves and the last apples on the trees in the orchards. Autumn and winter were not the best seasons to travel the roads of England, he thought, but travel he must. My lord Cardinal had instructed him. He drew his surcoat of mulberry velvet closer to him, thinking of the cold, damp mornings and evenings ahead which would accelerate the onset of his ague. The edges of the garment were clearly showing signs of wear. He did not consider himself to be a vain man, yet he had no wish to appear at court in clothes that would proclaim his penury far louder than any words could. His father had been known as Henry the Magnificent, not a sobriquet that history would ever bestow on *him*. And yet he was a Percy, one of the great border earls, and he had his pride.

He turned away from the window for the mellow autumn morning had done nothing to lift his spirits. He sat down at the desk again and resting his head in his hands tried to collect his thoughts. How would he feel being at court again? That hotbed of gossip and innuendo where everyone connived and jostled for power and position, and where there were so many spies that every move and gesture was noted, every word and con-versation was reported to someone? He did not relish any of that, and how would he feel witnessing Anne, whom he had yearned to see again, as the object of the King's desire? The beautiful, dark-eyed, vivacious Anne dressed in sumptuous gowns of velvet and cloth of gold, her graceful neck adorned with diamonds and pearls, constantly at the King's side? She was no longer *his* Anne. She would never again be *his* Anne, although he would never stop loving her. She was Henry Tudor's Anne now. Could he bear to see her laughing and flirting with the King? Could he stand by and watch the King kiss her as he himself had once done? Would he find himself riven by jealousy and despair? He sighed heavily; he was already being torn between that question and the fierce longing to see her again. But there was no remedy, he had to go. He could not refuse Wolsey's directive.

He reached for a sheet of parchment and the quill pen. He would have to reply to the Cardinal but he would also write to Will Chatton, asking that he accompany him to London for he would have need of a trustworthy, compassionate friend at his side.

The letters were completed and he was sealing them when the Countess was announced.

Henry looked up and noted that her pale features were composed in the usual expression of discontent. 'Good morning, madam. It has the promise of becoming a fair day,' he greeted her affably.

Mary nodded curtly by way of a reply but she was not to be deterred by such pleasantries. 'My lord, it pains me that I must come to you, but the Steward of the Household has informed me that once again there are insufficient funds—'

Henry stood up. 'Mary, you are fully aware of the Cardinal's instructions,' he interrupted sharply, his good humour disappearing.

'There are considerations that have arisen that my lord Cardinal has not envisaged, Henry!'

'Indeed there are, madam.' He picked up Wolsey's letter. 'And this is one of them. I am instructed to go to court to discuss with the King my duties as Lord Warden. It will mean that one of my houses in Newington Green must be opened up with all the attendant expenditure, but he does not inform me how I am to pay for it.'

Mary's expression changed; the news pleased her. 'So, we are to go to London.' It would be a very welcome diversion. She would enjoy going to court and as Countess of Northumberland she would be afforded the respect and attention to which she was entitled.

'No, Mary. *I* am to go to London,' Henry replied quietly.

She stared at him hard, her eyes narrowing. So, he had no intention of taking her with him. She was to be left here, conveniently forgotten, denied the pleasures of civilised society and the company of her peers. Left here while no doubt he sought to make the acquaintance once more of Mistress Anne Boleyn! She was fully aware that he had not forgotten *her*. From the day she had been married to him she had suspected that he still had feelings for Mistress Anne who was now, if everything she heard was to be believed, the King's mistress!

She laughed cuttingly as anger, disappointment and humiliation surged through her. 'So, I am to remain here? Think you to oust the King in Mistress Boleyn's affections?'

'It has nothing to do with Mistress Boleyn. It is my lord Cardinal's command and he states that I am to travel with the minimum of servants and expenditure. He makes no mention of my wife,' Henry replied, handing her the letter.

She glanced at it and then threw it on the desk. 'Do not take me for a fool, Henry! It may well be on the Cardinal's orders that you go but do not lie to me about Mistress Boleyn. In your heart you pray to see her again, do you deny it?' she snapped, her cheeks flushed with anger.

Henry refused to be drawn. 'I must do as the Cardinal asks.'

Mary snatched up the letter, tore it in two and flung it at him. 'You are a liar and a coward, Henry! You do not have the courage to tell me to my face what is in your heart. That you are rejoicing that you have been sent for and that I am to remain here, so you can spend every possible moment seeking out that . . . that low-born *whore*!'

Henry's temper was rising. 'Do not use such language, Mary! It does not become you,' he snapped coldly.

Her eyes were blazing as she faced him and her hands were clenched so tightly that her nails dug into her palms. 'You could not bestow the title "Countess" on her so she seeks to gain wealth and power from a different source, she seeks to take the Queen's place now. Are you such a naive fool that you believe she holds him off because she values her chastity? Mistress Anne who spent years at the French court and no doubt learned many ways of inflaming a man's lust, ways she now uses to keep the King chasing her as a huntsman chases a doe? Or do you think she will not submit to his ultimate desire because she still has some regard for you?' She laughed again, a shrill sound full of mockery and contempt. 'You cannot compete with *the King*, Henry. You have nothing to offer such as she. All you possess are empty coffers and a title that lacks the power and influence it once had.'

Throughout this tirade wave upon wave of anger had coursed through him at her vile innuendos. 'Would that I could have bestowed the title "Countess" on her for she is more worthy to bear it than you, madam, for all that you are the daughter of an earl. Your mind and thoughts are those of the sewer and you have the tongue of a viper! I rejoice that I am to go to London for it will afford me some relief from your poisonous presence and it *will* afford me great pleasure to see Mistress Anne Boleyn again.' He snatched up his letters from the desk and stormed out, leaving her white-faced and shaking.

'You will regret you ever admitted that you would have preferred marriage to her rather than to me, Henry Percy,' she cried but the door had slammed shut behind him.

She sank down in the chair beside the desk, her lips set in a line of bitter determination, and then she felt the child inside her quicken. That was what she had come to tell him, that she was carrying his heir and that provision must be made for the child, but he had insulted and humiliated her beyond all endurance. Her eyes narrowed. She would do everything in her power not to carry this child to full term. She would deny him his heir if at all possible.

Beverley, Yorkshire

Will was at home when the Earl's letter was brought by messenger and as he broke the seal he wondered if it contained more distressing news.

'Is his lordship well?' Joanna enquired, laying down the little shirt she was embroidering for Edward. The days were becoming shorter now and she had lit more candles to give a fuller light both for her needlework and the accounts Will had been examining. Supper was over, Edward asleep and Meg visiting the home of young Thomas Watford, to whom she had recently become betrothed. The room was warm and comfortable, the firelight and candlelight a cheerful contrast to the windy darkness beyond the latticed windows. Tyke, Edward's puppy, lay asleep before the hearth.

Will nodded, relieved that Henry's letter contained good news. 'He seems in good spirits. Since the imprisonment of

Worme at Alnwick he is relieved to be rid of at least one spy.'

Joanna nodded. 'Never was a man more aptly named.'

'Now it appears that he is once more in favour with the Cardinal for he has been commanded to go to court to see the King and give account of his dealings with the reivers.'

'Then that is good news indeed, Will. Perhaps now he will be allowed to live in a more comfortable fashion. Is the Countess Mary to go with him? Poor lady, she does not enjoy living in the North Country and with so little money.'

Will quickly scanned the lines of the Earl's rather untidy writing. 'He makes no mention of the Countess but he asks that I accompany him. We will reside in Brook House.'

Joanna's dark brows rose questioningly. 'Why does he wish you to go, Will, but not her ladyship?'

Will frowned. 'I do not know, unless he truly feels – as he writes – that he will have need of a loyal, trustworthy companion.'

'But what of Lord Arundel and the other gentlemen who were his companions?'

'Lord Arundel he can trust but' – he shrugged – 'who knows how things now stand at court? And then there is . . .'

'Mistress Anne,' Joanna added quietly. 'It will be . . . painful for him to see her again.'

Will carefully folded the letter. 'I fear so but he cannot refuse.'

'Can you spare the time?'

Will nodded. 'I shall use it profitably to visit merchants and my agent when his lordship does not need me.'

Joanna picked up her sewing and smiled. 'And Master Aske. Do not forget Robert, Will.'

He smiled back at her. 'I shan't, and I shall bring both you and Meg some fine cloth for winter gowns and a collar of tooled leather for Tyke.' He rose and took the writing materials from their cupboard and placed them on the table. 'I have letters to write. They must be ready for dispatch in the morning. I'll make arrangements for the journey then too.'

Joanna nodded, and turned back thoughtfully to her sewing. Although she disliked him being away from home she was glad Lord Henry would have his company. She had no wish to go with them: she was content with her life in Beverley. Neither the magnificence nor the intrigues of Henry Tudor's court had ever really appealed to her. Besides, when Will returned she would hear at first hand of everything that was taking place there. That would be sufficient.

Chapter Thirty-Five

Brook House, Newington Green, London

THE JOURNEY HAD BEEN arduous for the first days of November had been bitterly cold and wet and the roads muddy. In places they had become waterlogged and impassable and they had been forced to ride on the uneven, slippery verges, hoping their mounts would not stumble, damage a leg and go lame. As on that other journey five years ago, they had stayed at monasteries overnight although Will realised that the Earl's memories of that previous sojourn were hazy.

It was a relief to them both when they finally rode through the gates and into the courtyard of Brook House on Newington Green.

'I hope there is a good fire and a cup of spiced wine awaiting you, my lord,' Will commented as he dismounted. They were cold, wet and stiff. Their clothes were liberally spattered with mud but the journey had taken more of a toll on the Earl than on himself, he noted.

'I hope there is hot water to wash with too for I do not intend to tarry long here,' Henry replied as the grooms took his and Will's horses and the Earl's marcher escorts led their mounts to the stables.

Will was surprised. 'You intend to go to York Place today, my lord?'

'I do. I would not have my lord Cardinal berate me for being tardy in attending him,' Henry answered as they entered the stone corridor on the ground floor at the end of which a staircase led up to the Earl's chambers. He was thankful that the place was reasonably warm and had obviously been cleaned in preparation for this visit. What he had told Will was not strictly the truth, he thought. Wolsey would not hear of his arrival in London for hours, maybe not until tomorrow morning. He wished to find out at which of his palaces the King was at present residing and glean what news he could of Anne. No doubt Wolsey would ensure that they obtained an audience with the King sometime tomorrow and then . . . then he would see her again. A surge of joy ran through him despite his creeping weariness.

'Surely, my lord, the Cardinal will realise that you must rest after such a lengthy and hazardous journey. He would not wish your health to suffer from it,' Will ventured.

'My health did not greatly concern him the last time he commanded me to take to the roads, so I doubt he will give much thought to it now,' Henry answered caustically.

'Do not forget, my lord, that even the walls have ears,' Will reminded him quietly.

Henry smiled. 'I had almost forgotten that, Will. I see I was wise indeed to ask you to accompany me.'

York Place, London

Two hours later, after washing, changing their clothes and dining, they rode out again into Newington Green and through the streets of the city towards York Place.

Will stared around him; little seemed to have changed in five years, he thought. The streets were still crowded and filthy, beggars still abounded as did the half-starved dogs and cats scavenging in the gutters. It would have been an easier and infinitely more pleasant journey by river, he mused. Tomorrow, when his lordship was at court, he had arranged to call upon Robert Aske and perhaps they would take a tankard of ale together – somewhere a little more salubrious than the Waterman's Arms, he hoped.

Eventually they reached the gardens of Wolsey's palace and Will's mind went back to the day he had first brought Joanna to walk in them. Then the trees had been laden with blossom, the breeze from the river stirring the new green leaves, the sunlight playing on the water cascading from the many fountains. Today the trees were almost bare, just a few ragged leaves adhered to their skeletal branches and a cold wind tore at their cloaks; even the fountains appeared dull and cold.

Henry too was remembering the days he'd spent here in the Cardinal's household. Days spent whiling away the hours, gaming, composing poems, taking part in masques with Tom Arundel, Hal Norris, Francis Weston, Tom Wyatt, George Boleyn, Margaret Fairfax, Margaret Wyatt and . . . Anne.

Soon, so very soon now, he would learn where she was and how she was faring and when he might be able at last to see her. All thoughts of Mary, her anger and virulent assassination of Anne's character, were far from his mind. Despite the knowledge that everything he said and did would be noted by Wolsey's spies, he was glad he had been allowed to return.

As they mounted the stairs that led to the gallery where Henry had been so publicly berated by both his father and the Cardinal, Will could not help but contrast the luxury and grandeur that surrounded them with the austerity in which the Earl was now forced to live and he prayed that Thomas Wolsey would relax his stringent strictures on his lordship's expenditure. Compared to the people who were waiting in the gallery in the hope of an audience with the Cardinal, his lordship's clothes looked slightly shabby, although Henry appeared to be oblivious to the fact. Will permitted himself a smile; no doubt his former master's thoughts were fully occupied by Anne Boleyn.

After a brief wait they were ushered into the Cardinal's presence. Will thought the King's Chief Minister had gained more weight. He looked older, too, and more preoccupied. However, the hooded eyes were as cold and as reptilian as ever.

'My lord of Northumberland, you are welcome,' Wolsey greeted Henry affably enough.

'Thank you, my lord. Will Chatton – no longer my squire but a successful merchant – has accompanied me; we arrived but two hours since,' Henry informed him.

'At my own expense, my lord,' Will's tone was respectful but he held Wolsey's speculative gaze steadily, determined that the Cardinal be aware that he knew of Wolsey's treatment of his former master.

Wolsey smiled slowly and nodded, appraising Will's clothes and the fine gold ring he wore on his right hand. 'So, it would appear that I am not the only man in this chamber of humble birth who has risen in the world by means of his own accomplishments.' He did not clearly remember the man, he had been a mere squire after all, but it pleased him to hear that he had achieved a degree of wealth and status. Chatton, like himself, had not inherited his wealth as Henry Percy and so many others at court had done. He smiled cynically to himself. Although in young Percy's case all he had inherited were the debts of a criminally wasteful and extravagant father.

'I hope your affairs of business will not suffer in your absence, Master Chatton,' he probed, his tone implying that Will was a fool if he had accompanied Henry Percy out of loyalty alone.

'Indeed not, my lord. I have a great many things to attend to in the city, things I have perhaps neglected for too long,' Will replied courteously, very much aware of what the Cardinal meant.

'My lord Northumberland, I will speak with our sovereign lord the King, who no doubt will wish to learn the details of your administration of his laws upon the Border, although at present His Majesty has many onerous matters that command his attention, not least that of my lord Cardinal Campeggio, emissary of His Holiness the Pope, who arrived two weeks ago to consider … certain matters.' Wolsey was aware that news of the King's Secret Matter must by now have reached even the northern counties but he had no intention of enlightening Henry Percy as to its progress.

So, it was true. The case had gone as far as Rome and the

Pope had sent Campeggio to deliberate upon it, Henry thought, wondering if he dare openly enquire after Anne's whereabouts and thereby perhaps learn more of her involvement with the King. He decided against it. 'Thank you, my lord. I would not wish to impinge upon His Majesty's time to any great length. A brief audience should suffice to answer His Grace's questions and assure him of my most loyal and diligent service.'

'You will be most cordially received, I can assure you, my lord,' Wolsey replied unctuously, turning away.

Henry was aware that the interview was at an end and he felt deflated. He was to learn nothing of Anne from Wolsey, that was clear.

Will realised it too. 'My lord Cardinal, may I be so bold as to ask at which of his palaces the King's Majesty is currently residing? Tomorrow, I have planned to meet an . . . associate . . . at the Inns of Court while his lordship attends the King. Of course I wish firstly to accompany my lord of Northumberland to court, but I would be most grateful if I knew from which palace I should set out.'

'His Majesty is at present at Greenwich, as is the Queen,' Wolsey replied guardedly. Chatton had no need to accompany Henry Percy to Greenwich – he would do that himself – the question was clearly an excuse to try to ascertain the whereabouts of Mistress Anne. She who was leading the King a merry dance and becoming more and more arrogant and sure of her position each day.

Will dutifully thanked him and they were escorted out into the gallery.

'I am afraid that ploy didn't work, my lord. He was well

aware of my intention to try to find out where Mistress Boleyn is. I'm sorry.'

'He is a cautious and devious man, Will. I shall have to wait until tomorrow to find out if she is with the King or at some other residence in the city,' Henry replied. He could not hide the disappointment in his voice.

Will noticed George Cavendish, Wolsey's secretary, making his way towards them.

'My lord of Northumberland, it is good to see you again after so long – and you too, Chatton,' Cavendish greeted them amiably.

Henry smiled politely. 'I am pleased to be here.'

Will nodded and Cavendish walked on but Will turned and followed him. 'Master Cavendish, I would ask a favour of you. It is so long since I was in London and news travels very slowly to the North Country. What news is there of matters at court? How fare the King and Mistress Anne Boleyn?'

Cavendish glanced around him quickly. 'The King is the epitome of good health and Mistress Boleyn fares well indeed.' He lowered his voice. '*Very* well indeed. You have heard that the King is greatly enamoured of her?'

Will nodded. 'She is with the King at Greenwich?'

Cavendish was surprised. 'No. It was thought prudent for Mademoiselle Anne to return to Hever while Cardinal Campeggio is here in London.' He glanced furtively around again. 'It must appear that the King observes the formality of presiding over the court with the Queen, not one of her ladies. I doubt she will return until the Cardinal has departed.'

It was not what Will had wanted to hear but he thanked the man and strode quickly after Henry.

'What news, Will?' Henry asked tentatively.

'So as not to offend Cardinal Campeggio's sensibilities and to appear to be considerate of those of the Queen, Mistress Anne has been sent to Hever. She is not here, my lord. I am sorry. Cavendish thinks she will remain at Hever until Campeggio has gone.'

Henry's shoulders slumped as disappointment overwhelmed him. He had travelled so far and endured great discomfort, his spirits bolstered only by hope and the anticipation of once more seeing her and speaking to her. But it was not to be. His stay would be brief for Wolsey had implied that the King was more concerned about Campeggio's visit than the state of law and order on the Borders. He did not know how long it would be before she returned and he would have no reason to prolong his stay at Brook House; he would have to go back north. And then . . . then how long would it be before he would be summoned again to court – if ever? The King was consumed with his passion for Anne. Henry Tudor would not tolerate him lingering indefinitely at court – a constant reminder that she had once loved him.

Will remained silent. Nothing he could say would alleviate the Earl's dejection.

Hever Castle, Kent

'Mistress Anne, your father has arrived. He will attend you when he has washed and changed his clothes,' Semmonet announced, finding her mistress sitting staring discontentedly into the flames of the fire that burned cheerfully in the hearth. She had grown in both beauty and confidence this last year, she thought, and it was fitting. Mistress Anne was by far the most attractive, witty, well educated and graceful woman at the English court, which she, as a Frenchwoman, would always compare unfavourably to the court of King Francis. It seemed to her only natural that her mistress had found favour with King Henry – the man was not a fool – but she was not totally sure that Anne would succeed in persuading him to put aside his wife and take her as his Queen. In France it was a great honour to be the King's mistress but it was not enough for Anne, and she hoped that it would not all end in disappointment and shattered dreams.

She poured wine into a goblet and handed it to Anne, smiling. 'To fortify you for whatever news your father brings.'

Anne took it and sipped it thoughtfully, 'I hope it will cheer me for I am bored. I find the winter days in the country long and tedious. There is so little to amuse me.'

Semmonett tutted and shook her head. 'You are like a *papillon* – a butterfly – a creature of the summer who dances and plays in the sunlight and thrives upon the gaiety at court.' Her quiet words held no note of censure. In her gown of blue velvet and silver tissue, the neckline bordered with jewels and her matching hood studded with pearls and diamonds, Anne did indeed look like an exotic butterfly – or a queen, the older woman thought fondly.

Anne rose and placed the now empty goblet on a cupboard. 'Time passes so slowly, Semmonet. I do not want to remain buried here while the King presides daily over the court with the Queen. I am impatient to be at his side again.'

Semmonet nodded. She knew very well that this waiting was taking its toll on Anne.

'Perhaps that is what your father has come to tell you. That you are to return.'

Anne smiled at her. 'I hope so.'

There was no further conversation for a squire announced that Sir Thomas was ascending the stairs.

'You are well, I trust, daughter,' Sir Thomas greeted her as both the squire and Semmonet withdrew.

'As well as can be expected being exiled here. Is there news, Father? Has the King sent for me?' she demanded.

He shook his head. 'Unfortunately not, but I bring both letters and his fond wishes. He has spoken at length to Cardinal Campeggio about the annulment.'

She was disappointed and did not hide it. 'And what has the Cardinal had to say on the matter?'

'He procrastinates and deliberates on the scriptures and canon law. He is old and suffers greatly from the gout but the King, too, is impatient, Anne. He cannot bear to be parted from you, such is his deep affection for you.'

She laughed cuttingly, throwing back her head, the diamonds on her hood flashing in the firelight. 'Such is his desire to bed me!'

'You have a sharp and careless tongue, Anne, and the King cannot abide a scold.'

She turned away from him so he would not see the anger in her eyes. *He* was not the one who had to endure the waiting. *He* did not have to encourage the King's advances and yet try to deter him from becoming too passionate. *He* was reaping the rewards without having to endure being kept away from court. How long was this situation to continue? It was taking a terrible toll on her nerves but no matter how long she must wait she was determined that she would settle now for nothing less than a crown. 'Can Wolsey do nothing to hasten Campeggio?'

Sir Thomas looked sceptical. 'I fear not and I do not think he is aware that if – *when* . . .' he hastily amended, seeing her dark brows rush together in a frown, 'the King obtains the annulment he intends to make you his Queen. The Cardinal has no liking for me, your Uncle Norfolk or you. He is jealous of his position and power.'

She gazed at him steadily, her dark eyes hard. How she had changed. Driven by ambition, she was no longer the pliable girl she had been but a woman filled with determination.

'Then I think, my lord father, that it is time he found out. I beg you to inform the King of my desire to return to Court. Tell him that I am pining for him, that I cannot eat, cannot sleep and must surely succumb to my . . . abject misery . . . at being parted from him for so long. I trust you to make sure he fully understands for do you not see that the longer I am forced to reside here, the greater the chance that he might be swayed from his desire to marry me? Wolsey will do all in his power to delay the matter, for, as you have just reminded me, he is jealous of his power and Campeggio answers not to the King but to the Pope, who in his turn relies for his security and influence upon the Emperor Charles – the Queen's nephew. I *must* return to court soon, Father!'

Sir Thomas nodded. This was no foolish girl, as Wolsey had once described her. She was clever and had a clear grasp of affairs, unlike her sister Mary. 'I will do all in my power to persuade him, Anne, I promise.'

She smiled, relieved. It was in his interests too that she

return. All their ambitions were bound up with her own. When she was Queen of England the Howards and Boleyns would wield the power – not men such as Thomas Wolsey.

Chapter Thirty-Six

1529
Prudhoe Castle, Northumberland

Henry made his way quickly through the round archway towards the chamber block built against the east wall of the keep and entered the stone passageway via a thick oak door, heading for the stairs that led to the chambers above. Although spring had officially commenced a month ago it came late to Northumberland and the pale April sunlight was still weak and lacking warmth.

It wasn't just the chill in the air, he thought, the castle seemed quieter than usual and he sensed that few fires had been lit of late. He hadn't been expected to return so soon from Alnwick, which was no great distance away, but the perpetrators of the most recent case of reiving had been speedily dealt with. At Alnwick he had also received word that that treacherous

Scot, Archibald Douglas, the Earl of Angus, was to be allowed by King Henry to take refuge in England.

Angus and his brother, George Douglas, were as slippery as eels and as cunning as foxes, Henry mused. He was aware that they had openly encouraged Sir William Lysle and the English outlaws and the blame for much of the violence carried out on the Borders could be laid at their feet. Angus was constantly at odds with his King, James, and most of the Scottish nobility too; matters had reached such a pitch of late that Angus had written to King Henry seeking sanctuary. The Cardinal had urged the King to agree, which to James's chagrin he had done, and now Wolsey had instructed that he meet Angus when he arrived in Newcastle with his followers and that he greet him 'in as loving wise as could be, all the gentlemen of Northumberland there being assembled.' This was why he had returned to Prudhoe. It would be many weeks yet before Angus arrived but there was much to do.

He was surprised when he reached his chamber to find his brother Thomas awaiting him. 'I was not aware that you intended to make the journey from Cumberland to visit me, Thomas. How fares my lady mother?'

'She is well; Lady Cumberland defers to her instructions regarding the household most amiably, but it is not our mother that I have come to discuss with you, Henry, and I was not aware that you had left Alnwick. I was en route to visit you there but decided to rest my horse and have dinner here first. I arrived but a short time ago.' Thomas's tone was belligerent. He strode across to the square stone fireplace and looked with disgust at the empty hearth. 'God's wounds, could they not have lit a fire, the lazy churls!'

Henry removed his bonnet and gauntlets and placed them on a press. Thomas hadn't changed, he thought, and he had a fair idea why he had come. 'They did not expect me. You cannot expect them to possess the power of foresight and, besides, I would not have them waste fuel. It costs money.'

'Why *have* you returned?' Thomas demanded, ignoring his brother's reference to money, the subject he intended to raise.

'I have received instructions from Cardinal Wolsey to prepare to welcome the Earl of Angus when he arrives in Newcastle. A banquet is to take place in his honour,' Henry stated flatly.

'A banquet to *honour* that treacherous knave!' Thomas exploded.

'The King has given him permission to take up residence in England, where as yet I have no knowledge, but he is to be greeted cordially and by all the noblemen of the shire.'

'And you have agreed to this?'

Henry nodded. 'Whatever I may think of Angus and his followers, I have little choice but to obey the King.'

'Well, Brother, I do!' Thomas retorted angrily.

'You would disobey the King, Thomas? You are courting danger.'

'Do not forget, Henry, that I am not officially a nobleman of this shire and therefore under no obligation. It was Wolsey who instructed that I reside with Henry Clifford, after all. And who, pray, is to pay for this banquet, may I ask?'

'The Cardinal, for as well you know, Thomas, my coffers are empty. I am still paying our father's debts so I hope your journey has not been in vain, for I can do little to increase the amount apportioned either to yourself or Ingram.'

Thomas was infuriated that Henry had realised he had come to ask for money and was about to denounce both Wolsey and his deceased father when a servant entered clutching a letter.

'My lord, a messenger has just arrived bearing this from my lord of Shrewsbury.'

'Shrewsbury? Is it not for the Countess?' Henry asked, puzzled as to why his wife's father was writing to him.

'No, my lord. It cannot be, the Countess is not here,' the man answered, looking furtive.

'Where is she?' Henry demanded. Mary was in the last month of her pregnancy – she was soon to be confined.

'She ... she left, my lord. Five days since.'

'*What!* Did no one try to dissuade her? In her condition she should not travel. Where has she gone?'

The man looked uneasy. 'My lord, who here would try to dissuade the Countess? She rode with her servant and three marcher men to Sheffield to my lord of Shrewsbury's house.'

Henry broke the seal, his stomach churning with misgivings, and as he read Shrewsbury's letter he sank down in the chair beside the empty hearth and groaned, letting the parchment slip to the floor.

'What is it, Henry? What is amiss? Is it ... Mary?' Thomas demanded.

Henry nodded. He felt cold and numb with shock. 'The child was born ... dead. It was a boy,' he informed his brother brokenly.

'And the Countess?' Thomas asked.

'In poor health and spirits. The physician is in constant attendance.'

'What possessed her to go? What drove her to ride to

365

Sheffield and her time so near? Was there another argument, Henry?'

'I was not here for her to argue with, Thomas. I was at Alnwick,' Henry reminded him bitterly. Had she done it deliberately, seeking to spite him? She had said often enough that she wished she were not carrying this child. But surely she did not hate him so much that she would put her own child's life in danger? But she had and she had risked her own life too. She must be a tormented soul indeed, he thought sadly. There would be no more children, he knew that. He would not sire babies that she had so little regard for that she would seek to cut short their lives. It was a bitter loss indeed.

'So, her decision to ride to Sheffield has cost you your son. She is a headstrong fool, Henry. When she returns you must take her to task about it,' Thomas urged harshly, turning away so his brother, who had always been able to see through his dissembling, would not see his true reaction to the news. Henry now had no heir, Mary and Wolsey between them had made his brother's life a misery and his health was poor. In time the Earldom of Northumberland would be his.

'My lord, shall I fetch wine?' the servant asked. His lordship looked pale and ill, no doubt shocked by the tragic news, as he was himself.

'Yes, and parchment, a quill and ink. See that the messenger is fed and when he has rested I shall require him to take letters back to his master and . . . my wife.' He would write to them both but he would also write to Tom Arundel and Will Chatton. Then he would instruct that Masses be said in the chapel for the soul of his baby son.

Greenwich Palace, London

'Margaret, sing with me and Madge shall accompany us on the lute. The words are not my own, but your brother Tom's, so they will please us all and I have need of a distraction,' Anne instructed as they sat in the gardens of the palace. The June sunlight was strong and warm. A low, neatly clipped box hedge bordered the fountain whose cascading waters usually had a calming effect on her – but not today, she was too tense. All morning she had been preoccupied and anxious although she hid it well. To passing servants and courtiers the three young women appeared to be in high spirits.

Anne always took great care with her appearance but this morning she had spent even longer choosing the brocade gown, the sleeves of which were lined with gold tissue. Her hood was studded with diamonds, pearls and rubies. Around her neck she wore four ropes of matchless river pearls and from her kirtle was suspended, on a gold chain, the large table diamond the King had presented her with yesterday. Today she must look like a queen, she had told herself. It was important that when Henry returned he should see her looking the very equal of Katherine.

Madge had picked up the beribboned lute but Margaret Wyatt gently laid a hand on her arm and Madge looked up questioningly.

'I think perhaps we should leave our madrigals until later, Anne,' Margaret said quietly. 'Your aunt, Her Grace of Norfolk, is approaching.'

Anne's eyes narrowed. She did not like her aunt, Elizabeth Howard, who was a staunch supporter of the Queen and who was walking rapidly and purposefully towards them. Judging by the expression on her face she was the bearer of bad news, she thought grimly.

Both Margaret and Madge rose. 'Do you wish us to leave you, Anne?' Margaret whispered.

Anne nodded and the two girls left her side, bowing courteously to the Duchess.

'What brings you back to Greenwich, Aunt? Do you not attend the Queen at the Legatine Court?' Anne asked coldly. She wasn't alone in her dislike of Elizabeth Howard, she thought. Her Uncle Norfolk could not abide his wife either. He had taken Bess Holland, a member of his wife's household, as his mistress and there were frequent, violent and public arguments between her aunt and uncle.

The older woman eyed her with open hostility. 'The Queen has already returned to the palace from Blackfriars, Niece. I hastened to find and inform you of the fact.'

Anne's dark eyes widened in surprise. Campeggio had at last convened the long-awaited Legatine Court in the great hall of the priory and both the King and Queen were to attend to be examined by the cardinals. It was a public occasion and had caused great interest for it was the first time a king and queen had been summoned before a court. Upon the decision of this court hung the fate of the annulment of Henry's marriage to Katherine. It was a day that was of utmost importance for her future. 'Has the Queen been taken ill?' she asked.

'Indeed not. Quite the opposite,' Elizabeth Howard stated firmly. She had no liking for her niece whom she considered an arrogant, ruthless adventuress. She would enjoy this interview. She would relish seeing the girl's hopes of filling the shoes of her mistress the Queen greatly diminished and there were many women in the country who would join her. It was disgraceful that Henry Tudor should seek to put aside Katherine, a princess of Spain, for such as Mistress Anne Boleyn. 'When she was summoned into the court she did not take her seat in the chair of estate as directed, but went and knelt before the King, declaring that she had been a true wife to him. That when she had married him she had been a virgin, without touch of man, and the truth of which she put to his own conscience.'

Anne was trying hard to disguise her irritated frustration but the slight flush that spread over her cheeks gave her away. Katherine was determined to be obstinate, she fumed. She had already refused to go into a convent, as had been suggested by both Henry and Campeggio, should the court find in favour of an annulment, a refusal which had infuriated Henry.

The Duchess did not conceal her pleasure at her niece's annoyance. 'Her Grace continued that should the King persist in this course she would commit her cause to God and then she rose and walked out. She ignored the calls that she come back into court and when the people waiting outside the priory learned of this do you know what occurred, Niece?'

Anne glared at her, her anger increasing. 'How could I, Aunt, when I have been here these last hours?'

The Duchess smiled triumphantly. 'They cheered and applauded her. Their cries of "God Bless Queen Katherine" could be heard by all in the court.'

'That would not please the King,' Anne answered furiously. She knew the common people disliked and mistrusted her. When she had been hunting with the King a month ago, they had hissed and jeered as she had passed by.

'It did not but it will remind him that the Queen is greatly loved and admired.'

'And you hastened to inform me of all this. I can see that it gives you much pleasure, Aunt,' Anne snapped.

The Duchess refused to be goaded. 'I thought you should be aware of it.' She lowered her voice. 'You are not his wife yet, Anne, there are still many obstacles in the path of your ambition, not least the Queen's determination that you shall have neither her husband nor her crown. And she has the support of the people, which you do not. I shall leave you now to contemplate the consequences of this morning's events on your position.'

Anne stared at her retreating back with a feeling akin to hatred. She had come too far along this road to turn aside now. What cared she for the opinions of the common people? So, they loved and supported the Queen, did that matter so much to her? She was loved and supported by the King, they were but *his* subjects. Her power was growing; now it was to her the courtiers flocked, seeking favours and advancement, not Katherine. Henry would make her his Queen no matter what the cost, she was certain of it. He had sworn an oath that he would and she did not doubt him. She would *not* let him break that promise. On his return she would greet him most lovingly. She would soothe his outraged feelings, his wounded pride and dignity, and remind him of the delights that lay ahead when she became his wife – and, most importantly, the promise of a son. She fingered the diamond he had so recently given her, determined to put out of her mind her aunt's vituperative remarks. It was she whom Henry loved passionately and he was determined to rid himself of Katherine, she told herself. But despite the heat of the day, she shivered. It was as if the sun had suddenly been hidden by a cloud.

Beverley, Yorkshire

'What news from London did Robert have, Will?' Joanna asked, rising awkwardly from her seat as her husband entered the chamber on his return from a visit to York. She was six months into her second pregnancy now and became tired late in the evening. While Will had been away she had been helping Meg to finalise the arrangements for her forthcoming marriage to Thomas Watford. Her mother-in-law and Thomas Tamford were travelling from Lund for the occasion and would need to be accommodated here in Beverley and Meg was having a fine new gown and hood of pink damascene made for the day – a gown Joanna had insisted on making for her sister-in-law. Will's trip to York had been to purchase a necklace as a wedding gift for his sister, as well as for business and to meet his friend Robert Aske.

Will poured himself a goblet of wine, thinking Joanna looked a little tired even though the rays of the slowly setting July sun pouring in through the window caught her cheeks, making them glow softly with warmth. There were dark circles beneath her eyes. 'A great deal. But you look weary, have you been exerting yourself too much with Meg's gown?'

She smiled. 'No, but there are still things to be arranged. What did you buy for Meg?'

He drew a small leather pouch from a pocket in his doublet. 'This. Tell me if you think she will like it?'

Carefully she extracted the gold chain from which hung a

sapphire pendant surrounded by seed pearls. 'I'm sure she will be delighted with it. It is beautiful. Now, what did Robert have to tell you of the King's Secret Matter? It is far from being "secret" any more, I fear.'

'That Cardinal Campeggio has suddenly and unexpectedly adjourned the Legatine Court to Rome. It seems that the King is not to have his decision on the annulment as speedily as he hoped and the Queen has appealed to her nephew, the Emperor. He is said to be furious about it and holds Thomas Wolsey responsible, and my lord of Suffolk declared loudly to all that we were never merry in this country while there are cardinals amongst us.'

'And what says Mistress Anne?' Joanna's tone was sharp. Over the months when it had become known that when the King's marriage to Queen Katherine was annulled the King intended to marry Anne Boleyn, her opinion of Anne had changed. Like nearly every married woman in the country she thought it disgraceful and unjust that a loyal and devoted wife – a princess of noble birth – be cast aside for a lowly girl who was twenty-one years younger than her.

Will shrugged. 'I think she will have a great deal to say. It is reported that she too holds the Cardinal responsible and remember, Joanna, this is not the first time Thomas Wolsey has had a hand in thwarting her desires. Robert says she is much changed from the girl we knew and Lord Henry loved. Now the King does as she commands, such is her influence over him.'

She nodded slowly, remembering how Henry Percy had adored the sixteen-year-old Anne Boleyn. She must indeed have changed in these past years. Often she wondered how he felt when he heard the news from London concerning her and the King. Fate had been so cruel to him. She would never forget the shock and grief she had felt when they had learned of the circumstances of his son's birth and tragic premature death. The Countess had eventually returned home but Will had told her that their marriage had deteriorated further. It was common knowledge that their relationship was bitter, resentful and strained. 'And did Robert have any news of my lord of Northumberland and the Countess?'

'Robert has learned that the Countess Mary's sister, the Lady Elizabeth Dacre, has taken up residence with her until she regains her health and spirits. She attended the Countess Mary at her wedding, if you recall?'

Joanna did. 'That will give the Countess great comfort, I am sure, although I fear that the Lady Dacre was not happy with her sister's marriage either. She spoke coldly to his lordship that day, I remember.'

Will sighed. 'I fear that the Earl and that lady's husband are at odds too. There is an old grudge between the Percys and the Dacres. It is to be hoped that the presence of his in-laws under Lord Henry's roof does not make things worse.'

'I'm sure the Countess will recover soon and then there will be no need for them to continue to stay.' She smiled at him. 'Will, I am so glad that we live far away from London and do not have to witness this . . . this humiliating treatment of the Queen.'

'Nor the over-weaning ambition and growing arrogance of Mistress Anne, abetted by her family and friends,' Will added.

She reached across and took his hand. 'I am so thankful too that we have found such happiness and contentment and now we shall have a second baby, unlike the poor Earl and his Countess. I thank God each day for my good fortune. I bless the day you pulled me from the river, you are a good man, Will, and I love you dearly.'

He smiled and kissed her hand. 'We are indeed blessed, my love. Let us hope that Meg will be equally happy with her husband for many are not. I wonder, if Mistress Anne becomes the King's wife, will she be content with her husband?'

Joanna said nothing. Only time would tell.

Chapter Thirty-Seven

1530
Greenwich Palace, London

THOMAS HOWARD TURNED AWAY from the fire that burned fiercely in the carved stone fireplace in his sumptuously furnished privy chamber. He'd spent the last half-hour staring into the flames, preoccupied by the problem that now confronted him and which was one of some magnitude. His hearing was excellent so he had heard the faint creak as the door to the chamber was opened slowly and with care. He smiled grimly; his visitor was a man to whom caution was second nature.

'I was not sure whether you would be here or still engaged . . . elsewhere . . . on other matters, your grace. I received word that you were seeking me.'

'Indeed, there is something of note I must discuss with you. Come in, Thomas, and take some wine with me. I trust you did not observe anyone loitering outside in the passageway?' he asked. His question was a mere formality; Thomas Boleyn was far too cautious and devious a man to let himself be observed entering – unannounced – the chambers of the Duke of Norfolk so late at night and in such a furtive manner.

He poured a goblet of rich Burgundy and handed it to his guest, indicating that he be seated. He did not particularly like his brother-in-law and it rankled that last December Boleyn had been elevated by the King to Earl of Wiltshire and Ormonde and had now been appointed Lord Privy Seal and a member of the Privy Council. Of course it had been at the instigation of his niece Anne. It would not do for the woman who had every expectation of becoming Queen to remain the daughter of a mere viscount. No indeed, so her father had been given an earldom and she was now Lady Anne Rochford and holding court as if she were Queen already. He smiled cynically to himself as he took a deep draught from his own goblet, his pale aesthetic features partly in shadow, his dark eyes watchful. My lord of Wiltshire had risen high in the service of the King – thanks mainly to his two daughters – although he grudgingly admitted that the man was an astute, experienced diplomat and was proving to be an efficient member of the Privy Council. He was also devious and unscrupulous in the pursuit of his ambitions, the foremost of which was to put his elder daughter on the throne of England. It was an ambition they shared for he had ever espoused any cause which would advance himself and the House of Howard.

Thomas Boleyn seated himself close to the fire and relished both the warmth and the fine quality of the wine. Beyond the palace walls a sleet-laden, bitter February gale blew downriver from the sea and hurled itself against the walls and windows, its icy draughts creeping down chimneys, through ill-fitting casements and along the wide galleries, but here in Norfolk's apartments it was comfortable and warm.

'I can assume that this interview is . . . confidential?' he asked cautiously.

The Duke nodded and handed him a letter. 'I received this a few hours since, directly from the hand of my lord of Shrewsbury.'

'Shrewsbury! George Talbot's loyalties lie with Queen Katherine; it is well known he opposes our influence and dislikes Anne intensely.'

'Talbot's foremost loyalty is to himself. He is not fool enough to openly antagonise the King but I agree he is no friend of ours,' Norfolk commented dryly.

'Then why does he write to you, your grace?' Thomas was deeply suspicious. In his experience he'd never found it prudent to trust anyone completely. He was wary now of Norfolk. Even though Anne was Norfolk's niece he would not be surprised if the Duke withdrew his support from their cause should he find it expedient to do so.

The Duke was aware of his companion's unease. 'He did not. You will note that it is not addressed to me but to Shrewsbury himself.'

Thomas frowned. 'You confuse me, your grace, I thought you said . . .'

The Duke refilled his goblet. 'I said it was given to me by Shrewsbury. Read it,' he instructed curtly. He watched his companion closely as he scanned the lines of the missive. Boleyn's expression changed from one of wary confusion to astonishment and finally anger.

'The ravings of a hysterical woman! But what she is implying does not bode well for Anne or for . . . us.'

The Duke nodded slowly. 'I agree, and quite obviously Shrewsbury had no wish to bring this matter to the attention of the King, as his weak-minded daughter instructs him to. Abetted by her sister, Lady Dacre, no doubt. Lady Dacre and her husband harbour malice towards my lord of Northumberland.'

Thomas stared at him hard, wondering if the Duke had already decided upon a course of action to have brought the letter to his attention so soon.

'You are aware that Mary Percy has left her husband and returned to her father's house in Sheffield?'

Boleyn shook his head. He turned his half-empty goblet slowly between his hands as he digested the Countess of Northumberland's revelations.

'Amidst accusations of ill treatment and allegations of poisoning. The stillbirth has obviously weakened her constitution, to say naught of her mind. Of course it is all without foundation. Harry Percy does not have the temperament to try to rid himself permanently of his wife in such a manner. Indeed I have but recently received a letter from him complaining of intolerable interference from his in-laws in what was already an insufferable relationship and denying all his wife's allegations. I know him well enough – he is my godson, after all – and I believe him.'

Thomas Boleyn wiped perspiration from his forehead. Suddenly the heat of Norfolk's chamber wasn't so welcome. 'But what are we to do about these . . . ravings? The woman is dangerous. Her accusations obviously derive from jealousy and spite but there are those who will seize upon them in order to discredit Anne in the eyes of the King and deny her the crown.' Fear and fury were crying for precedence in his reaction. That fool, Mary Percy, had vowed that there had been a pre-contract between her husband and his eldest daughter. She had written that Henry Percy had told her quite plainly that he would have preferred to have taken Anne as his wife, rather than herself, and that Anne was more fitted to have been a countess than she; she demanded that her father inform the King of these facts. A pre-contract between Anne and Henry Percy would put an end to any hope Henry Tudor had of making her his wife. 'With the matter of the annulment far from settled the King will have no wish to be told of anything which may serve to deny him what he desires most. He will be furious. I see now why Shrewsbury didn't take this letter to him.'

'Indeed, he did not wish the wrath of our sovereign lord to descend upon his head. He values it too much to risk it being severed from his body. But you are right, Thomas, the woman is dangerous and Shrewsbury is a fool not to keep her under closer restraint. We will have to show the letter to Anne – she must at least be aware of these allegations. And we must find a way to refute them.'

Thomas Boleyn rose and drew the folds of his fur-lined velvet surcoat closely around him. He smiled grimly. 'Fore-warned is forearmed, your grace. I will seek her out at once, there is no time for delay. You know how quickly rumours fly – be they true or false.'

'Be discreet about it,' the Duke warned.

Thomas nodded. 'I will bring her to my chambers before I make mention of it. Do you wish to speak with her too?'

'I wish to hear what she has to say upon the matter,' the Duke replied bluntly.

'Then I bid you to go there and wait as soon as I have departed,' Boleyn urged, leaving as quietly as he had arrived.

Less than half an hour later Thomas Boleyn entered his chambers with his daughter at his side. Norfolk rose from the table at which he had been seated, the letter in his hand.

'I understand that there is a matter of some importance you wish to discuss with me, Uncle?' Anne demanded imperiously, annoyed that she had been interrupted. She had been playing cards with her ladies and she had been winning. 'The King was not a little disconcerted at my departure for he does not like to be parted from me for even a short while.'

'I begged his indulgence most humbly, I assure you, your grace,' her father assured the Duke, irritated by her attitude.

Norfolk ignored him and handed her the parchment. 'I think you should read this, Niece.'

The jewels in the rings that adorned her fingers sparkled in the candlelight as she unfurled it and Norfolk mused that in the gown of purple velvet studded with precious stones and edged with fur and the diadem adorned with nineteen diamonds, a recent gift from the King, she looked regal. The fact that the gown was purple – the colour reserved exclusively for royalty – was a clear indication of how high in Henry Tudor's affections she now stood.

She read it quickly, her brows drawn together in a frown of concentration. When she'd finished she looked up at her uncle, her dark eyes narrowing. 'It is a pack of lies born of vicious spite! Did I not swear to you, Father, that I am still a maid?

Henry Percy had no carnal knowledge of me. That so called "contract" was invalid. It was *de futuro*, not legal and binding unless consummated. We were both young and foolish but he behaved honourably towards me.'

Norfolk, who had been studying her reactions carefully, could not help but admire her refusal to become dismayed or panicked by Mary Percy's allegations.

Her father was clearly relieved by her refutation. 'So, what action are we to take? Shrewsbury did not wish to bring this to the King's attention, fearing his wrath.'

'I shall take the letter myself to the King and demand that my lord of Northumberland be summoned to refute these lies,' she announced, her chin raised determinedly.

'Is that wise, Anne?' her father cautioned. 'It may be that *you* will incur his anger and suspicion.'

The smile she bestowed upon him was full of confidence and not a little arrogance, Norfolk thought.

'The King is never angry with me, Father. He is captivated by me. He is mine to command – so he frequently tells me – and I can do naught wrong in his eyes. The whole court is aware of it. Would you have me say nothing and let Mary Percy's spiteful accusations place all our hopes in jeopardy?'

'You would have Harry Percy summoned and confront him? Is *that* wise, Niece?' Norfolk asked gravely. He did not have her confidence in the hold she had over the King; he could remember a time when Katherine of Aragon could do naught wrong in her husband's eyes either. 'If indeed young Percy does still have feelings for you might he not betray them in his speech or manner? The King is an astute judge of men; he would quickly become aware of such sentiments.'

Anne shook her head as she folded the parchment. 'No, Harry Percy would not do such a thing. Besides, it was a long time ago and I doubt he still thinks of me with any affection. However, I shall ensure that I do not see him or he me, and that the King does not examine him. It is a matter for the bishops for it involves canon law. I shall speak with the King immediately.' She nodded curtly, tucking the parchment into the wide hanging sleeves of her purple gown. 'I bid you both good night.'

As she made her way back towards the King's apartments a little dart of anxiety stabbed her. Did Harry still think he was in love with her? If so, would he collude with his jealous, venomous wife and say they had indeed once been contracted? She pushed the thoughts away; she would *not* think such things. The contract had been declared invalid. Had it been otherwise his marriage to Mary Talbot would certainly not have been sanctioned by both the King and the Cardinal. Surely any feelings of love he had for her would be long dead? What she had felt for him certainly was. She would always think of him with a little affection, but nothing more even though she had once promised to be his wife. He had been her first love and a girl always remembered her first sweetheart fondly, even when she had been a wife and mother for many years. He would feel the same, she was certain, and would pose no threat to her. Harry Percy would not betray her: he would not want to hurt her, any more than she would ever hurt him if it was in her power to avoid it. And she felt, at the moment, that her power was a force others would have to reckon with.

Palace of Westminster, London

Norfolk was taken aback by his godson's appearance when Henry was ushered into the Council chamber. He corresponded regularly with the Earl but he had not seen him for some time. How old was he now? he pondered. Certainly no older than twenty-eight but he looked like a man approaching middle age. His shoulders were rounded like those of an old man who sat permanently hunched before the fire. He was pale; there were lines of suffering etched on his face and around the deep set dark eyes; and the hands that held the edges of his fur-lined surcoat close to him shook slightly as though he was afflicted with an ague. Fate, illness and the harsh climate of the North had indeed taken their toll, Norfolk thought.

'Your grace of Norfolk, I am come in response to the summons of our sovereign lord the King and the Council,' Henry greeted him formally. The journey from Alnwick in the harsh winter weather had been slow and hard but he had been forced to make it. How could he refuse? It had been with shock and dismay that he'd read Norfolk's letter. This was Mary's doing. When she'd left him, screaming hysterically that she would stay no longer and suffer his cruelty or risk death at his hand, she had vowed that she would do all in her power to discredit and harm him. He'd thought her threats idles, born out of disillusionment, dislike and a disappointment that had finally turned to bitter hatred, engendered by her state of mind and the malice her sister and her husband bore him. Her jealousy of Anne had increased and this was her attempt to prevent Anne from becoming Queen. The need to clear his name was an urgent one, and he felt all the gravity of the situation as he stood before the grave-faced assembly.

'Your diligence is to be commended, my lord of Northumberland. I pray you, be seated,' Norfolk replied solemnly. The young man didn't look capable of standing to answer the questions about to be put to him.

Henry was grateful for Norfolk's consideration. He felt far from well but was determined to face the Lords of the Privy Council and the Archbishops of Canterbury and York – resplendent in their gold and white robes – who were assembled before him, truthfully and with dignity.

'You are aware of the reason why you have been summoned?' Norfolk asked. He was certain that his godson would not be fool enough to admit to anything which could throw doubt upon the legitimacy of Anne's position. In fact he had hinted at it subtly in his letter.

'I am, your grace. It has been alleged by my wife that there was a pre-contract between myself and the Lady Anne Rochford. It is a lie, my lords,' Henry replied firmly. He refused to allow himself to think about that night, so long ago now, when he had asked her to marry him and she had agreed. He had never been as happy in his life before then – or since. He refused to allow himself to think of the utter despair and heartbreak he'd felt when he'd been informed that their betrothal was invalid in law because he had not slept with her. If he had he could have married her, despite his father and Wolsey. His life would have been a happy and fulfilled one and he would not be here now.

'We understand, my lord, that there existed a *de futuro* betrothal that was not consummated, making it invalid under canon law?' Norfolk stated, glancing in the direction of the archbishops, who both nodded their agreement.

Slowly Henry too nodded. He wished suddenly that he had asked Will Chatton to accompany him as he had done on his last visit to London. He had need of a trusted companion to bolster his spirits; being compelled to answer these questions resurrected such feelings of pain and unhappiness that it was hard to quell them. He had considered it but had dismissed the idea for not only was his former servant fully occupied with his business affairs and his two young sons, but Will knew all the details of his love affair with Anne and he had feared that Will would be examined by the Council concerning his knowledge of it.

'And furthermore, your marriage to the Lady Mary Talbot was sanctioned by Cardinal Wolsey and the King – which would not have been the case had there been a legal and binding pre-contract.'

Again Henry nodded. 'It was, your grace.'

'Are you willing to swear before my lords the Archbishops that everything you have said is the truth before God?'

Henry rose slowly and knelt before the two clergymen, folding his hands as if in prayer. 'I do swear to Almighty God before you, my lord Archbishops, that there was no valid pre-contract between myself and the Lady Anne Rochford and that when this hearing is over I shall hear Mass and take the Sacred Host to give further credence to the substance and sanctity of my oath.'

Both men rose and William Warham, Archbishop of Canterbury, raised Henry to his feet. 'My lord of Northumberland, no man would put his immortal soul in such peril as to swear a false oath and then take the Sacrament. We are satisfied that you have spoken the truth and will convey this to the King. You may return to your home. Go, with God's blessing.'

Henry thanked him with some relief and was grateful when Norfolk took his arm and led him from the chamber. It had been an ordeal he could well have done without.

'I will accompany you to Mass, Henry,' Norfolk said, more affable now the formalities were over. 'Although that gesture was not necessary, they believed what you told them.'

'It was not a mere gesture, your grace, and I am thankful the matter is now closed and I can return home,' Henry replied.

'It is a matter that should never have arisen at all. You have your wife and her sister to thank for the suffering of body and spirit you have endured.'

'I know it. I cannot conceive why she hates me so much. I never wished her harm; I never ill treated her.'

'Jealousy and spite. I am well acquainted with them both,' Norfolk replied grimly.

'Careless words spoken in anger during an argument, of which I have to admit there were many,' Henry said ruefully. 'But I am grateful for your consideration. The journey has caused me not a little hardship.'

'I warrant that you do not miss Lady Northumberland's presence?' Norfolk mused aloud, thinking that he would think himself most fortunate if Elizabeth, Duchess of Norfolk, would take herself off to some distant house and remain there indefinitely. She was a constant thorn in his side.

'I wish I could say I do, but it would be a lie. There was never any . . . affection . . . between us. Then, after the child was born dead . . . you are aware of how things deteriorated. I have no heir; my brother Thomas will inherit.'

Norfolk looked sceptical. 'I would not put too much faith in Thomas, Henry. His reputation goes before him. He is of a rebellious nature; I have heard that his dealings with the treacherous Kerrs will not stand close scrutiny. Be wary in your dealings with him.'

Henry frowned. Norfolk obviously had spies in the North Country but he had heard nothing of his brother's involvement with the Scottish clan, who resided mainly in Teviotdale and whom he considered little more than outlaws. He sighed: was he never to know peace within his home and family?

As they entered the chapel Norfolk turned to him. 'You have at least removed any doubts the King had concerning Anne and she will be grateful for it.' He lowered his voice. 'The Cardinal is in disgrace. He no longer enjoys the position and influence he once had. He no longer enjoys his many palaces and vast wealth either. Five of them and their contents now belong to the King and he has not seen Wolsey in person since last summer, although he still corresponds with him. The Lady Anne will not allow it and the King listens to her now and no one else – as many are finding to their cost and dismay. She lays the blame for the slowness in obtaining the annulment and Katherine's continuing obstinacy at the Cardinal's feet, something she reminds the King of almost daily.'

Henry didn't reply. Although Wolsey had been instrumental in bringing so much grief and heartache into his life he did not hate him for it. It was not in his nature to harbour feelings of bitterness and revenge. It appeared that now the wolves were snapping at the Cardinal's heels, ready to tear him to pieces.

He just wanted to return home, to do his duty as Lord Warden and to try to find a small measure of peace, away from the intrigues, plotting and ruthless pursuit of wealth and ambition which seemed of paramount importance to men like the Earls of Shrewsbury and Wiltshire, the Duke of Suffolk – and his godfather, Thomas Howard.

Chapter Thirty-Eight

Topcliffe, Yorkshire

'MASTER CHATTON, THIS IS indeed a surprise but you are most welcome,' Maynard greeted Will cordially as he hurried down the steps into the courtyard, at the same time gesturing assertively for grooms to attend to the horses and servants to take the visitors' saddlebags into the castle.

Will smiled at him. On his last visit here he'd found the Steward of the Household hospitable, honest and unswervingly loyal to his master. 'I trust our descending upon you without warning will not cause any inconvenience but I fear the weather is fast closing in.' He shivered and glanced upwards at the ponderous grey clouds just visible through the deepening November dusk. They were heavy with either sleet or snow, he thought.

'Of course not. I fear it would be unwise to travel further tonight. I will have a chamber prepared for you and inform the

Earl of your arrival,' Maynard replied agreeably. 'But first you must eat and warm yourselves.'

Will and his travelling companion were ushered along the passageway in the undercroft and then up a staircase which led to the great hall. Already the cressets on the wall had been lit and Will was heartened by their glow. Supper was over but Maynard led them to the fire and instructed that spiced ale be served immediately whilst two serving maids were sent in haste to the kitchens to procure food.

'As you say, it would have been foolhardy to continue our journey. We were within a few miles' distance but I was unsure if his lordship would be here. Is he well, Maynard?'

The steward raised his eyes to the hammer-beamed roof. 'As well as can be expected, Master Chatton, considering the harshness of the weather and the perpetual upheaval of travelling. I pray that the unrest on the Border does not deteriorate to such an extent that my lord is required to venture up there.'

Will nodded and introduced his companion. 'Master Steward, this is my stepfather, Thomas Tamford. I am returning to Beverley and he to Lund; we have come from Morpeth.'

'Indeed, you are also most welcome, Master Tamford,' Maynard replied courteously. He had been wondering who the old man was for he was well past the age to be Will Chatton's servant and it was obvious that the journey had taken its toll on him; he looked close to exhaustion. 'When you have dined I will have you shown to your chamber. There will be a warm comfortable bed for you this night, Master Tamford.'

'That be much appreciated, sir, these old bones do not take kindly to riding any distance these days and I feel the cold keenly,' Thomas answered, a little in awe of the efficient

Maynard and his present grand surroundings. He was more at ease in the stone cottage in Lund where he'd lived ever since he'd married Will's mother. Bone-weary and longing for the warm comfortable bed the steward had promised he had no wish to find himself in the presence of the great Earl of Northumberland. He was a man of humble birth, as was Will, but he had none of his stepson's confidence.

'From Morpeth? Had you business there, Master Chatton?'

Will shook his head. 'No. Sadly my mother died last week and it was her wish to be buried in Morpeth where she was born and where her kin also lie. We could not deny her that last request but it has been a far from easy journey – for many reasons.'

'My condolence on your loss. I hope she did not suffer greatly,' Maynard replied gravely.

'No indeed, she went peacefully. Thomas cared for her most devotedly during the last weeks.'

Thomas nodded sadly. 'She was a good woman and she wanted for nothing, thanks to Will. Her latter years were comfortable and peaceful as mine have been but I will miss her sorely.'

The serving maids appeared, bearing bowls and dishes, and Maynard left them briefly to make sure his instructions concerning their guests' accommodation had been carried out. When he returned it was to inform Will that Lord Henry wished to see him in his privy chamber and to conduct Will's stepfather to the hastily prepared bedchamber.

Henry was genuinely pleased to see his former squire and shook Will warmly by the hand. 'It was fortunate that you were travelling close at hand, Will, for the snow is falling heavily now, although Maynard has informed me of the circumstances that prompted your journey. My sincere condolences.'

'Thank you, my lord. Death is something we must all face but she went with dignity and in comfort.'

Henry poured two goblets of wine and handed one to Will and bade him be seated. 'What news of your family, Will?'

'Joanna is well; the children are thriving, my lord. My sister Margaret appears content with her new husband and I shall continue to ensure that my stepfather has comfort and security in his remaining years. He cared greatly for my mother. Business too is good, thank God. How fare your lady mother, sisters and brothers, Lord Henry?'

Henry frowned. 'Mother and my sisters are well but . . . but Thomas and Ingram . . .' He sighed heavily. 'I fear they continue to embroil themselves in the incessant mischief-making on the Border and with the Clan Kerr. I swear they will both feel the force of my anger if it continues. Thomas petitioned me for the position of Deputy Warden of either the East or Middle Marches but I refused him. He is arrogant and foolhardy and would not use his powers wisely. Instead the post has been given to Lord Ogle whom I trust. The decision has not been received favourably by many and least of all by my brother.'

Will looked grave. 'Clan Kerr! Known, I believe, as "the brigands of Teviotdale"?'

Henry nodded. 'I can but hope that the Kerrs do not follow Angus's example and beg the King for sanctuary when their behaviour becomes intolerable to King James. I have Angus safely ensconced at Norham but confined to his allotted chambers. He does not have the freedom to roam at will and thereby acquaint himself with the castle's fortifications and defences, such as they are. I still do not trust him. Who knows when he will decide to turn his coat again and return to Scotland, swearing allegiance to James?'

'The King is aware of all this, my lord?' Will queried.

Henry nodded curtly, swiftly pushing all thoughts of Henry Tudor to the back of his mind, for to dwell on the King was to be reminded of Anne.

They sat in silence for a while, drinking wine and staring into the fire until they were interrupted by Maynard.

'My lord, we have another visitor. Sir Walter Walshe has arrived, having come from London at the behest of the King's Privy Council,' he announced, looking decidedly uneasy.

Henry rose, his dark eyes filled with grave concern. 'Bring him to me, Maynard. I would find out what matter is so important that he has travelled so far.'

The steward nodded, glancing surreptitiously at Will who had also risen.

'You will wish to see Sir Walter in private, my lord,' Will stated.

Henry shook his head. Whatever news Walshe had brought he was certain it would not be welcome and he was glad Will Chatton was here. 'No, I wish you to remain, Will.'

Will resumed his seat as Maynard departed. 'You think it is something . . . ?'

Henry smiled grimly. 'News from London is never good these days, I fear. I pray it is not a summons for me to go to court.'

Walter Walshe was a tall, middle-aged man with a rather florid complexion, which was heightened by the exertions of his long and arduous journey and the inclement weather. He had been greatly relieved to have reached Topcliffe before the snow had become too heavy. 'Lord Northumberland, I bring urgent instructions from the Privy Council,' he greeted Henry, eyeing Will suspiciously.

'Anything you have to say, Sir Walter, can be said before Master Will Chatton. He is a respected merchant of Beverley and my former squire and companion,' Henry said firmly.

Walshe nodded curtly. 'It concerns the Lord Cardinal, Thomas Wolsey. You are instructed, my lord, to go with all haste to Cawood and arrest the Cardinal on a charge of treason. I have here the warrant but you are instructed that under no circumstances is Wolsey to be allowed to read the warrant for his arrest. You are then to send him without delay, in the care of Sir Roger Lassells, to the Earl of Shrewsbury at Sheffield. My lord of Shrewsbury will then escort him to London to stand trial. Those are my instructions, my lord.'

Henry stared at him, trying to digest his words and shaking his head. 'Treason? What treason has the Cardinal committed?' Of course he had heard that Wolsey had fallen from favour, that his wealth and palaces had been confiscated by the King, who had finally allowed him to travel north to take up his position as Archbishop of York, after the Dukes of Norfolk and Suffolk had divested him of his seals of office.

'Letters have been obtained that clearly show he has been secretly corresponding with Rome and therefore he is charged with treasonously inviting foreign rulers to interfere in the governance of the King's Realm and undermine our sovereign lord's authority.'

'Letters! By whom were these letters "obtained"?' Henry asked quietly, still unable to believe that the once great Cardinal was now to be arrested and sent like a common felon to London.

'I believe, my lord, they were obtained by the Lady Anne Rochford,' Walshe replied, his expression unreadable.

Will, despite his own astonishment at the news of Wolsey's fate, was watching Henry closely. He could only guess at the turmoil Walshe's words were causing his former master.

Henry strove to hide his feelings from his companions, taking the parchment from Walshe and breaking the seal. So, she had at last triumphed over Wolsey. She had somehow obtained proof of the crime of which he was now accused. Letters from Rome – but were they legitimate or mere forgeries? He would probably never find out. Did she assume he still bore the Cardinal malice for past wrongs as she undoubtedly did? He was unlikely to find the answer to that question either. He scanned the instructions and then folded them again.

'Thank you, Sir Walter. You must now dine and rest. I assume you are to accompany me to Cawood?' Henry placed the parchment carefully on a table.

'I am, my lord, and I thank you for your hospitality,' Walshe replied, relieved the interview was over and the responsibility for the Cardinal's arrest now lay firmly with the Earl of Northumberland.

When he'd shown the man out Henry picked up the warrant and sat down, facing his friend. 'How the mighty are fallen, Will.'

'Indeed. He will have no fair and just trial, he will be executed, Lord Henry, we both know that.'

Henry shook his head sadly. 'He is an old man now and I

hear he is sick. I bear him no malice no matter what . . . others may think. I feel nothing but pity for him, for he served his master well. He does not deserve to be treated thus.'

Will marvelled at Henry's generosity of spirit. He himself could not be so forgiving. 'He treated you very badly, my lord. I cannot forget that he forbade you to attend your father's funeral, took control of your finances – forcing you to live in penury – and filled your household with spies. At every turn he sought to thwart and humiliate you.'

Henry rose and refilled their goblets. 'I do not bear grudges, Will, nor do I let bitterness and the desire for revenge gnaw away at me. There is enough suffering in life to contend with.' He gazed sadly into the fire, thinking of the futility of his efforts to bring peace and justice to the Border, his failed marriage, his dead son, his brother's jealousy and rebelliousness and the ailments that afflicted him with increasing severity.

'But I fear the Lady Anne Rochford does, my lord,' Will said quietly.

'As do every one of her family. My godfather Norfolk always hated and despised Wolsey and was envious of the power he once held. I fear they will all have encouraged her to bring about his downfall.' He still could not find it in his heart to blame her entirely. He could not equate the woman who had brought Wolsey down, by all accounts a self-centred and imperious creature with her sights fixed implacably on a crown, with the charming, generous and endearing young girl he'd known.

Will didn't reply. He was aware of how much the Lady Anne had changed from the girl Henry had loved, even if Henry seemed oblivious to it. There were too many tales of her growing arrogance and merciless ambition and the power she now had over the King. The power that Thomas Wolsey once exercised. Will too wondered if it was upon her instructions that Henry had been ordered to arrest the Cardinal. If so, then she was certainly seeking revenge for the hurt and humiliation Wolsey had caused her all those years ago. And of course she blamed the Cardinal for attempting to thwart her latest ambition: to become Queen of England. 'Do you wish me to accompany you to Cawood, my lord?' he asked.

Henry considered it. It was a journey he was reluctant to make but like so many things in his life he had no choice. He had no desire to witness the old man's shame and despair, for Wolsey would know that only an ignominious death awaited him. He would welcome Will's company. 'What of your stepfather?' he asked tentatively.

'I shall ask Thomas to go first to Beverley to inform Joanna that I have been . . . delayed. I shall urge him to rest there, to await my return. I should not wish either Joanna or the old man to be worried by my absence. I shall tell him that you have need of my services but that is all, my lord. News of the Cardinal's arrest will spread quickly enough once we reach Cawood.'

Henry nodded, relieved. 'I bid you to retire now, Will. There is much we must do tomorrow. Thankfully Cawood is no great distance away. We should be there the day after tomorrow, and you should be back in Beverley in a few days.'

Will rose and placed his empty goblet on a press. The candles had burned down and Henry's face was partly in shadow. ''Tis but a short space of time to lose, Lord Henry, and it is something I wish to witness. The Cardinal has been no friend to you, my lord, and I do not have the same capacity for forgiveness as you.'

Henry remained silent as Will withdrew, trying to focus on the preparations he must make next morning while striving to keep at bay the thought of what awaited the Cardinal in London. He could lay most of the unhappiness in his life at the feet of Thomas Wolsey but it never helped to hark back to the past. All he could do now was pray that both he and the Cardinal could find the courage to face the future.

Cawood Manor, Yorkshire

The snow had melted by the time they left Topcliffe although it was still bitterly cold. Henry was muffled in a cape of soft leather lined with fur over a shirt of fine wool and a doublet of padded brocade. Thick gauntlets protected his hands and leather boots his feet but beneath his warm garments he shivered uncontrollably. It had little to do with the weather, it was an affliction he suffered more and more frequently, unconnected with the ague which reoccurred during the winter months. Will rode beside him, equally muffled up, against the cold, while Sir Walter rode behind and was followed by two dozen armed marcher men in the Earl's employ.

Will had made sure that his stepfather had enough food and warm clothing for the journey to Beverley and had given him a letter for Joanna, urging him to stay with her until he returned. Henry had instructed a groom and two retainers to accompany the old man to ensure no harm befell him.

They reached the manor of Cawood, which lay some nine miles south of the city of York, by early afternoon of the next day. It was cold, grey and blustery with flurries of sleet born on the biting wind but as they passed through the gates Will noted that although obviously chilled and tired Henry looked to be calm and in control of his emotions.

The large stone house built of yellowish-coloured local stone was a fraction of the size of York Place, the Cardinal's magnificent London palace, now in possession of the King. It was substantial, Will mused, but certainly not huge or ostentatious. The porter came out to greet them, his expression one of consternation upon seeing the armed men, their livery emblazoned with the crescent moon emblem of the Earl of Northumberland.

Henry reined in his horse. 'Master Porter, I demand that you give up to me the keys to the gates.'

'My lord, I cannot give up the keys. Not without the permission of the Lord Cardinal, my master,' the man replied stubbornly.

'Do as you are bid, we come in the name of the King!' Walshe demanded harshly.

The porter held his ground but looked uncertainly from the Earl to Walshe. 'My lord, I dare not.'

Henry nodded. 'You are a faithful servant to your master. Keep the keys but let no one leave without my express permission. Now, I bid you send word to your master that I wish to speak to him.'

Walshe looked decidedly uneasy as the man departed and Will wondered if Henry had been wise. The Cardinal seemed to have a great number of retainers and servants here, he saw, and since their arrival many had either come out into the courtyard or been peering through the windows at the Earl's party.

At length the man returned. 'My lord of Northumberland, my master bids you welcome and asks that you join him.'

Henry dismounted as did his entourage and both Will and Walshe followed him into the manor house.

If it was not as big as York Place or Hampton Court, Cawood was almost as richly furnished, Will thought as they were led up the staircase to Wolsey's apartments. The Cardinal was certainly not living in reduced circumstances. The last time he had seen Thomas Wolsey had been when Lord Henry had gone to London to report to the King upon the state of law and order on the border, when the Cardinal had still been high in the King's favour. He wondered if the Cardinal would be as little changed in person as he appeared to be in circumstance, at least outwardly.

Henry too was glancing around, taking in the rich tapestries that covered the walls, the carved presses and cupboards, the silver plate and candlesticks. He stopped abruptly as the Cardinal came from his chambers to greet them. Wolsey was still lavishly attired in scarlet silk and velvet but the flesh had fallen from his bones: his skin was sallow and hung loosely. But the deep-set eyes had not changed.

'My lord of Northumberland, you are most welcome. Alas, dinner is over but I have commanded that the table stand, although I fear there is no more good fish. But come to the fire while a chamber is prepared and your trunks are brought up. It is a cold day to be travelling.'

Although age and the signs of illness were upon him, Wolsey had not lost his air of command or arrogance, Will observed as the Cardinal embraced Lord Henry. Did he really not understand how far from grace he had fallen? Did such an astute man not wonder why Henry was here and with a retinue of armed men? Wolsey's serpentine gaze alighted on him and he nodded curtly in recognition. Will stiffened. He could not forgive or forget the way Wolsey had publicly humiliated Henry, broken his heart and his spirit that day in the long gallery at York Place, even if his former master could.

'Ah, my lord, I see you have taken to heart the advice I gave you when you were with me at York Place many years ago. You have kept faith with your old friends and retainers; may they serve you faithfully and well. Come, take your ease in my chamber,' Wolsey urged, indicating that Henry join him in his private apartments.

Will noticed Walshe's hand tighten on the hilt of his sword.

Henry did not follow Wolsey, instead he stood quite still. Now that the time had come, he prayed his voice would betray none of the emotions he was experiencing for he, too, had been forcefully reminded of that day in the long gallery. He took a deep breath, laid a hand on Wolsey's arm and said quietly, 'My lord, I arrest you for high treason.'

Wolsey stared at him in utter astonishment, bereft of speech.

Will's fingers closed over the handle of the dagger he wore suspended from his belt. A ripple of shock ran through the room as the Cardinal's servants and those of the Earl shifted uneasily, eyeing each other with open hostility.

Wolsey found his voice. His sallow skin was suffused with the blood of anger and the dark eyes glinted with undisguised scorn. 'I will not submit to this arrest, my lord! It is the malice you and your forebears harbour against me for words and deeds long past that drives you to this course. Unless I see the warrant for my arrest I shall not submit.'

Henry stared at him coldly, the pity he had felt evaporating. He had not expected such a display of stubborn arrogance. 'It has naught to do with events long past and scarce recalled. When I was sworn Lord Warden of the Marches, it was you who impressed upon me the fact that I might arrest all men who are guilty of crimes – except the King. You are accused of high treason, my lord, and I have the warrant for your arrest, signed by the King himself.'

His words and the quiet but calm tone seemed to deflate the bubble of the Cardinal's defiance and the colour drained from Wolsey's face. 'As a member of the Apostolic See I am subject to no temporal authority, I answer only to God and His representative on earth: the Pope.'

Henry remained silent.

Wolsey turned to Walshe. 'I appeal to you, sir?'

Walshe did not flinch. 'My lord of Northumberland speaks the truth. He holds the warrant for your arrest, which he has been most firmly instructed to keep private from yourself. He bears no malice towards you, my lord. His orders come directly from the King. I brought them from the court but two days since.'

It was as if all the fight had drained from the Cardinal, Will thought.

Wolsey turned his back on Henry. He knew who had instigated this, she whom he had once dismissed as a 'foolish girl of little estate'. Underestimating her had possibly been the gravest mistake he had ever made. She had plotted his downfall ever since the day he had denied her the opportunity of

becoming Countess of Northumberland. Now, despite everything, she would become Queen of England. He was certain
that it was she who had chosen Henry Percy to arrest him: it
was of a piece with her vindictive nature. Well, he would not
afford her such satisfaction. It would be his last act of defiance.

'I will not submit to you, my lord of Northumberland. I will
submit instead to Walter Walshe, a lowly servant of the Privy
Council.'

'So be it,' Henry replied curtly. 'Sir Walter, I command that
my lord Cardinal be attended upon by his own servants and
retainers.'

Walshe looked quickly at the Cardinal's scarlet-clad back
and lowered his voice. 'My lord, is that wise? They outnumber
us and if—'

'I would heap no more humiliations upon the Lord
Cardinal's head, Sir Walter,' Henry interrupted. 'His servants
shall attend him and he shall be allowed to make his farewells
to his tenants and bestow his blessings upon them as befits a
prince of the Church. Tomorrow he may say Mass and then Sir
Roger Lasselles will escort him to Sheffield.' Henry turned and
walked away, leaving Wolsey alone to contemplate his fate.

'My lord, you have dealt with him more justly and kindly
than I warrant he deserves,' Will said to Henry as they
descended the staircase. 'I fear his over-weaning self-importance has not decreased. He still fails to comprehend that he
rose so high only because he was befriended by the King. And
it is the King who holds the power of life and death.'

'Let the man have his last moments of dignity, Will, for
disgrace and death await him,' Henry replied, thankful that
tomorrow he would turn the Cardinal over to Roger Lassells,

depart from Cawood and return north. Most probably he would go to Warkworth, for that castle set on the wild rugged Northumberland coast would afford him much-needed isolation. He wanted no further part in the machinations of the Boleyns. The events of the past few days had stirred memories and emotions he had thought to leave buried. It seemed that Anne, however distant, still had the power to throw his carefully ordered thoughts into turmoil.

Chapter Thirty-Nine

1532
Windsor Castle, Berkshire

'THERE, YOU ARE PERFECT!' Mary Carey put down the hairbrush and stood back smiling with undisguised admiration at her elder sister. She had never seen Anne looking so . . . so *majestic*, she thought. Her crimson velvet gown with its elegant wide hanging sleeves lined with silver tissue was studded all over with precious gems and edged with ermine. There were diamonds around her throat and wrists and two huge pear-shaped gems hung from her earlobes. Her dark hair cascaded loosely around her shoulders reaching almost to her waist and had a rich glossy sheen to it. Her sister seemed almost incandescent with beauty. 'But are you not just a little nervous, Anne?' she whispered.

Anne laughed, a tinkling sound filled with excitement, delight and supreme confidence. 'What is there to be nervous about, Mary? Is not a great honour to be bestowed upon me this day? Am I not to become the Lady Marquess of Pembroke? A lady of high estate in my own right.' She lifted her head in a gesture of quiet satisfaction. 'I shall no longer be dependent upon whatever title Father holds for my status.'

Mary nodded, although she could still not quite believe that her sister really *was* destined to become the King's wife and Queen of England: Anne had risen to such unimaginable heights. There were times when Mary realised how foolish she had been in falling headlong into the King's arms and bed. But she had loved him; she had wanted only to be his adored mistress, not his wife. She had gained very little from so willingly achieving that goal while Anne had gained everything by denying him. She had been cast aside after a brief while; Anne had captivated him for years and had far more influence over him than she had ever had. She wondered if her sister truly loved Henry Tudor. She swore she did but Mary was not certain she spoke the truth. Such a man as he could offer everything: power, wealth, position beyond all imagining – what woman would refuse all that?

She was now a widow with two small children, poor William Carey had died of the sweating sickness four years ago, and she was dependent upon Anne for her position at court, indeed for everything. Yet her sister had never reminded her of her foolishness in not securing a better position and future for herself or her children.

'Lady Carey, it is time for the Lady Anne to proceed to the presence chamber,' Eleanor, Countess of Rutland, instructed briskly while the Countess of Sussex carefully draped the crimson velvet cloak edged with ermine over the right arm of

Lady Mary Howard, the Duke of Norfolk's young daughter, who was to walk behind her cousin Anne carrying the gold coronet in her left hand.

Mary stepped back and went to take her place amongst the ladies of her sister's retinue. She held no grand title, she was really of very little importance now but somehow that knowledge did not upset or dismay her. She would be content to live quietly at Hever with Catherine and Henry; she adored her children and fretted when she was away from them. She loved the countryside; she never found it quiet and boring as Anne did. She was not jealous of Anne.

Although it was a triumphant day for her sister there were some ladies, steadfastly loyal to Queen Katherine, who had refused to attend this ceremony, notably the King's sister Mary Tudor, Dowager Queen of France and Duchess of Suffolk, and their aunt, Elizabeth Howard, Duchess of Norfolk. And they were perhaps the two most important ladies in the realm, apart from Katherine and Anne herself. Mary felt some pity for Katherine who had been ignominiously banished to Ampthill with a greatly reduced household and separated from her precious daughter the Princess Mary, but who was still adamantly declaring that her marriage to the King was lawful. They had heard how on her journey to Ampthill the common people had flocked from the towns and villages to cheer and call blessings upon Katherine their Queen as she passed by. They had little affection for Anne whom they called 'Nan Bullen' or worse. When she heard of Katherine's triumphant progress Anne had been furious, crying out that it was a disgrace and an insult to the King. He had banished Katherine so she should not be fêted in such a manner, but there had been little she could do. She could not make the people love her and she had told Mary she didn't care. She had the love and affection of the King and that mattered more than the feelings of the common people and she'd sworn that when she was Queen her court would be as decorous and devout as Katherine's had been.

The procession moved slowly towards the door to the presence chamber, which had been opened wide. Beyond it the ancient stone walls were hung with tapestries and pennants and the September sun streamed into the chamber, illuminating the rich attire of the guests the King had invited to witness the elevation of the woman he worshipped.

As she passed through the doorway and entered the chamber Anne caught her first glimpse of the glittering assembly that awaited her. The French Ambassador; the Venetian Ambassador; the Imperial Ambassador; Charles Brandon, Duke of Suffolk; her Uncle Norfolk; Thomas Cromwell, the new Lord Chancellor who had replaced Wolsey – who had cheated the executioner by dying at Leicester. Thomas Cranmer, destined to be the new Archbishop of Canterbury, surrounded by all the archbishops and bishops in their magnificent robes who were supportive of the King's position. Her father, now an Earl, and her brother George, now a baron, looked proudly on. But although they had both been elevated beyond their highest expectations it was she they had come to honour today. She had secured her own destiny without relying on their assistance. She would leave this chamber a marquess: a noblewoman with lands and palaces of her own and the sum of one thousand pounds a year to maintain her high estate.

Her heart beat faster with excitement as she walked slowly

and with great dignity between the ranks of the assembled nobility and bishops towards the raised dais where, on the chair of estate beneath the richly embroidered canopy of state, sat the King. She smiled at him; she felt and looked radiant. Henry was raising her to the position of Lady Marquess because he knew that most of the universities had declared in his favour regarding the annulment and he was confident that he could now pressurise Pope Clement into granting it very soon – and then he would make her his Queen. He had instructed Thomas Cromwell to begin to set out the Appeals Statute which forbade any future matrimonial disputes to be referred to Rome. He was taking her to France next month as his consort – a magnificent display of pomp and wealth was planned – and she would be received and treated as the equal of the royal ladies of Francis's court. She was nearing the end of that long road she had set her foot upon years before.

She had been a most dutiful daughter. She had raised the Boleyns from humble knights to the highest positions in the land and she was now approaching the pinnacle of her ambition. Henry adored her, he could not bear to be apart from her, he listened to her opinions and advice, he delighted in her wit and her accomplishments, he debated the new religious teachings with her. How could she ever have thought that she would have been content as the wife of Harry Percy? A mere countess, forced to reside in those bleak, remote fortress castles in the North with few comforts, jewels or fine clothes and no standing at all, save that of wife to an impoverished husband? Now, only the finest, the richest, the most costly gowns, furs and precious gems were good enough for Anne Boleyn, the future Queen of England.

She had reached the dais and sank slowly into a deep curtsy, bowing her head so that her raven-dark, shining tresses fell becomingly about her shoulders. She had caught Henry's benign smile as he stepped towards her. She glimpsed in his eyes the love and admiration he felt and knew that never had he seen her look so beautiful or so regally elegant. She knew too that never had he desired her more. The crimson gown that encased her slim body emphasised her narrow waist and then flared over her hips. Its low square neckline bordered with diamonds and goldsmith's work showed the soft mounds of her breasts pushed high by the boned stays of her bodice. Her slender neck was adorned with diamonds and her huge dark eyes were shining with love and pride. She was certain now that he would defy everyone, the Pope included, to make her his wife and *soon*.

He took her hands in his and raised her up as the patent of creation was read out by the Bishop of Winchester. Then he took the ermine-trimmed cloak from Mary Howard and placed it around her shoulders; the gold coronet he placed on her head. What sons she would bear him, she thought. Strong, lusty, handsome. Perhaps with his red-gold hair and her dark eyes and their combined intelligence, shrewdness and ambition. Sons who would make England a nation to be admired and feared throughout Europe. And what pleasure he would derive from their conception. Pleasure she had promised for so many long years.

City of London

Outside the Quill Tavern's walls a thick mist was descending, enveloping the narrow streets and muffling the cries of the Watch, but inside the hostelry it was well lit, warm and crowded, mainly with the clerks and a few lawyers from the Inns of Court.

Will pushed his way through the throng carrying two tankards of ale to where Robert Aske sat at a table made of scarred oak planks. Will's mulberry worsted doublet braided with black satin and his intricately embroidered white lawn undershirt set him apart from the clerks in their sombre black gowns.

'I fear the dampness of the fog from the river has driven many folk to seek refuge,' Aske remarked cheerfully. 'It is seldom as crowded as this.'

Will set the tankards down, nodding. 'I had forgotten how chill the October mists can be and that it is not only in the North that we suffer from them.'

'When do you return there, Will?'

'In two days' time.'

'Then you will have supper with me at Mistress Brookes's house tomorrow? She will be pleased to see you and learn how Joanna and the boys are faring. She remembers Joanna with great fondness.'

'I should be most happy to do so, Robert, and Joanna would not forgive me if I refused. She begged me to find the time to call upon her.'

'Then it is settled. How fares trade?'

'The Flemish merchants are still paying well for good

quality English woollen cloth and the trade in fine wines brings in handsome profits. Let us hope that peace with both France and the Emperor long continues. Wars do no good to anyone, least of all traders,' Will replied.

Aske raised his tankard. 'Spoken like a true merchant! To peace and prosperity and your continued good health.'

Will grinned. 'Your good health and fortune, Robert.'

'I doubt you have need to fear for your trade in wines, Will. Not while our sovereign lord entertains and sports with King Francis and the Lady Anne delights the gentlemen of the French court, although I hear that certain aspects of the visit have not gone to plan, much to her annoyance.'

Will raised his eyebrows. Robert heard things well before they became common knowledge in the North.

He elaborated. 'Indeed, the royal ladies of France refused to meet her. King Francis's wife is the Emperor's sister – Queen Katherine is her aunt – and I hear tell that Francis's own sister declared she would not meet "the King's whore".'

'So creating her a Lady Marquess has not had the desired effect,' Will replied dryly. 'So, what did King Henry have to say on this matter?'

Aske shrugged. 'There was little he could say. He travelled alone to meet Francis, leaving the Lady Anne in Calais until he returned with Francis and the gentlemen. Then he held a huge banquet for them with the Lady Anne as hostess although I doubt it served to soothe her feelings.'

Will pondered this. It must have been both humiliating and disappointing for her, he mused, but both his and Joanna's sympathies lay with Queen Katherine. 'And there is still no word from Rome concerning the annulment?'

'I fear there will be serious conflict with Pope Clement over it but I also fear that the King will marry her despite everything. He is besotted with her. Some whisper he is bewitched.'

'He would risk a bigamous marriage and excommunication?'

Again Aske shrugged. 'There are those at court who encourage him to defy Clement. Those who say the King and not the Pope should be head of the Church in England and . . .' He lowered his voice. '. . . and I have heard that the Lady Anne encourages him to look favourably upon the New Learning. She has obtained books that are banned and has brought them to his attention, debating the merits of them with him.'

'Surely that is dangerous? Has not the King declared Luther to be a heretic?'

'He did but such is her hold over him . . . and now that Archbishop Warham is dead and Cranmer – ever the King's man – ready to step into his shoes, I truly fear for our faith, Will.'

Will shook his head. 'The King is a devout Catholic; he would not jeopardise his immortal soul by risking excommunication.'

'The King desires a male heir above all else, Will. Queen Katherine failed in that respect. The Lady Anne is young and healthy and his passion for her has not abated.'

Will drank deeply, wondering if his friend was right. If he was, it did not bode well for the future of the Catholic faith in England and in the northern counties that faith was very strongly adhered to.

'When you return north, will you have occasion to see my lord of Northumberland?' Aske enquired.

'You think Lord Henry should be made aware of . . . events?'

Will did not particularly wish to enlighten Henry of Anne's continuing rise.

'I think he should be aware of the changing attitudes regarding the Church that are being voiced here in London. He has always been a devout man.'

'Perhaps you are right, but I have no wish to add to his concerns. As Lord Warden he has trouble enough to contend with. His brothers have become embroiled with the Clan Kerr and the increasing violence of the Scots and he is still wary of Angus.'

Aske sighed heavily. 'Will there ever be peace on the Border?'

'I doubt we will see it in our lifetime, Robert, or in my children's either,' Will replied but he resolved that he would visit Lord Henry if only to ensure he was in fairly good health and to forewarn him of the growing unease concerning the Church that Aske had relayed to him.

Warkworth Castle, Northumberland

Henry sat before the fire in the great chamber. Heavy tapestries covered the thick stone walls, his books and manuscripts were stacked neatly on a table. Two large silver candlesticks were set on a press beside the hearth, the candlelight playing on the rough grey coats of the two wolfhounds asleep at his feet. The sweet but mournful sound of the Northumbrian pipes filled the room as the Earl's piper played one of Henry's favourite ballads. The sound drowned out the November wind that swept in off the North Sea, a few miles distant, and howled and keened around the battlements. Supper was over and although he had letters to write he felt little inclination to commence work upon them, enjoying the few rare moments of comparative peace and solitude that could be obtained in a large household.

He had not found the sense of isolation he had craved on his return from Cawood. He had many worries, not least those caused by his brothers, who were still consorting with the Kerrs and harassing Lord Ogle's tenants. On Thomas's part it was no doubt out of sheer spite that it was Ogle and not himself who had been made Deputy Warden. The young Scottish Earl of Bothwell had followed Angus's example and was seeking to change his allegiance to Henry Tudor.

King James himself was in residence at Coldingham, just to the north of Berwick-upon-Tweed, with his new Warden of the Scottish Marches – the Earl of Moray – and three thousand men, although Angus had reliably informed him that James was in dire financial straits and could not afford to invade England. Money he had been promised by the Emperor Charles had not been forthcoming. James had, however, written to King Henry accusing Henry's Lord Warden of sanctioning the burning of church lands and the murder of honest men, which was totally untrue. The King's reply to those charges lay with the other documents on a nearby table. The Carlisle Herald had been dispatched to James with King Henry's letter accusing James of giving sanctuary to outlaws and brigands in Scotland.

Henry sighed and signalled that another log be thrown on to the fire. There seemed to be no respite from the intrigues and machinations of the Scots, the outlaws of Teviotdale and Tynedale – and his brothers. Just a few days ago, that blackguard Mark Kerr had had the audacity to send word to him that he intended to burn one of the villages so close to Warkworth itself that the flames would give enough light for the Lord Warden to dress himself by even at midnight. Henry had dismissed that threat with the contempt it warranted.

Amongst the correspondence that awaited his attention was a letter from Will Chatton in which he stated his intention to ride north to Warkworth as soon as he had concluded certain affairs of business. It was a letter he must stir himself to reply to, Henry thought. It was a long journey and a harsh one at this time of year and he suspected that Will had gleaned news from court for his former squire wrote that he had been in London on business and had spent some time with Robert Aske.

He sighed wearily and poured more wine into his goblet. He had heard of Anne's elevation to Lady Marquess of Pembroke and of the King's visit to France on which she had accompanied him. Last year he had employed a gentleman, Sir Reginald Carnaby, to act as a confidential messenger, carrying his letters to and from the King. Carnaby was a pleasant, gregarious young man, who brought him news as well as correspondence from London, and Henry was always glad to see him and to hear his news.

He had inferred from her newly bestowed title and estates that Henry Tudor did indeed intend to marry Anne and that it would be soon regardless of whether the Pope granted an annulment or not. Queen Katherine had been banished to a manor house in Bedfordshire and it was now Anne who presided at court in her place. The news had given him no pleasure; it had only deepened his depression. He had not seen her since the day they had been parted and he could neither envisage nor bear to contemplate the woman she was rumoured to have become. He had also heard of the rumours concerning the drafting of an Appeals Statute, instigated by Cromwell, and of her leanings towards the New Learning, no doubt encouraged and influenced by both Thomas Cromwell and Thomas Cranmer, and that had disturbed him greatly. He had always been devout, as had she when he had known her, but he considered the new doctrines false and invidious – a threat to the faith he held sacred.

He sighed again, dragging himself out of his reverie and signalling that his writing materials be brought and placed before him. There was no need for Will Chatton to make the arduous journey north. He was aware of recent events in London and had no wish to be reminded of them.

Two hours later the letters were finished and, physically tired and mentally weary, Henry thought to seek the comfort of his bed. He finished his wine and brushed the sand from the last of the letters and was in the act of sealing it, when shouts and cries from the outer ward of the castle disturbed the peace of the chamber. He rose stiffly and crossed to one of the windows, peering down into the darkness, but was unable to see who or what was causing the commotion. Then came the sound of feet pounding up the stone stairs and he turned and crossed to the door, consternation in his eyes.

As he reached the door he flung it open and was confronted by Marsham, his Captain of the Earl's Guard.

'My lord! Word has just reached us that Mark Kerr and thirty mounted men have attacked the village of Whittle,' the man informed him.

'God's wounds! Whittle is but four miles away and there are

no more than six houses there! What hope have so few against thirty men?' Henry cried. 'Light the beacon, man! Light the beacon! We must raise the alarm before they move on.'

'It is being done, my lord, but they have already murdered four men and a woman,' the captain replied grimly.

'A woman?' Henry repeated, anger rising in him.

'The wife of a villager and she great with child. They declared they would burn all the houses so that the light would be seen here at the castle, my lord, but the fools had brought nothing with them with which to kindle a flame. They demanded kindling but the villagers had none and so in vicious spite they stabbed the woman to death and then cut down four men.'

Anger surged through Henry as he thought of the poor woman and her unborn child and of the message Mark Kerr had sent him. 'Make haste and send word to every deputy to raise his levies and block every road and track to the border. I want Mark Kerr and his murdering kin brought to justice! I will have the goodwife of Whittle avenged!' he cried. And if either Thomas or Ingram had had a part in this atrocity he would see them brought to justice too and he would disinherit them both, leaving his estates to the Crown. As Lord Warden it was his duty to protect these poor people – his tenants. If ever Thomas became Earl what kind of protection or justice could they expect from him?

The captain and the man who had accompanied him turned and hastened down the stairs, their boots clattering on the stones, and Henry went back into the chamber. From the windows he could now see the flames of the beacon leaping high into the black night sky, knowing that a score or more beacons would be lit on the surrounding hills. His hands, shaking from his affliction and the fury that was consuming him, gripped the stone sill tightly. Regardless of his health and the inclement weather, he vowed that if the Kerrs escaped this night and reached Teviotdale he would take up arms and pursue them himself – across the border into Scotland – and then, by God's blood, Mark Kerr would rue the day he had boasted to the Earl of Northumberland of burning villages. He would raze every cottage, house, manor, pele and castle in Berwickshire to the ground.

Chapter Forty

Alnwick Castle, Northumberland

THE FLAMES FROM THE chain of beacons had lit up the dark wintry night sky from Warkworth to Norham, alerting the men of Northumberland to the attack. Within hours they had ridden out, fully armed and prepared to block every known route to the border, but somehow the renegade Kerrs had eluded them, reached the Waterbreak and escaped safely into Scotland. But this latest instance of murderous reiving had so inflamed the countryside that hundreds had flocked to join Henry as he had ridden in haste from Warkworth to Alnwick, determined to carry out his threat to follow the Kerrs across the border in pursuit of justice.

Three days later, on a bitterly cold November morning, the inner bailey was crowded with grim-faced men. The air was clear and still sharp with frost; pale winter sunlight glinted on the burnished steel blades of swords, battle-axes, helmets and breastplates. It caught and played on the trappings of restless horses whose breath rose like steam in the raw air and as Henry mounted his horse he felt his determination deepen. The burning fury that had consumed him when news of the atrocity and of the Kerrs' escape had been brought to him had given way to a quieter, colder anger. His tolerance had reached breaking point.

'All are ready to ride, my lord,' Marsham, the Captain of the Earl's Guard, informed him. 'And a party of Scots horsemen have arrived to join us under the command of Sir George Douglas,' he added, casting a suspicious glance over his shoulder in the direction of the group.

'Indeed. Give orders, Marsham, that they be watched closely. It is never wise to trust a Douglas no matter that they come in the guise of friends and allies. We ride for Berwick, then on to Coldingham, although I have news that King James has left there in some haste.'

The man nodded curtly and Henry raised his right hand in its leather gauntlet. Pressing lightly on his spurs, he urged his destrier forward. As its great iron-shod hooves clattered and struck sparks crossing the drawbridge he was forcefully reminded of the day he'd ridden out with his father for Redesdale. He'd been a boy of eleven then, sickly, cold and afraid of what the day would bring. What was he now? he mused grimly. A man of thirty, still suffering ill health, still cold but at least unafraid of what danger today might hold. There was no place for fear now in his heart, only anger and determination that justice be done.

The murder of women and children was not uncommon on the Border, more was the pity of it, but the cold-blooded killing of this woman and her unborn child had affected him deeply. It was a senseless, spiteful and needless act of savagery perpetrated by brutal men. The sole purpose of that barbaric crime had been to openly and arrogantly taunt him as Lord Warden, and to flout the King's laws. He vowed that Mark Kerr and his kin would pay dearly and he thanked God that his brothers had had no part in it.

They were covering the miles towards Berwick rapidly beneath a sky that was still clear and blue although the sun held little warmth. He sat erect in the saddle although the lower edge of his breastplate felt uncomfortable against his diaphragm and his fingers were becoming numb and stiff in their thick leather gauntlets. Ignoring his discomfort he thought of his own son. It was something he tried not to do frequently but the fate of that poor child of Whittle had prompted it. It had been Mary's impetuous and foolhardy ride to Sheffield that had brought on her labour but he had come to accept the sad fact that it was God's will the boy had not lived. Mayhap the child had already been dead in her womb but that child in the womb of the goodwife of Whittle had been alive. It had had a God-given right to life and it was not the right of men like Kerr to wantonly extinguish it.

His thoughts returned to that winter's day in Redesdale and to the way Will Chatton had fought with nothing but his bare hands to defend his father. Did not all his tenants deserve the chance to live in peace, to work their land and raise their families without fear of molestation and murder? Did they not deserve the chance to live a useful life and perhaps better themselves as Will had? It was his sworn duty as Lord Warden to uphold the King's law on the Border but it was his moral duty to protect and obtain retribution for the poor people of Northumberland.

The wind had freshened now, grey clouds were moving ominously in from the sea bringing the threat of sleet and the sun had disappeared. Henry began to experience the all-too-familiar ache in his bones: the debilitating ague was returning. He steeled himself against it; his anger would sustain him, he told himself firmly. He would have justice for every one of his tenants afflicted by the pernicious practice of reiving. This day the Kerrs would feel the full weight of his justifiable wrath.

The horses were tiring, their flanks heaving and flecked with sweat, for they had been ridden hard on the thirty miles from Alnwick and Henry was chilled to the bone and shivering as they entered Berwick, the great fortress town on the south bank of the Tweed. Coldingham was ten miles to the north, now abandoned by James and his army, but the towns of Blackhill and Branerdegast and many villages lay between. Dismounting stiffly in the castle yard Henry gave orders that the animals were to be rested and watered, and the men to find food, but he warned that the respite would be brief; they would ride on before noon.

The wind had eased but the sky was heavy with cinereous clouds. The light was dismal and already beginning to fade although it was still only early afternoon. The November dusk would fall prematurely and obliterate all landmarks, Henry mused as they rode towards the small town of Blackhill, a dark blur in the distance. In the villages they'd passed through every inhabitant swore they had seen no sign of the Kerrs in months. Their loud protestations had not been believed for the men from Berwick had recognised some of them as distant kinsfolk of Mark Kerr. Their lives had been spared but their sacks of corn had been commandeered, their beasts driven off and their homes put to the torch.

The village of Reston had fared no better, nor had Blackhill, but as they approached Coldingham horsemen were observed riding out of the town gates. Peering through the ever-deepening gloom Henry rose in his stirrups to get a clearer view. 'Do they think to escape like rats from a stricken ship?' he murmured, more to himself than to Marsham, who rode beside him.

'I think, my lord, that they be riding towards us, not away from us.'

Henry could now see that his captain spoke the truth.

George Douglas had come up on Henry's left side. 'Then I doubt they are of the Clan Kerr! Thieves, blackguards and murderers they undoubtedly are, Lord Henry, but also muckle black cowards!' The stocky dark-haired Scot's voice was filled with scorn. ' 'Tis more than likely that those men were sent out to try to delay us while they sneak away in the gloaming to try to reach the fastness of the Lammamuir Hills.'

'Then there is no time to be lost. We ride on and at speed, Sir George. Marsham! We advance!'

The captain turned in his saddle, his face set and his eyes cold and hard as he signalled for the standard of the Earl of Northumberland to be brought up. Within seconds the cry of *'Espérance! Espérance en Dieu!'*, the centuries-old rallying cry of the Percys, rang out across the surrounding fields and as the horses were spurred into a gallop the ground beneath them began to shake under the pounding of hundreds of hooves. Henry had drawn his sword and he held it high above his head

424

as his destrier charged forward, mane flying, eyes rolling and huge feathered hooves thundering on the hard-packed earth.

'They're turning, Lord Henry! They're running!' George Douglas yelled above the din.

Henry nodded grimly; the horsemen ahead were wheeling their mounts around and galloping back towards the town.

The Earl's forces reached the walls seconds later and as there had been no time to close the gates, women grabbed their children and ran screaming in terror to barricade themselves in their houses. The townsmen had all armed themselves with knives, billhooks, pikes and even short swords and the retreating horsemen now turned in the narrow streets to face the onslaught of the Earl and his men. For a few minutes a fierce fight raged as men hacked at each other and horses collided and screamed in pain as those on foot stabbed and slashed at their legs and bellies. Blood turned the cobbles slippery, making them increasingly hazardous for men and beasts. It soon became obvious that the townsmen were outnumbered and they began to fall back, retreating into the maze of narrow side streets.

Henry, wiping the sweat and blood from his face with the back of his left hand, yelled to Marsham to send men to search every building for the Kerrs and to round up the wounded and take prisoner all those who had taken up arms against them. 'There will be those here who know of their whereabouts, though they swear on God's blood they don't!' he cried, cleaning the blood from his sword on his mount's saddlecloth and sheathing it before leaning back in the saddle. He was shaking with a mixture of fatigue and illness, he felt light-headed and the all-pervading stench of blood made him nauseous but his task was not yet finished. Around him there were still shouts and groans from angry or wounded men but also the hysterical screams of women and the high, terrified cries of children. With a supreme effort he dragged himself up in his stirrups and yelled to George Douglas.

'Sir George, I command that no harm be done to any woman or child upon pain of hanging! It is because of the death of a woman and child that we are here; I will countenance no murderous acts of reprisal on innocents!'

The mayhem around him seemed to continue unabated as men were driven or dragged from their homes. Added to the din was the lowing of cattle, the squealing of pigs, the frightened bleating of sheep and goats as the animals were driven from their pens. The men of Northumberland were heaving sacks of corn, barlcy and oats on to the rough carts they had commandeered plus anything else of value they could find. All too often in the past it had been their belongings that had been loaded on to carts and carried away; they clearly felt justified in their actions.

Henry forced himself to sit erect as Marsham and a company of his men at last reappeared, herding a group of bloodied and bruised men towards him from one of the narrow side lanes.

'They be not boasting now of burning villages, my lord! We found them cringing like curs in a loft above a stable and they put up a poor fight.' Marsham prodded one none too gently with the tip of his sword. 'This one be the braggart Mark Kerr!'

Henry leaned forward and stared at the man, his eyes as hard as flint; his face was pale but his expression was set and unforgiving. 'Mark Kerr and your kinsmen and followers, in the name of our sovereign lord King Henry, I arrest you for the murder of the men of Whittle and of the woman and her unborn child you slaughtered. I arrest you for March Treason. You will be tried and sentenced to be hanged, cut down and disembowelled whilst still alive, your bodies quartered and your heads severed upon the orders of the King.'

Their faces drained of colour as the horror of the manner of their deaths was impressed upon them. Kerr and his followers sank to their knees in the blood and dirt, their hands outstretched in supplication. 'Have pity! My lord, have pity! We humbly beg the King's gracious pardon for our crimes!' they pleaded, wild-eyed.

Henry ignored them and turned to George Douglas. 'See they are kept under close guard. They will be tried at Berwick.'

The Scot nodded. 'A good day's work, Lord Henry.'

Henry nodded briefly before turning his horse's head away towards the town gate.

'What of the town, my lord?' Douglas called after him.

'Burn it!' Henry instructed flatly.

It was the answer Douglas had expected. When they returned to Berwick he estimated it would be with sixty horses, over four hundred head of cattle, pigs and sheep, almost a thousand marks' worth of grain and close to seventy prisoners. The heads of the Kerrs would be set on pikes above the gates of Berwick and Newcastle as a reminder of the fate of those who were guilty of March Treason. He doubted anyone would risk the wrath of Henry Percy again for many months.

Henry left Berwick after the trial and sentencing and returned to Alnwick, intending to travel south to Wressle as soon as he was able. He was again suffering from his old illness and had neither the desire nor stamina to witness the execution of the Kerrs. He longed only for the comparative comfort of Wressle, but a bare three weeks later, as he was slowly beginning to recover, word reached him that the Earl of Moray, the Scottish Warden, was riding south to inflict reprisals for Henry's burnings of the towns of Blackhill and Coldingham.

Hastily written letters had been dispatched to Sir Arthur Darcy, Sir Thomas Clifford and the Earl of Angus, who was still swearing loyalty to King Henry and residing at Norham, instructing them to raise a detachment each and ride north to the border, crossing at the separate but strategic points Henry had set out. The Earl himself had raised 2,500 men but as he prepared to lead his contingent north to engage the Scots he still felt ill, wearied by the escalating scale of violence.

Again he needed all his willpower and stamina to overcome the shivering and weakness in his bones and sit erect in the saddle as he rode out at the head of his men, Marsham behind him. George Douglas had taken his followers and had gone to join his brother Angus at Norham.

December was always harsh in the North Country, the roads frozen to the hardness of iron, the wind sweeping in from the North Sea or across from the Cheviot Hills, raw and biting, cutting through the heaviest of clothing like a knife through butter. His men were all marcher bred and bore the adverse conditions stoically but Henry's constitution had been weakened by years of debilitating illness and heartache. He suffered greatly on the long, cold, uncomfortable, bone-shaking journey. From the small but vicious attack of Mark Kerr on the hamlet of Whittle which had claimed six lives, he thought miserably, hundreds more would now be killed or wounded, their homes burned, their goods and animals taken, their families left to try to survive the winter months as best they could. It was a spiral of death and destruction which seemed to have no end and the futility of it all and his unavoidable part in it served to darken his mood still further. Only his sense of duty as Lord Warden gave him the will and purpose to carry on and he determined that when this battle was over he would try to draw some good from it. He would petition the King to revive the ancient right of the Lord Warden to knight men who distinguished themselves in the field. It was yet another of the many privileges Thomas Wolsey had been responsible for stripping from him, he thought. The last time a Lord Warden had conferred knighthoods had been at Flodden, when King Henry had been away in France and Queen Katherine had stood Regent in his absence. How greatly times had changed – and not for the better, he mused despondently. Although the one thing that seemed constant was the continual warfare and bloodshed on the Border.

Chapter Forty-One

1533
York Place, London

THE DENSE INKY DARKNESS of the January night enveloped the dead Cardinal's former palace. It was past midnight and at last the large, noisy household was settling down for the night, but in a seldom-used chamber high in the west turret candles had been lit. Fresh rushes had been strewn on the floor and tapestries and Turkey carpets hung from the walls. The flickering candlelight cast long shadows across the chamber but illuminated the faces of the four men gathered there: the Reverend Rowland Lee, Henry Norris and Thomas Heanage, both gentlemen of the King's privy chamber, and Henry Tudor himself, clad in a doublet and breeches of cloth of gold studded with jewels, over which he wore a black velvet surcoat lined with sable fur. A black velvet bonnet studded with table diamonds and rubies the size of small eggs sat at a jaunty angle on his head and his expression was that of a man anticipating a great event but striving to keep his exuberance in check.

The icy chill of the chamber was somewhat dispelled by the heat radiating from the two braziers that stood against one wall but the Reverend Lee looked sombre and ill at ease as he tucked his cold hands inside the sleeves of his vestments. His demeanour was distinctly at odds with that of the King. He had not sought to officiate at this ceremony; he had been given no choice. It had been pointed out to him that since Thomas Cranmer had not yet been consecrated Archbishop of Canterbury it was not expedient for him to undertake it. Nor had the Appeals Statute, the means by which the King's divorce would be legalised in England, been passed by Parliament, all of which made him view this ceremony with more than a little concern. In his heart he seriously doubted the validity of the outcome of the King's intentions this night but therein lay his dilemma. Henry Tudor *was* the King and he a mere subject. He was also aware of the fact that the lady was already with child.

'It would appear that the Lady Anne is availing herself of the time-honoured tradition of keeping us waiting, Hal,' Henry remarked jovially to Henry Norris, unable to suppress his childlike excitement.

Norris smiled. He could not miss the note of triumph in the King's voice but, like Lee, wondered if the outcome of the night's event would be deemed valid. Mentally he shrugged; Luther had irreverently declared that 'Squire Harry will play God and do as he pleases' and he would appear to have been right. This gathering was shrouded in secrecy; only a small handful of people knew that tonight the King would marry

Anne Boleyn – Lady Pembroke, he corrected himself – and all were sworn to silence for Henry Tudor's son and heir must be born without a hint of illegitimacy.

The sound of footsteps on the narrow stone stair outside brought him quickly out of his reverie. 'I think the bride has arrived, sire,' he stated. As he crossed towards the door Henry's gaze followed his movements eagerly.

Anne had ostentatiously retired after supper but had devoted the intervening hours to her appearance. She had dismissed all her ladies apart from Anne Savage, who was to be her witness and who had helped her to dress. This was a momentous occasion, though there would be few to see it, and she had chosen to wear a purple and gold damask gown heavily embroidered with goldsmith's work and diamonds, the wide hanging sleeves lined with gold tissue. Over it she had donned a sleeveless surcoat of rich purple velvet edged with miniver and on her head she wore the diadem Henry had given her, studded with nineteen diamonds, thinking pleasurably of the far more magnificent crown that would in time replace it.

As she had slowly climbed the spiral stairs, one hand resting on her already swelling belly, she had felt a surge of satisfaction. She had achieved everything she had set her sights upon. Within the hour she would become the King's dearly beloved wife and Queen of England. She already carried his child in her belly and was certain that it was a boy. She had finally capitulated in the face of Henry's ardent passion when they had been delayed by storms in Calais and had been a little surprised that she had become pregnant so quickly. Henry had promised her a magnificent coronation in the spring. No expense would be spared, he'd enthused devotedly, delighted by her pregnancy.

It would be a coronation befitting his consort and the mother of the long-awaited Prince, heir to the throne of England. She would be the wife of a king and the mother of a king. She would be untouchable and could at last rest secure in the knowledge that her enemies – and she admitted that their number was increasing – would never prevail against her. She had raised herself and her family to an estate such as even her Uncle Norfolk had not envisaged.

As she finally reached the door she paused to steady her breathing, which had become a little laboured with the exertion of her ascent.

'My lady, all is well?' Anne Savage enquired anxiously in a whisper as the door was opened by a smiling Henry Norris.

Beyond him Anne caught sight of the tall, gloriously attired figure of the King, his face flushed and ruddy in the light of candles and braziers, his small blue eyes shining with expectation and desire. She inclined her head gracefully, and then bestowed on her future husband a radiant smile, her dark eyes glowing with pride and gratification. 'All is well, Anne. In truth I declare all is *very* well indeed.'

Temple Bar, City of London

'Robert, this is wonderful!' Joanna Chatton cried delightedly as she leaned forward and gazed out of the upper storey of the half-timbered building. 'It is so generous of you to have provided us with such a place from which to view the procession.' Robert Aske had gone to great pains, bargaining long and hard with the owner to rent it out for a few hours so that Will and his family could get a close view of Anne's triumphant journey through the streets of London to Westminster Hall. Tomorrow the Lady Anne was to be anointed and crowned in the church at Westminster.

Will's agent of many years had recently become ill and had passed his business affairs to his son. Thinking it prudent to visit the young man Will had decided to take lodgings and combine this business visit to London with a rare trip for his family. He had rented a house in Newington Green, not far from the closed and shuttered Brook House.

Meg and her new husband Tom had made the journey too and both were extremely excited as it was their first visit to the capital.

'Oh, I am so glad that we came with you, Joanna, and the day could not be fairer!' she enthused. 'Isn't it a blessing that the sun is shining and there are blossoms on the trees? It would have been terrible for it to have been cold or raining or blustery.'

Joanna nodded her agreement. 'Chill grey skies would certainly have dampened the occasion but today is beautiful and tomorrow begins the month of June, so that bodes well for the coronation.'

Meg pointed in wonder to the houses opposite. 'Look at all the rich hangings the people opposite have draped from their windows. Everything is so . . . so colourful and bright! Folk here must indeed be wealthy to own such carpets and tapestries.'

'Not all, Meg. I'm afraid there are many paupers and beggars too in London,' Will informed his sister.

Joanna was settling little Arthur on her knee while Meg had lifted young Edward on to hers. Will looked down into the street. A great deal of work had been done by the civic officials to transform the place. The streets along which the new Queen would progress had been cleaned and liberally strewn with fresh gravel and railed off on one side. Tapestries, carpets and brightly coloured arrases had been provided to drape from windows and balconies. At vantage points across the city the guilds and merchant companies had erected extravagant tableaux extolling the virtues of Queen Anne. Musicians played along the route, children scattered petals and wine ran freely from the conduits and fountains. A pageant was to be staged here at Temple Bar, Robert had informed him, which meant that Anne's procession would pause to watch it and they would have longer to view all the dignitaries and their entourages.

'How long will we have to wait for our first sight of her?' Meg asked impatiently, craning her neck in an attempt to peer further along the route.

Will laughed. 'Have a little patience, Meg. We will hear the music, the commotion and the cheering before the procession actually comes into view.'

Joanna too leaned forward. 'I think I hear the sounds of trumpets and timbales, though they are still some distance away.'

Robert exchanged a grin with Will and young Tom Watford. 'At least these two ladies are eager to see the spectacle.' He had begged Mistress Brookes to join them but she had flatly refused, declaring that in her mind there was only one Queen of England – Queen Katherine – and that she had no wish to see the King's 'concubine' fêted and honoured as if she were a virtuous woman and rightful Queen. She doubted that there would be many who would take off their caps and cheer for 'Nan Bullen' either, she'd stated vehemently.

'Indeed they are,' Will affirmed. 'We heard she went by barge to the Tower yesterday.'

Robert Aske nodded. 'In a splendid procession accompanied by hundreds of barges – fifty alone from the Haberdashers' Company – all draped in rich cloths and flying banners. Some were full of musicians; others contained strange dragon creatures that belched flames. It was indeed a sight to behold. And when they reached the Tower the noise from the volleys of cannon fired in her honour was deafening. She looked very regal and I heard tell that she was gracious to all, thanking the citizens for their kindness to her. I also heard that the renovations of the royal apartments where she resided last night cost a small fortune. Men have been working on them for months.'

Will nodded. 'The King is spending a great deal to honour her.'

Aske raised his eyebrows. 'Some are saying far too much. Some are wondering if all this . . . extravagance . . . is just to try to reconcile people to his new wife.'

Will did not have time to reply for both Meg and Joanna cried out aloud as the procession came into view and everyone craned forward.

At first both Joanna and Meg exclaimed and clapped in delight as knights, ambassadors and their servants, judges, doctors and abbots, bishops, the Lord Chancellor, dukes, earls and noblemen rode by arrayed in blues, yellows, violets, greens, gold, scarlet and silver; at length they were so overcome by the myriad of colours and magnificence of the multitude that they lapsed into stunned silence. Even Will, who had been at the

Cardinal's court with Lord Henry and had accompanied him often to King Henry's court and had witnessed the splendour of both, admitted to his companions that he had never seen anything quite like this display.

Meg found her voice as Anne's litter at last came into view. 'Oh, Joanna! *Look! Oh, look!*'

The litter was borne by sixteen knights and was covered with cloth of gold shot with silver. Anne sat regally staring ahead of her, a smile on her lips. Her gown was of silver tissue and over it she wore an ermine-trimmed mantle of the same costly material. Sunlight caught the hundreds of silver threads in her garments and the jewels she wore and she appeared to the two women as a glittering, shimmering vision that dazzled them both. Her long dark hair cascaded over her shoulders and on her head she wore a gold coronet set with rubies. Behind her rode her Chamberlain and Master of Horse, both richly attired, then seven ladies, two chariots, seven more ladies in velvet and silk, more chariots and dozens of servants.

Neither Meg nor Joanna had eyes for the members of the vast retinue, however. Meg clutched her sister-in-law's arm tightly, her eyes wide. 'Never have I seen such a gown or such . . . robes! I could not even imagine something so . . . wondrous! She . . . she *sparkles* like sunlight! Is she not the most beautiful lady, Joanna?' she cried breathlessly.

Joanna smiled at her. 'She is indeed beautiful, Meg, and her clothes are wonderful.' She turned and looked up at Will. 'But she was always beautiful, was she not, Will?'

He nodded his agreement. Anne *was* still beautiful and she looked every inch a queen but he could find in this woman no trace of the young girl he remembered. That girl, dressed in a plain dark green gown and hood, who had attended his wedding Mass at Lord Henry's side no longer existed. In her place was an elegant, dazzlingly attired, proud and supremely confident woman, although her smile looked fixed and a little brittle, he thought. The streets resounded to the sounds of the procession and were thronged with people, but the crowds who stood three and four deep were silent. There were no caps being snatched off and thrown into the air. There were no cries and cheers of 'God Save Queen Anne', no blessings were being called down upon her. King Henry might love and revere her but the people quite obviously did not.

Anne was all too acutely aware of the silence that accompanied her progress but she continued to hold her head high and forced herself to smile. The pageants that had already been presented to her had pleased her; for them, as she'd listened to her praises being extolled, her smile had been genuine. But as she'd progressed the sullen silence of the people lining the streets had begun to rankle and then infuriate her. This was her day of triumph. Henry had promised her a coronation that would be marvelled at throughout Christendom and he had not failed her, but he could not make the people love and accept her. She would be relieved finally to reach Westminster Hall and leave the hostile populace behind, she thought as the procession halted at Temple Bar, here to witness another pageant.

A young man had stepped forward, ready to read his verses from a gilded parchment scroll and she leaned slightly forward in the litter to listen to the words. She glanced upwards for a second and caught sight of the small group seated at an open window above her. One of the young women waved and suddenly called out a blessing and Anne smiled radiantly up at her. So not everyone viewed her with enmity, she thought, feeling happier. Perhaps it would encourage others to cheer her.

A puzzled expression clouded her eyes for a second as a memory flitted through her mind. There was something familiar about the other young woman but she could not remember what. She was comely, with olive skin and dark hair beneath a scarlet hood, but she had met so many attractive young women in her life. She focused her attention on the unfolding pageant but her mind began to wander as she listened to the youth. Unfortunately his verses were rather pedestrian and his voice far from melodious. Her gaze was drawn upwards again. The woman was standing now, holding up a small boy and looking down at her with dark, almond-shaped eyes so very like her own . . . and then she remembered. Years ago she had attended her wedding; she had worn a veil of lace in the Spanish style. Mistress . . . Olivarez . . . but now Mistress . . . what? She could not remember but then a man reached forward and took the child from her. The name came suddenly. Chatton! Will Chatton, Harry's squire. She shivered and looked away, fixing her attention on the youth still reading his verses. She had no wish to be reminded of Harry Percy today. She was Queen of England now and Harry Percy had been a lifetime away.

Joanna was almost certain that she had seen a flash of recognition in the Queen's eyes before she had turned, but maybe she had just imagined it. It was so many years ago now and Anne had changed, that much was oh so obvious, and she was also clearly very pregnant. Even her sumptuous gown and loose-fitting mantle could not totally hide the swelling of her belly.

She hoped Anne was happy. She did not agree with what she had done, nor could she condone it – not even for the sake of a male heir for the King. She had been taken aback when Meg had suddenly called out 'God Bless Queen Anne!' but she had not reprimanded her. Meg had been carried away by the excitement of the occasion and she did not have the heart to scold her but she would never utter those words herself. For her, like so many, Katherine would always be Queen and Anne but the upstart usurper, although she did not wish her harm and hoped that she would bear a healthy child.

She turned to Will. 'The procession is about to move onwards. Shall we make our way back to our lodgings before the boys become fractious?'

'Wait a while and take some refreshments, the streets will still be very crowded,' Aske urged.

'Thank you, Robert. We will return by way of the river, it will be safer. No doubt folk will take full advantage of the free wine,' Will stated.

'Aye, they will. Though they did not raise their voices, I noted,' Aske replied flatly as he turned away from the window, his expression grave.

Chapter Forty-Two

Greenwich Palace, London

S HE LAY TWISTING AND writing on the pallet bed with its linen sheets and fine crimson canopy. The bedclothes were stained and strands of her dark hair were plastered to her forehead and cheeks with sweat. The cloying smell of the herbs that had been cast on to the fire to dissipate the odours of the lying-in chamber were making her feel sick. Her labour had begun so long ago that she could not now recollect just when the first pains had assailed her.

The light in the chamber was diffused by the panels of tapestry that covered the walls and windows and candles afforded the women sufficient illumination to carry out their ministrations. She had however grown tired of gazing upon the figures of St Ursula and her seemingly endless entourage of virgins that looked down on her from the walls. None of them had ever had to endure childbirth and she stared with increasing exasperation at the ethereal features of the saint. St Ursula's sweet but slightly vacuous expression was infuriating.

Her restless gaze fell next upon the magnificent, heavily carved and gilded bed which Henry had ordered to be placed in the chamber and which stood beside the one on which she now lay. She would not rest in it until this agony was over, her soiled, malodorous garments stripped from her, her body cleansed with rose water and her hair dried and brushed. Then, dressed in a robe of embroidered lawn and lace, covered by a bed gown of silk and velvet, she would be suitably attired to greet her husband and present him with his son.

The women continued to fuss around her like a flock of cackling hens, she thought as she once again sank her teeth into her lower lip. Fresh waves of agony claimed her before diminishing, leaving her gasping and weak.

'The pains are coming closer, it cannot be long now. Is the urge to bear down becoming overpowering, madam?' the midwife asked anxiously. She, too, was perspiring heavily and would be greatly relieved when the Queen's labour was over and the child safely delivered.

Anne could only nod, she was exhausted. She had never experienced such pain before nor had she imagined that it would be so intense, gruelling or prolonged. It was of little comfort to her to realise that all women must endure this seemingly unending agony and many times over. Men could not begin to countenance the suffering women experienced, she thought savagely. They enjoyed all the pleasure but endured none of the pain.

Henry had spent weeks planning the lavish entertainments he would host to celebrate the birth of his son, she thought fretfully, banquets, jousts and masques, while she had been shut up in these claustrophobic chambers since the last week of August with just her women for company, and now today was, what . . . the seventh day of September? She was unsure.

The entertainments had not been the only thing that had absorbed his attention, she recalled bitterly as she twisted to try to find a position which would afford her some grain of comfort. It had reached her ears that he had embarked upon an affair with one of the ladies of the court. She had been furious, hurt and humiliated and had confronted and upbraided him.

Had he not sworn that she was his 'most beloved wife'? Had he not divorced Katherine, defied the Pope and alienated many of his subjects to make her such? Was she not about to bear him his longed-for son and heir? How could he now hurt and shame her thus? she had demanded furiously. His reply had not been what she had expected. Far from begging her forgiveness and seeking to placate and soothe her, he had faced her, his blue eyes hard, and had replied in a voice filled with coldness, 'Madam, you will shut your eyes and endure as your betters have done.' She had rounded on him angrily only to be met with the chilling retort that as he had raised her, so he could cast her down. His words had shocked her into silence and since then there had existed an uneasy truce between them. She was certain, however, that when she presented him with a prince he would abandon his mistress and revert back to his former adoring self.

The agony began again and she twisted the strip of linen which had been affixed to the head of the bed around her hand and dragged hard upon it.

'Push, madam! Push as hard as you can! I can see the child's head,' the midwife urged.

The contraction subsided and another of the women wiped the sweat from her brow with a damp linen cloth. She tried to muster what little strength she had left, praying only that the ordeal would be over soon. She did not even care at this moment what sex the child was; just that it would quickly and safely make its entry into the world before she expired from agony and sheer exhaustion.

This time she could not bite back the screams or ignore the intense urge to bear down. Finally with a groan of relief she felt the baby slide from her in a rush of blood and mucus and she fell back against the damp, stained pillows and closed her eyes.

'Praise be to God and His holy mother, it is over!' she gasped wearily. The blessed relief of sleep was threatening to claim her when the high-pitched wail of her child, shocked into taking its first breaths by a slap on the buttocks from the midwife, dragged her back from the brink. She raised herself up on one elbow. 'It is healthy and perfectly formed?'

The baby was being wrapped in a towel but she could see the soft red-gold down that covered its tiny head.

'You have a fine, healthy . . . daughter, madam,' the midwife announced rather hesitantly.

She stared at the woman as though she had not understood and then waves of dismay washed over her. It was not the longed-for prince she had been so certain she was carrying and upon whom so much depended. It was a girl, a princess – *another* princess! She closed her eyes; she did not wish to begin to contemplate Henry's reaction or his bitter disappointment.

The midwife placed the baby in her arms and as she looked down into the little face, the eyes tightly shut, the tiny rosebud mouth pursed, she felt a surge of joy and protectiveness engulf her, obliterating all her earlier feelings. This was her baby, her daughter, and she loved her.

Wressle Castle, Yorkshire

Sir Reginald Carnaby had ridden hard from London with letters which would inform the Earl of the truce that had been signed by the King and King James of Scotland which was intended to restore peace to the Border, and also of the news of the birth of the Princess. He entered the Earl's chamber to find his master pacing the floor looking disturbed and anxious. The words he had intended to use to announce this latter joyful event were instantly forgotten.

'My lord, is all not well?' he enquired courteously, handing over to Henry the rolls of sealed parchment he had carried in his saddlebags.

Henry shook his head but bade his courier to avail himself of a goblet of wine. He liked the young man: he was pleasant, well mannered and loyal. He trusted him too, although he was aware that many of his servants disliked Carnaby and both his brothers believed him to be an agent of the King, his purpose to spy on them all.

'I fear not,' Henry answered frowning. 'Young Sir Humphrey Lysle is hell bent on causing trouble even though he has but recently been released from the Tower and his lands and title restored to him. Despite my warnings, he is consorting with the Fenwicks, Swinburns and Shaftoes to create all manner of mischief.' Henry pressed two fingers to the bridge of his nose to try to alleviate the ache behind his eyes.

'He is the boy whose life you begged the King to spare when his father was executed for March Treason, is he not?' Carnaby said quietly. He had made it his business to acquaint himself with the history of the North Country. 'How old is he?'

'Eighteen, and it pains me that he has not learned sense.' Henry helped himself to wine and then stood close to the fire, staring into the flames. Even though this first month of autumn was proving mild he always felt chilled and frequently was plagued with a nervous trembling in his hands.

He did not enlighten Carnaby of the fact that he blamed his brother Thomas for encouraging young Humphrey Lysle's behaviour or that both his brothers were seriously engaged in the latest bout of trouble-making. They had even resorted to defying him by urging their tenants not to rise in arms should he require and command them to. This he viewed as intolerable, an act of blatant insubordination against the authority of the King who had appointed him Lord Warden. He had raised an army against the Scots and continued to maintain it, but the men were in need of paying and the King had advanced him nothing so he had been forced to pay them himself, although he could ill afford it. Now he must write to King Henry to urge recompense. He was beset by worries on all sides.

'We must hope that he comes to his senses soon, lest he find himself again incarcerated in the Tower,' Carnaby agreed. 'My lord, I have news from London concerning . . . the Queen.'

Henry turned and looked at him enquiringly.

'She was delivered of a healthy daughter three days ago. A fair child who much resembles her father, it is said.'

Henry turned away again. So, there was no son. It was a girl; how disappointed she must be. She had gambled everything on providing the King with a son. 'And the King?' he ventured. Henry Tudor had moved heaven and earth to marry her – some muttered bigamously – pinning his hopes of vindication for his actions on the birth of a male heir.

'It is said that he received the news in silence, my lord, but although disappointed he is confident a son soon will follow. The Princess is to be given an opulent christening this very day in the church of the Observant Friars at Greenwich with Archbishop Cranmer her godfather and the Dowager Duchesses of Norfolk and Dorset her godmothers.'

'And what name is she to be given?' Henry asked. This child would now take precedence over the Princess Mary.

'Elizabeth, my lord,' Carnaby replied.

Henry nodded slowly. Named for her grandmothers Elizabeth of York and Elizabeth Boleyn, he thought. He did not wish to dwell further on the matter. 'Pray leave the letters, I shall peruse them shortly. I thank you for delivering them speedily. You must be hungry and weary, Sir Reginald. Seek out my steward, and when you are refreshed I will inform you if there are replies to be drafted and then taken back.'

The young courier left. He hoped he would not be required to make the journey to London again in the very near future.

1534
Beverley, Yorkshire

A blustery April wind rattled the casement and Joanna shivered a little as she put another log on the fire. The evenings were still cool and the weather unpredictable. She had lit the candles half an hour ago and the room looked comfortable and welcoming. She had changed into a fine wool gown of dark green trimmed with scarlet braid for Will was bringing Robert Aske for supper. She had not seen their friend since the coronation almost a year ago. He was becoming a very successful lawyer and she enjoyed his company and hearing of his life in London. Downstairs in the kitchen Cook and Amy were preparing the supper and both boys were in bed asleep.

Of course she had heard of the birth of the Princess Elizabeth, who was reputed to be a healthy bonny child, much admired at court and doted on by both her parents, although last December when she had been barely three months old she had been given her own household at Hatfield in Hertfordshire and placed in the care of Lady Bryan. She could not envisage what it must be like to be parted from her children, she would miss them unbearably, but it was the royal custom for princes and princesses to have their own establishments.

She had wondered whether Anne had been very disappointed that her child had not been a boy, and in the market place she had heard many women declare that it was the judgement of God upon the King for putting aside his lawful wife and supplanting her with that whore Nan Bullen. She had not spoken her thoughts aloud for Will had counselled her against it, but she had pitied the poor Princess Mary – or the 'Lady' Mary as she must now be called. She who had been revered as a princess all her life was now separated from her mother. Her household had been disbanded after Christmas and she had been forced to reside at Hatfield and wait upon her baby half-sister, who now took precedence over her. She had even been commanded to give up her jewels to the new Queen. Joanna had also heard in the market place that whenever the King visited the Princess Elizabeth he refused to see his elder daughter. How could he be so heartless?

The sound of voices and then footsteps on the stair drove away all thoughts of the plight of Mary Tudor and she hastened to greet Will and his companion.

'Something in the kitchen smells exceptionally good! I trust I find you well, Joanna?' Aske greeted her cordially as she ushered both men in and bade them sit beside the hearth.

'You do indeed, Robert. Supper will be served as soon as you have rested and taken some wine. It is so good to see you again after all these months.'

'Robert has been keeping me abreast of events in London. He is becoming a very busy man.' Will smiled at his wife as she checked that the table was laid out to her satisfaction.

'I am glad to hear that. Do you have business in York, Robert?' she enquired, repositioning a pewter goblet a little more to the left of the trencher.

'Not really, I fear my father is in poor health now and I have been remiss in visiting him of late – and I thought it prudent to absent myself from London for a while,' he stated, looking grave.

Joanna did not press him for Amy had appeared carrying a tray upon which reposed a large pie and two covered dishes.

'Cook makes the best coney and leek pie in the county,' Will stated, sniffing appreciatively as Joanna took the dishes and urged the men to come to the table.

'And there are fresh vegetables to accompany it, bought this morning in the market, and a ginger syllabub to follow,' she smiled.

'A veritable feast,' Aske beamed, taking his seat and thinking how restful it was to have supper with friends in their well-kept house far away from the noise, dirt and increasing tensions of the capital.

When the meal was nearing its completion Joanna looked questioningly at the young lawyer. 'And what news from London, Robert? How fares the little Princess?'

Aske refilled his goblet, feeling he had need of sustenance; news never seemed good these days. 'She is thriving and a new act has been passed which in effect places her first in the line of succession, above the Princess Mary – the Lady Mary,' he corrected himself.

Joanna shook her head. 'I will always think of her as "Princess Mary". Why can they not both be named Princess? The King is their father.' It did not seem such an impossible thing to her.

'Sadly, Joanna, for Mary to continue to be named Princess means that Katherine must be recognised as Queen and there cannot be two Queens of England,' Aske explained.

'There will only ever be one rightful Queen in my mind and heart, and that is Katherine,' Joanna stated firmly.

'And there are many who would agree,' Will added. 'There is more to this Act of Supremacy than declaring Princess Elizabeth heir to the throne and it is causing some dissent. Every loyal subject is required to swear on oath to recognise the King as Supreme Head of the Church in England and the legality of his marriage to Queen Anne. Both Katherine and Mary have of course flatly refused.'

'As in all conscience one would expect them to,' Will interrupted.

'Do you think we will be commanded to swear this oath, Robert?' Joanna asked, frowning.

He shook his head. 'The wording states "when required".'

'So the King seeks only the approval of noblemen and churchmen, not clerks, tradesmen or merchants?' Will surmised.

'For the present, but who knows how far the King, encouraged by Master Secretary Cromwell, will pursue it in the future. Many of the bishops and noblemen have indeed sworn, including my lord of Norfolk who I always thought to be a firm supporter of Rome and Queen Katherine.'

Will looked puzzled. 'But Queen Anne is his niece.'

'I have heard that he stormed out of her presence in a great rage, declaring to all that he would not be spoken to as if he were a dog. It is said that he has lost patience with her arrogance and now shuns her. As to his adherence to Rome, he has declared that he has not read the Scriptures and will never do so, but he is no lover of the New Learning.'

Will was mulling all this over in his mind. 'So for now we will not be asked to swear this oath.'

Aske shook his head slowly. 'No, but I do not know how long it will be before I am required to swear it.'

'And will you, Robert?' Joanna asked.

'The honest answer is that I do not know. I have no wish to become a martyr so I can only pray that I shall not be required to do so, but I do not think I can stand silently by while the beliefs I have cherished all my life are cast down and trampled upon. Both Bishop Fisher and Sir Thomas More have refused,' he informed them.

'They are men of firmly held convictions so one must only admire them,' Will commented soberly.

'They have been committed to the Tower and the Bishop is now an old man,' Aske stated bluntly.

Both Will and Joanna gasped in shock. Both men were widely respected and revered – and not just in parliamentary and court circles. 'The Tower! But is Sir Thomas not an old and trusted friend of the King? What will happen to them?' Joanna cried.

Aske shook his head. 'I do not know but to refuse to swear is to be accused of treason.'

'Pray God the King will show mercy,' Will said fervently.

'Pray God the King will come to his senses,' Aske replied bluntly.

Joanna said nothing but she felt that suddenly a dark cloud had cast a shadow over the peace and stability of her life. All this would never have come to pass had Henry Percy been allowed to marry Anne Boleyn. He had genuinely loved her, and she had, Joanna was sure, felt a tenderness for him. If only those two young people had been able to follow the dictates of their hearts, instead of those of their politicking parents, all their worlds would have been so different.

Chapter Forty-Three

❖⋯❖⋯❖

1535
Topcliffe Castle, Yorkshire

MAYNARD ENTERED THE EARL'S privy chamber. He looked irritated but anxious too.

Henry looked up from the letter he had just finished writing. He had returned to Topcliffe a few days ago seeking a respite from the worries that beset him and had been thankful to adjust to the more tranquil life in Yorkshire and the warmth of the July days. At the spring Warden Court at Alnwick he had had no alternative but to sentence Humphrey Lysle and Alexander Shaftoe to death, both having been found guilty of March Treason. It had saddened him greatly that Lysle had utterly disregarded his warnings and instigated a savage raid on a village just across the border, thereby violating the truce between the two countries. He had had no alternative but to condemn him. When word had reached him that both hell-raisers had somehow escaped from their prison and fled to the comparative safety of Teviotdale he had written to the Scottish Warden demanding their immediate capture and return, and then, leaving the matter in the capable hands of his deputy Lord Ogle, had journeyed to Topcliffe to recover from the recurrence of his old illness that had afflicted him immediately after the Warden Court.

'There is something that requires my attention, Maynard?' he asked.

'My lord, Master Robert Aske has arrived and wishes to speak with you on a matter he informs me is of the utmost importance,' the steward informed him.

Henry frowned. 'Aske is here?'

'Indeed, my lord. He has ridden in great haste – so he says.'

'Then bring him to me.'

Maynard nodded. 'I have instructed that his horse be taken to the stables and that food be prepared for him; I trust that is in order, my lord?'

Henry nodded, wondering what was so important that it would force Aske to leave his law practice and ride north in such haste.

As the young lawyer entered Henry could see immediately that something was very wrong. 'Master Aske, you have had a hard journey. Pray be seated and take a cup of wine.' Aske's dark clothes were covered in dust, as was his hat, which he had removed. Obviously his steward had already provided water for the young man's face and hands were devoid of dirt but his expression was one of grave concern and in his eyes Henry thought he saw great sorrow. Had some tragedy occurred?

Aske took the proffered goblet and drank deeply. 'My lord,

the rigours of the journey are as naught compared to the news I bring. News I thought you would wish to hear before it becomes the main topic of discussion in the market place and ale house. Tragic news, I fear.'

Henry frowned. 'It concerns me personally?'

'It concerns us all, my lord. Bishop Fisher and Sir Thomas More have been executed for refusing to take the Oath of Supremacy. Sir Thomas – that revered and saintly man – was beheaded on Tower Hill but three days since and Bishop Fisher last month. All London is shocked and grieving.'

Henry paled; the hand holding the goblet began to tremble slightly. 'The entire country will be shocked and grieving, as I am. I was aware that Bishop Fisher was loud in his defiance but Sir Thomas . . . he would not speak out against the King. He was obdurate in maintaining his silence.' More had been a close friend of the King and he could not understand how Henry Tudor could have ordered his execution.

'It was upon the evidence of one of Master Secretary Cromwell's minions – a Master Richard Rich – that he was convicted. I fear that evidence was suspect. On the scaffold he declared, "I am the King's good servant, but God's first." Bishop Fisher declared that he was dying to preserve the honour of God. It was known, my lord, that the Pope had but recently conferred upon him the Cardinal's hat.'

'May God have mercy upon them both,' Henry said, reverently crossing himself and adding silently, And may God have mercy upon Cromwell and Rich when their times come. He closed his eyes and murmured, '*In Paradisum deducant te Angeli.*'

Aske nodded, recognising the words of the burial service.

'May angels lead them into Paradise indeed, my lord. *Requiem aeternam donaeis, Domine.*'

'Amen,' Henry sighed, getting to his feet. The sunlight seemed less bright, the day more sombre. 'I thank you for coming in person to impart these tragic tidings, Master Aske. I would no doubt have heard them in time. Sir Reginald Carnaby is here at Topcliffe with me at present; had he been in London he would have brought me the news. He is a personable and gregarious young man, but not always . . . sensitive in his manner of speech.'

'My lord, I fear the consequences of this act upon us all in time.'

Henry stared at him hard. 'You think all men will be forced to swear the oath upon pain of death?'

Aske nodded. 'You will have heard, my lord, that Master Cromwell has deputised a Thomas Legh and a Richard Layton to visit all abbeys, monasteries and priories to ascertain their worthiness with a view to dissolving those they find to be godless, fraudulent or licentious. It is rumoured, however, that it is their wealth he is primarily interested in.'

This disturbed Henry. Thomas Cromwell was Anne's protégé and had risen high in the King's favour. 'To what purpose?'

'To enrich the King's coffers. My lord, what will happen if the monks and nuns are dispossessed? Where will the sick, the needy and the pilgrims find succour? I fear there will be great suffering and great resentment – and then, should men be commanded to swear the oath on pain of death, I fear rebellion. I myself could not in all conscience stand idly by while such events unfolded.'

Henry sighed heavily. He had not been aware of this but if what Aske said was true it did indeed bode ill for the ecclesiastical establishments. It would cause great distress and generate immense anger. It would be seen as yet another attack upon the Catholic faith by the adherents of the New Learning. 'All we can do, I fear, Master Aske, is wait and see what transpires and put our trust in the Almighty. But if these things do come to pass, I beg you to consider your position carefully.'

By the time the young man rose to take his leave Henry knew that the peace of mind he had sought at Topcliffe was going to prove elusive. He mistrusted both Cromwell and Cranmer and was beginning to wonder what kind of a hornet's nest Anne and the King had stirred up.

Windsor Castle, Berkshire

Anne was relieved that the summer progress was over. They had returned to Windsor, arriving but an hour ago. It had been entertaining at first when the royal party with its large entourage had set out for Reading, Abingdon, Woodstock and Sudeley. By the end of July they had arrived at Tewkesbury and had lodged at Painswick Manor where both she and Henry had enjoyed the days spent hunting; relations between them had improved considerably and he came to her bed more frequently than he had been wont to do of late. She had been delighted to find when they had arrived at Acton Court that Sir Nicholas Poyntz had added a whole new wing to the house, especially to accommodate herself and the King. His uncle, Sir John, was a trusted member of her household and their stay had been pleasant and amicable.

She had been as relieved to leave Windsor and go on progress as she was to return, for over the past year she had been under a great deal of strain. Henry had bitterly regretted the death of Thomas More and had blamed her; this she had felt was deeply unfair, and had told Henry so. He had been adamant that More and Fisher would not defy him, she had reminded him. Had he not signed the warrant himself? It was unjust that she now be held responsible.

She had been deliberately and publicly slighted by the French Ambassador, she had failed to become pregnant again, and her relations with Henry had deteriorated for he had still been consorting with that strumpet he had dallied with whilst she had been pregnant with Elizabeth. She had quarrelled violently with both her Uncle Norfolk and Thomas Cromwell and now she mistrusted them both. Sometimes she felt as if her nerves were stretched like catgut and the strain had begun to show in her face and manner. She was aware that her position was becoming increasingly insecure, and would remain so until she gave Henry the thing he desired most: a healthy son. There were few people she could trust: only Margaret Wyatt remained a true and loyal friend. She had become angry with her sister Mary, who had married again, secretly and far beneath her, a soldier by the name of William Stafford and had been banished from court. Anne resented the fact that Mary was proving to be fertile while she was not.

There were even times of late when she wondered if her life would have been happier had she been allowed to marry Harry Percy. She would not have held such an exalted position or wielded great power and influence, nor lived in such luxury, but she would not have had to endure the constant anxieties and tensions or the humiliation of her husband's infidelities. Harry Percy would never have treated her so, she was sure of it.

She sank thankfully into a velvet-covered chair in her privy chamber as wine and wafers were brought by her ladies and Margery Horsman, Mistress of her Wardrobe, supervised the maids unpacking her clothes. From Acton Hall they had journeyed to the home of Sir Edward Baynton, her vice-chamberlain, and it had been a very pleasant sojourn but she certainly had not enjoyed the three nights they had spent at Wulfhall at the invitation of Sir John Seymour.

She had not failed to notice – and she was certain that no one else had either – that Henry had lavished a great deal of attention upon their host's daughter Jane, one of her ladies-in-waiting and a young woman she had always considered decidedly plain and devoid of grace, wit or personality. The girl was dowdy in her manner of dress, adhering to the cumbersome, unattractive gable hood and the old-fashioned style of gown. In reply to Henry's compliments and flattery Mistress Seymour had cast her eyes down modestly and smiled in what Anne considered to be a sickeningly sanctimonious manner but which Henry thought charmingly virtuous. His behaviour had infuriated her and they had again quarrelled for she was beginning to realise that her husband was incapable of remaining faithful. It was not how she had expected to be treated nor would she countenance it. She was not Katherine who had ignored his infidelities, maintaining her silence and dignity even when he flaunted his mistress beneath her very nose – as he had done with her sister Mary.

Suddenly, as she sipped the sweet hippocras wine, a wave

of nausea overtook her and she pressed her hand to her mouth.

'My lady, you are ill? You are as pale as a linen sheet,' young Mary Howard cried, gently taking the gold-encrusted Venetian glass goblet from her mistress's hand.

'Do not fuss, Mary. I am but weary from travelling, that is all, it is passing,' Anne replied, thankful that the sickly feeling was beginning to diminish.

The girl passed the goblet back and turned to resume her tasks and Anne twisted the delicate stem between her fingers. She had not felt truly well these past days and she had assumed it was merely anxiety caused by Henry's interest in Mistress Seymour, but now . . . A slow, triumphant smile spread across her face. It had to be! The faintness and nausea, the tiredness, the absence of her 'curse' . . . she was pregnant! Oh, pray God this time it would be a boy and that he would be delivered safely. Then she could once again feel secure. She could stop worrying, stop wondering just what Henry was doing. If she was pregnant she was invulnerable. The sly Mistress Seymour with her insipid looks and falsely pious manner would prompt no anxiety or anger in her now. She was carrying the King's son and she would not allow anything to upset her and put at risk this child she carried.

Greenwich Palace, London

The great hall had been decorated with boughs of holly and twisting, trailing fronds of ivy and was illuminated by hundreds of candles. The huge Yule log burned fiercely in the carved stone fireplace and the brilliance of both candle and firelight picked out the red, green, blue and gold paint of the carvings of heraldic beasts and flowers that adorned the hammer-beamed roof.

The room resounded with sprightly tunes from the musicians and the laughter and gaiety of the assembled court enjoying the copious amounts of food and drink provided at this Christmas banquet. The tantalising odours of roast meats, pastries and all the delicacies the kitchens could provide mingled with the smells of sweet spiced wines and pungent herbs.

Anne leaned back in her gilded chair and rested a hand over the swelling mound of her belly, partly disguised by the folds of her purple velvet, ermine-trimmed gown. She would have to be laced less tightly in the days ahead, she thought with some satisfaction. From her place here on the dais beside Henry she had an excellent view of the entire hall and knew that to all who were seated at the trestle tables below, from the noblemen and women, the knights, the officers of the royal household, the clerks and the more lowly servants, it appeared that the King and Queen were merry and enjoying each other's company. She knew otherwise. Perhaps on Henry's part the bonhomie, the jesting, the lively repartee was not entirely a charade, she could not be sure, but she was barely suppressing the humiliation and anger that simmered in her breast.

Despite the fact that he had been both relieved and happy that she was once again carrying his child, his pursuit of the whey-faced and conniving Mistress Seymour had not abated. Mistress Seymour, however, was still playing the virtuous maid. Henry constantly sought her company and it had come to her ears that he had sent small gifts and tokens, all of which had been regretfully returned. Her dark eyes clouded at the memory of Henry walking with the girl, deep in some earnest discussion, along the gallery but a few days ago, but she quickly stifled her rancour as her husband turned towards her, an expression of solicitude on his face.

'Madam, are the festivities not to your liking? They are perhaps tiring you?'

She sat up and reached for her gold, ruby-studded goblet, shaking her head and forcing herself to smile as if she did not know that his seemingly pleasant and assiduous request hid an ulterior motive. He wished her to agree that she was fatigued and to retire, leaving him free to partner *her* when the dancing commenced. 'No, my lord, I am not tired and the festivities are a delight.'

The expression of concern disappeared and he turned away from her. She watched him rise and go to seek out Chapuys, the Imperial Ambassador. She frowned as she sipped her wine. Of late he had become friendlier with Chapuys, who was naturally an adherent and ally of Katherine. What did he hope to gain? she wondered. A closer allegiance with the Emperor, Katherine's nephew? It made her uneasy. She wished she had agreed to retire for her back had begun to ache and she felt a lassitude creeping into her limbs. She certainly had no desire to watch Henry partnering Mistress Jane in the dance.

Resolving not to allow her emotions to overwhelm her she turned and smiled at her Uncle Norfolk, who was seated a little to her left. They were barely on speaking terms but she would not sit here in silence and isolation.

'The King appears to be on quite amicable terms with Ambassador Chapuys, does he not, Uncle?'

Norfolk could not ignore her although he wished he were able to. They had scarce spoken two civil words these past weeks. He smiled cynically. 'I would say *most* amicable, madam. Did I not observe His Majesty walking through the presence chamber in earnest conversation with the Ambassador this morning, his arm about Chapuys's shoulder? All who beheld it marvelled at such a display of friendship.'

'Indeed,' Anne replied icily, 'and would you venture a reason for this new-found amiability?'

Norfolk shrugged. 'I would not care to do so, madam.'

Anne seethed at the rebuff but then to her surprise the Duke leaned towards her.

'There *is* something. What whispers have you heard, Uncle?' she demanded.

Norfolk permitted himself a moment to word his reply. The reason for the King's recently improved friendship with the Ambassador and his subsequently increased conviviality was a fact that privately saddened him but she would come to hear of it soon, no doubt. 'It is said, Madam, that the Princess Dowager is dying.'

Anne caught her breath and took another sip of wine. Katherine was dying! A great wave of relief surged through her. With Katherine dead both she and Henry would at last be free of the threat of war with Spain and its Empire. There could no longer be any doubt or dissent as to the legality of her marriage or Elizabeth's legitimacy, no denying that she was the rightful Queen of England. No wonder Henry had become so well disposed towards Chapuys. She tried hard to hide the relief Norfolk's words had evoked.

'I cannot say I regret to learn of this, Uncle. I will not be hypocritical, but I am not inhuman. I do feel some . . . pity for her at this time, despite the fact that she has always been most obdurate in her opposition to me.'

Norfolk looked away. 'That is most generous of you, madam,' he replied sarcastically.

1536
Greenwich Palace, London

On the seventh day of the New Year the news of Katherine's death at Kimbolton Castle was brought to the King. Henry wept but Anne felt she had at last been delivered from a rival whose very existence had been a threat to the security of her position. She was also relieved when Henry refused to accept some of the items Katherine had requested be sent to him, although he had read the last letter she had written to him, still signing herself 'Katherine, the Queen'. Both she and Henry had donned purple velvet mourning and then, in deference to Katherine's Spanish origins, the yellow and white satin favoured by the Spanish court on such occasions.

The atmosphere at court had lightened considerably as Henry had given banquets and planned jousts and carried Elizabeth into Mass to a fanfare of trumpets.

His obsession with jousting had resulted in a serious fall and she still remembered vividly the feeling of shock speedily followed by horror that she had experienced when Norfolk had rushed into her chamber to inform her that Henry had been unhorsed and that his mount – an armoured destrier – had fallen upon him. Henry had been carried unconscious from the field and it had been feared he would not live, but thanks to

God's mercy he had recovered. She did not want to relive those hours of fear and uncertainty, she thought, pushing the memory from her mind.

Today Katherine was to be buried at Peterborough and Henry had dressed in black and gone to attend a Requiem Mass in the chapel. She would be thankful when the day was over and all memory of his former wife could then be cast from her mind and she could concentrate her thoughts entirely upon the son she was carrying.

She summoned Lady Lisle and asked that she read to her from her copy of Coverdale's New Testament translated into English, bound in costly vellum and printed with her name in red and gold. Today she felt it would be appropriate. Her gown had been loosened and her hood removed and she closed her eyes as she leaned back in her chair. Lady Lisle's quiet, well-modulated tones were calming.

After fifteen minutes she gasped aloud as a spasm of pain gripped her. She arched her back to try to relieve the discomfort.

Lady Lisle quickly laid aside the book and was on her feet. 'Madam! What is amiss?'

Anne's features were contorted and beads of perspiration had broken out on her forehead as she gripped Lady Lisle's hands tightly.

'Madam, is it the child? Shall I summon assistance?' The older woman's voice betrayed her acute anxiety.

Anne groaned pitifully as she pressed her hands to her belly. No! No, please God, no! She could not lose this baby, she *must* not miscarry her son, but as another spasm ripped through her she felt the first trickle of blood seep from her and slide slowly down her thighs. God was not listening. Henry's persistent, blatant courtship of Jane Seymour followed by the shock of his fall had caused this, she thought hysterically. There would be no son and heir for Henry Tudor. She had failed yet again.

Chapter Forty-Four

———◆———

Brook House, Newington Green, London

WILL HAD COVERED THE distance from the water stairs to the courtyard of Brook House on foot and as rapidly as he could, avoiding the carts, street vendors, beggars and groups of apprentice boys but noting the knots of people who had congregated outside ale houses and shops, huddled together in tense, shocked conversations. Yesterday those same people had gone out and gathered greenery, there had been dancing and feasting and at the palace there had been jousting to celebrate May Day. Now all vestige of festivity had disappeared, he thought grimly.

The Thames lightermen always seemed to know what was going on in the city before the majority of the citizens and it had been the man rowing the lighter he'd hailed at Westminster Stairs who'd informed him of the arrests almost as he'd stepped into the boat. It was news he was hastening to impart to the

Earl before it was blurted out by either the crass and tactless Carnaby or one of the servants.

It had been convenient for him to accompany Lord Henry to London for he had matters of importance to discuss with his agent and had sent an immediate reply to the Earl's letter accepting the invitation. Henry had decided to pay one of his rare visits to the capital, prompted by the growing concern he felt for Cromwell's plans to investigate and dissolve the ecclesiastical establishments and to try to ascertain at what rate the New Learning was increasing amongst the people of the southern counties. The people of the North violently opposed it and he felt, like Aske, that there would be great anger should it be imposed upon them. They had arrived three days ago but as yet the Earl had not paid a visit to court as he was still fatigued from the journey.

He was concerned by Lord Henry's state of health, which seemed to him to be deteriorating. The years spent contending with both the climate and the turbulent conditions on the Border had taken their toll. Although still only thirty-four years old, as he was himself, the Earl could be mistaken for a man far advanced in years and he feared that the latest appalling news would further increase his afflictions.

The courtyard appeared peaceful enough, he thought as he crossed towards the door that led into the long corridor off which were the buttery and pantries and the staircase leading to the Earl's chambers on the first floor. The few servants he encountered were dutifully going about their tasks in the quiet warmth of the late afternoon. Supper would be served later now the evenings were lengthening.

Henry was reading, seated comfortably beside a window

looking out over the gardens, the high wall of which kept at a distance the tumult, odours and dirt of the city streets beyond.

Henry laid aside the volume as his former squire entered. 'Will, I did not expect you to return so soon. Your business is concluded?'

'Not quite, Lord Henry, I must finalise some details tomorrow. I was not agreeable to some of the percentages being suggested.'

Henry nodded. Will had become astute in matters of commerce. 'You will take some wine; you appear to be in need of refreshment.'

Will thanked him and poured wine from the silver jug into two goblets. He was aware that he was flushed and perspiring, owing to the warmth of the afternoon and his exertions to reach Brook House quickly. He was also aware that Henry himself was going to need some fortification after the news he was about to impart.

He handed him the goblet. 'Lord Henry, when I left the lighter at the water stairs I walked back in great haste. I fear there is news that is spreading like wildfire throughout the city and I did not wish you to hear it bruited in the coarse manner of a servant.'

Henry frowned as he sipped the wine. 'It is grave news, I can tell by your expression, Will.'

'My lord, it is almost . . . unbelievable. I fear that the Queen has been taken under arrest to the Tower.'

Henry stared at him aghast. 'The *Queen*! Arrested!'

Will nodded slowly. 'Sir Henry Norris and Lord Rochford, her brother, are also under arrest and a musician by the name of Smeaton – Mark Smeaton.' He did not add that it was widely rumoured that Sir Francis Weston, William Brereton and the Lord alone knew who else were under suspicion.

Henry was trying to make sense of it all. 'What has she been charged with, Will? What charges are levelled against Hal Norris and George Boleyn?'

Will braced himself before he answered; there was no easy way to say this. 'She is charged with treason against the King's person, my lord.'

'Treason!' Henry cried incredulously.

Will took a deep draught of wine. 'She is accused of adultery with Norris and Smeaton and . . . and Rochford.'

Henry stared at him in horror. It was utterly inconceivable! Adultery with Norris, Smeaton – a musician – and . . . and her own brother? She had always been close to George but . . . but *incest*! Never!

'It is monstrous, Lord Henry. It defies belief and I do not believe it of her. It is a tissue of lies,' Will said vehemently.

Henry sipped his wine but it tasted as bitter as gall in his mouth. 'I do not believe it of her either. She strived for so long and sacrificed her integrity to achieve her goal; she would not be so foolish as to place herself in such a predicament. And we have both been at the court, Will, it is virtually impossible to be alone. You are constantly surrounded by people; there is no privacy. These . . . liaisons, had they existed, would have been observed and reported to the King long before now, not least by her enemies who look to find the smallest fault or misdemeanour.' Henry shook his head, still unable to comprehend the magnitude of the charges being levelled at her. 'No, I refuse to believe these calumnies. They are without foundation, without credibility. I fear it is because she has failed to give him a son and he has grown tired of her. His . . . interest in Mistress Seymour is well known. He now wishes to rid himself of her, as he did Queen Katherine. Who has brought these charges against her, is it known?'

'Master Secretary Cromwell. The musician has confessed to it, my lord. According to the boatman he was observed being taken under guard to the Tower yesterday.'

'And no doubt tortured! No man ever spoke the truth under torture,' Henry retorted scathingly.

'My lord, if they find her guilty . . . the penalty for treason . . .' Will could not continue.

Henry's eyes clouded with disbelief as the horrendous realisation swept over him. 'By the Blood of Christ, surely they will not demand that she ... *die*! It would be nothing less than murder! She is an anointed Queen!'

Will felt equally outraged but shook his head. 'I do not think it will come to that, my lord. All Christendom would be appalled by such an act and the King vilified by all men, princes and commoners. I fear she will be divorced and mayhap incarcerated in a nunnery for the rest of her life, unless Master Cromwell sees fit to abolish all such establishments.'

Henry placed the half-full goblet down on the press beside him and stared bleakly out of the window. 'Pray God you are right, Will. I . . . I pity her. She is responsible for much dissent and is not without her faults but she is alone now, without friends, family and surrounded by those who wish to see her cast down.'

Will sat down on a stool opposite his former master and childhood companion and twisted the stem of his empty goblet between his fingers. The evening sunlight lit the chamber with a roseate glow but the brightness was superficial, the atmosphere now chill and filled with foreboding.

'The boatman said he had spoken with someone who had witnessed her arrival at the Tower. A fellow lighterman.'

'Was she . . . distraught?' Henry asked. He could not stop himself from picturing her as the young girl he remembered. She must have been petrified when they had taken her through the water gate into that grim fortress.

'So I believe, my lord, but we can only pray that when she is brought to trial these evil lies will be disproved.'

Henry did not reply. If the King wished to be rid of her he doubted she would be declared innocent of the charges. Her reputation, her name would be defamed. She would be reviled and imprisoned – somewhere – as Katherine had been and left to decline in penury and isolation and that would break her. Hal Norris and George Boleyn, although innocent as he firmly believed them to be, would die, as would the musician Smeaton. He felt the weight of sorrow and depression descend upon his shoulders. Both Hal and George had been friends and companions in those distant, happier days and as for Anne . . . he had loved her deeply.

The Tower of London

'Madam, it is time,' Sir William Kingston, the Constable of the Tower, announced quietly.

Anne clasped her hands tightly together to disguise their trembling as she turned to face him. He was a kindly man and she was grateful for it. When she had stepped out of the barge on to the slippery stone steps around which lapped the turgid waters of the Thames, she had been almost hysterical with terror and had asked him if she was to be confined in a dungeon. Gently but firmly he had assured her that she was to be lodged in the chambers where she had resided before her coronation.

He had had the Holy Sacrament brought and placed in her privy chamber, at her request, but he had been unable to banish to the outer chambers the women Cromwell had instructed be set to wait upon her. Set to watch and listen, for all were Cromwell's creatures. Mistress Stoner, Mistress Coffin, Lady Kingston, her aunt Anne, Lady Shelton, and another aunt, Elizabeth, wife of her father's brother James who had been a friend of the deceased Katherine. She had no privacy at all; Mistress Stoner even slept in her chamber.

The thirteen days she had been here she had spent in prayer and in wondering what her fate would be. There were times when she could not suppress her fears and she would fall to weeping inconsolably. At others she looked sadly back over the years and wondered where her youth and happiness had gone, when and how things had changed so drastically. But a few short years ago she had been Henry's beloved sweetheart and then wife, from whom he could not bear to be parted. He had adored and admired her wit, her intelligence, her grace and accomplishments. He had had her crowned and anointed Queen. But she had failed to give him a son and he had turned against her.

Never would she forget the look in his eyes when he had visited her after she had miscarried of a boy in January. 'I see that God will not give me male children. When you are up, madam, I shall speak to you,' he had said coldly before turning and leaving. But he had not and since then he had avoided her, increasingly seeking the company of Mistress Seymour. How had everything gone so wrong between them that she should be brought to this? That he accused her of such hideous crimes, even thought her capable of them? That she was now to stand trial – maybe even for her very life? Terror once again washed over her and she reached for her small velvet-covered prayer book.

'Madam, I urge you. It is not wise to keep my lords waiting,' Lady Kingston reminded her gently, holding open the door.

She nodded and walked towards the corridor. Twenty-six of her peers, presided over by her Uncle Norfolk, were awaiting her in the King's Hall here in the Tower. They would judge her case and as far as she could ascertain none were her avowed enemies. She squared her slim shoulders and held her head erect. She had dressed in a gown of plain black velvet with no elaborate trimmings, her hood was also of black velvet and bordered only with black silk braid. She wore no jewels at her throat or wrists and no rings adorned the fingers that tightly clasped her much-used prayer book.

It would take all the courage she possessed to speak the words she had composed and memorised for her defence, and speak them calmly and clearly with no hint of hysteria or fear in her voice, but she would do it. On those words depended so much. Her virtue and reputation, her fate and that of her child, Elizabeth.

The King's Hall, Tower of London

When the summons had arrived it had rendered Henry speechless and devastated. After Anne's arrest and those of Francis

Weston, William Brereton, Thomas Wyatt and Richard Page which had followed, he had determined to leave the city and return north, for all the men involved had been his friends and he felt unable to contend with the magnitude of the unfolding tragedy. His plans had been abandoned when he read Cromwell's directive. He was commanded by the King to attend her trial and sit in judgement upon her.

'Is there no possibility at all of declining, my lord?' Will Chatton asked when he'd been informed of the fact. The summons was as abhorrent to him as it was to Henry.

'None, Will.'

'Could you not plead ill health? It is not untrue.' Henry did indeed look ill, he'd thought. This matter was weighing heavily upon him; even the most unobservant dolt could see that.

'I fear I would have to be prostrate and delirious with fever to be excused,' Henry had replied hopelessly.

'Then I shall accompany you, my lord. I would be grateful if you could obtain permission for me to wait in some outer chamber in the Tower,' Will had said firmly. He had no desire at all to set foot in that sinister fortress-palace but he realised that this was going to be perhaps the greatest ordeal Henry had had to face since the day his dreams of marrying Anne had been so cruelly shattered and his life and happiness blighted for ever.

He had accompanied Henry to the Tower but had taken leave of him at the entrance to the King's Hall and gone to wait in a small ante-chamber. He had glimpsed through the open door the rows of scaffolding that had been erected for the lords now assembling to be seated upon. He had no great confidence that Anne would be found innocent but at least there would be one man in that hall who would support her plea.

As Henry entered the hall he caught sight of Norfolk seated beneath the canopy of state, the King's usual place. Of course of Henry Tudor there was no sign, he would distance himself from these proceedings, declaring he was the injured party. Norfolk's eldest son, the Earl of Surrey, was standing talking to his father, but he had no wish to speak to his godfather or Surrey and so he followed the usher who was directing the noblemen to their seats.

He nodded curtly to the Earls of Arundel, Oxford, Westmorland, Rutland, Sussex and Derby beside whom he was placed. The Duke of Suffolk, the Marquis of Exeter, the Lords Audley, Morley, Montague, Clinton and many others sat to his left. All were looking sombre and conversations were stilted. The atmosphere was taut with nervous anticipation, he thought, but was it not to be wondered at? A Queen of England was to be tried for treason.

Conversation ceased as Sir William Kingston ushered her into the chamber and Henry looked for the first time in thirteen years at the woman he had loved so passionately and had never been able to forget. He was shocked by her appearance. She was still beautiful and elegant but she was so thin; the black velvet dress and hood made her skin look dull and sallow. Anxiety, he saw, had aged her. She appeared calm and dignified but her dark eyes held a hunted, wary expression. The vivacity that had been such a vital part of her character and which had captivated him had disappeared. He could not look at her without recalling the moments they had shared, the touch of her hand, her lips warm against his, and his heart was filled with bitter regrets.

He looked down and plucked at the edge of his crimson

velvet robe, vowing to keep his eyes cast down throughout the proceedings, but he could not help himself. He looked up. Her gaze was sweeping slowly and hesitantly over those assembled to judge her. As their eyes met hers widened in recognition and a tremor ran through him. For a brief instant he saw again the young girl he had loved but also caught a glimpse of her fear, her shame that he would hear in detail the vile things of which she was accused, the pain of realisation that he was now to sit in judgement on her, and a flash of . . . betrayal? He longed to shout aloud that he refused to believe the lies and could not – would not betray her, but he could only hold her dark gaze and pray that she would read in his eyes the affection, the pity and the loyalty that he felt for her and to which he would always hold fast. As she at last looked beyond him he closed his eyes, praying that she had understood his unspoken belief in her innocence.

The evidence was of the flimsiest, he concluded as the trial progressed. Surely it must be obvious to everyone that this was so? They could not hope to convict her on proofs obtained by torture, mere hearsay and the vicious spite of George Boleyn's wife, the vituperative Jane Rochford whose sanity he seriously doubted, for what wife would accuse her husband of such a crime?

He leaned forward as Anne stepped forward to defend herself, willing her to declare her innocence in such a manner that no man there could disbelieve her.

Anne spoke calmly, clearly and succinctly, inwardly praying that not only could she maintain her composure but that her words would be believed. 'My lords, I will not say your sentence is unjust nor presume that my reasons can prevail against your convictions and I am willing to believe that you have sufficient reasons for what you have done but that they must be other than those produced in this court for I am clear of all the offences you have laid to my charge.' She paused briefly, her eyes fixed upon Norfolk. 'I have ever been a faithful wife to the King though I do not say I have always shown him the humility which his goodness to me and the honours to which he raised me merited. I confirm that I have had jealous fancies and suspicions of him which I have not discretion enough or wisdom to conceal at all times but God knows and is my witness that I have not sinned against him in any other way.'

Henry admired her spirit and courage and did not doubt her words of denial. He wished only that the entire deadly charade were at an end for he felt sick at her plight.

She had concluded; Norfolk was speaking now and his voice grated on Henry's nerves. Suddenly he looked up, alert; he stared hard at his godfather as the meaning of the Duke's words now became crystal clear to him. This was not a *trial*! This was a mere travesty of one! They were not required to weigh the evidence and come to a decision. All that was required of them was their agreement to the fact that she was guilty! She had already been declared so by the King! And he would have their assent to the fact so no blame could be apportioned solely to him. Henry Tudor would be rid of her. He would have her dead!

Slowly and purposefully he rose to his feet, gripping the rail in front of him for support. He felt faint and was fighting the waves of horror and revulsion that were threatening to overwhelm him. He would *not* sit here a moment longer. He would *not* be party to this – this most atrocious and abominable of crimes. He breathed in deeply, willing himself not to succumb to his feelings of outrage and disgust. The dizziness began to fade and with an effort that required every ounce of strength and courage he possessed he straightened his back and squared his shoulders. As he glanced quickly around he encountered the curious, uneasy glances of his fellow peers.

He stepped down from the raised platform and turned to face Norfolk, who was staring at him warily.

'You wish to speak, my lord of Northumberland?' the Duke asked curtly.

Henry remained silent, holding that harsh gaze unflinchingly.

'You are unwell, my lord?' Norfolk persisted, his unease deepening. Harry Percy certainly looked ill, he thought, judging from his pallor and the trembling that was afflicting his limbs. In fact it seemed that he was only remaining on his feet by sheer willpower.

'The answer to both your questions, your grace, is "no",' Henry replied steadily before turning away from his godfather and walking slowly and resolutely towards the door.

'Lord Northumberland, you do not have the court's permission to leave! Your presence is required!'

Henry ignored Norfolk's belligerent command and fixed his eyes firmly on the large oak doors that led from the hall. He would not let her think that he in any way colluded with their perfidious verdict yet he could not bear to glance in her direction again. He knew if he did all his resolve would desert him. The aggrieved mutterings of the other scarlet-robed peers assaulted his ears like the buzzing of a swarm of angry bees, but he did not turn or look back. He walked doggedly onwards, feeling that the very air in the chamber was choking him.

As the doors slammed behind him he felt sweat break out on his forehead and his trembling increased violently. He stumbled and clung for support to the carved door post.

Will, having heard the commotion surrounding Henry's exit, had hastened from the ante-chamber. 'Lord Henry!' he cried, startled at the Earl's appearance.

'I refuse to be a party to that, though I may suffer the King's wrath and lose my liberty because of it! It is a travesty, a mere pretence! A . . . a wicked charade! She is innocent and I will not betray her like this. I will not set my hand to any document that condemns her. I will *not* have her blood on my hands! She is already judged guilty and they will have her dead!' Henry's voice cracked with despair.

Will stared at him, unable to believe what he was hearing. 'They . . . they have pronounced sentence already, my lord?'

'It is a foregone conclusion and but a matter of time before Norfolk utters the word "guilty". By God's wounds, he is her uncle! The King is her husband, the father of her child and he wishes her *dead*! I cannot conceive of the evil that exists in these men's hearts and I will remain no longer in this accursed place!' Henry thought of all his former friends and companions confined now within these walls, many destined to pay with their lives for their alleged crimes. How had they all been sucked into this maelstrom of murderous destruction? At least Tom Arundel was not amongst them. Nor was Francis Bryant; indeed Bryant could be counted as one of her enemies. But Tom Wyatt, her friend from childhood, was one of their number, a man he liked and admired. He prayed that Tom would be spared.

Despite his shock Will realised that not only had the Earl placed himself in extreme danger but also that the ordeal had made him ill. Henry was shaking uncontrollably now; his skin was the colour of parchment and glistened with sweat. He offered the Earl his arm for support. 'We shall leave with all haste, my lord. We shall return home, to the North.'

Henry leaned heavily on Will's arm. 'I could not condemn her, she is innocent. Innocent!' he repeated. He would rather face death himself than do such a thing to the woman who had once been the love of his life and whom he would always hold in his heart with affection. He would never believe the lies they had manufactured to bring about her downfall. He would always hold in contempt the weak and self-serving peers who had bowed to the King's commands. All his life he had upheld the concepts of loyalty and justice and he would not renounce them now. Not even the wrath of the King could make him sign away her innocence and her life, and if he were to forfeit his liberty and his own life because of it, then so be it.

'*Espérance! Espérance en Dieu!*' he muttered as Will helped him towards the doors leading outside to the green.

Epilogue

Friday 19 May 1536
Tower Green, London

ANNE REMOVED HER PLAIN black brocade hood and placed the small cap of white linen over her hair, which had been pinned high on her head. Her hands shook slightly and for an instant she fumbled with the fastenings. She had never imagined, even in her darkest hours after she had been found guilty, that it would come to this. That on this beautiful May morning, when the sun shone so brilliantly, the new green leaves rustled in the soft breeze and birdsong filled the air, that here on the green in front of the chapel of St Peter ad Vincula she would die.

But so it was. She had had time to prepare for it and now she was ready to meet her Maker. She had spoken her final words to the few people whom Henry had permitted to witness her death and she had been careful not to accuse, blame or vilify him. She had called him a gentle and merciful prince and exhorted people to obey and serve him. He had afforded her the small mercy of a swordsman from France and not the axe.

She had dispensed alms, thanked her ladies for their

kindness towards her and asked that prayers be said for her soul. She had bestowed her forgiveness on her executioner as he had knelt before her. She was resigned now to her fate. She had forgiven those who had falsely condemned her. They had all signed away her life – all save one. Harry Percy. When she had seen him there in the King's Hall she had felt dismayed. He looked an aged and broken man. His features bore the imprint of great suffering but when he had held her gaze in that instant she had felt a frisson of hope. In his eyes she had seen sadness and pity but also tenderness and, she'd felt, a belief in her innocence. When he had risen and, defying her Uncle Norfolk, had walked out of the chamber, she had murmured '*Espérance*' and 'hope' had again surged through her. He at least did not believe the vile calumnies and by his refusal to remain in that room had proclaimed his steadfast loyalty. He had not betrayed or deserted her and for that she blessed him, requesting that somehow her treasured prayer book could be given to him as a token of her affection and esteem.

Her thoughts turned for the last time to her child. Elizabeth was not yet three years old, so young to be left motherless and in such circumstances. She had prayed fervently that Henry would not look on her with malice, that her half-sister Mary would be kind to her and that God would protect and guide her throughout her life. There was nothing left to do now but to kneel and submit.

She removed the robe that covered her gown and handed it to one of her ladies whilst another placed the blindfold over her eyes. She knelt, bending her head so the rough wood of the block received it. This is where it all ends, she thought, but in my end is my beginning.

'To Jesus Christ I commend my soul,' she prayed aloud as she extended her arms in the proscribed signal to the executioner.

Sunlight flashed briefly on the blade as it descended.

Brook House, Newington Green, London

As he lay prostrated by illness in his bed Henry could not forget her face on that terrible day in the King's Hall, or the courage with which she had stood up to them all. He had once loved her devotedly, he would never forget her. Yet there was another image even more clear in his mind: the face of the lovely sixteen-year-old girl in whose dark eyes he believed he had seen true happiness and love as she had promised to become his wife that night in the chapel of the Queen she had supplanted. He did not wish to remember her as she'd looked the day she had been condemned to die, he thought as waves of anguish engulfed him. In his memory she would remain young, beautiful, kind and loyal – for ever. He was dimly aware that Will Chatton kept vigil beside his bed and gleaned a little comfort from the fact, for Will too had known her then.

The booming of a cannon fired from the Tower shattered the oppressive silence in the chamber and Henry shuddered violently, although it was the sound for which he had been waiting. He turned his face away from the window, his grief overcoming him entirely.

Will crossed himself devoutly and bowed his head. 'May God have mercy upon her soul,' he said quietly.

Henry closed his eyes. '*Requiescat in pace, Anna Regina.*'

Author's Note

The author of historical fiction is allowed more licence than a historian compiling a factual account, but historical facts must still be closely adhered to, particularly in the case of so well known a figure as Anne Boleyn. I have conducted my research I hope methodically and accurately, but for any mistakes I do apologise.

There is some dissent amongst historians as to whether Anne was the elder or the younger Boleyn daughter, there being no recorded dates of birth for either, but I think I have to agree with Retha M. Warnicke who believes that Anne was the oldest for the two convincing reasons she examines in her excellent book *The Rise and Fall of Anne Boleyn*. Firstly, Anne was afforded what was for that era – and for a girl – a very prestigious education, being sent at the age of six to the court of the Regent of the Netherlands, where she shared the schoolroom with the young Archduchesses, whereas it would appear that Mary Boleyn received only a modest education.

Secondly, whilst Sir Thomas endeavoured to arrange a match between Anne and James Butler, heir to the Earldom of Ormonde, Mary was married off to the much less exalted Sir William Carey. Mary did however spend some time in France which may have given rise to the rumours concerning Francis I.

The recorded evidence of the life of Henry Percy, Sixth Earl of Northumberland (named 'the Unlucky'), is unfortunately very limited, but from what does exist it would appear that he was a sensitive, cultured and honourable young man born in an era where greed, ambition, intrigue and extreme violence were commonplace. He was therefore unsuited to the age in which he lived and the duties and responsibilities demanded of him. He suffered ill health from childhood, the recurring 'agues' – bouts of fever accompanied by uncontrollable shivering – were possibly malaria, but as to the illness that afflicted him so severely in adulthood and which proved to be fatal there are no decisive clues.

Henry Percy survived for only a year after Anne Boleyn's execution. Although adamant in his refusal to become embroiled in the great rebellion of the northern counties against the dissolution of the monasteries and the encroaching doctrines of Protestantism known as the Pilgrimage of Grace, he was nevertheless accused of treason and commanded to journey to London to stand trial even though he was in the throes of his final illness. This was possibly a reprisal for his conduct at Anne's trial and the fact that he had refused in a letter, dated 12 May 1536, to admit that there had indeed been a pre-contract between him and Anne, when Cromwell had been seeking a context upon which Anne's marriage to the

King could be declared invalid. (The marriage was nevertheless pronounced invalid on 17 May 1536, two days before she was executed.)

Henry Percy died at his home in Newington Green on 29 June 1537, aged thirty-five, alone save for one manservant and in poverty, having willed his lands and title to the Crown. He was buried in the parish church at Hackney with no member of his family present. A monument was erected over his grave but of this and the church nothing now remains.

His brother Lord Thomas Percy was beheaded at Tyburn for his part in the Pilgrimage of Grace and Lord Ingram Percy was imprisoned in the Tower for some months but later released. Robert Aske, as one of the principal instigators and leaders of the Pilgrimage of Grace, was hanged in chains in York.

Will Chatton and his family are purely fictitious characters but through them I have endeavoured to give the reader an insight into the lives of the common folk of Tudor England and particularly the lawlessness and violence that existed at that time on the Border. With his experience of the vicissitudes of life and of the court and his somewhat cautious nature, I think Will would have had more sense than to become embroiled in the Pilgrimage of Grace, the aftermath of which resulted in hundreds of Henry Tudor's northern subjects being executed by the Duke of Norfolk on the King's orders. I would also like to think that the lone servant who attended Henry Percy on his deathbed would have been Will Chatton.

After Henry Percy's death, his widow, Mary Talbot, nagged her father Lord Shrewsbury into obtaining an audience for her with the King. When it was finally granted she asked that the allowance her late husband had provided her with continue to be paid by the Crown, the King now being in possession of her late husband's estates. Henry Tudor was not sympathetic. 'Madam, how can you desire any living from your husband's lands when your father gave nothing to your husband at your marriage,' was his curt reply. And with that she had to be satisfied.

Anne Boleyn's prayer book is in the library at Alnwick Castle, although now too fragile to be on public display. It would appear that it was purchased by either the First Duchess of Northumberland in the eighteenth century or the Fourth Duke of Northumberland in the nineteenth century. It is bound in faded velvet, has clasps of silver-gilt and on both covers bears the royal arms in enamel.

Of Topcliffe and Wressle Castles no vestige now remains. Warkworth, Prudhoe and Norham Castles still stand as impressive ruins, administered by English Heritage. Alnwick Castle, seat of the Tenth Duke of Northumberland, is today still very much a family home although altered in some respects from the castle Henry Percy the Sixth Earl would have known. It is well worth visiting, having been the residence of the Percy family for seven hundred years and containing many artefacts and treasures, as is the magnificent Alnwick Garden, which has been completely renovated by the present Duchess.

Select Bibliography of Historical Works

The Estates of the Percy Family: J. M. W. Bean. Oxford University Press 1958

A History of the House of Percy: Gerald Brenan & W. A. Lindsay. Freemantle & Co. 1902

Anne Boleyn: Marie Louise Bruce. Coward, McCann & Geoghegan 1972

The Cotton Manuscripts. National Archives

The Life & Death of Cardinal Wolsey: George Cavendish

Henry Percy and Henry VIII: Kathleen Davies. Longman 1967

The Annals of the House of Percy Vol. 1: E. B. DeFonblanque. Freemantle 1902.

Duke of Northumberland's Papers: Historic Mss Commission (The Third Report)

Norham Castle: English Heritage

Prudhoe Castle: English Heritage

Warkworth Castle: English Heritage

Tudor Rebellions: Anthony Fletcher & Diarmaid MacCulloch, Longman 1997

Anne Boleyn: Paul Friedmann. MacMillan 1884

Northumbrian Castles: the Coast: Frank Graham. Butler Publishing 1987

Alnwick: a Short History & Guide: Frank Graham

Sex in Elizabethan England: Alan Haynes. Sutton 1997

Death, Religion and Family in Tudor England 1480–1570: R. A. Houlbrooke. Oxford University Press 1998

Annotations upon the Ecclesiastes, DNP MS 465. Christopher Hunwick, Archivist to the Duke of Northumberland

The Life and Death of Anne Boleyn: Eric Ives. Oxford 2004

Alnwick Castle: Colin Shrimpton & Clare Baxter. Heritage House 2008

Six Wives: The Queens of Henry VIII: David Starkey. Chatto & Windus 2003

The Royal Palaces of Tudor England: Simon Thurley. Yale University Press 1993

Tudor Women: Queens & Commoners: Alison Plowden. Atheneum 1979

The Rise and Fall of Anne Boleyn: Retha M. Warnicke. Cambridge University Press 1989

Henry VIII: King and Court: Alison Weir. Vintage 2008

I am indebted to all these authors for historical fact and background material.

Lyn Andrews
Isle of Man 2011